Anonymous

Typical selections from the best English writers

With introductory notices. Vol. 1, second Edition

Anonymous

Typical selections from the best English writers
With introductory notices. Vol. 1, second Edition

ISBN/EAN: 9783337278014

Printed in Europe, USA, Canada, Australia, Japan

Cover: Foto ©Andreas Hilbeck / pixelio.de

More available books at **www.hansebooks.com**

Clarendon Press Series

TYPICAL SELECTIONS.

London

MACMILLAN AND CO.

PUBLISHERS TO THE UNIVERSITY OF

Oxford

Clarendon Press Series

TYPICAL SELECTIONS

FROM THE

BEST ENGLISH WRITERS

WITH

INTRODUCTORY NOTICES

SECOND EDITION

VOL. I

LATIMER, A. D. 1490 — BERKELEY, A. D. 1684

Oxford

AT THE CLARENDON PRESS

M DCCC LXXVI

PREFACE.

THE Select Extracts, of which a second and greatly enlarged edition is now offered to the public, are designed to serve as a higher Reading Book for the use of Schools. The selection has been limited to the works of authors distinguished for excellence of style, and an endeavour has been made, in each case, to give passages which exhibit his characteristic features, and the manner or manners in which he has best succeeded, and which entitle him to be regarded as an example of style, and as illustrating a period in the development of the English Language. The notices prefixed to each author are partly historical and partly critical. It is hoped that while the comments on style will aid the young reader's judgment and taste, the biographical outlines will help him to recognise the relative position of each author to the others and to the general history of English Literature. With this view the Series has been chronologically arranged. It may be proper to add that the selections have been made, and the notices accompanying them written, by many different persons. Among these contributors are the Very Rev. A. P. Stanley, Dean of Westminster; the Rev. Canon Mozley, Regius Professor of Divinity; the Rev. Mark Pattison, Rector of Lincoln College; Professor Goldwin Smith; the late Professor Conington; Professor C. H. Pearson; Professor Nichol, and the Rev. G. D. Boyle. To these gentlemen and to others who have given valuable assistance the best thanks of the Editor are due.

E. E. S.

OXFORD,
Jan. 4, 1876.

a 3

CONTENTS.

I.

HUGH LATIMER.

HUGH LATIMER sprang, as one of the extracts which follow implies, from a worthy though humble parentage. He was born in 1490 or 1491 at Thurcaston in the county of Leicester. Foxe tells, 'that his parents having him left for their only son, and seeing his ready, prompt and sharp wit, purposed to train him up in erudition and knowledge of good literature, wherein he so profited in his youth at the common schools of his own country, that at fourteen years he was sent to the University of Cambridge, where, after some continuance of exercises in other things, he gave himself to the study of such divinity as the ignorance of that age did suffer.' He was remarkable in the university for 'sanctimony of life,' as well as for his studious habits. Latimer was at this time a fervent and zealous Papist, and a bitter opponent of all who favoured the Reformation, insomuch that the oration which he made when he proceeded to the degree of Bachelor of Divinity, in 1524, was directed against Philip Melancthon and his opinions. At this period Bilney, seeing the zeal and piety of Latimer, sought to win him to the new doctrine. It is told that Bilney came to Latimer's study and asked him to receive his confession, and that Latimer, granting the request, was so touched by the hearing of the confession that he forsook his former studies and became 'a true scholar in the true divinity.' Latimer now devoted himself more earnestly to the work of the ministry. He employed himself in visiting the sick and prisoners, and in preaching both to the clergy in Latin and to the people in

English, and many were won to the new doctrine by his instru-
mentality. The doctors and friars became alarmed, and induced
the Bishop of Ely to prohibit Latimer from preaching within the
churches of the university. He however obtained leave to preach
in the church of the Augustine Friars—that being exempt from
episcopal jurisdiction. Complaint was next made of Latimer to
the Pope's legate, Cardinal Wolsey, by whom he was summoned
to London to give an account of his teaching. The Cardinal
considered the complaints frivolous, and dismissed Latimer with
gentle admonition, giving him licence to preach throughout
England, and other marks of confidence. In Feb. 1529-30
Latimer was one of the delegates appointed by the Senate to
determine the validity of Henry the VIII's marriage with Cathe-
rine of Arragon, and the day on which the decree of the Senate
was presented he preached before the King. From this time
forward Latimer ceased to reside in Cambridge. He was appointed chaplain to Anne Boleyn and presented by the Crown to
the living of West Kington in Wiltshire. Although he was
diligent in the discharge of pastoral duty, he frequently preached
in London, and some of his sermons both there and elsewhere,
in which he attacked the practices of Rome, raised much controversy and met with occasional condemnation.

In August, 1535, the bishopric of Worcester was conferred
upon him; he held that see until July, 1539, when Cromwell
informed him that it was the King's pleasure that he should
resign his bishopric. Latimer had been twice imprisoned when
the accession of Edward VI set him free in 1547.

He went to reside with Archbishop Cranmer at Lambeth, and
refused peremptorily to be reinstated in his see or to accept any
other bishopric. At this time he showed that he was not above
the persecuting spirit of his age by the part he took in proceedings
against Joan Bochêr, who was burnt for heresy. Very shortly after
the accession of Queen Mary, Latimer was again committed to
prison, and after six months spent in the Tower, was removed
with Cranmer and Ridley to Oxford for the purpose of holding
disputations concerning heresy. At the close of these disputations the three prelates were excommunicated, condemned, and

committed to separate confinement. In September, 1555, after sixteen months of imprisonment, Latimer and Ridley were brought before commissioners empowered by Cardinal Pole to try them for heresy, and were sentenced to death. A fortnight later, on the 16th of October, 1555, Latimer, together with Ridley, was burnt in front of Balliol College, and not far from the Bocardo—the gaol of the city. Cranmer, who had been in the same prison, ascended to the roof of the gaol to see the spectacle, and kneeling down prayed to God to strengthen them. Such was the end of Hugh Latimer, whose brave words are in the mouth of every English child, ' Be of good comfort, Master Ridley, and play the man ; we shall this day light such a candle, by God's grace, in England, as I trust shall never be put out.'

Hugh Latimer was the chief preacher of the English Reformation, and if any single book be taken as giving a picture of the manners, thoughts, and events of that period, it would be his Sermons, which should be studied by all who wish to become acquainted with his time. Excepting Disputations and Letters he left little else. Latimer was, as has been already said, a man of the humbler class ; he never became a very learned man, and was often indiscreet, but he was earnest and fearless, had great natural eloquence, and much homely wit. He exercised no episcopal functions after his resignation of his see in 1539, but remained a kind of watchdog of the Reformation at the Court of Edward VI and the Palace of his friend Archbishop Cranmer. His theology was too practical to allow him to mix deeply in the special controversies of the time, and he was a man rather of blunt and courageous honesty than of deep thought or tender feeling.

---

1. A Yeoman's Estate.

My father was a yeoman, and had no lands of his own, only he had a farm of three or four pound a year at the uttermost, and hereupon he tilled so much as kept half a dozen men. He had walk for a hundred sheep; and my mother milked thirty kine. He was able, and did find the

king a harness, with himself and his horse, while he came to
the place that he should receive the king's wages.   I can
remember that I buckled his harness when he went unto
Blackheath field.   He kept me to school, or else I had not
been able to have preached before the king's majesty now.
He married my sisters with five pound, or twenty nobles
apiece; so that he brought them up in godliness and fear of
God.   He kept hospitality for his poor neighbours, and
some alms he gave to the poor.—*First Sermon preached
before King Edward the Sixth.*

2. Zeal in a Bad Cause.

AND now I would ask a strange question: who is the
most diligentest bishop and prelate in all England, that
passeth all the rest in doing his office?   I can tell, for I
know him who it is; I know him well.   But now I think I
see you listening and hearkening that I should name him.
There is one that passeth all the other, and is the most
diligent prelate and preacher in all England.   And will ye
know who it is?   I will tell you: it is the devil.   He is the
most diligent preacher of all other; he is never out of his
diocess; he is never from his cure; ye shall never find him
unoccupied; he is ever in his parish; he keepeth residence
at all times; ye shall never find him out of the way, call
for him when you will he is ever at home; the diligentest
preacher in all the realm; he is ever at his plough: no
lording nor loitering can hinder him; he is ever applying
his business, ye shall never find him idle, I warrant you.
And his office is to hinder religion, to maintain superstition,
to set up idolatry, to teach all kind of popery.   He is ready
as he can be wished for to set forth his plough; to devise
as many ways as can be to deface and obscure God's glory.
Where the devil is resident, and hath his plough going, there

away with books, and up with candles; away with bibles, and
up with beads; away with the light of the gospel, and up
with the light of candles, yea, at noon-days. Where the
devil is resident, that he may prevail, up with all superstition
and idolatry; censing, painting of images, candles, psalms,
ashes, holy water, and new service of men's inventing; as
though man could invent a better way to honour God with
than God himself hath appointed. Down with Christ's cross,
up with purgatory pickpurse, up with him, the popish purgatory, I mean. Away with clothing the naked, the poor
and impotent; up with decking of images, and gay garnishing
of stocks and stones : up with man's traditions and his laws,
down with God's traditions and his most holy word. Down
with the old honour due to God, and up with the new god's
honour. Let all things be done in Latin: there must be
nothing but Latin; not so much as *Memento, homo, quod cinis
es, et in cinerem reverteris :* 'Remember, man, that thou art
ashes, and into ashes thou shalt return:' which be the words
that the minister speaketh unto the ignorant people, when he
giveth them ashes upon Ash-Wednesday; but it must be
spoken in Latin: God's word may in no wise be translated
into English.—*Sermon of the Plough.*

3. Contemplation and Action.

WE read a pretty story of St. Anthony, who being in the
wilderness, led there a very hard and strict life, insomuch as
none at that time did the like, to whom came a voice from
heaven, saying, 'Anthony, thou art not so perfect as is a
cobbler that dwelleth at Alexandria.' Anthony hearing this,
rose up forthwith, and took his staff and travelled till he
came to Alexandria, where he found the cobbler. The
cobbler was astonished to see so reverend a father come to
his house. Then Anthony said unto him, 'Come and tell

me thy whole conversation, and how thou spendest thy time.'
'Sir,' said the cobbler, 'as for me, good works have I none,
for my life is but simple and slender; I am but a poor
cobbler: in the morning when I rise, I pray for the whole
city wherein I dwell, especially for all such neighbours and
poor friends as I have: after, I set me at my labour, where
I spend the whole day in getting my living, and I keep me
from all falsehood, for I hate nothing so much as I do
deceitfulness: wherefore, when I make any man a promise,
I keep it, and perform it truly; and thus I spend my time
poorly, with my wife and children, whom I teach and instruct,
as far as my wit will serve me, to fear and dread God.
And this is the sum of my simple life.'—*Sermon on
Christmas Day.*

4. What Card to Play.

A TRUE and faithful servant, whensoever his master commandeth him to do any thing, he maketh no stops nor
questions, but goeth forth with a good mind: and it is not
unlike he, continuing in such a good mind and will, shall
well overcome all dangers and stops, whatsoever betide him
in his journey, and bring to pass effectually his master's will
and pleasure. On the contrary, a slothful servant, when his
master commandeth him to do any thing, by and by he will
ask questions, 'Where?' 'When?' 'Which way?' and so
forth; and so he putteth every thing in doubt, that although
both his errand and way be never so plain, yet by his
untoward and slothful behaviour his master's commandment
is either undone quite, or else so done that it shall stand to
no good purpose. Go now forth with the good servant, and
ask no such questions, and put no doubts. Be not ashamed
to do thy Master's and Lord's will and commandment. Go,
as I said, unto thy neighbour that is offended by thee, and

reconcile him (as is afore said) whom thou hast lost by thy unkind words, by thy scorns, mocks, and other disdainous words and behaviours; and be not nice to ask of him the cause why he is displeased with thee: require of him charitably to remit; and cease not till you both depart, one from the other, true brethren in Christ.

Do not, like the slothful servant, thy master's message with cautels and doubts: come not to thy neighbour whom thou hast offended, and give him a pennyworth of ale, or a banquet, and so make him a fair countenance, thinking that by thy drink or dinner he will shew thee like countenance. I grant you may both laugh and make good cheer, and yet there may remain a bag of rusty malice, twenty years old, in thy neighbour's bosom. When he departeth from thee with a good countenance, thou thinkest all is well then. But now, I tell thee, it is worse than it was, for by such cloaked charity, where thou dost offend before Christ but once, thou hast offended twice herein: for now thou goest about to give Christ a mock, if he would take it of thee. Thou thinkest to blind thy master Christ's commandment. Beware, do not so, for at length he will overmatch thee, and take thee tardy whatsoever thou be; and so, as I said, it should be better for thee not to do his message on this fashion, for it will stand thee in no purpose. 'What?' some will say, 'I am sure he loveth me well enough: he speaketh fair to my face.' Yet for all that thou mayest be deceived. It proveth not true love in a man, to speak fair. If he love thee with his mind and heart, he loveth thee with his eyes, with his tongue, with his feet, with his hands and his body; for all these parts of a man's body be obedient to the will and mind. He loveth thee with his eyes, that looketh cheerfully on thee, when thou meetest with him, and is glad to see thee prosper and do well. He loveth thee with his tongue, that speaketh well by thee behind thy back, or giveth thee good counsel. He loveth thee with his feet, that is willing to go to help thee out of trouble and business. He loveth thee with his hands, that will help thee in time of necessity, by giving some alms-deeds, or with any other occupation of the hand. He loveth thee with his body, that will labour with his body, or put his body in danger to do good for thee, or to deliver thee from adversity: and so forth, with the other members of his body. And if thy neighbour will do according to these sayings, then thou mayest think that he loveth thee well; and thou, in like wise, oughtest to declare and open thy love unto thy neighbour in like fashion, or else you be bound one to reconcile 'the other, till this perfect love be engendered amongst you.

It may fortune thou wilt say, 'I am content to do the best for my neighbour that I can, saving myself harmless.' I promise thee, Christ will not hear this excuse; for he himself suffered harm for our sakes, and for our salvation was put to extreme death. I wis, if it had pleased him, he might have saved us and never felt pain; but in suffering pains and death he did give us example, and teach us how we should do one for another, as he did for us all; for, as he saith himself, 'he that will be mine, let him deny himself, and follow me, in bearing my cross and suffering my pains.' Wherefore we must needs suffer pain with Christ to do our neighbour good, as well with the body and all his members, as with heart and mind.

Now I trust you wot what your card meaneth: let us see how that we can play with the same. Whensoever it shall happen you to go and make your oblation unto God, ask of yourselves this question, 'Who art thou?' The answer, as you know, is, 'I am a christian man.' Then you must again ask unto yourself, What Christ requireth of a christian man?

By and by cast down your trump, your heart, and look first
of one card, then of another. The first card telleth thee,
thou shalt not kill, thou shalt not be angry, thou shalt not be
out of patience. This done, thou shalt look if there be any
more cards to take up; and if thou look well, thou shalt see
another card of the same suit, wherein thou shalt know that
thou art bound to reconcile thy neighbour. Then cast thy
trump upon them both, and gather them all three together,
and do according to the virtue of thy cards; and surely
thou shalt not lose. Thou shalt first kill the great Turks,
and discomfort and thrust them down. Thou shalt again
fetch home Christ's sheep that thou hast lost; whereby thou
mayest go both patiently and with a quiet mind unto the
church, and make thy oblation unto God; and then, without
doubt, he will hear thee.—*Sermons on the Card.*

II.

SIR WALTER RALEGH.

1552-1618.

SIR WALTER RALEGH was born in 1552. He was descended
from an old Devonshire family, who held an estate called Fardel,
in the parish of Cornwood in that county. After his first education at school, Walter Ralegh became a commoner of Oriel
College, Oxford, where he distinguished himself both by the
strength and vivacity of his genius and by his application to his
studies. He left the University at the end of three years without
having taken a degree, and immediately, at the age of seventeen,
went to France as one of the select troop of a hundred gentlemen
whom Queen Elizabeth permitted to volunteer for the assistance
of the Protestant grievances there. Ralegh remained in France for
six years, studying the art of war and the languages and manners
of men. Soon after his return to England in 1575 his active
temper drew him into the wars in the Low Countries and the
service of the Prince of Orange against the Spaniards. In 1579,
Ralegh embarked in an unsuccessful expedition to Newfoundland
—the first of the many voyages to the New World in which his
name was afterwards to become so famous. For the two years
which followed Ralegh served in Ireland, chiefly as Captain
under the Earl of Ormond, against the Desmonds and other
chieftains in the rebellion of Munster and in the sieges of forts
held by the Spaniards in support of the rebels. In the many
desperate encounters of this time, Ralegh acquired a reputation
for the chivalrous gallantry which belonged to his nature. On his
return to England, Ralegh was introduced at Court, and gained

the favour of Queen Elizabeth, which, with but one interruption, he retained until her death in 1603. Public service and private adventure filled these eventful years of Ralegh's life. In 1584, under the sanction of Queen Elizabeth, he discovered and took possession of Virginia. In the next year he was knighted, and chosen knight of the shire for his own county of Devon, and made a considerable figure in Parliament. He took a gallant part in the destruction of the Spanish Armada in 1588, accompanied the armament to restore the King of Portugal in the following year, and led the expedition against the Spaniards in Panama in 1592. In 1596 he had a chief command, and much distinguished himself at the taking of Cadiz. A second expedition to Newfoundland, two to Florida, one in search of the North-west passage, five to Virginia, and two to Guiana, were among the undertakings which Ralegh devised or conducted. His eager and active spirit was ever intent and improving the knowledge of navigation, and extending the power of England in the New World. The introduction of tobacco and of the potato are the most familiar results of his enterprises.

With the accession of James I Ralegh's fortune changed. He was accused of taking part in a plot against the King, tried at Winchester for treason, and sentenced to death, which for some time he daily expected. He was however reprieved and committed prisoner to the Tower, where he lay for twelve years. There he devoted the greater part of his time to reading and writing, and composed his great work of the History of the World. In 1616 Ralegh was released, and sent by the King on an expedition to explore gold mines in Guiana. This expedition, though unsuccessful, much exasperated the Spaniards, and on his return in 1618 Ralegh was, to please them, at once thrown into prison; no wrong being found against him, it was resolved to sacrifice him to Spain by calling him down to judgment upon the former sentence passed fifteen years before. This was done at Westminster on the 28th of October, and on the following day he was executed. It is told that taking leave of Lord Arundel and the other gentlemen on the scaffold he said, ' I have a long journey to go, and therefore will take my leave.' He then called to the executioner for the axe, 'I prithee let me see it, dost thou think I am afraid of it?' and having it in his hands he felt along the edge, and smiling, said to the sheriff, 'This is a sharp medicine, but a cure for all diseases.' Then being asked which way he would lay himself on the block, he answered, 'so the heart is right it is no matter which way the head lies.'

Though Ralegh's career had been active and adventurous, he was nevertheless a diligent student and a voluminous writer on history, politics and government, geography, military and naval tactics, and the records of travel. In describing events in which he had taken part, or in the discussion of moral questions, his style is rich and eloquent; it is often, and naturally, dry and cold in his great compilation, *The History of the World.* The attempt of Ralegh, says Johnson respecting this work, in a paper in the Rambler, is deservedly celebrated for the labour of his research and the elegance of his style, but he has endeavoured to exert his judgment more than his genius, to select facts rather than adorn them; he has produced a historical dissertation, but has seldom risen to the dignity of history.

---

1. Action at the taking of Cadiz.

HAVING, as aforesaid, taken the leading, I was first saluted by the fort called Philip, afterward by the ordnance on the curtain, and lastly by all the galleys in good order. To show scorn to all which, I only answered first the fort, and afterward the galleys, to each piece a blur with a trumpet; disdaining to shoot one piece at any one or all of those esteemed dreadful monsters. The ships that followed beat upon the galleys so thick as they soon betook them to their oars, and got up to join with the galleons in the strait, as aforesaid; and then, as they were driven to come near me, and enforced to range their sides towards me, I bestowed a benediction amongst them.

But St. Philip, the great and famous admiral of Spain, was the mark I shot at; esteeming those galleys but as wasps in respect of the powerfulness of the other ; and being resolved to be revenged for the Revenge, or to second her with mine own life, I came to anchor by the galleons; of which the Philip and Andrew were two that boarded the Revenge. I was formerly commanded not to board, but was promised fly-boats, in which, after I had battered a while, I resolved to join unto them.

My lord Thomas came to anchor by me, on the one hand, with the Lion; the Mary Rose, on the other, with the Dreadnought; the marshal toward the side of Puntall; and towards ten of the clock my lord general Essex, being impatient to abide far off, hearing so great thunder of ordnance, thrust up through the fleet, and headed all those on the left hand, coming to anchor next unto me on that side; and afterward came in the Swiftsure, as near as she could. Always I must, without glory, say for myself, that I held single in the head of all.

Now after we had beaten, as two butts, one upon another almost three hours, (assuring your honour that the volleys of cannon and culverin came as thick as if it had been a skirmish of musketeers,) and finding myself in danger to be sunk in the place, I went to my lord general in my skiff, to desire him that he would enforce the promised fly-boats to come up, that I might board; for as I rid, I could not endure so great a battery any long time. My lord general was then coming up himself; to whom I declared that if the fly-boats came not, I would board with the queen's ship; for it was the same loss to burn or sink, for I must endure the one. The earl finding that it was not in his power to command fear, told me that whatsoever I did, he would second me in person upon his honour. My lord admiral, having also a disposition to come up at first, but the river was so choked as he could not pass with the Ark, came up in person into the Nonparilla, with my lord Thomas.

While I was thus speaking with the earl, the marshal, who thought it some touch to his great esteemed valour, to ride behind me so many hours, got up ahead my ship; which my lord Thomas perceiving, headed him again, myself being but a quarter of an hour absent. At my return, finding myself from being the first to be but the third, I presently let slip anchor, and thrust in between my lord Thomas and the marshal, and went up further ahead than all them before, and thrust myself athwart the channel, so as I was sure none should outstart me again for that day. My lord general Essex, thinking his ship's sides stronger than the rest, thrust the Dreadnought aside, and came next the Warspite on the left hand, ahead all that rank but my lord Thomas. The marshal, while we had no leisure to look behind us, secretly fastened a rope on my ship's side towards him, to draw himself up equally with me; but some of my company advertising me thereof, I caused it to be cut off, and so he fell back into his place; whom I guarded, all but his very prow, from the sight of the enemy.

Now if it please you to remember, that having no hope of my fly-boats to board, and that the earl and my lord Thomas both promised to second me, I laid out a warp by the side of the Philip to shake hands with her: (for with the wind we could not get aboard:) which when she and the rest perceived, finding also that the Repulse (seeing mine) began to do the like, and the rear-admiral my lord Thomas, they all let slip, and came aground, tumbling into the sea heaps of soldiers, so thick as if coals had been poured out of a sack in many ports at once, some drowned and some sticking in the mud. The Philip and the St. Thomas burnt themselves:

the St. Matthew and the St. Andrew were recovered by our
boats ere they could get out to fire them. The spectacle
was very lamentable on their side; for many drowned themselves; many, half-burnt, leaped into the water; very many
hanging by the ropes' ends by the ships' sides, under the
water even to the lips; many swimming with grievous
wounds, strucken under water, and put out of their pain;
and withal so huge a fire, and such tearing of the ordnance
in the great Philip, and the rest, when the fire came to them,
as, if any man had a desire to see hell itself, it was there
most lively figured. Ourselves spared the lives of all after
the victory; but the Flemings, who did little or nothing in
the fight, used merciless slaughter, till they were by myself,
and afterward by my lord admiral, beaten off.—*Relation of
Cadiz Action.*

2. Of the last refuges of the Devil to maintain his kingdom.

Now the Devil, because he cannot play upon the open
stage of this world, (as in those days,) and being still as
industrious as ever, finds it more for his advantage to creep
into the minds of men; and inhabiting in the temples of
their hearts, works them to a more effectual adoration of
himself than ever. For whereas he first taught them to
sacrifice to monsters, to dead stones cut into faces of beasts,
birds, and other mixed natures; he now sets before them
the high and shining idol of glory, the all-commanding
image of bright gold. He tells them that truth is the
goddess of dangers and oppressions; that chastity is the
enemy of nature; and lastly, that as all virtue, in general,
is without taste, so pleasure satisfieth and delighteth every
sense: for true wisdom, saith he, is exercised in nothing else

than in the obtaining of power to oppress, and of riches to maintain plentifully our worldly delights. And if this arch-politician find in his pupils any remorse, any fear or feeling of God's future judgment, he persuades them that God hath so great need of men's souls, that he will accept them at any time and upon any conditions; interrupting by his vigilant endeavours all offer of timeful return towards God, by laying those great blocks of rugged poverty and despised contempt in the narrow passage leading to his divine presence. But as the mind of man hath two ports, the one always fre-quented by the entrance of manifold vanities, the other desolate and overgrown with grass, by which enter our charitable thoughts and divine contemplations; so hath that of death a double and twofold opening; worldly misery passing by the one, worldly prosperity by the other: at the entrance of the one we find our sufferings and patience to attend us; (all which have gone before us to prepare our joys;) at the other our cruelties, covetousness, licentiousness, injustice, and oppressions, (the harbingers of most fearful and terrible sorrow,) staying for us. And as the Devil, our most industrious enemy, was ever most diligent, so is he now more laborious than ever; the long day of mankind drawing fast towards an evening, and the world's tragedy and time near at an end.—*History of the World.*

3. Death.

FOR the rest, if we seek a reason of the succession and continuance of this boundless ambition in mortal men, we may add to that which hath been already said, that the kings and princes of the world have always laid before them the actions, but not the ends, of those great ones which preceded them. They are always transported with the glory of the one, but they never mind the misery of the other, till they find the experience in themselves. They neglect the advice of God, while they enjoy life, or hope it; but they follow the counsel of Death upon his first approach. It is he that puts into man all the wisdom of the world, without speaking a word, which God, with all the words˜of his law, promises, or threats, doth not infuse. Death, which hateth and destroyeth man, is believed; God, which hath made him and loves him, is always deferred: *I have considered*, saith Solomon, *all the works that are under the sun, and, behold, all is vanity and vexation of spirit;* but who believes it, till Death tells it us? It was Death, which opening the conscience of Charles the Fifth, made him enjoin his son Philip to restore Navarre; and king Francis the First of France, to command that justice should be done upon the murderers of the protestants in Merindol and Cabrieres, which till then he neglected. I is therefore Death alone that can suddenly make man to know himself. He tells the proud and insolent, that they are but abjects, and humbles them at the instant, makes them cry, complain, and repent, yea, even to hate their forepast happiness. He takes the account of the rich, and proves him a beggar, a naked beggar, which hath interest in nothing but in the gravel that fills his mouth. He holds a glass before the eyes of the most beautiful, and makes them see therein their deformity and rottenness, and they acknowledge it.

O eloquent, just, and mighty Death! whom none could advise, thou hast persuaded; what none hath dared, thou hast done; and whom all the world hath flattered, thou only hast cast out of the world and despised; thou hast drawn together all the far-stretched greatness, all the pride, cruelty, and ambition of man, and covered it all over with these two narrow words, *Hic jacet !—The History of the World.*

4. The Defence of Passes and Fords.

THE winning of this passage (of the river Granick by Alexander the Great) did greatly encourage the Macedonians, and brought such terror upon all those of the Lesser Asia, as he obtained all the ̈ kingdoms thereof without a blow, some one or two towns excepted. For in all invasions, where the nations invaded have once been beaten upon a great advantage of the place, as in defence of rivers, straits, and mountains, they will soon have persuaded themselves, that such an enemy, upon equal terms and even ground, can hardly be resisted. It was therefore Machiavel's counsel, that he which resolveth to defend a passage should with his ablest force oppose the assailant. And to say truth, few regions of any great circuit are so well fenced, that armies, of such force as may be thought sufficient to conquer them, can be debarred all entrance by the natural difficulty of the ways. One passage or other is commonly left unguarded; if all be defended, then must the forces of the country be distracted, and yet lightly some one place will be found that is defended very weakly. How often have the Alps given way to armies breaking into Italy! yea, where shall we find that ever they kept out an invader? Yet are they such as (to speak briefly) afflict with all difficulties those that travel over them; but they give no security to those that lie behind them, for they are of too large extent. The towns of Lombardy persuaded themselves that they might enjoy their quiet, when the warlike nation of the Switzers had undertaken to hinder Francis the French king from descending into the duchy of Milan; but whilst these patrons of Milan, whom their own dwelling in those mountains had made fittest of all other for such a service, were busied in custody of the Alps, Francis appeared in Lombardy, to so much the greater terror of the inhabitants, by how much the less they had expected his arrival. What shall we say of those mountains, which lock up whole regions in such sort, as they leave but one gate open? The straits, or (as they were called) the gates of Taurus in Cilicia, and those of Thermopylæ, have seldom been attempted, perhaps because they were thought impregnable; but how seldom (if ever) have they been attempted in vain. Xerxes, and long after him the Romans, forced the entrance of Thermopylæ; Cyrus the younger, and after him Alexander, found the gates of Cilicia wide open; how strongly soever they had been locked and barred, yet were those countries open enough to a fleet that should enter on the back side. The defence of rivers, how hard a thing it is, we find examples in all histories that bear good witness. The deepest have many fords, the swiftest and broadest may be passed by boats, in case it be found a matter of difficulty to make a bridge. He that hath men enough to defend all the length of his own bank hath also enough to beat his enemy; and may therefore do better to let him come over, to his loss, than by striving in vain to hinder the passage, as a matter tending to his own disadvantage, fill the heads of his soldiers with an opinion that they are in ill case, having their means of safeguard taken from them by the skill or valour of such as are too good for them. Certainly if a river were sufficient defence against an army, the isle of Mona, now called Anglesea, which is divided from North Wales by an arm of the sea, had been safe enough against the Romans invading it under conduct of Julius Agricola. But he wanting, and not meaning to spend the time in making vessels to transport his forces, did assay the fords. Whereby he so amazed the enemies attending for ships and such like provision by sea, that surely believing nothing could be hard or invincible to men which came so minded to war, they humbly entreated for peace, and yielded the island. Yet the Britains were men stout enough, the Persians very dastards.

It was therefore wisely done of Alexander to pass the river of Granick in face of the enemy, not marching higher to seek an easier way, nor labouring to convey his men over it by some safer means. For having beaten them upon their own ground, he did thereby cut off no less of their reputation than of their strength, leaving no hope of succour to the partakers and followers of such unable protectors.—*The History of the World.*

5. Great Commanders.

CERTAINLY the things performed by Xenophon discover as brave a spirit as Alexander's, and working no less exquisitely, though the effects were less material, as were also the forces and power of command by which it wrought. But he that would find the exact pattern of a noble commander must look upon such as Epaminondas, that encountering worthy captains, and those better followed than themselves, have by their singular virtue overtopped their valiant enemies, and still prevailed over those that would not have yielded one foot to any other : such as these are do seldom live to obtain great empires. For it is a work of more labour and longer time, to master the equal forces of one hardy and well-ordered state, than to tread down and utterly subdue a multitude of servile nations, compounding the body of a gross unwieldy empire. Wherefore these *parvo potentes*, men that with little have done much upon enemies of like ability, are to be regarded as choice examples of worth ; but great conquerors, to be rather admired for the substance of their actions, than the exquisite managing ; exactness and greatness concurring so seldom, that I can find no instance of both in one, save only that brave Roman Cæsar.—*The History of the World.*

6. Sea Fights.

CERTAINLY, he that will happily perform a fight at sea, must be skilful in making choice of vessels to fight in ; he must believe, that there is more belonging to a good man of war upon the waters, than great daring; and must know, that there is a great deal of difference between fighting loose, or at large, and grappling. The guns of a slow ship pierce as well, and make as great holes, as those in a swift. To clap ships together without consideration, belongs rather to a madman than to a man of war; for by such an ignorant bravery was Peter Strossie lost at the Azores, when he fought against the marquis of Santa Cruz. In like sort had the lord Charles Howard, admiral of England, been lost in the year 1588, if he had not been better advised, than a great many malignant fools were that found fault with his demeanour. The Spaniards had an army aboard them, and he had none; they had more ships than he had, and of higher building and charging; so that, had he entangled himself with those great and powerful vessels, he had greatly endangered this kingdom of England. For twenty men upon the defences are equal to an hundred that board and enter; whereas then, contrariwise, the Spaniards had an hundred for twenty of ours, to defend themselves withal. But our admiral knew his advantage, and held it ; which had he not done, he had not been worthy to have held his head. Here to speak in general of sea-fight, (for particulars are fitter for private hands than for the press,) I say, that a fleet of twenty ships, all good sailers and good ships, have the advantage, on the open sea, of an hundred as good ships and of slower sailing. For if the fleet of an hundred sail keep themselves near together, in a gross squadron, the twenty ships, charging them upon any angle, shall force them to give ground, and to fall back upon their next fellows, of which so many as entangle are made unserviceable, or lost. Force them they may easily, because the twenty ships, which give themselves scope, after they have given one broadside of artillery, by clapping into the wind, and staying, they may give them the other, and so the twenty ships batter them in pieces with a perpetual volley; whereas those that fight in a troop have no room to turn, and can always use but one and the same beaten side. If the fleet of an hundred sail give themselves any distance, then shall the lesser fleet prevail, either against those that are a-rear and hindmost, or against those that by advantage of over-sailing their fellows keep the wind; and if upon a lee-shore the ships next the wind be constrained to fall back into their own squadron, then it is all to nothing that the whole fleet must suffer shipwreck, or render itself. That such advantage may be taken upon a fleet of unequal speed, it hath been well enough conceived in old time, as by that oration of Hermocrates, in Thucydides, which he made to the Syracusians when the Athenians invaded them, it may easily be observed.—*The History of the World.*

III.

RICHARD HOOKER.

CIRCA 1553–1600.

RICHARD HOOKER was born at Heavitree, near Exeter, about
1553. His parents not being rich intended him for a trade, but
his schoolmaster at Exeter, recognizing his natural endowments,
prevailed with them to continue him at school, assuring them that
his talents and learning were so remarkable, that they would soon
attract the notice of some patron, who would free them from
further care and charge about him. The promise of his boyhood
induced his uncle, who was known to Jewel, Bishop of Salisbury,
to commend him to that prelate, and under his protection Hooker
was sent to the University of Oxford, and admitted as a clerk of
Corpus Christi College in the year 1567. In 1573 he was chosen
scholar, and in 1577 he was elected fellow of his college, and
about two years afterwards he was appointed deputy-professor of
Hebrew. During these years Isaak Walton tells us of Hooker's
attainments, 'that by his great reason and his industry' 'he did
not only know more of causes and effects, but what he knew he
knew better than other men;' 'his behaviour in his college was
mild, innocent and exemplary, and thus this good man continued
till his death, still increasing in learning, in patience and in
piety.' We hear of his intimacy at Oxford with Edwin Sandys,
George Cranmer, and Henry Savile, all men of mark and influence
in their day. In 1581 Hooker took orders, and in the same year
he first preached in London at St. Paul's. Soon after he married,
and took the living of Drayton Beauchamp, in Bucks. The

marriage was probably a hasty one ; at any rate, it brought little
felicity. From his appointment as Master of the Temple, 1585,
Hooker's reputation as a divine may be said to date. He now
commenced his long controversy with the Nonconformist divines;
after some years of keen strife he exchanged the Mastership of
the Temple for the living of Boscombe, in Wiltshire. In 1595
he was presented by the Crown to Bishopsborne, in Kent,
where, in 1600, he died, at the early age of forty-seven. ,

Hooker undertook the defence of the ritual and polity of the
Church of England against the attacks of the Puritans, and dedicated to this object his great work on the *Laws of Ecclesiastical
Polity*. His style is grave, close, and full, and in general possesses
little ornament or finish, consulting the practical purposes of a
controversialist and the efficient statement of argument and fact,
rather than the ear or delicate taste of the reader. Particular
passages, however, are highly elaborated, and wrought up not
only to great majesty and grandeur of diction, but even to a
musical sweetness and rhythm. Solidity and compactness, however, are always preserved, and his most exalted eloquence is still
grave and severe, weighted with balance of clauses and intricacies
of construction. With the inspiration which springs up from
deep feeling and the sense of great truths, he combines occasionally an acute and powerful sarcasm, which he introduces
dexterously and with ease into the fitting place ; thus exhibiting
all the resources and the full armour of a theologian and controversialist.

---

1. Creation and the Law of Nature.

THIS world's first creation, and the preservation since of
things created, what is it but only so far forth a mani-
festation by execution, what the eternal law of God is
concerning things natural ? And as it cometh to pass in
a kingdom rightly ordered, that after a law is once published, it presently takes effect far and wide, all states

framing themselves thereunto; even so let us think it fareth
in the natural course of the world: since the time that God
did first proclaim the edicts of his law upon it, heaven and
earth have hearkened unto his voice, and their labour hath
been to do his will: He 'made a law for the rain;' He
gave his 'decree unto the sea, that the waters should not
pass his commandment.' Now if nature should intermit
her course, and leave altogether though it were but for a
while the observation of her own laws; if those principal
and mother elements of the world, whereof all things in this
lower world are made, should lose the qualities which now
they have; if the frame of that heavenly arch erected over
our heads should loosen and dissolve itself; if celestial
spheres should forget their wonted motions, and by irregular
volubility turn themselves any way as it might happen; if
the prince of the lights of heaven, which now as a giant
doth run his unwearied course, should as it were through
a languishing faintness begin to stand and to rest himself;
if the moon should wander from her beaten way, the times
and seasons of the year blend themselves by disordered
and confused mixture, the winds breathe out their last gasp,
the clouds yield no rain, the earth be defeated of heavenly
influence, the fruits of the earth pine away as children at
the withered breasts of their mother no longer able to
yield them relief: what would become of man himself,
whom these things now do all serve? See we not plainly
that obedience of creatures unto the law of nature is the
stay of the whole world?

If here it be demanded what that is which keepeth
nature in obedience to her own law, we must have recourse
to that higher law whereof we have already spoken, and
because all other laws do thereon depend, from thence we
must borrow so much as shall need for brief resolution in

this point.   Although we are not of opinion therefore, as some are, that nature in working hath before her certain exemplary draughts or patterns, which subsisting in the bosom of the Highest, and being thence discovered, she fixeth her eye upon them, as travellers by sea upon the pole-star of the world, and that according thereunto she guideth her hand to work by imitation: although we rather embrace the oracle of Hippocrates, that 'each thing both in small and in great fulfilleth the task which destiny hath set down;' and concerning the manner of executing and fulfilling the same, 'what they do they know not, yet is it in show and appearance as though they did know what they do; and the truth is they do not discern the things which they look on:' nevertheless, forasmuch as the works of nature are no less exact, than if she did both behold and study how to express some absolute shape or mirror always present before her; yea, such her dexterity and skill appeareth, that no intellectual creature in the world were able by capacity to do that which nature doth without capacity and knowledge; it cannot be but nature hath some director of infinite knowledge to guide her in all her ways.   Who the guide of nature, but only the God of nature?   'In him we live, move, and are.'   Those things which nature is said to do, are by divine art performed, using nature as an instrument; nor is there any such art or knowledge divine in nature herself working, but in the Guide of nature's work.—*Of the Laws of Ecclesiastical Polity.*

2.   The Law of Reason.

Now the due observation of this Law which Reason teacheth us cannot but be effectual unto their great good that observe the same.   For we see the whole world and each part thereof so compacted, that as long as each thing performeth only that work which is natural unto it, it thereby preserveth both other things and also itself. Contrariwise, let any principal thing, as the sun, the moon, any one of the heavens or elements, but once cease or fail, or swerve, and who doth not easily conceive that the sequel thereof would be ruin both to itself and whatsoever dependeth on it? And is it possible, that Man being not only the noblest creature in the world, but even a very world in himself, his transgressing the Law of his Nature should draw no manner of harm after it? Yes; 'tribulation and anguish unto every soul that doeth evil.' Good doth follow unto all things by observing the course of their nature, and on the contrary side evil by not observing it; but not unto natural agents that good which we call Reward, not that evil which we properly term Punishment. The reason whereof is, because amongst creatures in this world, only Man's observation of the Law of his Nature is Righteousness, only Man's transgression Sin. And the reason of this is the difference in his manner of observing or transgressing the Law of his Nature. He doth not otherwise than voluntarily the one or the other. What we do against our wills, or constrainedly, we are not properly said to do it, because the motive cause of doing it is not in ourselves, but carrieth us, as if the wind should drive a feather in the air, we no whit furthering that whereby we are driven. In such cases therefore the evil which is done moveth compassion; men are pitied for it, as being rather miserable in such respect than culpable. Some things are likewise done by man, though not through outward force and impulsion, though not against yet without their wills; as in alienation of mind, or any the like inevitable utter absence of wit and judgment. For which cause, no man did ever think the hurtful actions of furious men and innocents to be punishable. Again, some things we do neither against nor without, and yet not simply and merely with our wills, but with our wills in such sort moved, that albeit there be no impossibility but that we might, nevertheless we are not so easily able to do otherwise. In this consideration one evil deed is made more pardonable than another. Finally, that which we do being evil, is notwithstanding by so much more pardonable, by how much the exigence of so doing or the difficulty of doing otherwise is greater; unless this necessity or difficulty have originally risen from ourselves. It is no excuse therefore unto him, who being drunk committeth incest, and allegeth that his wits were not his own; inasmuch as himself might have chosen whether his wits should by that mean have been taken from him. Now rewards and punishments do always presuppose something willingly done well or ill; without which respect though we may sometimes receive good or harm, yet then the one is only a benefit and not a reward, the other simply an hurt not a punishment. From the sundry dispositions of man's Will, which is the root of all his actions, there groweth variety in the sequel of rewards and punishments, which are by these and the like rules measured: 'Take away the will, and all acts are equal: That which we do not, and would do, is commonly accepted as done.' By these and the like rules men's actions are determined of and judged, whether they be in their own nature rewardable or punishable.—*Of the Laws of Ecclesiastical Polity.*

3. Faith, Hope, and Charity, Supernatural Law.

CONCERNING Faith, the principal object whereof is that eternal Verity which hath discovered the treasures of hidden

wisdom in Christ; concerning Hope, the highest object
whereof is that everlasting Goodness which in Christ doth
quicken the dead; concerning Charity, the final object
whereof is that incomprehensible Beauty which shineth in
the countenance of Christ the Son of the living God: concerning these virtues, the first of which beginning here with
a weak apprehension of things not seen, endeth with the
intuitive vision of God in the world to come; the second
beginning here with a trembling expectation of things far
removed and as yet' but only heard of, endeth with real
and actual fruition of that which no tongue can express;
the third beginning here with a weak inclination of heart
towards him unto whom we are not able to approach,
endeth with endless union, the mystery whereof is higher
than the reach of the thoughts of men; concerning that
Faith, Hope, and Charity, without which there can be no
salvation, was there ever any mention made saving only
in that law which God himself hath from heaven revealed?
There is not in the world a syllable muttered with certain
truth concerning any of these three, more than hath been
supernaturally received from the mouth of the eternal God.

Laws therefore concerning these things are supernatural,
both in respect of the manner of delivering them, which is
divine; and also in regard of the things delivered, which
are such as have not in nature any cause from which they
flow, but were by the voluntary appointment of God ordained
besides the course of nature, to rectify nature's obliquity
withal.

Laws being imposed either by each man upon himself, or
by a public society upon the particulars thereof, or by all the
nations of men upon every several society, or by the Lord
himself upon any or every of these; there is not amongst
these four kinds any one but containeth sundry both natural

and positive laws.　Impossible it is but that they should fall
into a number of gross errors, who only take such laws for
positive as have been made or invented of men, and holding
this position hold also, that all positive and none but positive
laws are mutable.　Laws natural do always bind; laws
positive not so, but only after they have been expressly and
wittingly imposed.　Laws positive there are in every of those
kinds before mentioned.　As in the first kind the promises
which we have passed unto men, and the vows we have made
unto God; for these are laws which we tie ourselves unto,
and till we have so tied ourselves they bind us not.　Laws
positive in the second kind are such as the civil constitutions
peculiar unto each particular commonweal.　In the third
kind the law of heraldry in war is positive: and in the last
all the judicials which God gave unto the people of Israel
to observe.　And although no laws but positive be mutable,
yet all are not mutable which be positive.　Positive laws are
either permanent or else changeable, according as the matter
itself is concerning which they were first made.　Whether
God or man be the maker of them, alteration they so far
forth admit, as the matter doth exact.

Laws that concern supernatural duties are all positive, and
either concern men supernaturally as men, or else as parts
of a supernatural society, which society we call the Church.
To concern men as men supernaturally is to concern them
as duties which belong of necessity to all, and yet could not
have been known by any to belong unto them, unless God
had opened them himself, inasmuch as they do not depend
upon any natural ground at all out of which they may
be deduced, but are appointed of God to supply the defect
of those natural ways of salvation, by which we are not
now able to attain thereunto.　The Church being a supernatural society doth differ from natural societies in this, that

the persons unto whom we associate ourselves, in the one are
men simply considered as men, but they to whom we be
joined in the other, are God, Angels, and holy men.   Again
the Church being both a society and a society supernatural,
although as it is a society it have the selfsame original
grounds which other politic societies have, namely, the
natural inclination which all men have unto sociable life, and
consent to some certain bond of association, which bond is
the law that appointeth what kind of order they shall be
associated in: yet unto the Church as it is a society supernatural this is peculiar, that part of the bond of their association which belongs to the Church of God must be a law
supernatural, which God himself hath revealed concerning
that kind of worship which his people shall do unto him.
The substance of the service of God therefore, so far forth
as it hath in it any thing more than the Law of Reason doth
teach, may not be invented of men, as it is amongst the
heathens, but must be received from God himself, as always
it hath been in the Church, saving only when the Church
hath been forgetful of her duty.—*Of the Laws of Ecclesiastical Polity.*

4. Music.

TOUCHING musical harmony whether by instrument or
by voice, it being but of high and low in sounds a due
proportionable disposition, such notwithstanding is the force
thereof, and so pleasing effects it hath in that very part
of man which is most divine, that some have been thereby
induced to think that the soul itself by nature is or hath in it
harmony.   A thing which delighteth all ages and beseemeth
all states; a thing as seasonable in grief as in joy; as decent
being added unto actions of greatest weight and solemnity,

as being used when men most sequester themselves from
action. The reason hereof is an admirable facility which
music hath to express and represent to the mind, more
inwardly than any other sensible mean, the very standing,
rising, and falling, the very steps and inflections every way,
the turns and varieties of all passions whereunto the mind is
subject; yea so to imitate them, that whether it resemble
unto us the same state wherein our minds already are, or
a clean contrary, we are not more contentedly by the one
confirmed, than changed and led away by the other. In
harmony the very image and character even of virtue and
vice is perceived, the mind delighted with their resemblances,
and brought by having them often iterated into a love of the
things themselves. For which cause there is nothing more
contagious and pestilent than some kinds of harmony; than
some nothing more strong and potent unto good. And
that there is such a difference of one kind from another we
need no proof but our own experience, inasmuch as we are
at the hearing of some more inclined unto sorrow and
heaviness; of some, more mollified and softened in mind;
one kind apter to stay and settle us, another to move and
stir our affections; there is that draweth to a marvellous
grave and sober mediocrity, there is also that carrieth as it
were into ecstacies, filling the mind with an heavenly joy
and for the time in a manner severing it from the body. So
that although we lay altogether aside the consideration of
ditty or matter, the very harmony of sounds being framed in
due sort and carried from the ear to the spiritual faculties of
our souls, is by a native puissance and efficacy greatly
available to bring to a perfect temper whatsoever is there
troubled, apt as well to quicken the spirits as to allay that
which is too eager, sovereign against melancholy and
despair, forcible to draw forth tears of devotion if the mind

be such as can yield them, able both to move and to moderate all affections.—*Of the Laws of Ecclesiastical Polity.*

5. Past and Present.

THERE is crept into the minds of men at this day a secret pernicious and pestilent conceit that the greatest perfection of a Christian man doth consist in discovery of other men's faults, and in wit to discourse of our own profession. When the world most abounded with just, righteous, and perfect men, their chiefest study was the exercise of piety, wherein for their safest direction they reverently hearkened to the readings of the law of God, they kept in mind the oracles and aphorisms of wisdom which tended unto virtuous life, if any scruple of conscience did trouble them for matter of actions which they took in hand, nothing was attempted before counsel and advice were had, for fear lest rashly they might offend. We are now more confident, not that our knowledge and judgment is riper, but because our desires are another way. Their scope was obedience, ours is skill; their endeavour was reformation of life, our virtue nothing but to hear gladly the reproof of vice; they in the practice of their religion wearied chiefly their knees and hands, we especially our ears and tongues.—*Of the Laws of Ecclesiastical Polity.*

IV.

SIR PHILIP SIDNEY.

1554-1586.

SIR PHILIP SIDNEY was born in 1554 at Penshurst, in Kent, of a noble family. His father was Sir Henry Sidney, Queen Elizabeth's Lord-Deputy in Ireland. His mother was Mary Dudley, the sister of the Earl of Leicester. His sister was the Countess of Pembroke, the subject of Ben Jonson's celebrated epitaph. He was early sent to a school at Shrewsbury, and from thence was removed at the age of fifteen to Christ Church, Oxford. He appears also to have studied at Cambridge. At this time we are told of Sidney that he cultivated not one art, or one science, but the whole circle of arts and sciences. 'Such,' says Fuller, 'was his appetite for learning, that he could never be fed fast enough therewith, and so·quick and strong his digestion that he soon turned it into wholesome nourishment, and throve healthfully thereon.'

In 1572 he obtained Queen Elizabeth's licence to travel, and went to Paris, where, in the month of August, he narrowly escaped death in the Massacre of St. Bartholomew, by taking refuge in the house of Walsingham, the English Ambassador. From Paris Sidney travelled to Frankfort, where he formed the friendship of the eminent Hubert Languet. Sidney went thence to Vienna, where he devoted himself to the learning of horsemanship, of arms and other manly and martial exercises, and before he left it he excelled in tilt and tournament, in the use of all sorts of weapons, and in such exercises as befitted a noble cavalier. In 1574 we find him in Italy at Venice, but chiefly at Padua, where he applied himself with his wonted diligence to the study of geometry and astronomy. After three years of travel Sidney returned to England, where he became the delight of the English Court. He was soon employed on a diplomatic mission to Vienna, and acquitted himself with ability and dignity of this embassage and of similar visits to other foreign courts. In 1580 he addressed a letter of great weight to Queen Elizabeth, dissuading her from the marriage with the Duke of Anjou, which was then under consideration, and did not thereby incur her royal displeasure, as was the case with some others. A quarrel with the Earl of Oxford in the same year, which he was forbidden to adjust by a duel, led Sidney to retire to Wilton, the seat of his brother-in-law, the Earl of Pembroke : while here he laid out the plan of his *Arcadia*, a romance of a heroic and pastoral character.

In the following year Sidney entered Parliament as knight of the shire for his native county of Kent, and in 1583 he married the only daughter of Sir Francis Walsingham, and had the honour of knighthood conferred upon him by the Queen. Sidney's energetic spirit led him in 1585 to conceive, and he was with difficulty restrained from conducting conjointly with Sir Francis Drake an expedition to attack the Spanish settlements in South America.

The expedition was stopped by Queen Elizabeth, who having taken the Protestants of the Netherlands under her protection promised to despatch a military force to their succour, and to employ Sidney in this service. Sir Philip Sidney was nominated Governor of Flushing in the same year, and at once engaged in military operations against the Spaniards. In the following year he met his death-wound in a victorious encounter with them under the walls of Zutphen, and died Oct. 7, 1586, at the early age of thirty-two. He was buried in St. Paul's on the 16 Feb., 1587, amid general mourning—a just tribute to the courage and devotion of which his life gave noble example.

Sidney's principal compositions were circulated in MS. during his life, but do not appear to have been printed until after his death. His sonnets appeared in 1591, his *Arcadia* in 1593, and

the *Defence of Poesy* in 1595. Of these, that which obtained the
largest share of favour in the age succeeding his death was the
Arcadia, an eloquent romance of Castilian and Elizabethan
chivalry thrown back into the time of the struggle of Sparta
with her Helots. This work abounds in vivid descriptive and
narrative passages, and though occasionally tainted with the
pedantic euphuism of the sixteenth century, it is a store-house
of poetic prose inferior to none which had preceded it in our
literature. Sidney's *Defence of Poesy* has had a longer, though a
more restricted, popularity. It is the great source from which
later advocates of imaginative composition in England have
drawn their arguments.

---

1. After a Wreck.

A LITTLE way off they saw the mast, whose proud height
now lay along, like a widow having lost her mate of whom she
held her honour: but upon the mast they saw a young man
(at least if he were a man) bearing shew of about eighteen
years of age, who sate (as on horseback) having nothing on
him but his shirt, which, being wrought with blue silk and
gold, had a kind of resemblance to the sea; on which the
sun (then near his western home) did shoot some of his
beams. His hair (which the young men of Greece used to
wear very long) was stirred .up and down with the wind,
which seemed to have a sport to play with it, as the sea had
to kiss his feet: himself full of admirable beauty, set forth
by the strangeness both of his seat and gesture; for, holding his head up full of unmoved majesty, he held a sword
aloft with his fair arm, which often he waved about his
crown, as though he would threaten the world in that
extremity.—*Arcadia*.

2. The Scenery of Arcadia.

THE third day after, in the time that the morning did strow roses and violets in the heavenly floor against the coming . of the sun, the nightingales (striving one with the other which could in most dainty variety recount their wrong-caused sorrow) made them put off their sleep, and rising from under a tree (which that night had been their pavilion) they went on their journey, which by and by welcomed Musidorus's eyes (wearied with the wasted soil of Laconia) with delightful prospects. There were hills which garnished their proud heights with stately trees; humble valleys, whose bare estate seemed comforted with the refreshing of silver rivers; meadows enamelled with all sorts of eye-pleasing flowers; thickets which being lined with most pleasant shade were witnessed so too by the cheerful disposition of many well-tuned birds: each pasture stored with sheep, feeding with sober security, while the pretty lambs with bleating oratory craved the dams' comfort: here a shepherd's boy piping as though he should never be old; there a young shepherdess knitting, and withal singing, and it seemed that her voice comforted her hands to work, and her hands kept time to her voice-music.—*Arcadia.*

3. Pamela and Philoclea.

THE elder is named Pamela, by many men not deemed inferior to her sister; for my part, when I marked them both, methought there was more sweetness in Philoclea, but more majesty in Pamela; methought love played in Philoclea's eyes and threatened in Pamela's; methought Philoclea's beauty only persuaded, but so persuaded as all hearts must yield; Pamela's beauty used violence, and such violence as no heart could resist. And it seems that such proportion is between their minds; Philoclea so bashful, as though her excellencies had stolen into her before she was aware; so humble that she will put all pride out of countenance; in sum, such proceedings as will stir hope, but teach good manners. Pamela of high thoughts, who avoids not pride with not knowing her excellencies, but by making it one of her excellencies to be void of pride; her mother's wisdom, greatness, nobility, but (if I can guess aright) knit with a more constant temper.—*Arcadia.*

4. The Poet.

THE Greeks named him ποιητήν; which name hath, as the most excellent, gone through other languages; it cometh of this word ποιεῖν, which is to make; wherein, I know not whether by luck or wisdom, we Englishmen have met with the Greeks in calling him Maker! which name, how high and incomparable a title it is, I had rather win honour by marking the scope of other sciences, than by any partial allegation. There is no art delivered unto mankind, that hath not the works of nature for his principal object, without which they could not consist, and on which they so depend, as they become actors and players, as it were, of what nature will have set forth. So doth the astronomer look upon the stars, and by that he seeth set down what order nature hath taken therein. So doth the geometrician and arithmetician, in their diverse sorts of quantities. So doth the musician, in tunes, tell you, which by nature agree, which not. The natural philosopher thereon hath his name; and the moral philosopher standeth upon the natural virtues, vices, or passions of man: and follow nature, saith he, therein, and thou shalt not err. The lawyer saith what men have determined. The historian, what men have done. The grammarian speaketh only of the rules of speech; and the rhetorician and logician, considering what in nature will soonest prove, and persuade thereon, give artificial rules, which still are compassed within the circle of a question, according to the proposed matter. The physician weigheth the nature of man's body, and the nature of things helpful and hurtful unto it. And the metaphysick, though it be in second and abstract notions, and therefore be counted supernatural, yet doth he, indeed, build upon the depth of nature. Only the poet, disdaining to be tied to any such subjection, lifted up with the vigour of his own invention, doth grow, in effect, into another nature: in making things either better than nature bringeth forth, or quite anew; forms such as never were in nature, as the heroes, demi-gods, cyclops, chymeras, furies, and such like; so as he goeth hand in hand with nature, not inclosed within the narrow warrant of her gifts, but freely ranging within the zodiack of his own wit. Nature never set forth the earth in so rich tapestry as diverse poets have done; neither with so pleasant rivers, fruitful trees, sweet-smelling flowers, nor whatsoever else may make the too much-loved earth more lovely. Her world is brazen, the poets only deliver a golden.—*The Defence of Poesy.*

5. The Praise of Poesy.

THE ending of all earthly learning being virtuous action, those skills which serve most to bring forth that, have a more just title to be princes over the rest: wherein if we can shew it rightly the poet is worthy to have it before any other competitors: among whom principally to challenge it step forth the moral philosophers; whom methinks I see coming towards me with a sullen gravity, as though they could not abide vice by daylight; rudely clothed, for to witness outwardly their contempt of outward things; with books in their hands against glory, whereto they set their names; sophistically speaking against subtilty, and angry with a man in whom they see the foul fault of anger. . . . . . . The historian scarce gives leisure to the moralist to say so much, but that he, loaden with old mouse-eaten records; better acquainted with a thousand years ago than with the present age; a wonder to young folks and a tyrant in table-talk—denieth, in a great chafe, that any man for teaching of virtue and virtuous actions is comparable to him. . . . . . The philosopher, therefore, and the historian are they which would win the goal, the one by precept, the other by example; but both not having both, do both halt. For the philosopher, sitting down with the thorny arguments, the bare rule is so hard of utterance, and so misty to be conceived, that one that hath no other guide but him shall wade in him until he be old, before he shall find sufficient cause to be honest. . . . On the other hand, the historian, wanting the precept, is so tied, not to what should be but to what is—to the particular truth of things and not the general reason of things—that his example draweth not necessary consequence, and therefore a less fruitful doctrine. Now doth the peerless poet perform both: for whatsoever the philosopher saith should be done he giveth a perfect picture of it, by some one by whom he presupposeth it was done; so as he coupleth the general notion with the particular example. . . . . . . Tully taketh much pains, and many times not without poetical helps, to make us know what force the love of our country hath in us: let us but hear old Anchises speaking in the midst of Troy's flames, or see Ulysses in the fulness of all Calypso's delights, bewailing his absence from barren Ithaca! Anger, the Stoics said, was a short madness; let but Sophocles bring you Ajax on a stage, killing or whipping sheep and oxen, thinking them the army of the Greeks, with their chieftains Agamemnon and Menelaus; and tell me if you have not a more familiar insight into anger than finding in the school-men its genus and difference.

Now, to that which is commonly attributed to the praise of history, in respect of the notable learning which is got by marking the success, as though therein a man should see virtue exalted, and vice punished; truly, that commendation is peculiar to Poetry, and far off from history; for, indeed, Poetry ever sets virtue so out in her best colours, making fortune her well-waiting hand-maid, that one must needs be enamoured of her. Well may you see Ulysses in a storm, and in other hard plights; but they are but exercises of patience and magnanimity, to make them shine the more in the near following prosperity. And, on the contrary part, if evil men come to the stage, they ever go out (as the tragedy-writer answered to one that misliked the shew of such persons) so manacled, as they little animate folks to follow them. But history being captived to the truth of a foolish world, is many times a terror from well-doing, and an encouragement to unbridled wickedness. . . . I conclude there-fore that he (the Poet) excelleth history, not only in furnish-ing the mind with knowledge, but in setting it forward to that which deserves to be called and accounted good: which setting forward, and moving to well-doing, indeed, setteth the laurel crown upon the poets as victorious, not only of the historian, but over the philosopher; howsoever in teach-ing it may be questionable. For suppose it to be granted, that which I suppose, with great reason, may be denied, that the philosopher, in respect of his methodical proceeding, teach more perfectly than the Poet, yet I do think that no man is so much φιλοφιλοσοφος, as to compare the philosopher in moving with the Poet. The philosopher showeth you the

way, he informeth you of the particularities, as well of the
tediousness of the way, as of the pleasant lodging you shall
have when your journey is ended, as of the many bye-
turnings that may divert you from your way; but this is
to no man but to him that will read him, and read him with
attentive, studious painfulness; which constant desire whosoever hath in him, hath already past half the hardness of the
way, and therefore is beholden to the philosopher but for the
other half.—But to be moved to do that which we know, or
to be moved with desire to know, hoc opus, hic labor est.

Now, therein, of all sciences, is our Poet the monarch. For
he doth not only shew the way, but giveth so sweet a prospect
into the way, as will entice any man to enter into it : nay, he
doth, as if your journey should lie through a fair vineyard, at the
very first, give you a cluster of grapes ; that, full of that taste,
you may long to pass further. He beginneth not with obscure
definitions, which must blur the margin with interpretations,
and load the memory with doubtfulness; but he cometh to
you with words set in delightful proportion, either accompanied with, or prepared for, the well enchanting skill of
music ; and with a tale forsooth, he cometh unto you, with a
tale which holdeth children from play, and old men from the
chimney corner ; and, pretending no more, doth intend the
winning of the mind from wickedness to virtue ; even as the
child is often brought to take most wholesome things, by
hiding them in such others as have a pleasant taste. So is it
in men (most of whom are childish in the best things, till
they be cradled in their graves); glad will they be to hear
the tales of Hercules, Achilles, Cyrus, Æneas ; and hearing
them, must needs hear the right description of wisdom,
valour, and justice; which, if they had been barely (that is to
say philosophically) set out, they would swear they be
brought to school again. Truly, I have known men, that

even with the reading of Amadis de Gaule, which, God knoweth, wanteth much of a perfect Poesy, have found their hearts moved to the exercise of courtesy, liberality, and especially courage. Who readeth Æneas carrying old Anchises on his back, that wisheth not it were his fortune to perform so excellent an act.

By these therefore examples and reasons, I think it may be manifest, that the Poet, with that same hand of delight, doth draw the mind more effectually than any other art doth. And so a conclusion not unfitly ensues : *that as virtue is the most excellent resting-place for all worldly learning to make his end of, so Poetry, being the most familiar to teach it, and most princely to move towards it, in the most excellent work, is the most excellent workman.—The Defence of Poesy.*

V.

FRANCIS BACON, LORD VERULAM.

1560–1626.

FRANCIS BACON, born Jan. 1560–1, was the youngest son of Sir Nicholas Bacon, Lord Keeper of the Great Seal. His grave and thoughtful habit in childhood, and his power of minute and detailed observation, gave token of his future intellectual eminence. It is told of him that he would steal away from his companions at play to study the singular echo in a brick conduit near his father's house, of which he speaks in one of his celebrated works. He matriculated Fellow Commoner at Trinity College, Cambridge, at the early age of twelve. In 1576 his father, having in view for him a public career, sent him to Paris in the employment of the Ambassador, Sir Amyas Paulett. But on the death of his father, finding himself left with only a slender fortune, he was compelled to enter the profession of the law, and was admitted barrister in 1582. Two years afterwards he entered the House of Commons as Member for Melcombe Regis.

For many years to come he was compelled to toil in a profession in which his heart was not. He writes to Burleigh, 'that he had contemplative ends as vast as his civil ends were moderate, for he had taken all knowledge to be his province;' and to the Queen, 'my mind turns upon other wheels than those of profit.' It might have been expected that Bacon's acknowledged talents, and his family connection with the Cecils, would have led him early to preferment. He attached himself however to the rival party at the Court of Queen Elizabeth, and found in its chief, the Earl of Essex, a warm and indefatigable friend, though an unsuccessful patron. The part which Bacon afterwards took in the prosecution of Essex is one of the most vexed questions of his history, and perhaps the hardest part of his conduct to explain or justify. Promotion was slow in reaching him, and scarcely came until the new reign had begun, but when it came it was rapid; he did not rise to be Attorney-General till 1613, and in March 1616-7 he received the Great Seal. He was created successively Baron Verulam and Viscount St. Alban.

He was disgraced on a charge of judicial corruption, but the extent of his culpability has been greatly exaggerated by party malice. A cold, caught in the process of an experiment to test the preserving qualities of snow, carried him off in April, 1626.

Bacon had wasted, in the pursuit of professional preferment, powers which were worthy to have been better employed. Yet he has left behind him a name which is hardly second to any in the annals of philosophy, as the inaugurator or restorer of the Inductive Method in Science. His eloquence and his far-reaching thoughts have powerfully affected both his own and succeeding generations, and the splendour of his style has given irresistible power to his ideas.

He wrote many works both in Latin and English; of the latter, the principal are, *Of the Proficience and Advancement of Learning, Essays Civil and Moral, History of the Reign of King Henry the Seventh,* and *The New Atlantis.*

---

1. Use of Reason in Religion.

THE use of human reason in religion is of two sorts: the former, in the conception and apprehension of the mysteries of God to us revealed; the other, in the inferring and deriving of doctrine and direction thereupon. The former extendeth to the mysteries themselves; but how? by way of illustration, and not by way of argument. The latter consisteth indeed of probation and argument. In the former we see God vouchsafeth to descend to our capacity, in the expressing of his mysteries in sort as may be sensible

unto us; and doth grift his revelations and holy doctrine
upon the notions of our reason, and applieth his inspirations
to open our understanding, as the form of the key to' the
ward of the lock.   For the latter, there is allowed us an use
of reason and argument, secondary and respective, although
not original and absolute.   For after the articles and principles of religion are placed and exempted from examination
of reason, it is then permitted unto us to make derivations
and inferences from and according to the analogy of them,
for our better direction.   In nature this holdeth not; for
both the principles are examinable by induction, though not
by a medium or syllogism; and besides, those principles or
first positions have no discordance with that reason which
draweth down and deduceth the inferior positions.   But yet
it holdeth not in religion alone, but in many knowledges,
both of greater and smaller nature, namely, wherein there
are not only *posita* but *placita;* for in such there can be no
use of absolute reason.   We see it familiarly in games of
wit, as chess, or the like.   The draughts and first laws of the
game are positive, but how?   merely *ad placitum*, and not
examinable by reason;   but then how to direct our play
thereupon with best advantage to win the game, is artificial
and rational.   So in human laws there be many grounds
and maxims which are *placita juris*, positive upon authority,
and not upon reason, and therefore not to be disputed: but
what is most just, not absolutely but relatively, and according to those maxims, that affordeth a long field of disputa-
tion.   Such therefore is that secondary reason, which hath
place in divinity, which is grounded upon the *placets* of
God.—*Of the Proficience and Advancement of Learning.*

2. Of Adversity.

IT was a high speech of Seneca (after the manner of the Stoics), *that the good things which belong to prosperity are to be wished ; but the good things that belong to adversity are to be admired.* *Bona rerum secundarum optabilia ; adversarum mirabilia.* Certainly if miracles be the command over nature, they appear most in adversity. It is yet a higher speech of his than the other (much too high for a heathen), *It is true greatness to have in one the frailty of a man, and the security of a God.* *Vere magnum habere fragilitatem hominis, securitatem Dei.* This would have done better in poesy, where transcendences are more allowed. And the poets indeed have been busy with it; for it is in effect the thing which is figured in that strange fiction of the ancient poets, which seemeth not to be without mystery; nay, and to have some approach to the state of a Christian; that *Hercules, when he went to unbind Prometheus* (by whom human nature is represented), *sailed the length of the great ocean in an earthen pot or pitcher ;* lively describing Christian resolution, that saileth in the frail bark of the flesh through the waves of the world. But to speak in a mean. The virtue of Prosperity is temperance, the virtue of Adversity is fortitude ; which in morals is the more heroical virtue. Prosperity is the blessing of the Old Testament; Adversity is the blessing of the New; which carrieth the greater benediction, and the clearer revelation of God's favour. Yet even in the Old Testament, if you listen to David's harp, you shall hear as many hearse-like airs as carols ; and the pencil of the Holy Ghost hath laboured more in describing the afflictions of Job than the felicities of Salomon. Prosperity is not without many fears and distastes; and Adversity is not without comforts and hopes. We see in needle-works and embroideries, it is more pleasing to have a lively work upon a sad and solemn ground, than to have a dark and melancholy work upon a lightsome ground: judge therefore of the pleasure of the heart by the pleasure of the eye. Certainly virtue is like precious odours, most fragrant when they are incensed or crushed: for Prosperity doth best discover vice, but Adversity doth best discover virtue.—*Essays and Counsels, Civil and Moral.*

3. Poesy.

POESY is a part of learning in measure of words for the most part restrained, but in all other points extremely licensed, and doth truly refer to the imagination; which, being not tied to the laws of matter, may at pleasure join that which nature hath severed, and sever that which nature hath joined; and so make unlawful matches and divorces of things; *Pictoribus atque poetis, &c.* It is taken in two senses in respect of words or matter. In the first sense it is but a character of style, and belongeth to arts of speech, and is not pertinent for the present. In the latter it is (as hath been said) one of the principal portions of learning, and is nothing else but feigned history, which may be styled as well in prose as in verse.

The use of this feigned history hath been to give some shadow of satisfaction to the mind of man in those points wherein the nature of things doth deny it, the world being in proportion inferior to the soul; by reason whereof there is, agreeable to the spirit of man, a more ample greatness, a more exact goodness, and a more absolute variety, than can be found in the nature of things. Therefore, because the acts or events of true history have not that magnitude which satisfieth the mind of man, poesy feigneth acts and events greater and more heroical. Because true history propoundeth the successes and issues of actions not so

agreeable to the merits of virtue and vice, therefore poesy
feigns them more just in retribution, and more according
to revealed providence. Because true history representeth
actions and events more ordinary and less interchanged,
therefore poesy endueth them with more rareness, and more
unexpected and alternative variations. So as it appeareth
that poesy serveth and conferreth to magnanimity, morality,
and to delectation. And therefore it was ever thought to
have some participation of divineness, because it doth raise
and erect the mind, by submitting the shows of things to
the desires of the mind; whereas reason doth buckle and
bow the mind unto the nature of things. And we see that
by these insinuations and congruities with man's nature and
pleasure, joined also with the agreement and consort it hath
with music, it hath had access and estimation in rude times
and barbarous regions, where other learning stood excluded.

The division of poesy which is aptest in the propriety
thereof (besides those divisions which are common unto it
with history, as feigned chronicles, feigned lives, and the
appendices of history, as feigned epistles, feigned orations,
and the rest) is into poesy narrative, representative, and
allusive. The narrative is a mere imitation of history, with
the excesses before remembered; choosing for subject
commonly wars and love, rarely state, and sometimes
pleasure or mirth. Representative is as a visible history;
and is an image of actions as if they were present, as history is of actions in nature as they are, (that is) past.
Allusive or parabolical is a narration applied only to express
some special purpose or conceit. Which latter kind of parabolical wisdom was much more in use in the ancient times,
as by the fables of Æsop, and the brief sentences of the
Seven, and the use of hieroglyphics may appear. And the
cause was, for that it was then of necessity to express any

point of reason which was more sharp or subtile than the
vulgar in that manner, because men in those times wanted
both variety of examples and subtilty of conceit. And as
hieroglyphics were before letters, so parables were before
arguments: and nevertheless now and at all times they
do retain much life and vigour, because reason cannot be
so sensible, nor example so fit.—*Of the Proficience and
Advancement of Learning.*

4.   The Delights of Learning.

Scilicet ingenuas didicisse fideliter artes
Emollit mores, nec sinit esse feros;

IT taketh away the wildness and barbarism and fierceness
of men's minds : but indeed the accent had need be upon
fideliter : [it must be a *true* proficiency:] for a little superficial learning doth rather work a contrary effect.   It taketh
away all levity, temerity, and insolency, by copious suggestion
of all doubts and difficulties, and acquainting the mind to
balance reasons on both sides, and to turn back the first
offers and conceits of the mind, and to accept of nothing but
examined and tried.   It taketh away vain admiration of any
thing, which is the root of all weakness.   For all things are
admired, either because they are new, or because they are
great.   For novelty, no man that wadeth in learning or contemplation throughly, but will find that printed in his heart
Nil novi super terram.   Neither can any man marvel at the
play of puppets, that goeth behind the curtain and adviseth
well of the motion.   And for magnitude, as Alexander the
Great after that he was used to great armies and the great
conquests of the spacious provinces in Asia, when he received letters out of Greece of some fights and services there,
which were commonly for a passage or a fort or some

walled town at the most, he said, *It seemed to him that he was advertised of the battles of the frogs and the mice, that the old tales went of:* so certainly if a man meditate much upon the universal frame of nature, the earth with men upon it (the divineness of souls except) will not seem much other than an ant-hill, whereas some ants carry corn, and some carry their young, and some go empty, and all to and fro a little heap of dust. It taketh away or mitigateth fear of. death or adverse fortune; which is one of the greatest impediments of virtue and imperfections of manners. For if a man's mind be deeply seasoned with the consideration of the mortality and corruptible nature of things, he will easily concur with Epictetus, who went forth one day and saw a woman weeping for her pitcher of earth that was broken, and went forth the next day and saw a woman weeping for her son that was dead; and thereupon said, *Heri vidi fragilem frangi, hodie vidi mortalem mori.* . . .

It were too long to go over the particular remedies which learning doth minister to all the diseases of the mind; sometimes purging the ill humours, sometimes opening the obstructions, sometimes helping digestion, sometimes increasing appetite, sometimes healing the wounds and exulcerations thereof, and the like; and therefore I will conclude with that which hath *rationem totius;* which is, that it disposeth the constitution of the mind not to be fixed or settled in the defects thereof, but still to be capable and susceptible of growth and reformation. For the unlearned man knows not what it is to descend into himself or to call himself to account, nor the pleasure of that *suavissima vita, in dies sentire se fieri meliorem.* The good parts he hath he will learn to shew to the full and use them dexterously, but not much to increase them : the faults he hath he will learn how to hide and colour them, but not much to amend them ; like an ill mower, that mows on still and never whets his scythe : whereas with the learned man it fares otherwise, that he doth ever intermix the correction and amendment of his mind with the use and employment thereof. Nay further, in general and in sum, certain it is that *veritas* and *bonitas* differ but as the seal and the print; for truth prints goodness, and they be the clouds of error which descend in the storms of passions and perturbations.

From moral virtue let us pass on to matter of power and commandment, and consider whether in right reason there be any comparable with that wherewith knowledge investeth and crowneth man's nature. We see the dignity of the commandment is according to the dignity of the commanded : to have commandment over beasts, as herdsmen have, is a thing contemptible ; to have commandment over children, as schoolmasters have, is a matter of small honour ; to have commandment over galley-slaves is a disparagement rather than an honour. Neither is the commandment of tyrants much better, over people which have put off the generosity of their minds : and therefore it was ever holden that honours in free monarchies and commonwealths had a sweetness more than in tyrannies ; because the commandment extendeth more over the wills of men, and not only over their deeds and services. . . . But yet the commandment of knowledge is yet higher than the commandment over the will ; for it is a commandment over the reason, belief, and understanding of man, which is the highest part of the mind, and giveth law to the will itself. For there is no power on earth which setteth up a throne or chair of estate in the spirits and souls of men, and in their cogitations, imaginations, opinions, and beliefs, but knowledge and learning. And therefore we see the detestable and extreme pleasure that arch-heretics and false prophets and impostors are transported with, when they once find in themselves that they have a superiority in the faith and conscience of men ; so great, that if they have once tasted of it, it is seldom seen that any torture or persecution can make them relinquish or abandon it. But as this is that which the author of the Revelation calleth the depth or profoundness of Satan ; so by argument of contraries, the just and lawful sovereignty over men's understanding, by force of truth rightly interpreted, is that which approacheth nearest to the similitude of the divine rule. . . . .

Again, for the pleasure and delight of knowledge and learning, it far surpasseth all other in nature : for shall the pleasures of the affections so exceed the senses, as much as the obtaining of desire or victory exceedeth a song or a dinner ; and must not of consequence the pleasures of the intellect or understanding exceed the pleasures of the affections ? We see in all other pleasures there is satiety, and after they be used, their verdure departeth ; which sheweth well they be but deceits of pleasure, and not pleasures ; and that it was the novelty which pleased, and not the quality. And therefore we see that voluptuous men turn friars, and ambitious princes turn melancholy. But of knowledge there is no satiety, but satisfaction and appetite are perpetually interchangeable ; and therefore appeareth to be good in itself simply, without fallacy or accident.—*Of the Proficience and Advancement of Learning.*

5. Of Superstition.

IT were better to have no opinion of God at all, than such an opinion as is unworthy of him. For the one is unbelief, the other is contumely : and certainly superstition is the reproach of the Deity. Plutarch saith well to that purpose : *Surely* (saith he) *I had rather a great deal men should say there was no such man at all as Plutarch, than that they should say that there was one Plutarch that would eat his*

children as soon as they were born; as the poets speak of
Saturn. And as the contumely is greater towards God, so
the danger is greater towards men. Atheism leaves a man
to sense, to philosophy, to natural piety, to laws, to reputation; all which may be guides to an outward moral virtue,
though religion were not; but superstition dismounts all
these, and erecteth an absolute monarchy in the minds of
men. Therefore atheism did never perturb states; for it
makes men wary of themselves, as looking no further: and
we see the times inclined to atheism (as the time of Augustus
Caesar) were civil times. But superstition hath been the
confusion of many states, and bringeth in a new *primum
mobile*, that ravisheth all the spheres of government. The
master of superstition is the people; and in all superstition
wise men follow fools; and arguments are fitted to practice,
in a reversed order. It was gravely said by some of the
prelates in the council of Trent, where the doctrine of the
schoolmen bare great sway, *that the schoolmen were like
astronomers, which did feign eccentrics and epicycles, and such
engines of orbs, to save the phaenomena; though they knew
there were no such things;* and in like manner, that the
schoolmen had framed a number of subtle and intricate
axioms and theorems, to save the practice of the church.
The causes of superstition are, pleasing and sensual rites
and ceremonies; excess of outward and pharisaical holiness;
over-great reverence of traditions, which cannot but load
the church; the stratagems of prelates for their own ambition
and lucre; the favouring too much of good intentions, which
openeth the gate to conceits and novelties; the taking an
aim at divine matters by human, which cannot but breed
mixture of imaginations: and, lastly, barbarous times, especially joined with calamities and disasters. Superstition,
without a veil, is a deformed thing; for as it addeth de-

formity to an ape to be so like a man, so the similitude of superstition to religion makes it the more deformed. And as wholesome meat corrupteth to little worms, so good forms and orders corrupt into a number of petty observances. There is a superstition in avoiding superstition, when men think to do best if they go furthest from the superstition formerly received; therefore care would be had that (as it fareth in ill purgings) the good be not taken away with the bad; which commonly is done when the people is the reformer.—*Essays or Counsels Civil and Moral.*

6. Of Studies.

STUDIES serve for delight, for ornament, and for ability. Their chief use for delight, is in privateness and retiring; for ornament, is in discourse; and for ability, is in the judgment and disposition of business. For expert men can execute, and perhaps judge of particulars, one by one : but the general counsels, and the plots and marshalling of affairs, come best from those that are learned. To spend too much time in studies is sloth; to use them too much for ornament is affectation; to make judgment wholly by their rules is the humour of a scholar. They perfect nature, and are perfected by experience : for natural abilities are like natural plants, that need pruning by study; and studies themselves do give forth directions too much at large, except they be bounded in by experience. Crafty men contemn studies; simple men admire them; and wise men use them: for they teach not their own use; but that is a wisdom without them, and above them, won by observation. Read not to contradict and confute; nor to believe and take for granted; nor to find talk and discourse; but to weigh and consider. Some books are to be tasted, others to be swallowed, and some few to be chewed and digested: that is, some books are to be read only in parts; others to be read, but not curiously, and some few to be read wholly, and with diligence and attention. Some books also may be read by deputy, and extracts made of them by others; but that would be only in the less important arguments, and the meaner sort of books; else distilled books are, like common distilled waters, flashy things. Reading maketh a full man; conference a ready man; and writing an exact man. And, therefore, if a man write little, he had need have a great memory; if he confer little, he had need have a present wit; and if he read little, he had need have much cunning to seem to know that he doth not. Histories make men wise; poets witty; the mathematics subtle; natural philosophy deep; moral grave; logic and rhetoric able to contend. *Abeunt studia in mores ;* nay, there is no stond or impediment in the wit, but may be wrought out by fit studies : like as diseases of the body may have appropriate exercises. Bowling is good for the stone and reins, shooting for the lungs and breast; gentle walking for the stomach; riding for the head and the like. So, if a man's wit be wandering, let him study the mathematics ; for in demonstrations, if his wit be called away never so little, he must begin again; if his wit be not apt to distinguish or find difference, let him study the schoolmen, for they are *Cymini sectores.* If he be not apt to beat over matters, and to call up one thing to prove and illustrate another, let him study the lawyers' cases; so every defect of the mind may have a special receipt.—*Essays or Counsels Civil and Moral.*

7. Character of King Henry the Seventh.

THIS King (to speak of him in terms equal to his deserving) was one of the best sort of wonders; a wonder for wise men. He had parts (both in his virtues and his fortune) not so fit for a common-place as for observation. Certainly he was religious, both in his affection and observance. But as he could see clear (for those times) through superstition; so he would be blinded now and then by human policy. He advanced church-men. He was tender in privilege of the sanctuaries, though they wrought him much mischief. He built and endowed many religious foundations, besides his memorable hospital of the Savoy: and yet was he a great alms-giver in secret; which shewed that his works in public were dedicated rather to God's glory than his own. He professed always to love and seek peace; and it was his usual preface in his treaties, that when Christ came into the world peace was sung, and when he went out of the world peace was bequeathed. And this virtue could not proceed out of fear or softness, for he was valiant and active; and therefore no doubt it was truly Christian and moral. . . . . As for the disposition of his subjects in general towards him, it stood thus with him; that of the three affections which naturally tie the hearts of the subjects to their sovereign,—love, fear, and reverence,—he had the last in height; the second in good measure; and so little of the first, as he was beholding to the other two.

He was a Prince, sad, serious, and full of thoughts and secret observations; and full of notes and memorials of his own hand, especially touching persons; as whom to employ, whom to reward, whom to inquire of, whom to beware of, what were the dependencies, what were the factions, and the like; keeping (as it were) a journal of his thoughts. There is to this day a merry tale; that his monkey (set on as it was thought by one of his chamber) tore his principal note-book all to pieces, when by chance it lay forth: whereat the court which liked not those pensive accounts was almost tickled with sport.

He was indeed full of apprehensions and suspicions.   But
as he did easily take them, so he did easily check them and
master them ; whereby they were not dangerous, but troubled
himself more than others.   It is true, his thoughts were so
many, as they could not well always stand together; but
that which did good one way, did hurt another.

For his pleasures, there is no news of them. . . . He did by
pleasures as great Princes do by banquets, come and look a
little upon them, and turn away.   For never Prince was
more wholly given to his affairs, nor in them more of himself: insomuch as in triumphs of jousts and tourneys and
balls and masks (which they then called disguises) he was
rather a princely and gentle spectator than seemed much to
be delighted.

No doubt, in him as in all men (and most of all in kings)
his fortune wrought upon his nature, and his nature upon
his fortune.   He attained to the crown, not only from a
private fortune, which might endow him with moderation;
but also from the fortune of an exiled man, which had
quickened in him all seeds of observation and industry.
And his times being rather prosperous, than calm, had
raised his confidence by success, but almost marred his
nature by troubles.   His wisdom, by often evading from
perils, was turned rather into a dexterity to deliver himself
from dangers, when they pressed him, than into a providence to prevent and remove them afar off.   And even
in nature, the sight of his mind was like some sights of
eyes; rather strong at hand, than to carry afar off.   For
his wit increased upon the occasion; and so much the
more, if the occasion were sharpened by danger.   Again,
whether it were the shortness of his foresight, or the
strength of his will, or the dazzling of his suspicions, or
what it was; certain it is, that the perpetual troubles of his

fortunes (there being no more matter out of which they grew) could not have been without some great defects, and many errors in his nature, customs, and proceedings, which he had enough to do to save and help, with a thousand little industries and watches. But those do best appear in the story itself.

He was a comely personage, a little above just stature, well and straight limbed, but slender. His countenance was reverend, and a little like a churchman : and as it was not strange or dark, so neither was it winning or pleasing, but as the face of one well disposed. But it was to the disadvantage of the painter; for it was best when he spake.

His worth may bear a tale or two, that may put upon him somewhat that may seem divine.

One day when King Henry the Sixth (whose innocence gave him holiness) was washing his hands at a great feast, and cast his eye upon King Henry, then a young youth, he said, This is the lad, that shall possess quietly that, that we now strive for. But that that was truly divine in him, was that he had the fortune of a true Christian, as well as of a great King, in living exercised, and dying repentant. So as he had an happy warfare in both conflicts, both of sin, and the cross.

He was born at Pembroke Castle, and lieth buried at Westminster, in one of the stateliest and daintiest monuments of Europe, both for the chapel, and for the sepulchre. So that he dwelleth more richly dead, in the monument of his tomb, than he did alive in Richmond, or any of his palaces. I could wish he did the like, in this monument of his fame.

—*History of the Reign of King Henry the Seventh.*

VI.

JOHN DONNE.

1573-1631.

JOHN DONNE, of Welsh extraction, was born in London in
1573. His mother was descended from the family of the famous
Sir Thomas More. When only eleven years old he entered Hart
Hall, Oxford, from which in three years he removed to Trinity
College, Cambridge. He took no degree at either University:
his parents having brought him up as a Roman Catholic, he was
precluded from taking the necessary oaths. At seventeen he
was admitted of Lincoln's Inn, but coming in to a small fortune
by the death of his father, he betook himself to the study of
theology, in which direction his taste had always lain. He was
led as the result of his studies to attach himself to the Anglican
Church, as established under Elizabeth.

In the year 1596 he accompanied the Earl of Essex on his
Spanish expedition, and remained some time abroad, principally
in Italy and Spain. In 1603 he became secretary to Sir Thomas
Egerton, the Lord Keeper, who was afterwards made Chancellor,
with the title of Lord Ellesmere, under James the First. Donne was
thus on the road to state preferment, being much esteemed by
those in power, until the marriage which destroyed his prospects.
The interesting story of his marriage, and of the narrow circumstances to which he was reduced, having expended his patrimony
in storing his mind, may be read in the delightful narrative of
Izaak Walton, given among the extracts from that author. He
entered holy orders at the age of forty, yielding to the repeated
exhortations of Morton, Bishop of Durham, and the wish of King

James the First. Besides other preferment, he was appointed in 1621 to the Deanery of St. Paul's, and died March 31st, 1631.

Donne left poems which were published after his death, but his reputation as an author rests upon his *Sermons* and *Devotions*. He writes with a mind and imagination charged with matter, which strives, as it were, to press itself into each sentence. Full as his periods are, we feel that the store has been but sparingly dealt out, and that much more remains, if he would have said it. Having shone as a wit, in an age of wit, and an age when wit was not confined to ludicrous associations, but extended to a higher skill of point and antithesis, his language, though not strictly speaking obscure, requires close and unbroken attention to follow its meaning. The latest Editor of Donne's Sermons, Dean Alford, says there are passages in them which ' in depth and grandeur even surpass the strings of beautiful expressions to be found in Jeremy Taylor, and are the recreations of a loftier mind, and while Taylor's similes are exquisite in their melody of sound and happy in external description, Donne enters into the inner soul of art and gives his readers more satisfactory and permanent delight.'

·   ————————————   ı

1. Heavenly Mansions.

AND then a third beam of this consolation is, that in this house of his Father's, thus by him made ours, there are mansions; in which word, the consolation is not placed, (I do not say, that there is not truth in it) but the consolation is not placed in this, that some of these mansions are below, some above stairs, some better seated, better lighted, better vaulted, better fretted, better furnished than others ; but only in this, that they are mansions; which word, in the original, and Latin, and our language signifies a remaining, and denotes the perpetuity, the everlastingness of that state. A state but of one day, because no night shall overtake, or determine it, but such a day, as is not of a thousand years, which is the longest measure in the Scriptures, but of a thousand millions of millions of generations: *Qui nec praeceditur hesterno, nec excluditur crastino,* A day that hath no *pridie,* nor *postridie,* yesterday doth not usher it in, nor to-morrow shall not drive it out. Methusalem, with all his hundreds of years, was but a mushroom of a night's growth, to this day, and all the four monarchies, with all their thousands of years, and all the powerful kings, and àll the beautiful queens of this world, were but as a bed of flowers, some gathered at six, some at seven, some at eight, all in one morning, in respect of this day. In all the two thousand years of nature, before the law given by Moses, and the two thousand years of law, before the Gospel given by Christ, and the two thousand of grace, which are running now, (of which last hour we have heard three quarters strike, more than fifteen hundred of this last two thousand spent) in all this six thousand, and in all those, which God may be pleased to add, *in domo patris,* in this house of his Father's, there was never heard quarter-clock to strike, never seen minute glass to turn. No time less than itself would serve to express this time, which is intended in this word mansions; which is also exalted with another beam, that they are *Multa, In my Father's house there are many mansions.—Sermons.*

2. Religion.

For religion in general, is natural to us; the natural man hath naturally some sense of God, and some inclination to worship that power, whom he conceives to be God, and this worship is religion. But then the first thing that this general pious affection produces in us, is zeal, which is an exaltation of religion. *Primus actus voluntatis est amor;* Philosophers and divines agree in that, that the will of man cannot be idle, and the first act that the will of man produces, is love ; for till it love something, prefer and choose something, till it would have something, it is not a will ; neither can it turn upon any object, before God. So that this first, and general, and natural love of God, is not begotten in my soul, nor produced by my soul, but created and infused with my soul, and as my soul ; there is no soul that knows she is a soul, without such a general sense of the love of God. But to love God above all, to love him with all my faculties, this exaltation of this religious love of God, is the first-born of religion, and this is zeal. Religion, which is the worship of that power which I call God, does but make me a man ; the natural man hath that religion ; but that which makes me a father, and gives me an offspring, a first-born, that is zeal : by religion I am an Adam, but by zeal I am an Abel produced out of that Adam. Now if we consider times not long since past, there was scarce one house, scarce one of us, in whom this first-born, this zeal was not dead. Discretion is the ballast of our ship, that carries us steady ; but zeal is the very freight, the cargason, the merchandise itself, which enriches us in the land of the living ; and this was our case, we were all come to esteem our ballast more than our freight, our discretion more than our zeal ; we had more care to please great men than God ; more consideration of an imaginary change of times, than of unchangeable eternity itself. And as in storms it falls out often that men cast their wares and their freights overboard, but never their ballast, so soon as we thought we saw a storm, in point of religion, we cast off our zeal, our freight, and stuck to our ballast, our discretion, and thought it sufficient to sail on smoothly, and steadily, and calmly, and discreetly in the world, and with the time, though not so directly to the right haven. So our first-born in this house, in ourselves, our zeal, was dead. It was; there is the comfortable word of our text. But now, now that God hath taken his fan into his hand, and sifted his church, now that God hath put us into a straight and crooked limbeck, passed us through narrow and difficult trials, and set us upon a hot fire, and drawn us to a more precious substance and nature than before; now that God hath given our zeal a new concoction, a new refining, a new inanimation by this fire of tribulation, let us embrace and nurse up this new resurrection of this zeal, which his own Spirit hath begot and produced in us, and return to God with a whole and entire soul, without dividing or scattering our affections upon other objects; and in the sincerity of the true religion, without inclinations in ourselves, to induce, and without inclinableness, from others, upon whom we may depend, to admit, any drams of the dregs of a superstitious religion; for it is a miserable extremity, when we must take a little poison for physic. And so having made the right use of God's corrections, we shall enjoy the comfort of this phrase, in this house, ourselves, our first-born, our zeal was dead; it was, but it is not.— *Sermons.*

3. For, where your Heart is, there is your Treasure also.

LITERALLY, primarily, radically, *thesaurus*, treasure, is no more but *Depositum in crastinum*, Provision for to-morrow; to show how little a proportion, a regulated mind, and a contented heart may make a treasure. But we have enlarged the signification of these words, provision, and, to-morrow: for, provision must signify all that can any way be compassed; and to-morrow must signify as long as there shall be a to-morrow, till time shall be no more: but waiving these infinite extensions, and perpetuities, is there any thing of that nature, as, (taking the word treasure in the narrowest signification, to be but provision for to-morrow) we are sure shall last till to-morrow? Sits any man here in an assurance, that he will be the same to-morrow, that he is now? You have your honours, your offices, your possessions, perchance under seal; a seal of wax; wax that hath a tenacity, an adhering, a cleaving nature, to show the royal constancy of his heart, that gives them, and would have them continue with you, and stick to you. But then, wax, if it be heat, hath a melting, a fluid, a running nature too: so have these honours, and offices, and possessions, to them that grow too hot, too confident in them, or too imperious by them. For these honours, and offices, and possessions, you have a seal, a fair and just evidence of assurance; but have they any seal upon you, any assurance of you till to-morrow? Did our blessed Saviour give day, or any hope of a to-morrow, to that man, to whom he said, *Fool, this night they fetch away thy soul?* Or is there any of us that can say, Christ sayed not that to him?—*A Lent Sermon.*

4. Sleep.

NATURAL men have conceived a two-fold use of sleep; that it is a refreshing of the body in this life; that it is a preparing of the soul for the next; that it is a feast, and it is the grace at that feast; that it is our recreation, and cheers us, and it is our catechism, and instructs us; we lie down in a hope, that we shall rise the stronger; and we lie down in a knowledge, that we may rise no more. Sleep is an opiate, which gives us rest; but such an opiate, as perchance, being under it, we shall wake no more. But though natural men, who have induced secondary and figurative considerations, have found out this second, this emblematical

use of sleep, that it should be a representation of death, God,
who wrought and perfected his work, before nature began
(for nature was but his apprentice, to learn in the first seven
days, and now is his foreman, and works next under him)
. God, I say, intended sleep only for the refreshing of man by
bodily rest, and not for a figure of death, for he intended not
death itself then. But man having induced death upon himself God hath taken man's creature, death, into his hand,
and mended it; and whereas it hath in itself a fearful form
and aspect, so that man is afraid of his own creature, God
presents it to him, in a familiar, in an assiduous, in an agreeable, and acceptable form, in sleep, that so when he awakes
from sleep, and says to himself, shall I be no otherwise when
I am dead, than I was even now, when I was asleep, he may
be ashamed of his waking dreams, and of his melancholy
fancying out a horrid and an affrightful figure of that death
which is so like sleep. As then we need sleep to live out
our threescore and ten years, so we need death, to live that
life which we cannot outlive. And as death being our
. enemy, God allows us to defend ourselves against it (for
we victual ourselves against death, twice every day, as often
as we eat) so God having so sweetened death unto us, as
he hath in sleep, we put ourselves into our enemy's hands
once every day, so far, as sleep is death: and sleep is as
much death as meat is life.—*Meditations.*

·5. The Passing Bell.

THE bell rings out, the pulse thereof is changed; the
tolling was a faint, and intermitting pulse, upon one side;
this stronger, and argues more and better life. His soul
is gone out; and as a man who had a lease of one
thousand years after the expiration of a short one, or an
inheritance after the life of a man, in a consumption, he

is now entered into the possession of his better estate. His soul is gone; Whither? Who saw it come in, or who saw it go out? Nobody; yet every body is sure, he had one, and hath none. If I will ask mere philosophers, what the soul is, I shall find amongst them, that will tell me, it is nothing, but the temperament, and harmony, and just and equal composition of the elements in the body, which produces all those faculties which we ascribe to the soul; and so, in itself is nothing, no separable substance, that overlives the body. They see the soul is nothing else in other creatures, and they affect an impious humility, to think as low of man. But if my soul were no more than the soul of a beast, I could not think so; that soul that can reflect upon itself, consider itself, is more than so. If I will ask, not mere philosophers, but mixt men, philosophical divines, how the soul, being a separate substance, enters into man, I shall find some, that will tell me, that it is by generation and procreation from parents, because they think it hard, to charge the soul with the guiltiness of original sin, if the soul were infused into a body, in which it must necessarily grow foul, and contract original sin, whether it will or no; and I shall find some that will tell me, that it is by immediate infusion from God, because they think it hard, to maintain an immortality in such a soul, as should be begotten and derived with the body from mortal parents. If I will ask, not a few men, but almost whole bodies, whole churches, what becomes of the souls of the righteous, at the departing thereof from the body, I shall be told by some, that they attend an expiation, a purification in a place of torment; by some, that they attend the fruition of the sight of God, in a place of rest; but yet, but of expectation; by some, that they pass to immediate possession of the presence of God. St. Augustine studied the nature of the soul, as much as any thing, but the salvation of the soul; and he sent an express messenger to St. Hierome, to consult of some things concerning the soul: but he satisfies himself with this: Let the departure of my soul to salvation, be evident to my faith, and I care the less, how dark the entrance of my soul, into my body, be to my reason. It is the going out, more than the coming in, that concerns us. This soul, this bell tells me, is gone out; Whither? Who shall tell me that? I know not who it is; much less what he was: the condition of the man, and the course of his life, which should tell me whither he is gone, I know not. I was not there in his sickness, nor at his death; I saw not his way, nor his end, nor can ask them who did, thereby to conclude, or argue, whither he is gone. But yet I have one nearer me than all these, mine own charity; I ask that, and that tells me, he is gone to everlasting rest, and joy, and glory: I owe him a good opinion, it is but thankful charity in me, because I received benefit and instruction from him when his bell tolled: and I, being made the fitter to pray, by that disposition, wherein I was assisted by his occasion, did pray for him; and I pray not without faith; so I do charitably, so I do faithfully believe, that that soul is gone to everlasting rest, and joy, and glory. But for the body, how poor a wretched thing is that! We cannot express it so fast, as it grows worse and worse. That body, which scarce three minutes since was such a house, as that that soul, which made but one step from thence to heaven, was scarce thoroughly content, to leave that for heaven: that body hath lost the name of a dwelling-house, because none dwells in it, and is making haste to lose the name of a body, and dissolve to putrefaction. Who would not be affected to see a clear and sweet river in the morning, grow a kennel of muddy land-water by noon, and condemned to the saltness of the sea by night? and how lame a picture, how faint a representation, is that, of the precipitation of man's body to dissolution! Now all the parts built up, and knit by a lovely soul, now but a statue of clay, and now these limbs melted off, as if that clay were but snow; and now, the whole house is but a handful of sand, so much dust, and but a peck of rubbish, so much bone. If he, who as this bell tells me, is gone now, were some excellent artificer, who comes to him for a cloak, or for a garment now? or for counsel, if he were a lawyer? If a magistrate for justice? Man, before he hath his immortal soul, hath a soul of sense, and a soul of vegetation before that: this immortal soul did not forbid other souls to be in us before, but when this soul departs, it carries all with it; no more vegetation, no more sense: such a mother-in-law is the earth, in respect of our natural mother; in her womb we grew; and when she was delivered of us, we were planted in some place, in some calling in the world; in the womb of the earth, we diminish, and when she is delivered of us, our grave opened for another, we are not transplanted, but transported, our dust, blown away with prophane dust, with every wind.— *Meditations.*

VII.

JOSEPH HALL, BISHOP OF NORWICH.

1574–1656.

JOSEPH HALL was born at Ashby-de-la-Zouch, July 1st, 1574. He was educated at the Grammar School of Ashby, and at the age of fifteen was entered at Cambridge, at Emmanuel College, of which College he became Scholar, and in 1595 Fellow. In 1598 he published his *Satires*, and established his fame as a genuine humourist. After taking his degree as Master of Arts, he held a lectureship in rhetoric, but resigned it, finding that it interfered with the study of theology, and soon afterwards he entered holy orders. His preaching soon attracted attention, and after obtaining some small pieces of preferment, he was made Dean of Worcester in 1616. Until this time, when he was upwards of forty years of age, Hall had suffered from poverty, and often, as he said, 'wrote books in order to buy books.' In 1618 he was a deputy at the Synod of Dort. In 1627 he was made Bishop of Exeter. In 1641 he was translated to the see of Norwich. Hall was a man of singular moderation, and great sweetness of character. In an age of fierce and truculent controversy, he set a noble example of charity in polemics. The Long Parliament deprived him of the revenue of his bishopric, and he died on the 8th of September, 1656, at Heigham, near Norwich. Bishop Hall did not escape altogether from the literary vice of his age. His pages are studded with conceits and sententious passages, which are too common, and repel many readers. At times, however, he rises to the very highest eloquence, and all his writings attest the sincerity and piety of his nature. The *Contem-*

plations on the principal passages of Holy Story are, perhaps, his most popular work, and display the powers of his thought and style in great perfection. Besides these he left many sermons and numerous treatises on moral, religious or polemical topics. He was suspected at one time of being a favourer of the Puritans, but though his principles were tolerant, he published, even when it was hazardous to do so, several able treatises in defence of the Liturgy and Discipline of the National Church of England.

It is observable that the later writings of Hall are in a simpler and more easy vein. The same progress, which has been noted in Clarendon's later efforts, may be traced in Hall's. During the long struggle of those eventful years, many colloquial expressions, formerly deemed inadmissible, seem to have crept by degrees into ordinary use, and to have found their place in literature. As a controversialist, Bishop Hall won a high place, and his modest yet manly defence of his own Church, is acknowledged to have had considerable influence with some of his Nonconformist adversaries. In times when the pulpit was too often degraded by the sallies and impertinencies of preachers, it is no slight praise to say, as may be said of Hall, that there is hardly a passage in his sermons which the most fastidious critic would desire to expunge.

---

1. David.

EVER since his anointing was David possessed with God's Spirit, and thereby filled both with courage and wisdom: the more strange doth it seem to him that all Israel should be thus dastardly. Those that are themselves eminent in any grace cannot but wonder at the miserable defects of others; and the more shame they see in others' imperfections, the more is their zeal in avoiding those errors in themselves.

While base hearts are moved by example, the want of

example is encouragement enough for an heroical mind: therefore is David ready to undertake the quarrel, because no man else dare do it. His eyes sparkled with holy anger, and his heart rose up to his mouth when he heard this proud challenger; *Who is this uncircumcised Philistine, that he should* revile the host *of the living God?* Even so, O Saviour, when all the generations of men ran away affrighted from the powers of death and darkness, thou alone hast undertaken and confounded them.

Who should offer to daunt the holy courage of David but his own brethren! The envious heart of Eliab construes this forwardness as his own disgrace: 'Shall I,' thinks he, 'be put down by this puisne? Shall my father's youngest son dare to attempt that which my stomach will not serve me to adventure?' Now therefore he rates David for his presumption, and instead of answering to the recompense of the victory, (which others were ready to give,) he recompenseth the very inquiry of David with a check. It was for his brethren's sake that David came thither, and yet his very journey is cast upon him by them for a reproach; *Wherefore camest thou down hither?* and when their bitterness can meet with nothing·else to shame him, his sheep are cast in his teeth: 'Is it for thee, an idle proud boy, to be meddling with our martial matters? Doth not yonder champion look as if he were a fit match for thee? What makest thou of thyself, or what dost thou think of us? Ywis it were fitter for thee to be looking to thy sheep than looking at Goliath; the wilderness would become thee better than the field: wherein art thou equal to any man thou seest, but in arrogance and presumption? The pastures of Bethlehem could not hold thee, but thou thoughtest it a goodly matter to see the wars: I know thee, as if I were in thy bosom, this was thy thought, "There is no glory to be got among fleeces, I will go seek it in arms; now are my brethren winning honour in the troops of Israel, while I am basely tending on sheep, why should I not be as forward as the best of them?" This vanity would make thee straight of a shepherd a soldier; and of a soldier, a champion: get thee home, foolish stripling, to thy hook and thy harp: let swords and spears alone to those that know how to use them.'

It is quarrel enough amongst many to a good action that it is not their own.

There is no enemy so ready or so spiteful as the domestical: the hatred of brethren is so much more as their blood is nearer: the malice of strangers is simple, but of a brother is mixed with envy. The more unnatural any quality is, the more extreme it is: a cold wind from the south is intolerable.

David's first victory is of himself, next of his brother: he overcomes himself in a patient forbearance of his brother; he overcomes the malicious rage of his brother with the mildness of his answer. If David had wanted spirit, he had not been troubled with the insultation of a Philistine. If he had a spirit to match Goliath, how doth he so calmly receive the affront of a brother? *What have I now done? Is there not a cause?* That which would have stirred the choler of another allayeth his: it was a brother that wronged him, and that his eldest; neither was it time to quarrel with a brother while the Philistines' swords were drawn, and Goliath was challenging. O that these two motives could induce us to peace! If we have injury in our person, in our cause, it is from brethren, and the Philistines look on. I am deceived if this conquest were less glorious than the following. He is fit to be God's champion that hath learned to be victor of himself.

It is not this sprinkling of cold water that can quench the fire of David's zeal; but still his courage sends up flames of desires; still he goes on to inquire and to proffer : he whom the regard of others' envy can dismay shall never do aught worthy of envy : never man undertook any exploit of worth and received not some discouragement in the way.—*Contemplations.*

2. The Happy Man.

HE is an happy man, that hath learned to read himself more than all books, and hath so taken out this lesson, that he can never forget it; that knows the world, and cares not for it; that, after many traverses of thoughts, is grown to know what he may trust to, and stands now equally armed for all events; that hath got the mastery at home; so as he can cross his will without a mutiny, and so please it, that he makes it not a wanton : that in earthly things wishes no more than nature; in spiritual, is ever graciously ambitious : that for his condition, stands on his own feet, not needing to lean upon the great; and can so frame his thoughts to his estate, that when he hath least he cannot want, because he is as free from desire as superfluity : that hath seasonably broken the headstrong restiness of prosperity, and can now manage it at pleasure; upon whom all smaller crosses light as hailstones upon a roof; and for the greater calamities, he can take them as tributes of life and tokens of love; and if his ship be tossed, yet he is sure his anchor is fast. If all the world were his, he could be no other than he is; no whit gladder of himself, no whit higher in his carriage; because he knows contentment lies not in the things he hath, but in the mind that values them. The powers of his resolution can either multiply or subtract at pleasure. He can make his cottage a manor or a palace when he lists; and his home-close a large dominion; his stained cloth, arras; his earth, plate; and can see state in the attendance of one servant : as one that hath learned, a man's greatness or baseness is in himself; and in this he may even contest with the proud, that he thinks his own the best. Or, if he must be outwardly great, he can but turn the other end of the glass, and make his stately manor a low and strait cottage; and in all his costly furniture, he can see, not richness, but use : he can see dross in the best metal; and earth through the best clothes : and in all his troop he can see himself his own servant. He lives quietly at home, out of the noise of the world; and loves to enjoy himself always; and sometimes his friend: and hath as full scope to his thoughts as to his eyes. He walks ever even, in the midway betwixt hopes and fears; resolved to fear nothing but God, to hope for nothing but that which he must have. He hath a wise and virtuous mind in a serviceable body, which that better part affects as a present servant and a future companion; so cherishing his flesh, as one that would scorn to be all flesh. He hath no enemies; not for that all love him, but because he knows to make a gain of malice. ·He is not so engaged to any earthly thing that they two cannot part on even terms; there is neither laughter in their meeting, nor in their shaking of hands tears. He keeps ever the best company; the God of spirits, and the spirits of that God; whom he entertains continually in an awful familiarity; not being hindered, either with too much light, or with none at all. His conscience and his hand are friends, and, what devil

soever tempt him, will not fall out: that divine part goes
ever uprightly and freely; not stooping under the burden
of a willing sin, not fettered with the gives of unjust
scruples.   He would not, if he could, run away from
himself or from God; not caring from whom he lies hid,
so he may look these two in the face.   Censures and
applauses are passengers to him, not guests; his ear is
their thoroughfare, not their harbour; he hath learned to
fetch both his counsel and his sentence from his own breast.
He doth not lay weight upon his own shoulders, as one
that loves to torment himself, with the honour of much
employment; but, as he makes work his game, so doth
he not list to make himself work.   His strife is ever to
redeem, and not to spend time.   It is his trade to do
good, and to think of it his recreation.   He hath hands
enow for himself and others; which are ever stretched
forth for beneficence, not for need.   He walks cheerfully
in the way that God hath chalked, and never wishes it
more wide or more smooth.   Those very temptations
whereby he is foiled strengthen him: he comes forth
crowned and triumphing out of the spiritual battles; and
those scars that he hath, make him beautiful.   His soul
is every day dilated to receive that God in whom he is;
and hath attained to love himself for God, and God for
his own sake.   His eyes stick so fast in heaven, that no
earthly object can remove them: yea, his whole self is
there before his time; and sees with Stephen, and hears
with Paul, and enjoys with Lazarus, the glory that he
shall have; and takes possession beforehand of his room
amongst the saints.   And these heavenly contentments
have so taken him up, that now he looks down displeasedly
upon the earth, as the region of his sorrow and banishment: yet, joying more in hope than troubled with the

sense of evils, he holds it no great matter to live, and his greatest business to die; and is so well acquainted with his last guest, that he fears no unkindness from him: neither makes he any other of dying than of walking home when he is abroad; or of going to bed when he is weary of the day. He is well provided for both worlds; and is sure of peace here, of glory hereafter; and therefore hath a light heart and a cheerful face. All his fellow-creatures rejoice to serve him: his betters, the angels, love to observe him: God himself takes pleasure to converse with him: and hath sainted him afore his death, and in his death crowned him.—*Characters of Virtues.*

3. The Deceit of Appearances.

SHOULD appearance be the rule, how scornfully would the carnal eye overlook the poor ordinances of God? What would it find here but foolishness of preaching, homeliness of sacraments, an inky letter, a priest's lips, a savourless message, a morsel of bread, a mouthful of wine, a handful of water, a slanderbeaten cross, a crucified Saviour, a militant Church, a despised profession? When yet this foolishness of preaching is the power of God to salvation; these mute letters the lively oracles of God; these vile lips, the cabinets of heaven to preserve knowledge; this unplausible message, *magnalia Dei;* this water, the water of life in the midst of the Paradise of God, ἄριστον μὲν ὕδωρ ; this bread, the manna of angels; this wine, heavenly nectar ; this Church, the King's daughter, all glorious within; this dying sacrifice, the Lord of life ; this cross, the banner of victory; this pro-fession, heaven upon earth: *Judge not therefore according to appearance.*

Should appearance be the rule, woe were God's children,

happy were his enemies. Who that had seen Cain standing
masterly over the bleeding carcass of Abel, Joseph in his
bonds, his mistress in her dress, Moses in the flags, Pharaoh
in the palace, David skulking in the wilderness, Saul com-
manding in the court, Elijah fainting under his juniper tree,
Jezebel painting in her closet, Micaiah in the prison, Zidkijah
in the presence, Jeremiah in the dungeon, Zedekiah in the
throne, Daniel trembling among the lions, the Median
princes feasting in their bowers, John's head bleeding in the
platter, Herod smiling at the revels, Christ at the bar, Pilate
on the bench, the disciples scourged, the scribes and elders
insulting; would not have said, O happy Cain, Potiphar's
wife, Pharaoh, Saul, Jezebel, Zidkijah, Zedekiah, Median
princes, Pilate, Herod, elders; miserable Abel, Joseph,
Moses, David, Elijah, Micaiah, Jeremiah, Daniel, John,
Christ, the disciples? Yet we know Cain's victory was
as woful as Abel's martyrdom glorious; Joseph's irons
were more precious than the golden tires of his mistress:
Moses' reeds were more sure than Pharaoh's cedars;
David's cave in the desert more safe than the towers of
Saul; Elijah's raven a more comfortable purveyor than all
the officers of Jezebel; Micaiah's prison was the guard-
chamber of angels, when Ahab's presence was the council-
chamber of evil spirits; Jeremiah's dungeon had moré true
light of comfort than the shining state of Zedekiah; Daniel
was better guarded with the lions than Darius and the
Median princes with their janisaries; John's head was
more rich with the crown of his martyrdom than Herod's
with the diadem of his tetrarchate; Christ at the bar gave
life and being to Pilate on the bench, gave motion to those
hands that struck him, to that tongue that condemned him,
and, in the mean while, gave sentence on his judge: the
disciples were better pleased with their stripes and weals

than the Jewish elders with their proud phylacteries. After this, who that had seen the primitive Christians; some broiled on gridirons, others boiled in lead ; some roasted, others frozen to death ; some flayed, others torn with horses ; some crashed in pieces by the teeth of lions, others cast down from the rocks to the stakes ; some smiling on the wheel, others in the flame ; all wearying their tormentors, and shaming their tyrants, with their patience : would not have said, ' Of all things I would not be a Christian ? ' Yet even this while, were these poor torturing-stocks higher, as Marcus Arethusius bragged, than their persecutors : dying victors ; yea, victors of death : never so glorious as when they began not to be : in gasping, crowned ; in yielding the ghost, more than conquerors : *Judge not therefore according to appearance.—Sermons.*

4. The Busybody.

His estate is too narrow for his mind, and therefore he is fain to make himself room in others' affairs ; yet ever, in pretence of love. No news can stir but by his door; neither can he know that which he must not tell. What every man ventures in Guiana voyage, and what they gained, he knows to a hair. Whether Holland will have peace, he knows ; and on what conditions, and with what success, is familiar to him, ere it be concluded. No post can pass him without a question ; and rather than he will lose the news, he rides back with him to appose him of tidings : and then to the next man he meets he supplies the wants of his hasty intelligence, and makes up a perfect tale ; wherewith he so haunteth the patient auditor, that, after many excuses, he is fain to endure rather the censure of his manners in running away, than the tediousness of an impertinent discourse. His speech is oft broken off with a succession of long parentheses, which he ever vows to fill up ere the conclusion ; and perhaps would effect it, if the other's ear were as unweariable as his tongue.   If he sees but two men talk, and read a letter in the street, he runs to them, and asks if he may not be partner of that secret relation ; and if they deny it, he offers to tell, since he may not hear, wonders ; and then falls upon the report of the Scottish mine, or of the great fish taken up at Lynn, or of the freezing of the Thames ; and, after many thanks and dismissions, is hardly entreated silence.   He undertakes as much as he performs little.   This man will thrust himself forward, to be the guide of the way he knows not ; and calls at his neighbour's window, and asks why his servants are not at work. The market hath no commodity which he prizeth not, and which the next table shall not hear recited.   His tongue, like the tail of Samson's foxes, carries firebrands, and is enough to set the whole field of the world on a flame. Himself begins tabletalk of his neighbour at another's board ; to whom he bears the first news, and adjures him to conceal the reporter : whose choleric answer he returns to his first host, enlarged with a second edition : so, as it uses to be done in the fight of unwilling mastiffs, he claps each on the side apart, and provokes them to an eager conflict.   There can no act pass without his comment ; which is ever far-fetched, rash, suspicious, dilatory.   His ears are long, and his eyes quick ; but most of all to imperfections, which as he easily sees, so he increases with intermeddling.   He harbours another man's servant ; and, amidst his entertainment, asks what fare is usual at home, what hours are kept, what talk passeth their meals, what his master's disposition is, what his government, what his guests : and when he hath by curious inquiries extracted all the juice and spirit of hoped intelligence, turns him off whence he came, and works on a new.   He hates constancy, as an earthen dulness, unfit for men of spirit; and loves to change his work and his place : neither yet can he be so soon weary of any place as every place is weary of him : for as he sets himself on work, so others pay him with hatred; and look, how many masters he hath, so many enemies; neither is it possible that any should not hate him but who know him not. So then he labours without thanks; talks without credit; lives without love; dies without tears, without pity; save that some say, 'It was pity he died no sooner.'—*Characters of Vices.*

5. Common Prayer.

THE liturgy of the church of England hath been hitherto esteemed sacred, reverently used by holy martyrs, daily frequented by devout protestants, as that which more than once hath been allowed and confirmed by the edicts of religious princes, and by your own parliamentary acts, and but lately being translated into other languages, hath been entertained abroad with the great applause of foreign divines and churches; yet now begins to complain of scorn at home.

The matter is quarrelled by some; the form by others; the use of it by both.

That which was never before heard of in the church of God, whether Jewish or Christian, the very prescription of the most holy devotion offendeth. Surely our blessed Saviour and his gracious forerunner were so far from this new divinity, as that they plainly taught taht which these men gainsay, a direct form of prayer; and such, as that part of the frame prescribed by our Saviour was composed of those forms of devotion then formerly usual. And God's people, ever since Moses's days, constantly practised it, and put it over until the times of the gospel: under which, while it is said that Peter and John went up to the temple at the ninth

hour of prayer, we know the prayer wherewith they joined
was not of an extemporary and sudden conception, but of
a regular prescription; the forms whereof are yet extant,
and ready to be produced. And the evangelical church
ever since thought it could never better improve her peace
and happiness, than in composing those religious models
of invocation and thanksgiving which they have traduced
unto us.

And can ye then with patience think that any ingenuous
Christian should be so far mistransported as to condemn
a good prayer because, as it is in his heart, so it is in his
book too?

Far be it from me to dishearten any good Christian from
the use of conceived prayer in his private devotions, and
upon occasion also in the public. I would hate to be guilty
of pouring so much water upon the Spirit, to which I shall
gladly add oil rather. No, let the full soul freely pour out
itself in gracious expressions of its holy thoughts into the
bosom of the Almighty. Let both the sudden flashes of our
quick ejaculations and the constant flames of our more fixed
conceptions mount up from the altar of a zealous heart unto
the throne of grace; and if there be some stops or solecisms
in the fervent utterance of our private wants, these are so far
from being offensive, that they are the most pleasing music
to the ears of that God unto whom our prayers come. Let
them be broken off with sobs and sighs and incongruities of
our delivery, our good God is no otherwise affected to this
imperfect elocution than an indulgent parent is to the clipped
and broken language of his dear child, which is more delightful to him than any other's smooth oratory. This is not to
be opposed in another, by any man that hath found the true
operation of this grace in himself.—*An Humble Remonstrance
for Liturgy and Episcopacy.*

VIII.

EDWARD HERBERT, LORD CHERBURY.

1581–1648.

EDWARD HERBERT was fourth in descent from Sir Richard, whose brother William was created Earl of Pembroke by Edward IV.

When twelve years old, Edward entered University College, Oxford, with some knowledge of Greek, Latin, and logic, and during the next six years pursued his studies there. While at Oxford he married, by the wish of his family, a cousin, the heiress of large estates, which it was desired to retain for the name of Herbert. He was barely twenty when he removed from Oxford with his wife to London, where, though favourably noticed at Court by the Queen, he devoted his time to serious studies, 'the more he learned adding still a desire to know more.'

On the accession of James he was made Knight of the Bath, and a few years later visited France, and there lived much with the Constable de Montmorenci and with Casaubon.

During the campaigns of 1610 and of 1614, he served with distinction in the Low Countries, under the Prince of Orange, against the Spaniards, and he then travelled through Germany to Italy.

From 1619 he acted with dignity and spirit as English Am-bassador at Paris, where in 1624 his first work, *De Veritate*, etc., was published, and attracted much attention.

The following year he was created a Peer of Ireland, and in 1631 of England, by the title of Lord Herbert, of Cherbury.

Lord Herbert sought at first to defend King Charles, but when the real struggle commenced he sided with the Parliament, and suffered much from the vengeance of the Royalists.

He died in 1648, knowing, as he says in the epitaph which he wrote for himself,

> 'That his immortal soul should find above
> With his Creator, peace, joy, truth and love.'

He was in his day no mean master of English, a truth-loving though somewhat sceptical philosopher, and a noble man ; brave as a knight-errant, never taking gift or reward, and even 'from childhood,' as he says, 'never choosing to stain his mind with telling a lie.'

His autobiography (first printed in 1764), and his *Life and Reign of King Henry the Eighth* (published in 1649), both deserve to be better known than they are.

His Latin treatises on *Natural Religion*, etc., prove him, says Leland, 'the most eminent of Deistical writers.' His *Occasional Poems*, published in 1665, show that he (like his brother George Herbert, of Bemerton) had in him something of a poet's feeling.

> 'The well accorded birds did sing,
>   Their hymns unto the present time,
>   And in a sweet concerted chime,
> Did welcome in the cheerful Spring.
> To which soft whispers of the wind,
>   And warbling murmur of a brook,
>   And varied notes of leaves that shook,
> A harmony of parts did bind.'

---

1. This Life and the Life to Come.

THE very furthest thing I remember is, that when I understood what was said by others, I did yet forbear to speak, lest I should utter something that were imperfect or impertinent. When I came to talk, one of the furthest inquiries I made was, how I came into this world? I told my nurse, keeper, and others, I found myself here indeed, but from what cause or beginning, or by what means, I could not imagine; but for this, as I was laughed at by nurse and some other women that were then present, so I was wondered at by others, who said, they never heard a child but myself ask that question; upon which, when I came to riper years, I made this observation, which afterwards a little comforted me, that as I found myself in possession of this life, without knowing anything of the pangs and throes my mother suffered, when yet doubtless they did not less press and afflict me than her, so I hope my soul shall pass to a better life than this without being sensible of the anguish and pains my body shall feel in death. For as I believe then I shall be transmitted to a more happy estate by God's great grace, I am confident I shall no more know how I came out of this world, than how I came into it. . . . .

And certainly, since in my mother's womb this plastica, or formatrix, which formed my eyes, ears, and other senses, did not intend them for that dark and noisome place, but, as being conscious of a better life, made them as fitting organs to apprehend and perceive those things which should occur in this world; so I believe, since my coming into this world my soul hath formed or produced certain faculties which are almost as useless for this life, as the above-named senses were for the mother's womb; and these faculties are hope, faith, love, and joy, since they never rest or fix upon any transitory or perishing object in this world, as extending themselves to something further than can be here given, and indeed acquiesce only in the perfect, eternal and infinite. I confess they are of some use here; yet I appeal to every body whether any worldly felicity did so satisfy their hope here, that they did not wish and hope

for something more excellent; or whether they had ever
that faith in their own wisdom, or in the help of man,
that they were not constrained to have recourse to some
diviner and superior power than they could find on earth,
to relieve them in their danger or necessity; whether ever
they could place their love on any earthly beauty, that it
did not fade and wither, if not frustrate or deceive them;
or whether ever their joy was so consummate in any thing
they delighted in, that they did not want much more than
it, or indeed this world can afford, to make them happy.
The proper objects of these faculties, therefore, though
framed, or at least appearing in this world, is God only,
upon whom faith, hope, and love were never placed in
vain, or remain long unrequited. But to leave these discourses, and come to my childhood again; I remember
this defluxion at my ears above-mentioned continued in
that violence, that my friends did not think fit to teach
me so much as my alphabet, till I was seven years old,
at which time my defluxion ceased, and left me free of
the disease my ancestors were subject unto, being the
epilepsy. My schoolmaster, in the house of my said lady
grandmother, then began to teach me the alphabet, and
afterwards grammar, and other books commonly read in
schools, in which I profited so much, that upon this theme
Audaces fortuna juvat, I made an oration of a sheet of
paper, and fifty or sixty verses in the space of one day.
I remember in that time I was corrected sometimes for
going to cuffs with two school-fellows, being both elder
than myself, but never for telling a lie, or any other fault;
my natural disposition and inclination being so contrary
to all falsehood, that being demanded whether I had committed any fault whereof I might be justly suspected, I did
use ever to confess it freely, and thereupon choosing rather

to suffer correction than to stain my mind with telling
a lie, which I did judge then, no time could ever deface;
and I can affirm to all the world truly, that from my first
infancy to this hour I told not willingly any thing that was
false, my soul naturally having an antipathy to lying and
deceit.—*Autobiography.*

2. Wolsey.

AT last the bishop (of Winchester) thinking how to better
his party, brought in this Thomas Woolsey; to which
purpose also Sir Thomas Lovell, Knight, and master of
the wards, assisted him. This man, though of mean birth,
being observed by them to be of a quick and stirring wit,
and particularly famous for a dispatch in Henry VII. his
time, wherein he used extraordinary diligence, was thought
a fit instrument for their purposes. He was already a
chaplain in the household, and almoner, and from thence
raised to the place of a counsellor. Being in this nearness,
he knew as well how to discourse with the king in matter
of learning, (the king being much addicted to the reading
of Thomas Aquinas) as to comply with him in his delights;
insomuch, as (saith Polydore) he would sing, dance, laugh,
jest, and play with those youths in whose attendance and
company the king much delighted. Briefly, (to use Polydore's words) he made his private house a receptacle for
pleasures of all kinds, where he frequently entertain'd the
king. He omitted not yet in the midst of all these jollities,
to speak seriously, representing so all businesses to the
king, as he got much credit with him. And this, again,
was confirm'd by those gallants, who contributed no little
thereunto. Whereupon he began to tell the king, that he
should sometimes follow his studies in school-divinity, and

sometimes take his pleasure, and leave the care of publick
affairs to him : promising that what was amiss in his kingdom
should be rectified. Likewise, he omitted not to infuse
fears and jealousies of all those whom he conceived the
king might affect. Whereby he became so perfect a
courtier, that he had soon attained the height of favour.
For as princes have arts to govern kingdoms, courtiers
have those by which they govern their princes, when
through any indisposition they grow unapt for affairs.
These arts being hopes and fears, which as doors and
passages to the heart, are so guarded by their vigilancy,
that they can both let themselves in, and keep all others
out : and therefore may be termed not only the two ends
of that thread upon which government depends, but
through their dexterous handling may be tyed upon
what knot they will.—*Life and Reign of King Henry
VIII.*

3. The Foundation of Christ Church.

The design for the college of Ipswich, was to erect only
a grammar-school, to train up the youth till they were
ready for the university; but that in Oxford (call'd first
Cardinal's, then King's College, now Christ's Church) was
nobler; for the building was intended most ample and
magnificent, as the foundations and first lines demonstrate,
the number of students, professors, etc. great; as appears
by a catalogue found among our records. . . .

I find also, that about 1524, he sought in Italy and
elsewhere, for able men to be his readers. Among whom
at this time the excellent John Ludovicus Vives (a Spaniard)
was sent to him to be professor of eloquence in Oxford.
And, for books, he sent to have the rarer sort copy'd out of
the pope's library.

These so great preparations, made the cardinal use many rigorous means of getting moneys, as by visitation of religious houses, etc. and at last by the ruin of divers. To perform this yet, he was to obtain the consent of the pope and his. king. The reasons represented to the pope, were, I suppose, of this nature :

That his holiness could not be ignorant what divers effects this new invention of printing had produc'd. For as it had brought in and restor'd books and learning, so together it had been the occasion of those sects and schisms which daily appeared in the world, but chiefly in Germany; where men began now to call in question the present faith and tenets of the Church, and to examine how far religion is departed from its primitive institution. And, that which particularly was most to be lamented, they had exhorted lay and ordinary men to read the Scriptures, and to pray in their vulgar tongue. That, if this were suffer'd, besides all other dangers, the common people at last might come to believe that there was not so much use of the clergy. For if men were persuaded once they could make their own way to God, and that prayers in their native and ordinary language might pierce heaven, as well as Latin; how much would the authority of the mass fall? How prejudicial might this prove unto all our ecclesiastical orders ?

That there were many things to be look'd to in these innovators, but nothing so much as this; since it was clear, that the keeping of the mysteries of religion in the hands of priests, had been a principal means in all ages, of making the priesthood sacred and venerable. That these mysteries and rites therefore, as the greatest secret and arcanum of church-government, should be preserv'd. Nay, that the clergy should rather fly to tropes and

allegories, if not to Cabala it self, than permit that all the
parts of religious worship, though so obvious, as to fall
easily within common understandings, should be without
their explication; since it might be well question'd, whether
the essence of religion, (consisting in the doctrine of good
life and repentance) might be held sufficient alone to exercise
even the most vulgar capacities; unless frequent traditions
concerning former times, and such obscure passages as
need interpretation, did concur. In which state of things
therefore, nothing remain'd so much to be done, as to
prevent further apostacy. For this purpose, since printing
could not be put down, it were best to set up learning
against learning; and, by introducing able persons to
dispute, to suspend the laity, betwixt fear and controversies. This, at worst yet, would make them attentive to
their superiors and teachers. All which being maturely
weigh'd by his holiness, it was not doubted but he would
advise, and commend to all Christian princes, the erecting
of new colleges and seminaries for the advancement of
learning; and here in England particularly, where many
favourers of Luther's sect, but especially of Zuinglius, did
appear. Yet because his holiness, by our ambassadors at
Rome, had divers times been inform'd of the great expences
of his king in the wars he had made with France and
Scotland, he did not think it the best course to desire
any money out of his purse. That therefore he had
thought of another expedient, which he humbly offer'd to
his holiness; which was, that in regard the number of
monasteries was greater in this kingdom, than that there
could be found learned men to supply them; that it were
not amiss to diminish the one a little, to increase the
other. That as this would take away the objection of
ignorance, wherewith the new sectaries in Germany had

so much branded the clergy, so it would furnish able persons to resist their doctrine, and uphold the credit and reputation of the Roman Church. Therefore he would be an humble suppliant to his holiness, to give him leave to throw down a few superfluous monasteries, and to imploy the revenues of them to the building of two colleges; one at Oxford, the other at Ipswich; and to believe, that all things being rightly considered, the fall of those few might be a means to keep up the rest, especially since, in this kingdom, the number of them was thought excessive.

To the king; as he needed not to use those motives, so he discreetly conceal'd such as might discover the secrets of ecclesiastical government. For certainly, what fault soever might be objected to the cardinal, he seem'd still a devout servant to his religion, as aspiring thereby unto the papacy. Therefore, he said little more unto the king, than that it was fit so learned a prince should advance learning, and maintain that faith, whereof the pope had made him the defender. For this purpose, he should advise him to found more colleges. Yet because his wars and other occasions had so exhausted his treasury, he would ask no more, than that the care thereof should be committed to him; who, if his highness so thought fit, would only suppress some little and unnecessary monasteries, and imploy the revenues to this use. King Henry also considering, that if, for his urgent occasions, he were necessitated at any time to seize on the other religious houses, he might this way discover how the people would take it, grants his request. Our king thus concurring with the pope, who, in favour of the cardinal, gave way to this suppression, that overture was first made, which being pursu'd afterwards by the king's sole authority, became the final ruin of all monasteries.—*Life and Reign of King Henry VIII.*

4. An Estimate of Wolsey.

AND thus concluded that great cardinal. A man in whom ability of parts and industry were equally eminent, though, for being employ'd wholly in ambitious ways, they became dangerous instruments of power in active and mutable times. By these arts yet he found means to govern not only the chief affairs of this kingdom, but of Europe; there being no potentate, which, in his turn, did not seek to him; and as this procur'd him divers pensions, so, when he acquainted the king therewith, his manner was, so cunningly to disoblige that prince who did fee him last, as he made way thereby oftentimes to receive as much on the other side. But not of secular princes alone, but even of the pope and clergy of Rome he was no little courted; of which therefore he made especial use, while he drew them to second him on most occasions. His birth being otherwise so obscure and mean, as no man had ever stood so single: for which reason also, his chief endeavour was not to displease any great person, which yet could not secure him against the divers pretenders of that time. For as all things pass'd through his hands, so they who fail'd in their suits generally hated him, all which, though it did but exasperate his ill nature, yet this good resultance follow'd, that it made him take the more care to be just; whereof also he obtain'd the reputation in his publick hearing of causes. For as he lov'd no body, so his reason carried him. And thus he was an useful minister of his king, in all points, where there was no question of disserving the Roman Church;

of which (at what price soever) I find he was a zealous servant; as hoping thereby to aspire to the papacy, whereof (as the factious times then were) he seem'd more capable than any, had he not so immoderately affected it. Whereby also it was not hard to judge of his inclinations. That prince, who was ablest to help him to this dignity, being ever preferr'd by him, which therefore was the ordinary bait by which the emperor and French king, one after the other, did catch him. And, upon these terms, he doubted not to convey vast treasures out of this kingdom, especially unto Rome, where he had not a few cardinals at his devotion. By whose help, though he could not obtain that supreme dignity he so passionately desir'd, yet he prevail'd himself so much of their favour, as he got a kind of absolute power in spiritual matters at home. Wherewith again he so serv'd the king's turn, as it made him think the less of using his own authority. One error seemed common to both, which was, that such a multiplicity of offices and places were invested in him. For as it drew much envy upon the cardinal in particular, so it derogated no little from the regal authority, while one man alone seem'd to exhaust all. Since it becometh princes to do like good husbandmen when they sow their grounds, which is, to scatter, and not to throw all in one place. He was no great dissembler, for so qualified a person; as ordering his business for the most part so cautiously, as he got more by keeping his word than by breaking it. As for his learning, (which was far from exact) it consisted chiefly in the subtilties of the Thomists, wherewith the king and himself did more often weary than satisfie each other. His style in missives was rather copious than eloquent, yet ever tending to the point. Briefly, if it be true (as Polydore observes) that no man ever did rise

with fewer vertues, it is as true, that few that ever fell
from so high a place had lesser crimes objected against
him. Though yet Polydore (for being at his first coming
into England committed to prison by him, as we have
said) may be suspected as a partial author., So that in
all probability he might have subsisted longer, when either
his pride and immense wealth had not made him obnoxious and suspected to the king, or that other than
women had oppos'd him: who as they are vigilant and
close enemies, so for the most part, they carry their businesses in that manner, they leave fewer advantages against
themselves, than men do.   In conclusion, as I cannot
assent to those who thought him happy for enjoying the
untimely compassion of the people a little before his end,
so I cannot but account it ˋa principal felicity, that during
his favour with the king, all things succeeded better than
afterwards; though yet it may be doubted whether the
impressions he gave, did not occasion divers irregularities
which were observ'd to follow.—*Life and Reign of King
Henry VIII.*

5. Indulgences.

PUNISHMENTS might have been left to God, but that they
serve to deter others.   But who would be afraid now, when
he knows at what rate he may put away his crimes? Of what
use would our threatenings for sins be, if they grow so
contemptible as that a little sum of money would discharge
them; is not this to make heaven venal? doth not this
reflect so much on Christian faith, that it makes a new
price for sin? Believe me, my lords, to make our faults cheap,
is to multiply them, and to take away not only that reverence is due to virtue, but to dissolve those bonds which

knit and hold together both civil and religious worship. For when men see what they are to pay for their faults, what will they care for other redemption? I would I could say we were not already fallen under some disesteem, when by our enjoyning of easie fasting, prayer, and some little alms, men find they suffer no more than what they would gladly endure to sin again; for who is the leaner or poorer for our penances: let us not then make the mysteries of salvation mercenary, or propose everlasting happiness on those terms, that it may be obtain'd for money, which we find so seldom yet without deceit or mischief. Let men's sins rather lie against them still than open such easie ways to remit them: and take this advice in good part, since it so much concerns us all.—*Life and Reign of King Henry VIII.*

6. Queen Katherine's Timely Submission.

Our king by proclamation did severely forbid the translation of the New Testament, by Tindal and Coverdale, or any other than is permitted by parliament: as also the English book of Frith, Wickliff, Tindal, etc. which our king most studiously supprest; both because he would have his subjects decline the bitter language and doctrine to be found in some of them, and that he would introduce his own, or at least a more sober reformation. Whereof also he was the more sensible, in that women began now ordinarily to dispute controversies, and urge the text: insomuch, that Anne Askew, a gentlewoman, defended herself therewith against her persecutors; though not so, but that she was burnt for it. Besides, the queen her self did this year run no little danger: for as she began about this time to give ear unto those who

declaim'd against the abuses of the Roman Church, she
thought herself so well instructed in religion, that she would
debate with the king thereof: which yet the king did but
impatiently hear; both as the anguish of a sore leg he had
at this time made him very froward, and as he lov'd not
to be contradicted in his opinions, especially, as he said,
in his old age, and by his wife.   This again was exaggerated
by Stephen Gardiner, Bishop of Winchester, so far, that by
representing the hazard she incurr'd by contravening the
six articles, and the late proclamation, in reading of forbidden books, and teaching openly her doctrine, the king
gave Winchester and Wriothesley the chancellor, and others,
leave to consult about the drawing of articles against her,
which they fail'd not to present unto the king, who sub-
scrib'd them: insomuch, that her enemies expected only
a warrant for carrying her by night to the Tower.   Which
the queen accidentally having notice of, fell into that passion,
and bitter bewailing her misfortune, that the king hearing
the perplexity she was in, sent his physicians, and after
came himself to her chamber, where compassionating her
estate, he us'd such kind words as did help to recover her.
Insomuch, that the next night, being attended by the Lady
Anne her sister, wife to Sir William Herbert, afterwards
Earl of Pembroke, she went unto the king's bed-chamber,
where he courteously welcomed her, and began to talk of
religion.

But she wittily excusing herself by the weakness of her
sex and judgment, said, 'She would refer her self in this
and all other causes to his majesty's wisdom.' 'Not so
(by Saint Mary)' quoth the king, 'you are become a doctor,
Kate, to instruct us (as we take it) and not to be instructed
or directed by us.'   But the queen replying, that 'what
she said was rather to pass away the time and pain of his

infirmity, than to hold argument; and that she hop'd by hearing his majesty's learned discourse, to receive some profit thereby.' The king answer'd, 'And is it even so (sweet-heart?) then are we perfect friends again.' Which also he confirm'd by divers testimonies. But as her maligners knew nothing of this reconcilement, they prepar'd the next day to carry her to the Tower, at a time limited by the king's warrant. This being come, and she happening to be merrily talking with him in his garden, the Lord Wriothesley, with forty of the guard, comes in; whom the king sternly beholding, and after calling to him, (at some distance from the queen) so expostulated the matter, as at last he reviled, and commanded him out of his sight and presence. Nevertheless, at the king's return, she was an humble suiter for his pardon. But the king answer'd no otherwise, than that 'she (poor soul) did not know how evil he deserv'd this grace at her hands.' And thus, by her opportune submission she escap'd: tho' yet some believe it was not so much the king's intention herein to use the rigour of the law, as to deter her from reading forbidden books. Howsoever, if he were not in earnest, it was thought a terrible jest, especially to a queen, that had the reputation of a vertuous, humble, and observant wife. But Winchester, who (it was thought) chiefly endeavoured her ruin, did himself, not long after, fall into the king's disfavour, as by his submission extant in our records doth appear. —*Life and Reign of King Henry VIII.*

7. A Knight of the Bath.

PASSING two or three days here, it happened one evening that a daughter of the duchess, of about ten or eleven years of age, going one evening from the castle to walk in the

meadows, myself, with divers French gentlemen, attended
her and some gentlewomen that were with her.   This young
lady wearing a knot of riband on her head, a French cheva-
lier took it suddenly, and fastened it to his hatband: the
young lady, offended herewith, demands her riband, but
he refusing to restore it, the young lady addressing herself
to me, said, 'Monsieur, I pray get my riband from that
gentleman;' hereupon going towards him, I courteously,
with my hat in my hand, desired him to do me the honour,
that I may deliver the lady her riband or bouquet again;
but he roughly answering me, 'Do you think I will give
it you, when I have refused it to her?' I replied, 'Nay
then, sir, I will make you restore it by force;' whereupon
also, putting on my hat and reaching at his, he to save
himself ran away, and, after a long course in the meadow,
finding that I had almost overtook him, he turned short,
and running to the young lady, was about to put the
riband on her hand, when I, seizing upon his arm, said
to the young lady, 'It was I that gave it.' 'Pardon me,'
quoth she, 'it is he that gives it me:' I said then, 'Madam,
I will not contradict you, but if he dare say that I did not
constrain him to give it, I will fight with him.' The French
gentleman answered nothing thereunto for the present, and
so conducted the young lady again to the castle. The
next day I desired Mr. Aurelian Townsend to tell the
French cavalier, that either he must confess that I constrained him to restore the riband, or fight with me; but
the gentleman seeing him unwilling to accept of this challenge, went out from the place, whereupon I following
him, some of the gentlemen that belonged to the constable
taking notice hereof, acquainted him therewith, who sending
for the French cavalier, checked him well for his sauciness,
in taking the riband away from his grandchild, and after-

wards bid him depart his house; and this was all that I
ever heard of the gentleman, with whom I proceeded in
that manner, because I thought myself obliged thereunto by the oath taken when I was made Knight of the
Bath, as I formerly related upon this occasion.—*Autobiography.*

IX.

THOMAS HOBBES.

1588—1679.

THOMAS HOBBES was born at Malmesbury in Wiltshire, in 1588. He received a careful early education at home and in the Grammar School of his native town. At fourteen he went to Oxford and entered at Magdalen Hall, where he spent five years, chiefly in the pursuit of philosophical studies. He is said to have assisted Lord Bacon in the translation into Latin of some of his English works. He became (1608) tutor in the Devonshire family, and travelled with his pupils at intervals during many years in France and Italy, forming the acquaintance of Galileo, Descartes, Gassendi, and other eminent men of the day. He returned to England in 1637, and resided at Chatsworth for some time, but the apprehension of civil war between King and Parliament made him think it safer to retire to Paris in 1641. He remained abroad for twelve years, and returned, in 1653, to England, where Cromwell ·permitted him to live undisturbed. He died in 1679 at the advanced age of ninety-one, having continued his literary activity to the last.

Hobbes was one of the most powerful and acute of English philosophical writers. The circumstances of his time, by directing his attention to the philosophy of politics and its foundation in morals and the nature of man, probably determined the subject of his principal writings. His career as an author did not commence till he had passed middle life. His two great works, the Treatise on Government, and Leviathan, appeared, the one when he was fifty-two, and the other when he was sixty-three years of age. Of his minor works the two most characteristic, Behemoth, an account of the Civil Wars, and The Dialogue of the Laws of England, were not published till after his death.

Hobbes may claim to be considered as the father of modern English philosophy. He was the precursor of the school of thought which may be traced in one direction through Locke and Bolingbroke, and in another through Berkeley and Hume. 'He proclaimed,' says Mr. Lewes, in his History of Philosophy, 'that Psychology is a science of observation, and that if we would understand the conditions and operations of our minds, we must patiently look inwards and see what passes there. All the reasoning in the world will not advance us one step, unless we first get a firm basis on fact.' In morals and law Hobbes was the progenitor of Bentham. Upon these great subjects he was the most powerful thinker of his age, and his theories, if sometimes imperfect, are full of profound and shrewd observation. Hobbes may fairly rank among the greatest writers England has produced. He is profound and clear in thought, weighty and strong in the expression of it. His style is vigorous and terse, enlivened by flashes of grotesque humour.

---

1. The Origin and Interpretation of Law.

WITHOUT law, every thing is in such sort every man's, as he may take, possess, and enjoy, without wrong to any man; every thing, lands, beasts, fruits, and even the bodies of other men, if his reason tell him he cannot otherwise live securely. For the dictates of reason are little worth, if they tended not to the preservation and improvement of men's lives. Seeing then without human law all things would be common, and this community a cause of encroachment, envy, slaughter, and continual war of one upon another, the same law of reason dictates to mankind, for their own preservation, a distribution of lands and goods, that each man may know what is proper to him, so as none other might pretend a right thereunto, or disturb him in the use of the same. This distribution is justice, and this properly is the same which we say is one's own; by which you may see the great necessity there was of statute laws, for preservation of all mankind. It is also a dictate of the law of reason, that statute laws are a necessary means of the safety and well-being of man in the present world, and are to be obeyed by all subjects, as the law of reason ought to be obeyed, both by King and subjects, because it is the law of God.

Now as to the authority you ascribe to custom, I deny that any custom of its own nature can amount to the authority of a law. For if the custom be unreasonable, you must, with all other lawyers, confess that it is no law, but ought to be abolished; and if the custom be reasonable, it is not the custom, but the equity that makes it law. For what need is there to make reason law by any custom how long soever, when the law of reason is eternal? Besides, you cannot find it in any statute, though *lex et consuetudo* be often mentioned as things to be followed by the judges in their judgments, that *consuetudines*, that is to say, customs or usages, did imply any long continuance of former time; but that it signified such use and custom of proceeding, as was then immediately in being before the making of such statute. Nor shall you find in any statute the word common-law, which may not be there well interpreted for any of the laws of England temporal; for it is not the singularity of process used in any court that can distinguish it, so as to make it a different law from the law of the whole nation.

It cannot be that a written law should be against reason; for nothing is more reasonable than that every man should obey the law which he hath himself assented to. But that is not always the law, which is signified by *grammatical* construction of the letter, but that which the legislature thereby intended should be in force; which intention, I confess, is a very hard matter many times to pick out of the words of the statute, and requires great ability of understanding, and greater meditations and consideration of such conjuncture of occasions and incommodities, as needed a new law for a remedy. For there is ·scarce anything so clearly written, that when the cause thereof is forgotten, may not be wrested by an ignorant grammarian, or a cavilling logician, to the injury, oppression, or perhaps destruction of an honest man. And for this reason the Judges deserve that honour and profit they enjoy.

For my part, I believe that men at this day have better learned the art of cavilling against the words of a statute, than heretofore they had, and thereby encourage themselves and others to undertake suits upon little reason. Also the variety and repugnancy of judgments of common-law, do oftentimes put men to hope for victory in causes, whereof in reason they had no ground at all: also the ignorance of what is equity in their own causes, which equity not one man in a thousand ever studied. And the lawyers themselves seek not for their judgments in their own breasts, but in the precedents of former judges: as the ancient judges sought the same, not in their own reason, but in the laws of the empire. Another, and perhaps the greatest cause of multitude of suits, is this, that for want of registering of conveyances of land, which might easily be done in the townships where the lands lay, a purchase cannot easily be had which will not be litigious.—*Dialogue of the Common Laws.*

2. Ethics of Subjects and Sovereigns.

B. IT seems you make a difference between the ethics of subjects, and the ethics of sovereigns.

A. So I do. The virtue of a subject is comprehended wholly in obedience to the laws of the commonwealth. To obey the laws, is justice and equity, which is the law of nature, and, consequently, is civil law in all nations of the world; and nothing is injustice or iniquity, otherwise, than it is against the law. Likewise, to obey the laws, is the prudence of a subject; for without such obedience the commonwealth (which is every subject's safety and protection) cannot subsist. And though it be prudence also in private men, justly and moderately to enrich themselves, yet craftily to withhold from the public or defraud it of such part of their wealth, as is by law required, is no sign of prudence, but of want of knowledge of what is necessary for their own defence.

The virtues of sovereigns are such as tend to the maintenance of peace at home, and to the resistance of foreign enemies. Fortitude is a royal virtue; and though it be necessary in such private men as shall be soldiers, yet, for other men, the less they dare, the better it is both for the commonwealth and for themselves. Frugality (though perhaps you will think it strange) is also a royal virtue: for it increases the public stock, which cannot be too great for the public use, nor any man too sparing of what he has in trust for the good of others. Liberality also is a royal virtue: for the commonwealth cannot be well served without extraordinary diligence and service of ministers, and great fidelity to their Sovereign; who ought therefore to be encouraged, and especially those that do him service in the wars. In sum, all actions and habits are to be esteemed good or evil by their causes and usefulness in reference to the commonwealth, and not by their mediocrity, nor by their being commended. For several men praise several customs, and that which is virtue with one, is blamed by others; and, contrarily, what one calls vice, another calls virtue, as their present affections lead them.

B. Methinks you should have placed among the virtues that, which, in my opinion, is the greatest of all virtues, religion.

A. So I have, though, it seems, you did not observe it.— *Behemoth.*

3. History of the House of Commons.

B. WHEN began first the House of Commons to be part of the King's great council?

A. I do not doubt but that before the Conquest some discreet men, and known to be so by the King, were called by special writ to be of the same council, though they were not lords; but that is nothing to the House of Commons. The knights of shires and burgesses were never called to Parliament, for aught that I know, till the beginning of the reign of Edward I, or the latter end of the reign of Henry III, immediately after the misbehaviour of the barons; and for aught any man knows, were called on purpose to weaken that power of the lords, which they had so freshly abused. Before the time of Henry III, the lords were descended, most of them, from such as in the invasions and conquests of the Germans were peers and fellow-kings, till one was made king of them all; and their tenants were their subjects, as it is at this day with the lords of France. But after the time of Henry III, the kings began to make lords in the place of them whose issue failed, titulary only, without the lands belonging to their title; and by that means, their tenants being no longer bound to serve them in the wars, they grew every day less and less able to make a party against the King, though they continued still to be his great council.

And as their power decreased, so the power of the·House of Commons increased; but I do not find they were part of the King's council at all, nor judges over other men; though it cannot be denied, but a King may ask their advice, as well as the advice of any other. But I do not find that the end of their summoning was to give advice, but only, in case they had any petitions for redress of grievances, to be ready there with them whilst the King had his great council about him. But neither they nor the lords could present to the King, as a grievance, that the King took upon him to make the laws; to choose his own privy-counsellors; to raise money and soldiers; to defend the peace and honour of the kingdom; to make captains in his army; to make governors of his castles, whom he pleased. For this had been to tell the King, that it was one of their grievances that he was King.— *Behemoth.*

4. Memory the Mother of the Muses.

Time and education beget experience; experience begets memory; memory begets judgment and fancy; judgment begets the strength and structure, and fancy begets the ornaments of a poem. The ancients therefore fabled not absurdly, in making Memory the mother of the Muses. For memory is the world, though not really, yet so as in a looking-glass, in which the judgment, the severer sister, busieth herself in a grave and rigid examination of all the parts of nature, and in registering by letters their order, causes, uses, differences, and resemblances; whereby the fancy, when any work of art is to be performed, finds her materials at hand and prepared for use, and needs no more than a swift motion over them, that what she wants, and is there to be had, may not lie too long unespied.

So that when she seemeth to fly from one Indies to the other, and from heaven to earth, and to penetrate into the hardest matter and obscurest places, into the future, and into herself, and all this in a point of time, the voyage is not very great, herself being all she seeks. And her wonderful celerity consisteth ·not so much in motion, as in copious imagery discreetly ordered, and perfectly registered in the memory; which most men under the name of philosophy have a glimpse of, and is pretended to by many, that grossly mistaking her, embrace contention in her place. But so far forth as the fancy of man has traced the ways of true philosophy, so far it hath produced very marvellous effects to the benefit of mankind. All that is beautiful or defensible in building; or marvellous in engines and instruments of motion; whatsoever commodity men receive from the observations of the heavens, from the description of the earth, from the account of time, from walking on the seas; and whatsoever distinguisheth the civility of Europe, from the barbarity of the American savages; is the workmanship of fancy, but guided by the precepts of true philosophy. But where these precepts fail, as they have hitherto failed in the doctrine of moral virtue, there the architect Fancy must take the philosopher's part upon herself. He, therefore, who undertakes an heroic poem, which is to exhibit a venerable and amiable image of heroic virtue, must not only be the poet, to place and connect, but also the philosopher, to furnish and square his matter; that is, to make both body and soul, colour and shadow of his poem out of his own store. . . .

There are some that are not pleased with fiction, unless it be bold; not only to exceed the *work*, but also the *possibility* of nature; they would have impenetrable armours, enchanted castles, invulnerable bodies, iron men, flying horses, and a thousand other such things, which are easily feigned by them that dare. Against such I defend you, without assenting to those that condemn either Homer or Virgil; by dissenting only from those that think the beauty of a poem consisteth in the exorbitancy of the fiction. For as truth is the bound of historical, so the resemblance of truth is the utmost limit of poetical liberty. In old time amongst the heathen, such strange fictions and metamorphoses were not so remote from the articles of their faith, as they are now from ours, and therefore were not so unpleasant. Beyond the actual works of nature a poet may now go; but beyond the conceived possibility of nature, never. I can allow a geographer to make in the sea, a fish or a ship, which by the scale of his map would be two or three hundred miles long, and think it done for ornament, because it is done without the precincts of his undertaking: but when he paints an elephant so, I presently apprehend it as ignorance, and' a plain confession of *terra incognita.* . . .

That which giveth a poem the true and natural colour, consisteth in two things; which are, *to know well,* that is, to have images of nature in the memory distinct and clear; and *to know much.* A sign of the first is perspicuity, propriety, and decency; which delight all sorts of men, either by instructing the ignorant, or soothing the learned in their knowledge. A sign of the latter is novelty of expression, and pleaseth by excitation of the mind; for novelty causeth admiration, and admiration curiosity, which is a delightful appetite of knowledge.—*Answer to Sir William Davenant.*

5. The Abuse of Oratory.

IT was noted by Sallust, that in Catiline, who was author of the greatest sedition that ever was in Rome, there was

Eloquentiæ satis, sapientiæ parum; eloquence *sufficient,* but
little wisdom. And perhaps this was said of Catiline, as
he was Catiline: but it was true of him as an author of
sedition. For the conjunction of these two qualities made
him not Catiline, but seditious. And that it may be understood, how want of *wisdom,* and store of *eloquence,* may
stand together, we are to consider, what it is we call wisdom,
and what eloquence. It is manifest that wisdom consisteth
in knowledge. Now of knowledge there are two kinds;
whereof the one is the remembrance of such things as we
have conceived by our senses, and of the order in which
they follow one another. And this *knowledge* is called *experience;* and the wisdom that proceedeth from it, is that
ability to conjecture by the present, of what is past, and to
come, which men call *prudence.* This being so, it is manifest presently, that the author of sedition, whosoever he
be, must not be prudent. For if he consider and take his
experiences aright, concerning the success which they have
had, who have been the movers and authors of sedition,
either in this or any other state, he shall find, that for one
man that hath thereby advanced himself to honour, twenty
have come to a reproachful end. The other kind of knowledge, is the remembrance of the names or appellations of
things, and how everything is called, which is, in matters
of common conversation, a remembrance of pacts and
covenants of men made amongst themselves, concerning
how to be understood of one another. And this kind of
knowledge is generally called science, and the conclusions
thereof truth. But when men remember not how things
are named, by general agreement, but either mistake and
misname things, or name them aright by chance, they are
not said to have science, but opinion, and the conclusions
thence proceeding are uncertain, and for the most part

erroneous. Now that science in particular, from which proceed the true and evident conclusions of what is right and wrong, and what is good and hurtful to the being, and well-being of mankind, the Latins call *sapientia*, and we by the general name of wisdom. For generally, not he that hath skill in geometry, or any other science speculative, but only he that understandeth what conduceth to the good and government of the people, is called a wise man. Now that no author of sedition can be wise in this acceptation of the word, is sufficiently proved, in that it hath been already demonstrated, that no pretence of sedition can be right or just. And therefore the authors of sedition must be ignorant of the right of state, that is to say, unwise. It remaineth therefore, that they be such, as name things, not according to their true and generally agreed upon names, but call right and wrong, good and bad, according to their passions, or according to the authorities of such as they admire, as Aristotle, Cicero, Seneca, and others of like authority, who have given the names of right and wrong, as their passions have dictated; or have followed the authority of other men, as we do theirs. It is required therefore in an author of sedition, that he think right, that which is wrong; and profitable, that which is pernicious; and consequently that there be in him *sapientiæ parum*, little wisdom.

Eloquence is nothing else but the power of winning belief of what we say. And to that end we must have aid from the passions of the hearer. Now to demonstration and teaching of the truth, there are required long deductions, and great attention, which is unpleasant to the hearer. Therefore they which seek not truth, but belief, must take another way, and not only derive what they would have to be believed, from somewhat believed already, but also, by aggravations and extenuations, make good and bad, right and wrong, appear great or less, according as shall serve their turns. And such is the power of eloquence, as many times a man is made to believe thereby, that he sensibly feeleth smart and damage, when he feeleth none, and to enter into rage and indignation, without any other cause, than what is in the words and passion of the speaker. This considered, together with the business that he hath to do, who is the author of rebellion, namely, to make men believe that their rebellion is just, their discontents grounded upon great injuries, and their hopes great; there needeth no more to prove, there can be no author of rebellion, that is not an eloquent and powerful speaker, and withal, as hath been said before, a man of little wisdom. For the faculty of speaking powerfully, consisteth in a habit gotten of putting together passionate words, and applying them to the present passions of the hearer.

Seeing then eloquence and want of discretion concur to the stirring of rebellion, it may be demanded, what part each of these acteth therein? The daughters of Pelias, king of Thessaly, desiring to restore their old decrepit father to the vigour of his youth, by the counsel of Medea, chopped him in pieces, and set him a boiling with I know not what herbs in a cauldron, but could not revive him again. So when eloquence and want of judgment go together, want of judgment, like the daughters of Pelias, consenteth, through eloquence, which is as the witchcraft of Medea, to cut the commonwealth in pieces, upon pretence or hope of reformation, which when things are in combustion, they are not able to effect.—*De Corpore Politico.*

6. Definitions.

WHEN two names are joined together into a consequence, or affirmation, as thus, *a man is a living creature;* or thus, *if he be a man, he is a living creature;* if the latter name, *living creature,* signify all that the former name *man* signifieth, then the affirmation, or consequence, is *true;* otherwise *false.* For *true* and *false* are attributes of speech, not of things. And where speech is not, there is neither *truth* nor *falsehood;* *error* there may be, as when we expect that which shall not be, or suspect what has not been; but in neither case can a man be charged with untruth.

Seeing then that truth consisteth in the right ordering of names in our affirmations, a man that seeketh precise truth had need to remember what every name he uses stands for, and to place it accordingly, or else he will find himself entangled in words, as a bird in lime twigs, the more he struggles the more belimed. And therefore in geometry, which is the only science that it hath pleased God hitherto to bestow on mankind, men begin at settling the significations of their words; which settling of significations they call *definitions,* and place them in the beginning of their reckoning.

· By this it appears how necessary it is for any man that aspires to true knowledge, to examine the definitions of former authors; and either to correct them, where they are negligently set down, or to make them himself. For the errors of definitions multiply themselves according as the reckoning proceeds, and lead men into absurdities, which at last they see, but cannot avoid, without reckoning anew from the beginning, in which lies the foundation of their errors. From whence it happens, that they which trust to books do as they that cast up many little sums into a greater, without considering whether those little sums were rightly cast up or not; and at last finding the error visible, and not mistrusting their first grounds, know not which way to clear themselves, but spend time in fluttering over their books;

as birds that entering by the chimney, and finding themselves enclosed in a chamber, flutter at the false light of a glass window, for want of wit to consider which way they came in. So that in the right definition of names lies the first use of speech; which is the acquisition of science: and in wrong, or no definitions, lies the first abuse; from which proceed all false and senseless tenets; which make those men that take their instruction from the authority of books, and not from their own meditation, to be as much below the condition of ignorant men, as men endued with true science are above it. For between true science and erroneous doctrines, ignorance is in the middle. Natural sense and imagination are not subject to absurdity. Nature itself cannot err; and as men abound in copiousness of language so they become more wise, or more mad than ordinary. Nor is it possible without letters for any man to become either excellently wise, or, unless his memory be hurt by disease or ill constitution of organs, excellently foolish. For words are wise men's counters, they do but reckon by them; but they are the money of fools, that value them by the authority of an Aristotle, a Cicero, or a Thomas, or any other doctor whatsoever, if but a man.—*Leviathan.*

7. Liberty.

THE liberty of subjects consists not in being exempt from the laws of the city, or that they who have the supreme power cannot make what laws they have a mind to. But because all the motions and actions of subjects are never circumscribed by laws, nor can be, by reason of their variety; it is necessary that there be infinite cases which are neither commanded nor prohibited, but every man may either do or not do them as he lists himself. In these, each man is said to enjoy his liberty; and in this sense liberty is to be understood in this place, namely, for that part of natural right which is granted and left to subjects by the civil laws. As water inclosed on all hands with banks, stands still and corrupts; having no bounds, it spreads too largely, and the more passages it finds the more freely it takes its current; so subjects, if they might do nothing without the commands of the law, would grow dull and unwieldy; if all, they would be dispersed; and the more is left undetermined by the laws, the more liberty they enjoy. Both extremes are faulty; for laws were not invented to take away, but to direct men's actions; even as nature ordained the banks, not to stay, but to guide the course of the stream. The measure of this liberty is to be taken from the subjects' and the city's good. Wherefore, in the first place, it is against the charge of those who command and have the authority of making laws, that there should be more laws than necessarily serve for good of the magistrate and his subjects. For since men are wont commonly to debate what to do or not to do, by natural reason rather than any knowledge of the laws, where there are more laws than can easily be remembered, and whereby such things are forbidden as reason of itself prohibits not of necessity, they must through ignorance, without the least evil intention, fall within the compass of laws, as gins laid to entrap their harmless liberty; which supreme commanders are bound to preserve for their subjects by the laws of nature.

It is a great part of that *liberty*, which is harmless to civil government and necessary for each subject to live happily, that there be no penalties dreaded but what they may both foresee and look for; and this is done, where there are either no punishments at all defined by the laws, or greater not required than are defined. Where there are none defined, there he that hath first broken the law, expects an indefinite or arbitrary punishment; and his fear is supposed boundless, because it relates to an unbounded evil. Now the law of nature commands them who are not subject to any civil laws, and therefore supreme commanders, that in taking revenge and punishing they must not so much regard the past evil as the future good; and they sin, if they entertain any other measure in arbitrary punishment than the public benefit. But where the punishment is defined; either by a law prescribed, as when it is set down in plain words that *he that shall do thus or thus, shall suffer so and so ;* or by practice, as when the penalty, not by any law prescribed, but arbitrary from the beginning, is afterward determined by the punishment of the first delinquent; (for natural equity commands that equal transgressors be equally punished); there to impose a greater penalty than is defined by the law, is against the law of nature. For the end of punishment is not to compel the will of man, but to fashion it, and to make it such as he would have it who hath set the penalty. And deliberation is nothing else but a weighing, as it were in scales, the conveniences and inconveniences of the fact we are attempting; where that which is more weighty, doth necessarily according to its inclination prevail with us. If therefore the legislator doth set a less penalty on a crime, than will make our fear more considerable with us than our lust, that excess of lust above the fear of punishment, whereby sin is committed, is to be attributed to the legislator, that is to say, to the supreme; and therefore if he inflict a greater punishment than himself hath determined in his laws, he punisheth that in another in which he sinned himself.

It pertains therefore to the harmless and necessary *liberty* of subjects, that every man may without fear enjoy the rights which are allowed him by the laws.— *Treatise concerning Government and Society.*

8. The Uses of Philosophy.

THE *end* or *scope* of philosophy is, that we may make use to our benefit of effects formerly seen; or that, by application of bodies to one another, we may produce the like effects of those we conceive in our mind, as far forth as matter, strength, and industry, will permit for the commodity of human life. For the inward glory and triumph of mind that a man may have for the mastering of some difficult and doubtful matter, or for the discovery of some hidden truth, is not worth so much pains as the study of philosophy requires; nor need any man care much to teach another what he knows himself, if he think that will be the only benefit of his labour. The end of knowledge is power; and the use of theorems (which, among geometricians, serve for the finding out of properties) is for the construction of problems; and, lastly, the scope of all speculation is the performing of some action, or thing to be done.

But what the *utility* of philosophy is, especially of natural philosophy and geometry, will be best understood by reckoning up the chief commodities of which mankind is capable, and by comparing the manner of life of such as enjoy them, with that of others which want the same. Now, the greatest commodities of mankind are the arts; namely, of measuring matter and motion; of moving ponderous bodies; of architecture; of navigation; of making instruments for all uses; of calculating the celestial motions, the aspects of the stars, and the parts of time; of geography, &c. By which sciences, how great benefits men receive is more easily understood than expressed. These benefits are enjoyed by almost all the people of Europe, by most of those of Asia, and by some of Africa: but the Americans, and they that live near the Poles, do totally want them.

But why? Have they sharper wits than these? Have
not all men one kind of soul, and the same faculties of
mind? What, then, makes this difference, except philosophy? Philosophy, therefore, is the cause of all these
benefits. But the utility of moral and civil philosophy is
to be estimated, not so much by the commodities we have
by knowing these sciences, as by the calamities we receive
from not knowing them. Now, all such calamities as
may be avoided by human industry, arise from war, but
chiefly from civil war; for from this proceed slaughter,
solitude, and the want of all things. But the cause of war
is not that men are willing to have it; for the will has
nothing for object but good, at least that which seemeth
good. Nor is it from this, that men know not that the
effects of war are evil; for who is there that thinks not
poverty and loss of life to be great evils? The cause,
therefore, of civil war is, that men know not the causes
neither of war nor peace, there being but few in the world
that have learned those duties which unite and keep men
in peace, that is to say, that have learned the rules of civil
life sufficiently. Now, the knowledge of these rules is moral
philosophy. But why have they not learned them, unless for
this reason, that none hitherto have taught them in a clear
and exact method? For what shall we say? Could the
ancient masters of Greece, Egypt, Rome, and others, persuade the unskilful multitude to their innumerable opinions
concerning the nature of their gods, which they themselves
knew not whether they were true or false, and which were indeed manifestly false and absurd; and could they not persuade the same multitude to civil duty, if they themselves had
understood it? Or shall those few writings of geometricians
which are extant, be thought sufficient for the taking away
of all controversy in the matters they treat of, and shall

those innumerable and huge volumes of *ethics* be thought unsufficient, if what they teach had been certain and well demonstrated? What, then, can be imagined to be the cause that the writings of those men have increased science, and the writings of these have increased nothing but words, saving that the former were written by men that knew, and the latter by such as knew not, the doctrine they taught only for ostentation of their wit and eloquence? Nevertheless, I deny not but the reading of some such books is very delightful; for they are most eloquently written, and contain many clear, wholesome and choice sentences, which yet are not universally true, though by them universally pronounced. From whence it comes to pass, that the circumstances of times, places, and persons being changed, they are no less frequently made use of to confirm wicked men in their purposes, than to make them understand the precepts of civil duties. Now that which is chiefly wanting in them, is a true and certain rule of our actions, by which we might know whether that we undertake be just or unjust. For it is to no purpose to be bidden in every thing to do right, before there be a certain rule and measure of right established, which no man hitherto hath established. Seeing, therefore, from the not knowing of civil duties, that is, from the want of moral science, proceed civil wars, and the greatest calamities of mankind, we may very well attribute to such science the production of the contrary commodities. And thus much is sufficient, to say nothing of the praises and other contentment proceeding from philosophy, to let you see the utility of the same in every kind thereof.—*Elements of Philosophy.*

9. Vain Philosophy.

AND whereas men divide a body in their thought, by numbering parts of it, and, in numbering those parts, number also the parts of the place it filled; it cannot be, but in making many parts, we also make many places of those parts; whereby there cannot be conceived in the mind of any man, more, or fewer parts, than there are places for: yet they will have us believe, that by the Almighty power of God, one body may be at one and the same time in many places; and many bodies at one and the same time in one place: as if it were an acknowledgment of the Divine Power to say, that which is, is not; or that which has been, has not been. And these are but a small part of the incongruities they are forced to, from their disputing philosophically, instead of admiring, and adoring of the divine and incomprehensible nature; whose attributes cannot signify what he is, but ought to signify our desire to honour him, with the best appellations we can think on. But they that venture to reason of his nature, from these attributes of honour, losing their understanding in the very first attempt, fall from one inconvenience into another, without end, and without number; in the same manner, as when a man ignorant of the ceremonies of court, coming into the presence of a greater person than he is used to speak to, and stumbling at his entrance, to save himself from falling, lets slip his cloak; to recover his cloak, lets fall his hat; and with one disorder after another, discovers his astonishment and rusticity.

Then for *physics*, that is, the knowledge of the subordinate and secondary causes of natural events; they render none at all, but empty words. If you desire to know why some kind of bodies sink naturally downwards toward the earth, and others go naturally from it; the Schools will tell you out of Aristotle, that the bodies that sink downwards, are *heavy;* and that this heaviness is it that causes them to descend. But if you ask what they mean by *heaviness,* they will define it to be an endeavour to go to the centre of the earth. So that the cause why things sink downward, is an endeavour to be below : which is as much as to say, that bodies descend, or ascend, because they do. Or they will tell you the centre of the earth is the place of rest, and conservation for heavy things; and therefore they endeavour to be there: as if stones and metals had a desire, or could discern the place they would be at, as man does; or loved rest, as man does not; or that a piece of glass were less safe in the window, than falling into the street. —*Leviathan.*

X.

IZAAK WALTON.

1593—1683.

IZAAK WALTON was born at Stafford, 1593. He followed the trade of a seamster. He was twice married, the second time to Ann Ken, sister of Dr. Ken, Bishop of Bath and Wells. In 1643 he retired from business with a small competency, and lived partly at Stafford and partly in various families of eminent clergymen, of whom, says Anthony Wood, he was much beloved.

It was during those visits that he collected the information which enabled him to write the lives of Dr. Donne, Sir Henry Wotton, Hooker, George Herbert, and Bishop Sanderson. His favourite recreation, both while he lived in London and afterwards, was angling, and in 1653 he published ' The Complete Angler, or The Contemplative Man's Recreation.' He lived to a good old age, and died in December, 1683, at Winchester, in the house of Dr. Hawkins, Prebendary of the Cathedral there.

The Complete Angler may be almost said to be an eclogue in prose. It conveys the precepts of the art and the Natural History of our river fish in the form of Dialogue, interspersed with charming pictures of rustic life and rural scenery. Its simplicity, its sweetness, its natural grace, and the fidelity with which it represents the features of English peasant life of the time, have given this book a permanent place in our literature, though the technical instruction belongs to a by-gone age of angling. The art of angling with the rod is of great antiquity in England, having been practised by clerics before the Reformation, but Walton's Manual, though not the first treatise published, was the first complete collection of the traditions of the ' gentle craft.'

1. The Praise of Angling.

AND let me tell you, that Angling is of high esteem, and of much use in other nations. He that reads the *Voyages* of Ferdinand Mendez Pinto, shall find that there he declares to have found a king and several priests a fishing.

And he that reads *Plutarch*, shall find, that Angling was not contemptible in the days of Mark Antony and Cleopatra, and that they, in the midst of their wonderful glory, used Angling as a principal recreation. And let me tell you, that in the *Scripture*, Angling is always taken in the best sense; and that though hunting may be sometimes so taken, yet it is but seldom to be so understood. And let me add this more: he that views the ancient *Ecclesiastical Canons*, shall find hunting to be forbidden to Churchmen, as being a turbulent, toilsome, perplexing recreation; and shall find Angling allowed to Clergymen, as being a harmless recreation, a recreation that invites them to contemplation and quietness.

I might here enlarge myself, by telling you what commendations our learned *Perkins* bestows on Angling: and how dear a lover, and great a practiser of it, our learned Dr. *Whitaker* was; as indeed many others of great learning have been. But I will content myself with two memorable men, that lived near to our own time, whom I also take to have been ornaments to the art of Angling.

The first is Dr. *Nowel*, sometime dean of the cathedral church of St. Paul, in London, where his monument stands yet undefaced; a man that, in the *reformation* of Queen Elizabeth, (not that of Henry VIII.) was so noted for his meek spirit, deep learning, prudence, and piety, that the then Parliament and Convocation, both chose, enjoined, and trusted him to be the man to make a *Catechism* for public use, such a one as should stand as a rule for faith and manners to their posterity. And the good old man, (though he was very learned, yet knowing that God leads us not to heaven by many, nor by hard questions,) like an honest Angler, made that good, plain, unperplexed *Cate-chism* which is printed with our good old *Service-book.* I say, this good man was a dear lover and constant practiser of Angling, as any age can produce; and his custom, was to spend besides his fixed hours of prayer, (those hours which, by command of the church, were en-joined the clergy, and voluntarily dedicated to devotion by many primitive Christians,) I say, besides those hours, this good man was observed to spend a tenth part of his time in Angling; and, also, (for I have conversed with those which have conversed with him,) to bestow a tenth part of his revenue, and usually all his fish, amongst the poor that inhabited near to those rivers in which it was caught; saying often, ' That charity gave life to religion :' and, at his return to his house, would praise God he had spent that day free from worldly trouble; both harmlessly, and in a recreation that became a churchman. And this good man was well content, if not desirous, that posterity should know he was an Angler; as may appear by his picture, now to be seen, and carefully kept, in Brazennose College ; to which he was a liberal benefactor. In which picture he is drawn, leaning on a desk, with his Bible before him ; and on one hand of him, his lines, hooks, and other tackling, lying in a round; and, on his other hand, are his Angle-rods of several sorts; and by them this is written, 'that he died 13 *Feb.* 1601, being aged 95 years, 44 of which he had been Dean of St. Paul's church; and that his age neither impaired his hearing, nor dimmed his eyes, nor weakened his memory, nor made any of the

faculties of his mind weak or useless.' It is said that
Angling and temperance were great causes of these blessings. And I wish the like to all that imitate him, and
love the memory of so good a man.

My next and last example shall be that undervaluer of
money, the late provost of Eton College, Sir Henry Wotton,
(a man with whom I have often fished and conversed,) a
man whose foreign employments in the service of this nation,
and whose experience, learning, wit, and cheerfulness, made
his company to be esteemed one of the delights of mankind.
This man, whose very approbation of Angling were sufficient
to convince any modest censurer of it, this man was also
a most dear lover, and a frequent practiser of the art of
Angling; of which he would say, 'it was an employment
for his idle time, which was not then idly spent;' for
'Angling was, after tedious study, a rest to his mind, a
cheerer of his spirits, a diverter of sadness, a calmer of
unquiet thoughts, a moderator of passions, a procurer of
contentedness;' and 'that it begat habits of peace and
patience in those that professed and practised it.' Indeed,
my friend, you will find Angling to be like the virtue of
Humility, which has a calmness of spirit, and a world of
other blessings attending upon it. Sir, this was the saying
of that learned man.—*The Complete Angler.*

.

2. The Life of Richard Hooker.

As soon as he was perfectly recovered from his sickness,
he took a journey from Oxford to Exeter, to satisfy and see
his good mother, being accompanied with a countryman and
companion of his own College, and both on foot; which
was then either more in fashion, or want of money or their
humility made it so: But on foot they went, and took

Salisbury in their way, purposely to see the good Bishop, who made Mr. Hooker and his companion dine with him at his own table; which Mr. Hooker boasted of with much joy and gratitude when he saw his mother and friends : and at the Bishop's parting with him, the Bishop gave him good counsel, and his benediction, but forgot to give him money; which when the Bishop had considered, he sent a servant in all haste to call Richard back to him; and at Richard's return the Bishop said to him, ' Richard, I sent for you back to lend you a horse which hath carried me many a mile, and, I thank God, with much ease;' and presently delivered into his hand a walking-staff, with which he professed he had travelled through many parts of Germany. And he said, ' Richard, I do not give, but lend you my horse; be sure you be honest, and bring my horse back to me at your return this way to Oxford. And I do now give you ten groats, to bear your charges to Exeter; and here is ten groats more, which I charge you to deliver to your mother, and tell her, I send her a Bishop's benediction with it, and beg the continuance of her prayers for me. And if you bring my horse back to me, I will give you ten groats more, to carry you on foot to the College : and so God bless you, good Richard.'

And this, you may believe, was performed by both parties. But alas ! the next news that followed Mr. Hooker to Oxford was, that his learned and charitable patron had changed this for a better life. Which may be believed, for as he lived, so he died, in devout meditation and prayer; and in both so zealously, that it became a religious question, ' Whether his last ejaculations or his soul did first enter heaven ?'

And now Mr. Hooker became a man of sorrow and fear : of sorrow, for the loss of so dear and comfortable a patron; and of fear for his future subsistence. But Mr. Cole raised his spirits from this dejection, by bidding him go cheerfully to his studies, and assuring him, that he should neither want food nor raiment (which was the utmost of his hopes), for he would become his patron.

And so he was for about nine months, or not much longer; for about that time the following accident did befal Mr. Hooker.

Edwin Sandys (then Bishop of London, and after Archbishop of York) had also been in the days of Queen Mary forced, by forsaking this, to seek safety in another nation; where, for many years, Bishop Jewel and he were companions at bed and board in Germany; and where, in this their exile, they did often eat the bread of sorrow, and by that means they there began such a friendship, as time did not blot out, but lasted till the death of Bishop Jewel, which was in 1571. A little before which time the two Bishops meeting, Jewel began a story of his Richard Hooker, and in it gave such a character of his learning and manners, that though Bishop Sandys was educated in Cambridge, where he had obliged, and had many friends; yet his resolution was, that his son Edwin should be sent to Corpus Christi College in Oxford, and by all means be pupil to Mr. Hooker, though his son Edwin was then almost of the same age: For the Bishop said, 'I will have a tutor for my son, that shall teach him learning by instruction, and virtue by example; and my greatest care shall be of the last; and (God willing) this Richard Hooker shall be the man into whose hands I will commit my Edwin.' And the Bishop did so about twelve months after this resolution.

And doubtless, as to these two, a better choice could not be made; for Mr. Hooker was now in the nineteenth year of his age; had spent five in the University; and had, by a constant unwearied diligence, attained unto a perfection in

all the learned languages; by the help of which, an excellent
tutor, and his unintermitted study, he had made the subtilty
of all the arts easy and familiar to himself, and useful for
the discovery of such learning as lay hid from common
searchers. So that by these, added to his great reason, and his
industry added to both, *he did not only know more of causes
and effects; but what he knew he knew better than other men.*
And with this knowledge he had a most blessed and clear
method of demonstrating what he knew, to the great advantage of all his pupils (which in time were many), but
especially to his two first, his dear Edwin Sandys, and his as
dear George Cranmer: of which there will be a fair testimony in the ensuing relation.

This for his learning. And for his behaviour, amongst
other testimonies, this still remains of him, that in four years
he was but twice absent from the chapel prayers; and that
his behaviour there was such as showed an awful reverence
of that God which he then worshipped and prayed to;
giving all outward testimonies, that his affections were set on
heavenly things. This was his behaviour towards God; and
for that to man, it is observable, that he was never known to
be angry, or passionate, or extreme in any of his desires;
never heard to repine or dispute with Providence, but, by a
quiet gentle submission and resignation of his will to the
wisdom of his Creator, bore the burthen of the day with
patience; never heard to utter an uncomely word: And by
this, and a grave behaviour, which is a divine charm, he
begot an early reverence unto his person, even from those
that at other times and in other companies, took a liberty to
cast off that strictness of behaviour and discourse that is
required in a collegiate life. And when he took any liberty
to be pleasant, his wit was never blemished with scoffing, or
the utterance of any conceit that bordered upon or might

beget a thought of looseness in his hearers. Thus innocent and exemplary was his behaviour in his College; and thus this good man continued till death; still increasing in learning, in patience, and in piety.—*Life of Hooker.*

3. A Quiet Scene.

BUT turn out of the way a little, good scholar, towards yonder high honeysuckle hedge; there we'll sit and sing whilst this shower falls so gently upon the teeming earth, and gives yet a sweeter smell to the lovely flowers· that adorn these verdant meadows.

Look, under that broad beech-tree, I sat down, when I was last this way a-fishing, and the birds in the adjoining grove seemed to have a friendly contention with an echo, whose dead voice seemed to live in a hollow tree, near to the brow of that primrose-hill; there I sat viewing the silver streams glide silently towards their centre, the tempestuous sea; yet sometimes opposed by rugged roots, and pebble-stones, which broke their waves, and turned them into foam: and sometimes I beguiled time by viewing the harmless lambs, some leaping securely in the cool shade, whilst others sported themselves in the cheerful sun; and saw others craving comfort from the swollen udders of their bleating dams. As I thus sat, these and other sights had so fully possessed my soul with content, that I thought as the poet hath happily expressed it:

> I was for that time lifted above earth;
> And possess'd joys not promis'd in my birth.

The Complete Angler.

4. Marriage of Dr. Donne.

THESE promises were only known to themselves: and the friends of both parties used much diligence, and many arguments, to kill or cool their affections to each other : but in vain; for love is a flattering mischief, that hath denied aged and wise men a foresight of those evils that too often prove to be the children of that blind father; a passion that carries us to commit errors with as much ease as whirlwinds remove feathers, and begets in us an unwearied industry to the attainment of what we desire. And such an industry did, notwithstanding much watchfulness against it, bring them secretly together, (I forbear to tell the manner how,) and at last to a marriage too, without the allowance of those friends, whose approbation always was, and ever will be, necessary to make even a virtuous love become lawful.

And that the knowledge of their marriage might not fall, like an unexpected tempest, on those that were unwilling to have it so, and that pre-apprehensions might make it the less enormous when it was known, it was purposely whispered into the ears of many that it was so, yet by none that could affirm it. But, to put a period to the jealousies of Sir George, (doubt often begetting more restless thoughts than the certain knowledge of what we fear,) the news was, in favour to Mr. Donne, and with his allowance, made known to Sir George, by his honourable friend and neighbour Henry, earl of Northumberland : but it was to Sir George so immeasurably unwelcome, and so transported him, that, as though his passion of anger and inconsideration might exceed theirs of love and error, he presently engaged his sister, the lady Elsemore, to join with him to procure her lord to discharge Mr. Donne of the place he held under his lordship. This request was followed with violence; and though Sir George were remembered, that errors might be overpunished, and desired therefore to forbear till second considerations might clear some scruples; yet he became restless until his suit was granted, and the punishment executed. . . .

Immediately after his dismission from his service, he sent
a sad letter to his wife, to acquaint her with it; and after
the subscription of his name, writ,

John Donne, Anne Donne, Un-done.

And God knows it proved too true: for this bitter physic of
Mr. Donne's dismission was not strong enough to purge out
all Sir George's choler; for he was not satisfied till Mr. Donne
and his sometime compupil in Cambridge, that married him,
namely, Samuel Brook, (who was after doctor in divinity,
and master of Trinity college,) and his brother Mr. Christo-
pher Brook, sometime Mr. Donne's chamberfellow in Lincoln's Inn, who gave Mr. Donne his wife, and witnessed the
marriage, were all committed to three several prisons.

Mr. Donne was first enlarged, who neither gave rest to
his body or brain, nor to any friend in whom he might hope
to have an interest, until he had procured an enlargement
for his two imprisoned friends.

He was now at liberty, but his days were still cloudy;
and being past these troubles, others did still multiply upon
him; for his wife was (to her extreme sorrow) detained from
him; and though with Jacob he endured not an hard service for her, yet he lost a good one, and was forced to
make good his title, and to get possession of her by a long
and restless suit in law; which proved troublesome and sadly
chargeable to him, whose youth, and travel, and needless
bounty, had brought his estate into a narrow compass.

It is observed, and most truly, that silence and submission
are charming qualities, and work most upon passionate men;
and it proved so with Sir George; for these, and a general
report of Mr. Donne's merits, together with his winning behaviour, (which, when it would entice, had a strange kind of
elegant irresistible art;) these and time had so dispassionated
sir George, that as the world had approved his daughter's

choice, so he also could not but see a more than ordinary merit in his new son; and this at last melted him into so much remorse (for love and anger are so like agues, as to have hot and cold fits; and love in parents, though it may be quenched, yet is easily rekindled, and expires not till death denies mankind a natural heat,) that he laboured his son's restoration to his place; using to that end both his own and his sister's power to her lord; but with no success; for his answer was, ' That though he was unfeignedly sorry for what he had done, yet it was inconsistent with his place and credit, to discharge and readmit servants at the request of passionate petitioners.'

Sir George's endeavour for Mr. Donne's readmission was by all means to be kept secret : (for men do more naturally reluct for errors, than submit to put on those blemishes that attend their visible acknowledgment.)—But however it was not long before Sir George appeared to be so far reconciled, as to wish their happiness, and not to deny them his paternal blessing, but yet refused to contribute any means that might conduce to their livelihood.

Mr. Donne's estate was the greatest part spent in many and chargeable travels, books, and dearbought experience : he out of all employment that might yield a support for himself and wife, who had been curiously and plentifully educated; both their natures generous, and accustomed to confer, and not to receive, courtesies : these and other considerations, but chiefly that his wife was to bear a part in his sufferings, surrounded him with many sad thoughts, and some apparent apprehensions of want.

But his sorrows were lessened and his wants prevented by the seasonable courtesy of their noble kinsman, Sir Francis Wolly, of Pirford in Surrey, who entreated them to a cohabitation with him; where they remained with much freedom to themselves, and equal content to him, for some years; and as their charge increased, (she had yearly a child,) so did his love and bounty. . . .

Immediately after his return from Cambridge, his wife died, leaving him a man of a narrow unsettled estate, and (having buried five) the careful father of seven children then living, to whom he gave a voluntary assurance, never to bring them under the subjection of a step-mother; which promise he kept most faithfully, burying with his tears all his earthly joys in his most dear and deserving wife's grave, and betook himself to a most retired and solitary life.

In this retiredness, which was often from the sight of his dearest friends, he became *crucified to the world*, and all those vanities, those imaginary pleasures, that are daily acted on that restless stage; and they were as perfectly crucified to him. Nor is it hard to think (being passions may be both changed and heightened by accidents) but that that abundant affection which once was betwixt him and her, who had long been the delight of his eyes, and the companion of his youth ; her, with whom he had divided so many pleasant sorrows and contented fears, as common people are not capable of; not hard to think but that she being now removed by death, a commeasurable grief took as full a possession of him as joy had done ; and so indeed it did; for now his very soul was elemented of nothing but sadness; now grief took so full a possession of his heart, as to leave no place for joy; if it did, it was a joy to be alone, where, like *a pelican in the wilderness*, he might bemoan himself without witness or restraint, and pour forth his passions like Job in the days of his affliction : 'Oh that I might have the desire of my heart! Oh that God would grant the thing that I long for!' For then, *as the grave is become her house*, so I would hasten to make it mine also; *that we two might there make our beds together in the dark.* Thus, as the Israelites sat mourning by the rivers of Babylon, when they remembered Sion; so he gave some ease to his oppressed heart by thus venting his sorrows: thus he began the day, and ended the night; ended the restless night and began the weary day in lamentations: and thus he continued till a consideration of his new engagements to God, and St. Paul's 'Wo is me, if I preach not the gospel,' dispersed those sad clouds that had then benighted his hopes, and now forced him to behold the light.

His first motion from his house was to preach where his beloved wife lay buried, (in St. Clement's church, near Temple-bar, London,) and his text was a part of the prophet Jeremy's Lamentation: 'Lo, I am the man that have seen affliction.'

And indeed his very words and looks testified him to be truly such a man; and they, with the addition of his sighs and tears, expressed in his sermon, did so work upon the affections of his hearers, as melted and moulded them into a companionable sadness; and so they left the congregation; but then their houses presented them with objects of diversion, and his presented him with nothing but fresh objects of sorrow, in beholding many helpless children, a narrow fortune, and a consideration of the many cares and casualties that attend their education. . . .

His marriage was the remarkable error of his life—an error, which, though he had a wit able and very apt to maintain paradoxes, yet he was very far from justifying it; and though his wife's competent years, and other reasons, might be justly urged to moderate severe censures, yet he would occasionally condemn himself for it; and doubtless it had been attended with an heavy repentance, if God had not blessed them with so mutual and cordial affections, as in the midst of their sufferings made their bread of sorrow taste more pleasantly than the banquets of dull and low-spirited people—*Life of Dr. Donne.*

5. Birds.

THOSE little nimble musicians of the air, that warble forth their curious ditties, with which nature hath furnished them to the shame of art.

As first the lark, when she means to rejoice, to cheer herself and those that hear her; she then quits the earth, and sings as she ascends higher into the air, and having ended her heavenly employment grows then mute and sad, to think she must descend to the dull earth, which she would not touch, but for necessity.

How do the blackbird and thrassel, with their melodious voices, bid welcome to the cheerful spring, and in their fixed months warble forth such ditties as no art or instrument can reach to!

Nay, the smaller birds also do the like in their particular seasons, as, namely, the laverock, the titlark, the little linnet, and the honest robin, that loves mankind both alive and dead.

But the nightingale, another of my airy creatures, breathes such sweet loud music out of her little instrumental throat, that it might make mankind to think miracles are not ceased. He that at midnight, when the very labourer sleeps securely, should hear, as I have very often, the clear airs, the sweet descants, the natural rising and falling, the doubling and redoubling of her voice, might well be lifted above earth, and say, ' Lord, what music hast Thou provided for the Saints in Heaven, when Thou affordest bad men such music on earth?'—*Complete Angler.*

XI.

SIR THOMAS BROWNE.

1605—1682.

THOMAS BROWNE was born in St. Michael's, Cheapside, in the year 1605. He was sent to Winchester School, and studied and graduated in Arts at Oxford. Afterwards he practised medicine in the counties surrounding the University. He travelled in Ireland, France and Italy, and returning through Holland, took the degree of Doctor of Medicine at Leyden. In 1636 he settled in Norwich, where he lived for forty-six years practising his profession extensively. In 1637 he was incorporated M.D. at Oxford. He was married in 1641 ; his wife survived him. In 1664 he was chosen an Honorary Fellow of the College of Physicians, and received the honour of knighthood from Charles II on the occasion of his paying a visit to the city of Norwich in 1671. He died at Norwich in 1682 at the mature age of seventy-seven.

His writings are numerous, and generally desultory. The most remarkable and the best known are The Religion of a Physician, *Religio Medici*, and a treatise on Vulgar or Common Errors, *Pseudodoxia Epidemica*. The *Religio Medici* was written shortly after his return from travel, and during a residence of two or three years at Halifax, and was published soon after he went to reside at Norwich. The work excited immediate attention by the liberality of sentiment and the freedom from prejudice which marked it, as well as by its novel paradoxes, subtle disquisitions, strength of language, and dignity of style. Sir Kenelm Digby produced a volume of acute comment and mixed censure and speculation, which gave the work further importance.

Pseudodoxia appeared ten years later, and passed through six editions in the lifetime of its author; it is noteworthy as much for the strangeness of the errors as for the quaintness of the refutations.

In 1658 the discovery of some ancient urns in Norfolk gave rise to his treatise on Urn Burial, *Hydriotaphia*—a work full of antiquarian learning.

Sir Thomas Browne's style is flowing, rich with illustrations, and here and there poetical. It is marred by a want of uniformity. The reader is surprised by eccentric changes from polished thoughts to the most uncouth ideas. Coleridge has characterised Browne as 'rich in various knowledge, exuberant in conceptions and conceits, contemplative, imaginative, often truly great in his style and diction, though doubtless too often big, stiff, and hyperlatinistic. In him the humourist constantly mingles with the philosopher.'

If he combated errors he resisted innovations, not accepting the motion of the earth around the sun. Being a devout Christian he spoke with candour of the hard things of his faith, and so was deemed by some an atheist; and since he was a firm believer, with others he passed as superstitious. He was in truth a thoughtful and cultivated man, fearless in maintaining what he believed, desirous of attaining to truth, indifferent to blame; and in gentle charity with all men.

---

1. God and Nature.

THUS there are two books from whence I collect my divinity; besides that written one of God, another of his servant nature, that universal and public manuscript, that lies expans'd unto the eyes of all; those that never saw him in the one, have discovered him in the other. This was the Scripture and theology of the heathens; the natural

motion of the sun made them more admire him, than its
supernatural station did the children of Israel; the ordinary
effect of nature wrought more admiration in them, than in
the other all his miracles; surely the heathens knew better
how to join and read these mystical letters, than we
Christians, who cast a more careless eye on these common
hieroglyphics, and disdain to suck divinity from the flowers
of nature. Nor do I so forget God, as to adore the name
of nature; which I define not with the schools, the principle
of motion and rest, but that straight and regular line, that
settled and constant course the wisdom of God hath ordained the actions of his creatures, according to their several
kinds. To make a revolution every day, is the nature of
the sun, because that necessary course which God hath
ordained it, from which it cannot swerve, by a faculty from
that voice which first did give it motion. Now this course
of nature God seldom alters or perverts, but like an excellent
artist hath so contrived his work, that with the self same
instrument without a new creation he may effect his obscurest
designs. Thus he sweeteneth the water with a wood, preserveth the creatures in the Ark, which the blast of his
mouth might have as easily created: for God is like a
skilful geometrician, who when more easily and with one
stroke of his compass he might describe, or divide a right
line, had yet rather do this in a circle or longer way;
according to the constituted and forelaid principles of his
art: yet this rule of his he doth sometimes pervert, to
acquaint the world with his prerogative, lest the arrogancy
of our reason should question his power, and conclude he
could not; and thus I call the effects of nature the works
of God, whose hand and instrument she only is; and therefore to ascribe his actions unto her, is to devolve the honour
of the principal agent, upon the instrument; which if with

reason we may do, then let our hammers rise up and boast
they have built our houses, and our pens receive the honour
of our writing. I hold there is a general beauty in the
works of God, and therefore no deformity in any kind or
species of creature whatsoever : I cannot tell by what logic
we call a toad, a bear, or an elephant, ugly, they being
created in those outward shapes and figures which best
express those actions of their inward forms. And having
past that general visitation of God, who saw that all that
he had made was good, that is, conformable to his will,
which abhors deformity, and is the rule of order and beauty;
there is no deformity but in monstrosity, wherein notwithstanding there is a kind of beauty, nature so ingenuously
contriving the irregular parts, as they become sometimes
more remarkable than the principal fabric. To speak yet
more narrowly, there was never any thing ugly, or mis-
shapen, but the chaos; wherein, notwithstanding, to speak
strictly, there was no deformity, because no form, nor was
it yet impregnant by the voice of God: now nature is not
at variance with art, nor art with nature; they being both
the servants of his providence : art is the perfection of
nature : were the world now as it was the sixth day, there
were yet a chaos: nature hath made one world, and art
another. In brief, all things are artificial, for nature is the
art of God.—*Religio Medici.*

2. True Affection.

THERE are wonders in true affection, it is a body of
enigmas, mysteries and riddles; wherein two so become
one, as they both become two; I love my friend before
myself, and yet methinks I do not love him enough; some
few months hence my multiplied affection will make me

believe I have not loved him at all; when I am from him,
I am dead till I be with him; when I am with him, I am
not satisfied, but would still be nearer him: united souls
are not satisfied with embraces, but desire to be truly each
other, which being impossible, their desires are infinite, and
must proceed without a possibility of satisfaction. Another
misery there is in affection, that whom we truly love like
our own, we forget their looks, nor can our memory retain
the idea of their faces, and it is no wonder, for they are
ourselves, and our affection makes their looks our own.
This noble affection falls not on vulgar and common constitutions, but on such as are marked for virtue; he that
can love his friend with this noble ardour, will in a competent degree affect all. Now if we can bring our affections
to look beyond the body, and cast an eye upon the soul,
we have found out the true object, not only of friendship
but charity; and the greatest happiness that we can bequeath
the soul, is that wherein we all do place our last felicity,
salvation; which though it be not in our power to bestow,
it is in our charity and pious invocations to desire, if not
procure and further. I cannot contentedly frame a prayer
for myself in particular, without a catalogue for my friends,
nor request a happiness wherein my sociable disposition
doth not desire the fellowship of my neighbour. I never
hear the toll of a passing bell,.though in my mirth, without
my prayers and best wishes for the departing spirit: I
cannot go to cure the body of my patient, but I forget my
profession, and call unto God for his soul; I cannot see
one say his prayers, but instead of imitating him, I fall into
a supplication for him, who perhaps is no more to me than
a common nature: and if God hath vouchsafed an ear to
my supplications, there are surely many happy that never
saw me, and enjoy the blessing of mine unknown devotions.

To pray for enemies, that is, for their salvation, is no harsh
precept, but the practice of our daily and ordinary devotions.
I cannot believe the story of the Italian, our bad wishes
and uncharitable desires proceed no further than this life ;
it is the devil, and the uncharitable votes of hell, that desire
our misery in the world to come.—*Religio Medici.*

3. The Faithful Physician.

I FEEL not in me those sordid and unchristian desires
of my profession; I do not secretly implore and wish for
plagues, rejoice at famines, revolve ephemerides and
almanacks in expectation of malignant aspects, fatal conjunctions, and eclipses: I rejoice not at unwholesome
springs, nor unseasonable winters; my prayer goes with
the husbandman's; I desire everything in its proper season,
that neither men nor the times be put out of temper. Let
me be sick myself, if sometimes the malady of my patient
be not a disease unto me, I desire rather to cure his infirmities than my own necessities; where I do him no good
methinks it is scarce honest gain, though I confess it is
but the worthy salary of our well-intended endeavours : I am
not only ashamed, but heartily sorry, that besides death,
there are diseases incurable, yet not for my own sake, or
that they be beyond my art, but for the general cause
and sake of humanity whose common cause I apprehend
as mine own: and to speak more generally, those three
noble professions which all civil Commonwealths do honour,
are raised upon the fall of Adam, and are not any exempt
from their infirmities; there are not only diseases incurable
in physic, but cases indissoluble in laws, vices incorrigible
in divinity; if general councils may err, I do not see why
particular courts should be infallible, their perfectest rules

are raised upon the erroneous reasons of man, and the laws of one do but condemn the rules of another; as Aristotle ofttimes the opinions of his predecessors, because, though agreeable to reason, yet were not consonant to his own rules and logic of his proper principles. Again, to speak nothing of the sin against the Holy Ghost, whose cure not only, but whose nature is unknown; I can cure the gout or stone in some sooner than divinity, pride or avarice in others. I can cure vices by physic, when they remain incurable by divinity; and shall obey my pills, when they contemn their precepts. I boast nothing, but plainly say, we all labour against our own cure, for death is the cure of all diseases. There is no catholicon or universal remedy I know but this, which though nauseous to queasy stomacks, yet to prepared appetites is nectar, and a pleasant portion of immortality.

For my conversation, it is like the sun's with all men, and with a friendly aspect to good and bad. Methinks there is no man bad; and the worst best, that is, while they are kept within the circle of those qualities wherein there is good: there is no man's mind of such discordant and jarring a temper to which a tuneable disposition may not strike a harmony. *Magnae virtutes, nec minora vitia*, it is the poesy of the best natures, and may be inverted on the worst; there are in the most depraved and venomous dispositions certain pieces that remain untouched, which by an antiperistasis become more excellent, or by the excellency of their antipathies are able to preserve themselves from the contagion of their enemies' vices, and persist entire beyond the general corruption.—*Religio Medici.*

4. A Common Error.

But the mortallest enemy unto knowledge, and that which hath done the greatest execution upon truth, hath been a peremptory adhesion unto authority; and more especially, the establishing of our belief upon the dictates of antiquity. For (as every capacity may observe) most men, of ages present, so superstitiously do look upon ages past, that the authorities of the one exceed the reasons of the other. Whose persons indeed being far removed from our. times, their works, which seldom with us pass uncontrolled, either by contemporaries, or immediate successors, are now become out of the distance of envies; and, the farther removed from present times, are conceived to approach the nearer unto truth itself. Now hereby methinks we manifestly delude ourselves, and widely walk out of the track of truth.

For, first, men hereby impose a thraldom on their times, which the ingenuity of no age should endure, or indeed the presumption of any did ever yet enjoin. Thus Hippocrates, about two thousand years ago, conceived it no injustice, either to examine or refute the doctrines of his predecessors; Galen the like, and Aristotle the most of any. Yet did not any of these conceive themselves infallible, or set down their dictates as verities irrefragable; but when they either deliver their own inventions, or reject other men's opinions, they proceed with judgment and ingenuity; establishing their assertions, not only with great solidity, but submitting them also unto the correction of future discovery.

Secondly, Men that adore times past consider not that those times were once present, that is, as our own are at this instant; and we ourselves unto those to come, as they unto us at present: as we rely on them, even so will those on us, and magnify us hereafter, who at present condemn ourselves. Which very absurdity is daily committed amongst us, even in the esteem and censure of our own times. And, to speak impartially, old men, from whom we should expect the greatest example of wisdom, do most exceed in this point of folly; commending the days of their youth, which they scarce remember, at least well understood not, extolling those times their younger years have heard their fathers condemn, and condemning those times the gray heads of their posterity shall commend. And thus is it the humour of many heads, to extol the days of their forefathers, and declaim against the wickedness of times present. Which notwithstanding they cannot handsomely do, without the borrowed help and satires of times past; condemning the vices of their own times, by the expressions of vices in times which they commend, which cannot but argue the community of vice in both. Horace, therefore, Juvenal, and Persius, were no prophets, although their lines did seem to indigitate and point at our times. There is a certain list of vices committed in all ages, and declaimed against by all authors, which will last as long as human nature; which digested into common places, may serve for any theme, and never be out of date until dooms-day.

Thirdly, The testimonies of antiquity, and such as pass oraculously amongst us, were not, if we considered them, always so exact as to examine the doctrine they delivered. For some, and those the acutest of them, have left unto us many things of falsity; controllable, not only by critical and collective reason, but common and country observation.— *Pseudodoxia Epidemica.*

5. Wise Words.

THOUGH a contented mind enlargeth the dimension of little
things; and unto some it is wealth enough not to be poor;
and others are well content, if they be but rich enough to be
honest, and to give every man his due; yet fall not into that
obsolete affectation of bravery, to throw away thy money, and
to reject all honours or honourable stations in this courtly
and splendid world. Old generosity is superannuated, and
such contempt of the world out of date. No man is now
like to refuse the favour of great ones, or be content to say
unto princes, 'stand out of my sun.' And if any there be of
such antiquated resolutions, they are not like to be tempted
out of them by great ones; and 'tis fair if they escape the
name of hypocondriacks from the genius of latter times, unto
whom contempt of the world is the most contemptible
opinion; and to be able, like Bias, to carry all they have
about them were to be the eighth wise man. However,
the old tetrick philosophers looked always with indignation
upon such a face of things; and observing the unnatural
current of riches, power, and honour in the world, and withal
the imperfection and demerit of persons often advanced unto
them, were tempted unto angry opinions, that affairs were
ordered more by stars than reason, and that things went on
rather by lottery than election.

If thy vessel be but small in the ocean of this world, if
meanness of possessions be thy allotment upon earth, forget
not those virtues which the great disposer of all bids thee to
entertain from thy quality and condition; that is, submission,
humility, content of mind, and industry. Content may dwell
in all stations. To be low, but above contempt, may be high
enough to be happy. But many of low degree may be higher
than computed, and some cubits above the common com-

mensuration; for in all states virtue gives qualifications and allowances, which make out defects. Rough diamonds are sometimes mistaken for pebbles; and meanness may be rich in accomplishments, which riches in vain desire. If our merits be above our stations, if our intrinsical value be greater than what we go for, or our value than our valuation, and if we stand higher in God's, than in the censor's book; it may make some equitable balance in the inequalities of this world, and there may be no such vast chasm or gulph between disparities as common measures determine. The divine eye looks upon high and low differently from that of man. They who seem to stand upon Olympus, and high mounted unto our eyes, may be but in the valleys, and low ground unto His; for he looks upon those as highest who nearest approach His divinity, and upon those as lowest who are farthest from it.

When thou lookest upon the imperfections of others, allow one eye for what is laudable in them, and the balance they have from some excellency, which may render them considerable. While we look with fear or hatred upon the teeth of the viper, we may behold his eye with love. In venomous natures something may be amiable: poisons afford antipoisons: nothing is totally, or altogether uselessly bad. Notable virtues are sometimes dashed with notorious vices, and in some vicious tempers have been found illustrious acts of virtue; which makes such observable worth in some actions of king Demetrius, Antonius, and Ahab, as are not to be found in the same kind in Aristides, Numa, or David. Constancy, generosity, clemency, and liberality have been highly conspicuous in some persons not marked out in other concerns for example or imitation. But since goodness is exemplary in all, if others have not our virtues, let us not be wanting in theirs; nor scorning them for their vices whereof we are free, be condemned by their virtues wherein we are deficient.   There is dross, alloy, and embasement in all human tempers; and he flieth without wings, who thinks to find ophir or pure metal in any.   For perfection is not, like light, centred in any one body; but, like the dispersed seminalities of vegetables at the creation, scattered through the whole mass of the earth, no place producing all and almost all some.   So that 'tis well, if a perfect man can be made out of many men, and, to the perfect eye of God, even out of mankind.   Time, which perfects some things, imperfects also others.   Could we intimately apprehend the ideated man, and as he stood in the intellect of God upon the first exertion by creation, we might more narrowly comprehend our present degeneration, and how widely we are fallen from the pure exemplar and idea of our nature: for after this corruptive elongation from a primitive and pure creation, we are almost lost in degeneration; and Adam hath not only fallen from his Creator, but we ourselves from Adam, our tycho and primary generator.—*Christian Morals.*

6. Urn Burial.

WHEN the funeral pyre was out, and the last valediction over, men took a lasting adieu of their interred friends, little expecting the curiosity of future ages should comment upon their ashes; and, having no old experience of the duration of their relicks, held no opinion of such after-considerations.

But who knows the fate of his bones, or how often he is to be buried?   Who hath the oracle of his ashes, or whither they are to be scattered? . . .

In a field of Old Walsingham, not many months past. were digged up between forty and fifty urns, deposited in a dry and sandy soil, not a yard deep, nor far from one another.—Not all strictly of one figure, but most answering these described: some containing two pounds of bones, distinguishable in skulls, ribs, jaws, thigh bones, and teeth, with fresh impressions of their combustion; besides the extraneous substances, like pieces of small boxes, or combs handsomely wrought, handles of small brass instruments, brazen nippers, and in one some kind of opal.

Near the same plot of ground, for about six yards compass, were digged up coals and incinerated substances, which begat conjecture that this was the *ustrina* or place of burning their bodies, or some sacrificing place unto the *manes*, which was properly below the surface of the ground, as the *aera* and altars unto the gods and heroes above it.

That these were the urns of Romans from the common custom and place where they were found, is no obscure conjecture, not far from a Roman garrison, and but five miles from Brancaster, set down by ancient record under the name of Branodunum. . . .

Than the time of these urns deposited, or precise antiquity of these relicks, nothing of more uncertainty; for since the lieutenant of Claudius seems to have made the first progress into these parts, since Boadicea was overthrown by the forces of Nero, and Agricola put a full end to these conquests, it is not probable the country was fully garrisoned or planted before; and, therefore, however these urns might be of later date, not likely of higher antiquity. . . .

Whether they were the bones of men, or women, or children, no authentic decision from ancient custom in distinct places of burial. Although not improbably conjectured, that the double sepulture, or burying place of Abraham, had in it such intention. But from exility of bones, thinness of skulls, smallness of teeth, ribs, and thigh bones, not improbable that many thereof were persons of minor age, or women. Confirmable also from things contained in them. In most were found substances resembling combs, plates like boxes, fastened with iron pins, and handsomely over-wrought like the necks or bridges of musical instruments, long brass plates overwrought like the handles of neat implements, brazen nippers, to pull away hair, and in one a kind of opal, yet maintaining a bluish colour.

Now that they accustomed to burn or bury with them, things wherein they excelled, delighted, or which were dear unto them, either as farewells unto all pleasure, or vain apprehension that they might use them in the other world, is testified by all antiquity. . . .

Some men, considering the contents of these urns, lasting pieces and toys included in them, and the custom of burning with many other nations, might somewhat doubt whether all urns found among us, were properly Roman relicks, or some not belonging unto our British, Saxon, or Danish forefathers. . . . Many urns are red, these but of a black colour, somewhat smooth, and dully sounding, which begat some doubt whether they were burnt, or only baked in oven or sun, according to the ancient way in many bricks, tiles, pots, and testaceous works ; and as the word *testa* is properly to be taken, when occurring without addition, and chiefly intended by Pliny, when he commendeth bricks and tiles of two years old, and to make them in the spring. Nor only these concealed pieces, but the open magnificence of antiquity, ran much in the artifice of clay. Hereof the house of Mausolus was built, thus old Jupiter stood in the capitol, and the statua of Hercules, made in the reign of Tarquinius Priscus, was extant in Pliny's days. . . .

Among these urns we could obtain no good account of their coverings; only one seemed arched over with some kind of brick work. Of those found at Buxton, some were covered with flints, some, in other parts, with tiles, those at Yarmouth Caster were closed with Roman bricks, and some have proper earthen covers adapted and fitted to them. But in the Homerical urn of Patroclus, whatever was the solid tegument, we find the immediate covering to be a purple piece of silk: and such as had no covers might have the earth closely pressed into them, after which disposure were probably some of these, wherein we found the bones and ashes half mortared unto the sand and sides of the urn, and some long roots of quich, or dog's-grass wreathed about the bones.

No lamps, included liquors, lachrymatories, or tear-bottles, attended these rural urns, either as sacred unto the *manes*, or passionate expressions of their surviving friends. While with rich flames, and hired tears, they solemnized their obsequies, and in the most lamented monuments made one part of their inscriptions. Some find sepulchral vessels containing liquors, which time hath incrassated into jellies. For, besides these lachrymatories, notable lamps, with vessels of oils, and aromatical liquors, attended noble ossuaries; and some yet retaining a vinosity and spirit in them, which, if any have tasted, they have far exceeded the palates of antiquity. Liquors not to be computed by years of annual magistrates, but by great conjunctions and the fatal periods of kingdoms. The draughts of consulary date were but crude unto these, and Opimian wine but in the must unto them.

In sundry graves and sepulchres we meet with rings, coins, and chalices. Ancient frugality was so severe, that they allowed no gold to attend the corpse, but only that which served to fasten their teeth. Whether the Opaline stone in this were burnt upon the finger of the dead, or cast into the fire by some affectionate friend, it will consist

with either custom.   But other incinerable substances were
found so fresh, that they could feel no singe from fire.
These, upon view, were judged to be wood; but, sinking
in water, and tried by the fire, we found them to be bone
or ivory.   In their hardness and yellow colour they most
resembled box, which, in old expressions, found the epithet
of eternal, and perhaps in such conservatories might have
passed uncorrupted. . . .

Now since these dead bones have already out-lasted the
living ones of Methuselah, and in a yard under ground, and
thin walls of clay, out-worn all the strong and specious
buildings above it; and quietly rested under the drums and
tramplings . of three conquests: what prince can promise
such diuturnity unto his relicks, or might not gladly say,

Sic ego componi versus in ossa velim?

Time, which antiquates antiquities, and hath an art to make
dust of all things; hath yet spared these minor monuments.
In vain we hope to be known by open and visible conservatories when to be unknown was the means of their continua-
tion, and obscurity their protection. . . .

Oblivion is not to be hired.   The greater part must be
content to be as though they had not been, to be found in
the register of God, not in the record of man.   Twenty-
seven names make up the first story before the flood, and
the recorded names ever since contain not one living century.
The number of the dead long exceedeth all that shall live.
The night of time far surpasseth the day, and who knows
when was the equinox?   Every hour adds unto that current
arithmetick, which scarce stands one moment.   And since
death must be the *Lucina* of life, and even Pagans could
doubt, whether thus to live were to die; since our longest
sun sets at right descensions, and makes but winter arches,

and therefore it cannot be long before we lie down in darkness, and have our light in ashes; since the brother of death daily haunts us with dying mementos, and time that grows old in itself, bids us hope no long duration;—diuturnity is a dream and folly of expectation.—*Hydriotaphia.*

XII.

THOMAS FULLER.

1608—1661.

THOMAS FULLER was born at All Winkle in Northampton-
shire in 1608. His father, rector of that parish, was probably his
only teacher till at the age of twelve he sent him to Cambridge,
where in 1628 he took the degree of Master of Arts. At the
age of twenty-three he became prebend of Salisbury, and vicar
of Broad Windsor. . Here he spent some ten quiet years working
in his parish and writing his ' Holy War' and ' Pisgah-Sight of
Palestine.' Tidings came to him from time to time of the
struggle which was growing fiercer every day between the nation
and the king. To Fuller, the son of a High-churchman, and
.bred in the loyal University of Cambridge, devotion to the existing sovereign was the natural expression of allegiance to the King
of kings, and it was with grief and horror that he heard of his
country's apostasy. At last, impatient of inaction, he hastened to
London. There, in many pulpits, chiefly those of the Savoy and
the Inns of Court, he boldly preached submission to the Lord's
Anointed. His earnestness and brilliant wit attracted crowds to
listen to him, and drew upon him the observation of the Long
Parliament which was then sitting. In 1643, he was required to
sign a declaration that he would support the measures of Parliament. He signed, with too many reservations to satisfy the
authorities, and the oath was on the point of being tendered to
him again, when Fuller quietly betook himself to the king's
quarters at Oxford, saving thereby his conscience and losing his
preferment. Lord Hopton made him his chaplain, and he
became 'Preacher militant' to the king's soldiers. As he wan-

dered about with the army he gathered materials for his 'Worthies of England.' But such a life was less favourable to his 'Church History.' It is of no value as a history till it reaches his own times, and yet it charms by the wit which sparkles in every page. In the spring of 1644 he left the army and took refuge in Exeter. It was during this lull that he wrote his 'Good Thoughts in Bad Times.' On the surrender of Exeter Fuller obtained special terms from Fairfax, under which he returned to London. He was living in a small lodging, working at his Worthies and praying for the king's return, when 'that royal martyr was murdered,' and 'the foul deed' so completely crushed him that it was long before he could take heart to work again. After 1655 the Protector allowed him freely to preach, though other Royalists were silenced. On the Restoration he was made Chaplain extraordinary to Charles II, and Doctor of Divinity by the University of Cambridge at the king's request. He died on the 12th of Aug. 1661. He was twice married. His writings are full of graphic touches and deep wisdom, and though his quaint fancy often led him beyond the bounds of good taste, he was never irreverent in meaning. His piety and genial humour might well atone for greater faults. Few writers tell a story better : and none, perhaps, have equalled him in the art of conveying a truth under the guise of a familiar-sounding proverb. Fuller's style is free to a great extent from the Latinisms which form so large an element in those of most of his contemporaries. He is more idiomatic in diction, the structure of his sentences is simpler, and a larger proportion of the words are of Saxon derivation. Charles Lamb says, ' The writings of Fuller are usually designated by the title of quaint, and with sufficient reason, for such was his natural bias to conceits that I doubt not upon most occasions it would have been going out of his way to have expressed himself out of them. But his wit is not always *lumen siccum*—a dry faculty of surprising : on the contrary his conceits are oftentimes deeply steeped in human feelings and passion. Above all, his way of telling a story, for its eager liveliness and the perpetual running commentary of the narrator happily blended with the narration, is perhaps unequalled.'

1. King David fleeth from Jerusalem.

OVER the Southern part of Mount Olivet David fled from Absalom; for perceiving that his son by state-felony had stolen away his people's hearts he politicly resolved not to be pent in Jerusalem (where the land-flood of a popular mutiny might presently, drown him) but to retire to the uttermost bounds of his kingdom, meantime giving his subjects leisure and liberty to review what they had done, dislike what they reviewed, revoke what they disliked; that so on second debates they might seriously undo, what on first thoughts they had furiously attempted; knowing full well that Rebellion, though running so at hand, is quickly tired, as having rotten lungs, whilst well-breathed Loyalty is best at a long course. As David was flying this way the Priests proffered their service to carry the Ark along with them: indeed how could it well stay behind, and what should the Ark and Absalom, Religion and Rebellion, do together? Was it not fit that as once it was joyfully brought into Jerusalem with David's dancing, so now it should dolefully depart hence with David's weeping? Howsoever, he accepted their goodwill, and on better reason declined their attendance. Coming a little past the top of the hill Ziba meets him with a couple of asses, laden with bread, raisins, summer fruits and wine for the refection of David and his company. But O the bran in that Bread! rottenness in those raisins! dregs in that wine he brought! joining them with a false accusation of his Master Mephibosheth to be a Traitor whilst, alas! all the disloyalty that good man was guilty of, was only his lame legs, his lying servant; and his over-credulous sovereign David did rashly believe this information. A little farther eastward was Bahurim, where Shimei, lord of that place, cursed David, casting stones and dust at him. What meant the mad man thus to rail, being within reach of David's armies, except he intended to vent out his venom and life together? But causeless curses rebound on their authors, and Ziba's gifts did David more harm than Shimei's curses; for those betrayed him to an act of injustice, whilst these improved his patience. Indeed his railing gave an alarm to the martial spirit of Abishai, who desired a commission to take off the head of this dead dog (blood so let out in the neck-vein is the soonest and speediest cure of such a traitorous phrenzy). But David, who desired not that Shimei should be killed for his words but rather that his own heart should be mortified by them, by heavenly logic '*a majore ad minus*' argued his own soul into humility; that seeing his own son had conspired against him, the ill words of an open enemy ought patiently to be endured. Well! let Shimei know that though he pass unpaid for the present, yet either David himself or his executors, administrators or assignees, shall one day see this debt duly discharged.—*Pisgah-Sight of Palestine.*

2. Hooker and Travers.

HOOKER was born in Devonshire, bred in Oxford, Fellow of Corpus Christi College; one of a solid judgment and great reading. Yea, such the depth of his learning, that his pen was a better bucket than his tongue to draw it out: a great defender both by preaching and writing of the discipline of the Church of England. Yet never got, (nor cared to get) any eminent dignity therein; conscience not covetousness engaging him in the controversy. Spotless was his conversation; and though some dirt was cast, none could stick on his reputation. Mr. Travers was brought up in Trinity College in Cambridge. For seven years together he became Lecturer at the Temple, till Mr. Hooker became the Master thereof.

Mr. Hooker's voice was low, stature little, gesture none at all, standing stone-still in the pulpit, as if the posture of his body' were the emblem of his mind, unmoveable in his opinions. Where his eye was left fixed at the beginning, it was found fixed at the end of his sermon. In a word, the doctrine he delivered had nothing but itself to garnish it. His style was long and pithy, driving on a whole flock of several clauses before he came to the close of a sentence. So that when the copiousness of his style met not with proportionate capacity in his auditors, it was unjustly censured for perplexed, tedious, and obscure. His sermons followed the inclination of his studies, and were for the most part on controversies, and deep points of school-divinity.

Mr. Travers's utterance was graceful, gesture plausible, matter profitable, method plain, and his style carried in it *indolem pietatis*, 'a genius of grace' flowing from his sanctified heart. Some say, that the congregation in the Temple ebbed in the forenoon, and flowed in the afternoon; and that the auditory of Mr. Travers was far the most numerous,— the first occasion of emulation betwixt them. But such as knew Mr. Hooker, knew him to be too wise to take exception at such trifles, the rather because the most judicious is always the least part in all auditories.

Here might one on Sundays have seen almost as many writers as hearers. Not only young students, but even the gravest benchers, (such as Sir Edward Coke and Sir James Altham then were) were not more exact in taking instructions from their clients, than in writing notes from the mouths of their ministers. The worst was, these two preachers, though joined in affinity, (their nearest kindred being married together,) acted with different principles, and clashed one against another. So that what Mr. Hooker delivered in the forenoon, Mr. Travers confuted in the afternoon. At the building of Solomon's temple 'neither hammer, nor axe, nor tool of iron was heard therein,' 1 Kings vi. 7; whereas alas! in this temple not only much knocking was heard, but (which was the worst) the nails and pins which one master-builder drave in, were driven out by the other. Thus, much disturbance was caused, to the disquieting of people's consciences, the disgrace of the ordinance, the advantage of the common enemy, and the dishonour of God himself.

Here Archbishop Whitgift interposed his power and silenced Travers from preaching in the Temple or anywhere else. As for Travers's silencing, many which were well pleased with the deed done, were offended at the manner of doing it. For all the congregation on a Sabbath in the afternoon were assembled together, their attention prepared, the cloth (as I may say) and napkins were laid, yea, the guests set, and their knives drawn for their spiritual repast, when suddenly, as Mr. Travers was going up into the pulpit, a sorry fellow served him with a letter, prohibiting him to preach any more. In obedience to authority, (the mild and constant submission whereunto won him respect with his adversaries,) Mr. Travers calmly signified the same to the congregation and requested them quietly to depart to their chambers. Thus was our good Zacharias struck dumb in the Temple, but not for infidelity; impartial people accounting his fault at most but indiscretion. Meantime his auditory (pained that their pregnant expectation to hear him preach should so publicly prove abortive, and

sent sermonless home) manifested in their variety of passion, some grieving, some frowning, some murmuring, and
the wisest sort, who held their tongues, shook their heads,
as disliking the managing of the matter.—*Church History.*

3. Robert Thorn.

ROBERT THORN was born in this city [Bristol]. I see it
matters not what the name be, so that the nature be good.
I confess Thorns came in by 'man's curse' and our Saviour
saith, 'Do men gather grapes of thorns?' But this our
Thorn (God send us many coppices of them) was a blessing to our nation, and wine and oil may be said freely
to flow from him. Being bred a merchant-tailor in London
he gave more than four thousand four hundred and forty-
five pounds to pious uses; a sum sufficient therewith to
build and endow a college, the time being well considered,
being towards the beginning of the reign of King Henry
the Eighth.

I have observed some at the church door cast in sixpence
with such ostentation that it rebounded from the bottom,
and rung against both the sides of the basin (so that the
same piece of silver was the alms and the giver's trumpet);
whilst others have dropped down silent five shillings without
any noise. Our Thorn was of this second sort, doing his
charity effectually, but with a possible privacy. Nor was
this good Christian abroad worse (in the apostle-phrase)
than an infidel at home in not providing for his family,
who gave to his poor kindred (besides debts forgiven
unto them) the sum of five thousand one hundred and
forty-two pounds.— *Worthies of England.*

4. The Schoolmaster.

He studieth his scholars' natures as carefully as they their books. And ranks their dispositions into several forms. And though it may seem difficult for him in a great school to descend to all particulars, yet experienced schoolmasters may quickly make a grammar of boys' natures, and reduce them all (saving some few exceptions) to their general rules.

1. *Those that are ingenious and industrious.* The conjunction of two such planets in a youth, presage much good unto him. To such a lad a frown may be a whipping, and a whipping a death, yea when their master whips them once, shame whips them all the week after. Such natures he useth with all gentleness.

2. *Those that are ingenious and idle.* These think with the hare in the fable, that running with snails,—so they count the rest of their schoolfellows,—they shall come soon enough to the post, though sleeping a good while before their starting. O! a good rod would finely take them napping!

3. *Those that are dull and diligent.* Wines, the stronger they be the more lees they have when they are new. Many boys are muddy-headed till they be clarified with age, and such afterwards prove the best. Bristol diamonds are both bright and squared and pointed by nature, and yet are soft and worthless; whereas orient ones in India are rough and rugged naturally. Hard, rugged, and dull natures in youth acquit themselves afterwards the jewels of the country, and therefore their dulness at first is to be borne with, if they be diligent. That schoolmaster deserves to be beaten himself who beats nature in a boy for a fault. And I question whether all the whipping in the world can make their parts

which are naturally sluggish rise one minute before the hour nature hath appointed.

4. *Those that are invincibly dull and negligent also.* Correction may reform the latter, not amend the former. All the whetting in the world can never set a razor's edge on that which hath no steel in it. Such boys he assigneth over to other professions. Shipwrights and boatmakers will choose those crooked pieces of timber which other carpenters refuse. Those may make excellent merchants and mechanics who will not serve for scholars.—*Holy State.*

5.   The Bodleian Library.

If the schools may be resembled to the ring, the library may the better be compared to the diamond therein; not so much for the bunching forth beyond the rest, as the preciousness thereof, in some respects equalling any in Europe, and in most kinds exceeding all in England: yet our land hath been ever Φιλοβιβλος, much given to the love of books; and let us *fleet the cream* of a few of the primest libraries in all ages.

In the infancy of Christianity, that at York bare away the bell, founded by archbishop Egbert (and so highly praised by Alevinus in his epistle to Charles the Great); but long since abolished.

Before the dissolution of abbeys, when all cathedrals and convents had their libraries, that at Ramsey was the greatest Rabbin, spake the most and best Hebrew, abounding in Jewish and not defective in other books.

In that age of lay-libraries (as I may term them, as belonging to the city) I behold that pertaining to Guildhall as a principal, founded by Richard Whittington, whence three cart-loads of choice manuscripts were carried in the reign of king Edward the Sixth, on the promise of [never performed] restitution.

Since the Reformation, that of Bene't in Cambridge hath for manuscripts exceeded any (thank the cost and care of Matthew Parker) collegiate library in England.

Of late, Cambridge library, augmented with the Archepiscopal library of Lambeth, is grown the second in the land.

As for private libraries of subjects, that of treasurer Burleigh was the best for the use of a statesman, the lord Lumlie's for an historian, the late earl of Arundel's for an herald, Sir Robert Cotton's for an antiquary, and archbishop Usher's for a divine.

Many other excellent libraries there were of particular persons: lord Brudenell's, lord Hatton's, &c., routed by our civil wars; and many books which scaped the execution are fled [transported] into France, Flanders, and other foreign parts.

To return to Oxford library, which stands like Diana amongst her nymphs, and surpasseth all the rest for rarity and multitude of books; so that, if any be wanting on any subject, it is because the world doth not afford them. This library was founded by Humphrey the good duke of Gloucester; *con*founded, in the reign of king Edward the Sixth, by those who I list not to name; *re*-founded by worthy Sir Thomas Bodley, and the bounty of daily benefactors.—*Worthies of England.*

6. Julius Caesar Scaliger's The General Artist.

I know my choice herein is liable to much exception Some will make me the pattern of ignorance, for making this Scaliger the pattern of the general artist; whose own

son Joseph might have been his father in many arts. But,
all things considered, the choice will appear well-advised,
even in such variety of examples. Yet, let him know that
undertakes to pick out the best ear amongst an acre of
wheat, that he shall leave as good, if not a better, behind
him, than that which he chooseth.

He was born, *anno* 1484, in Italy, at the castle of Ripa,
upon *Lacus Benacus*, now called Lago di Garda, of the
illustrious and noble family of the Scaligers, princes, for
many hundreds of years, of Verona, till at last the Vene-
tians outed them of their ancient inheritance. Being about
eleven years old, he was brought to the court of Maximilian,
emperor of Germany; where, for seventeen years together,
he was taught learning and military discipline. I pass by·
his valiant performances achieved by him, save that this one
action of his is so great and strong, it cannot be kept in
silence, but will be recorded:—

In the cruel battle of Ravenna, betwixt the emperor and
the French, he not only bravely fetched off the dead bodies
of Benedictus and Titus, his father and brother, but also,
with his own hands, rescued the eagle, (the standard imperial,) which was taken by the enemies. For which his
prowess, Maximilian knighted him; and with his own hands
put on him the golden spurs and chain, the badges of knighthood.

Amidst these his martial employments, he made many a
clandestine match with the Muses; and whilst he expected
the tides and returns of business, he filled up the empty
places of leisure with his studies. Well did the poets
feign Pallas patroness of arts and arms; there being ever
good intelligence betwixt the two professions, and, as it
were, but a narrow cut to ferry over out of one into the
other. At last, Scaliger sounded a retreat to himself from

the wars, and wholly applied himself to his book; especially after his wandering life was fixed by marriage unto the beautiful Andietta Lobeiaca, with whom he lived at Agin, near Montpelier in France.

His Latin was twice refined, and most critical, as appears by his own writings, and notes on other authors. He was an accurate Grecian; yet began to study it when well nigh forty years old, when a man's tongue is too stiff to bow to words. What a torture was it to him, who flowed with streams of matter, then to learn words, yea, letters, drop by drop! But nothing was unconquerable to his pains, who had a golden wit in an iron body. Let his book of Subtleties witness his profound skill in logic and natural philosophy.

His skill in physic was as great as his practice therein was happy; insomuch that he did many strange and admirable cures.

As for his skill in physiognomy, it was wonderful. I know some will say, 'That cannot be read in men's faces which was never wrote there; and that he that seeks to find the disposition of men's souls in the figures of their bodies, looks for letters on the backside of the book.' Yet is it credibly averred, that he never looked on his infant son Audectus but with grief, as sorrow-struck with some sad sign of ill success he saw in his face; which child at last was found stifled in bed, with the embraces of his nurse, being fast asleep.

In mathematics he was no Archimedes, though he showed his skill therein with the best advantage, and stood therein on his tiptoes, that his learning might seem the taller.

But in poetry his over-measure of skill might make up this defect, as is attested by his book *De Arte Poeticâ.* Yet his own poems are harsh and unsmooth, (as if he rather snorted than slept on Parnassus,) and they sound better to the brain than ear. Indeed, his censure in poetry was incomparable; but he was more happy in repairing of poems, than in building them from the ground, which speaks his judgment to be better than his invention.

What shall I speak of his skill in history, whose own actions were a sufficient history? He was excellently versed in the passages of the world, both modern and ancient. Many modern languages, which departed from Babel in a confusion, met in his mouth in a method; being skilful in the Sclavonic tongue; the Hungarian, Dutch, Italian, Spanish, and French.

But these his excellent parts were attended with prodigious pride; and he had much of the humour of the Ottomans in him,—to kill all his brethren, and cry down all his equals, who were cor-rivals with him in the honour of arts, which was his principal quarrel with Cardan. Great was his spite at Erasmus, the morning-star of learning, and one by whom Julius himself had profited; though afterwards he sought to put out that candle whereat he had lighted his own. In the bickering betwixt them, Erasmus plucked Scaliger by the long locks of his immoderate boasting, and touched him to the quick. (A proud man lies pat for a jeering man's hand to hit!) Yea, Erasmus was a badger in his jeers; where he did bite, he would make his teeth meet. Nor came Scaliger behind him in railing. However, afterward Scaliger repented of his bitterness, and before his death was reconciled unto him.

Thus his learning, being in the circuit of arts, spread so wide, no wonder if it lay thin in some places. His parts were nimble, that, starting so late, he overtook, yea, over-ran his equals; so that we may safely conclude, that, making abatement for his military avocations, and late applying himself to study, scarce any one is to be preferred before him for generality of human learning. He died *anno* 1558, in the seventy-fifth year of his age.—*Holy State.*

7. Of Recreations.

RECREATIONS is a second creation, when weariness hath almost annihilated one's spirits. It is the breathing of the soul, which otherwise would be stifled with continual business. We may trespass in them, if using such as are forbidden by the—lawyer, as against the statutes—physician, as against health—divine, as against conscience.

MAXIM II.

Spill not the morning (the quintessence of the day!) in recreations.—For sleep itself is a recreation. ˙ Add not, therefore, sauce to sauce ; and *he* cannot properly have any title to be refreshed, *who* was not first faint. Pastime, like wine, is poison in the morning. It is then good husbandry to sow the head, which hath lain fallow all night, with some serious work. Chiefly, intrench not on the Lord's-day to use unlawful sports ; this were to spare thine own flock, and to shear God's lamb.

III.

Let thy recreations be ingenious, and bear proportion with thine age.—If thou sayest with Paul, 'When I was a child, I did as a child;' say also with him, 'But when I was a man, I put away childish things.' Wear also the child's coat, if thou usest his sports.

IV.

Take heed of boisterous and over-violent exercises.—Ringing oft-times hath made good music on the bells, and put men's bodies out of tune ; so that, by over-heating themselves, they have rung their own passing-bell.

VI.

Refresh that part of thyself which is most wearied.—If thy life be sedentary, exercise thy body; if stirring and active, recreate thy mind. But take heed of cozening thy mind, in setting it to do a double task, under pretence of giving it a play-day, as in the labyrinth of chess, and other tedious and studious games.

VIII.

Running, leaping, and dancing, the descants on the plain song of walking, are all excellent exercises.—And yet those are the best recreations which, besides refreshing, enable, at least dispose, men to some other good ends. Bowling teaches men's hands and eyes mathematics and the rules of proportion. Swimming hath saved many a man's life, when himself hath been both the wares and the ship. Tilting and fencing is war without anger ; and manly sports are the grammar of military performance.

XI.

Choke not thy soul with immoderate pouring-in the cordial of pleasures.—The creation lasted but six days of the first week. Profane they whose recreation lasts seven days every week. Rather abridge thyself of thy lawful liberty herein; ... and then recreations shall both strengthen labour, and sweeten rest; and we may expect God's blessing and protection on us in following them, as well as in doing our work. For he that saith grace for his meat, in it prays also to God to bless the sauce unto him. As for those that will not take lawful pleasure, I am afraid they will take unlawful pleasure, and, by lacing themselves too hard, grow awry on one side.—*Holy State.*

8. Of Apparel.

CLOTHES are for necessity; warm clothes, for health; cleanly, for decency; lasting, for thrift; and rich, for magnificence. Now there may be a fault in their—number, if too various—making, if too vain—matter, if too costly— and mind of the wearer, if he takes pride therein. We come therefore to some general directions.

MAXIM I.

It is a chargeable vanity to be constantly clothed above one's purse or place.—I say 'constantly;' for, perchance, sometimes it may be dispensed with. A great man, who himself was very plain in apparel, checked a gentleman for being over-fine; who modestly answered, 'Your lordship hath better clothes at home, and I have worse.' But, sure, no plea can be made when this luxury is grown to be ordinary. It was an arrogant act of Hubert archbishop of Canterbury, who, when king John had given his courtiers rich liveries, to ape the lion, gave his servants the like; wherewith the king was not a little offended. But what shall we say to the riot of our age? wherein (as peacocks are more gay than the eagle himself) subjects are grown braver than their sovereign.

II.

It is beneath a wise man, always to wear clothes beneath men of his rank.—True, there is a state sometimes in decent plainness. When a wealthy lord, at a great solemnity, had the plainest apparel, 'O!' said one, 'if you had marked it well, his suit had the richest pockets.' Yet it argues no wisdom, in clothes always to stoop beneath his condition. When Antisthenes saw Socrates in a torn coat, he showed a hole thereof to the people; 'And, lo!' quoth he, 'through this I see Socrates's pride!'

III.

He shows a light gravity who loves to be an exception from a general fashion.—For the received custom in the place where we live, is the most competent judge of decency; from which we must not appeal to our own opinion. When the French courtiers, mourning for their king Henry II, had worn cloth a whole year, all silks became so vile in every man's eyes, that if any were seen to wear them, he was presently accounted a mechanic or country-fellow.

IV.

It is a folly for one, Proteus-like, never to appear twice in one shape.—Had some of our gallants been with the Israelites in the wilderness, when for forty years their clothes waxed not old, (Deut. xxix. 5,) they would have been vexed, though their clothes were whole, to have been so long in one fashion. Yet here I must confess, I understand not what is reported of Fulgentius, that he used the same garment winter and summer, and never altered his clothes, *etiam in sacris peragendis.*

V.

He that is proud of the rustling of his silks, like a madman, laughs at the rattling of his fetters.—For, indeed, clothes ought to be our remembrancers of our lost innocency. Besides, why should any brag of what is but borrowed? Should the ostrich snatch off the gallant's feather, the beaver his hat, the goat his gloves, the sheep his suit, the silk-worm his stockings, and neat his shoes, (to strip him no farther than modesty will give leave,) he would be left in a cold condition. And yet it is more pardonable to be proud, even of cleanly rags, than, as many are, of affected sloven-liness. The one is proud of a molehill, the other of a dung-hill.

To conclude: Sumptuary laws in this land to reduce

apparel to a set standard of price and fashion, according to the several states of men, have long been wished, but are little to be hoped-for. Some think, private men's superfluity is a necessary evil in a State, the floating of fashions affording a standing maintenance to many thousands, who otherwise would be at a loss for a livelihood,—men maintaining more by their pride than by their charity.—*Holy State.*

9. Ben Jonson.

BENJAMIN JONSON was born in this city (Westminster). Though I cannot, with all my industrious inquiry, find him in his cradle, I can fetch him from his long coats. When a little child, he lived in Harts-horn-lane near Charing-cross, where his mother married a bricklayer for her second husband.

He was first bred in a private school in Saint Martin's church; then in Westminster school; witness his own epigram;

> ' Camden, most reverend head, to whom I owe
> All that I am in arts, all that I know;
> How nothing's that to whom my country owes
> The great renown and name wherewith she goes,' &c.

He was statutably admitted into Saint John's College in Cambridge (as many years after incorporated an honorary member of Christ Church in Oxford) where he continued but few weeks for want of further maintenance, being fain to return to the trade of his father-in-law. And let them blush not that have, but those who have not, a lawful calling. He helped in the new structure of Lincoln's-Inn, when, having a trowel in his hand, he had a book in his pocket.

Some gentlemen, pitying that his parts should be buried under the rubbish of so mean a calling, did by their bounty manumise him freely to follow his own ingenious inclinations. Indeed his parts were not so ready to run of themselves, as able to answer the spur; so that it may be truly said of him, that he had an elaborate wit wrought out by his own industry. He would sit silent in a learned company and suck in (besides wine) their several humours into his observation. What was *ore* in others, he was able to refine to himself.

He was paramount in the dramatic part of poetry, and taught the stage an exact conformity to the laws of comedians. His comedies were above the *volge* (which are only tickled with downright obscenity), and took not so well at the first stroke as at the rebound, when beheld the second time; yea, they will endure reading, and that with due commendation, so long as either ingenuity or learning are fashionable in our nation. If his later be not so spriteful and vigorous as his first pieces, all that are old will, and all that desire to be old should, excuse him therein.

He was not very happy in his children, and most happy in those which died first, though none lived to survive him. This he bestowed as part of an epitaph on his eldest son, dying in infancy:

'Rest in soft peace; and, ask'd, say here doth lye,
Ben Jonson his best piece of poetry.'

He died anno Domini 1638; and was buried about the belfry, in the abbey church at Westminster.—*Worthies of England.*

XIII.

EDWARD HYDE, EARL OF CLARENDON.

1608—1674.

EDWARD HYDE was born 1608, at Dinton in Wiltshire. He began his studies at Oxford in his thirteenth year, but resided only one year, his father having determined to bring him up to the law. He pursued this profession with considerable success, till his increasing interest in public business led him to retire from the practice of it. He was returned to the Long Parliament for the borough of Saltash. He took a prominent part in the suppression of the Earl Marshal's Court, and was chairman of the committee on the case of ship-money; he also supported the proceedings against Strafford. Clarendon seceded from the popular party on the passing of a Bill to prevent the dissolution of Parliament except with its own consent, and he ever after- wards adhered to the Royal cause, and for a time was one of the King's principal advisers.

He accompanied Prince Charles to Jersey, where he passed two years in study and in the production of political papers for the King. He afterwards represented the cause of the Stuarts at various foreign Courts until the Restoration, when his ability and integrity were of essential service in re-establishing order, while by his moderation he restrained the excessive zeal of the Royalists.

He was created a peer in 1660, and also elected Chancellor of the University of Oxford. His conduct in the sale of Dunkirk and other public questions was opposed to popular feeling, and in some cases also to the wishes of the King, and in 1667 he fell

into disgrace, was required to resign the Great Seal and all other
public offices of trust, and after an unsuccessful impeachment
for high treason by the Commons he received the Royal command to withdraw from the kingdom. From Calais he wrote
a letter, given below, resigning the Chancellorship of the University.

He never returned to England, and died at Rouen in 1674.
Clarendon's most important works are his History of the Rebellion, and his own Life.   His style is sometimes deficient both
in clearness and elegance, and betrays a want of care and
accuracy; but his sentiments are always noble and dignified,
and he shows peculiar skill and delicacy in the delineation of
character.   Of this, striking examples are found in the sketches
of eminent men which abound in his History.

***

1.   Character of George Villiers, Duke of Buckingham.

THIS great man was a person of a noble nature, and
generous disposition, and of such other endowments, as
made him very capable of being a great favourite to a
great king.   He understood the arts of a court, and all
the learning that is professed there, exactly well.   By long
practice in business, under a master that discoursed excellently, and surely knew all things wonderfully, and took
much delight in indoctrinating his young unexperienced
favourite, who, he knew, would be always looked upon
as the workmanship of his own hands, he had obtained
a quick conception, and apprehension of business, and
had the habit of speaking very gracefully and pertinently.
He was of a most flowing courtesy and affability to all
men who made any address to him; and so desirous to
oblige them, that he did not enough consider the value
of the obligation, or the merit of the person he chose to

oblige; from which much of his misfortune resulted. He
was of a courage not to be daunted, which was manifested
in all his actions. . . . .

His kindness and affection to his friends was so vehement, that they were as so many marriages for better
and worse, and so many leagues offensive and defensive;
as if he thought himself obliged to love all his friends,
and to make war upon all they were angry with, let the
cause be what it would. And it cannot be denied that
he was an enemy in the same excess, and prosecuted
those he looked upon as his enemies with the utmost
rigour and animosity, and was not easily induced to re-
conciliation. And yet there were some examples of his
receding in that particular. And when he was in the
highest passion, he was so far from stooping to any dissimulation, whereby his displeasure might be concealed
and covered till he had attained his revenge, (the low
method of courts,) that he never endeavoured to do any
man an ill office, before he first told him what he was
to expect from him, and reproached him with the injuries
he had done, with so much generosity, that the person
found it in his power to receive further satisfaction, in the
way he would choose for himself. . . . .

His single misfortune was, (which indeed was productive
of many greater,) that he never made a noble and worthy
friendship with a man so near his equal, that he would
frankly advise him for his honour and true interest, against
the current, or rather the torrent, of his impetuous passion;
which was partly the vice of the time, when the court was
not replenished with great choice of excellent men; and
partly the vice of the persons who were most worthy to
be applied to, and looked upon his youth, and his obscurity
before his rise, as obligations upon him to gain their friend-

ships by extraordinary application. Then his ascent was so quick, that it seemed rather a flight than a growth; and he was such a darling of fortune, that he was at the top before he was well seen at the bottom; and, as if he had been born a favourite, he was supreme the first month he came to court; and it was want of confidence, not of credit, that he had not all at first which he obtained afterwards; never meeting with the least obstruction from his setting out, till he was as great as he could be: so that he wanted dependants before he thought he could want coadjutors. Nor was he very fortunate in the election of those dependants, very few of his servants having been ever qualified enough to assist or advise him; and they were intent only upon growing rich under him, not upon their master's growing good as well as great: insomuch as he was throughout his fortune a much wiser man than any servant or friend he had.

Let the fault or misfortune be what or whence it will, it may reasonably be believed, that, if he had been blessed with one faithful friend, who had been qualified with wisdom and integrity, that great person would have committed as few faults, and done as transcendent worthy actions, as any man who shined in such a sphere in that age in Europe. For he was of an excellent disposition, and of a mind very capable of advice and counsel. He was in his nature just and candid, liberal, generous, and bountiful; nor was it ever known, that the temptation of money swayed him to do an unjust or unkind thing. . . .

If he had an immoderate ambition, with which he was charged, and is a weed (if it be a weed) apt to grow in the best soils; it doth not appear that it was in his nature, or that he brought it with him to the court, but rather found it there, and was a garment necessary for that air. Nor was it more in his power to be without promotion, and titles, and wealth, than for a healthy man to sit in the sun in the brightest dog-days, and remain without any warmth. He needed no ambition, who was so seated in the hearts of two such masters.—*History of the Rebellion.*

2. Character of Blake.

HE wanted no pomp of funeral when he was dead, Cromwell causing him to be brought up by land to London in all the state that could be ; and to encourage his officers to venture their lives, that they might be pompously buried, he was, with all the solemnity possible, and at the charge of the public, interred in Harry the Seventh's chapel, among the monuments of the kings. He was a man of a private extraction; yet had enough left him by his father to give him a good education; which his own inclination disposed him to receive in the university of Oxford; where he took the degree of a master of arts; and was enough versed in books for a man who intended not to be of any profession, having sufficient of his own to maintain him in the plenty he affected, and having then no appearance of ambition to be a greater man than he was. He was of a melancholic and a sullen nature, and spent his time most with good-fellows, who liked his moroseness, and a freedom he used in inveighing against the licence of the time, and the power of the court. They who knew him inwardly, discovered that he had an anti-monarchical spirit, when few men thought the government in any danger. When the troubles begun, he quickly declared himself against the king; and having some command in Bristol, when it was first taken by prince Rupert and the marquis of Hertford, being trusted with the command of a little fort upon the line, he refused to give it up, after the governor had signed the articles of surrender, and kept it some hours after the prince was in the town, and killed some of the soldiers; for which the prince resolved to hang him, if some friends had not interposed for him, upon his want of experience in war; and prevailed with him to quit the place by very great importunity, and with much difficulty. After this, having done eminent service to the parliament, especially at Taunton, at land,' he then betook himself wholly to the sea; and quickly made himself signal there. He was the first man that declined the old track, and made it manifest that the science might be obtained in less time than was imagined; and despised those rules which had been long in practice, to keep his ship and his men out of danger; which had been held in former times a point of great ability and circumspection; as if the principal art requisite in the captain of a ship had been to be sure to come home safe again. He was the first man who brought the ships to contemn castles on shore, which had been thought ever very formidable, and were discovered by him to make a noise only, and to fright those who could rarely be hurt by them. He was the first that infused that proportion of courage into the seamen, by making them see by experience, what mighty things they could do, if they were resolved; and taught them to fight in fire as well as upon water: and though he had been very well imitated and followed, he was the first that gave the example of that kind of naval courage, and bold and resolute achievements.—*History of the Rebellion.*

3. Lord Falkland.

HE had the advantage of a noble extraction, and of being born his father's eldest son, when there was a greater fortune in prospect to be inherited, (besides what he might reasonably expect by his mother,) than came afterwards to his possession. His education was equal to his birth, at least in the care, if not in the climate; for his father being deputy of Ireland, before he was of age fit to be sent abroad, his breeding was in the court, and in the university of Dublin; but under the care, vigilance, and direction of such governors and tutors, that he learned all those exercises and languages, better than most men do in more celebrated places; insomuch as when he came into England, which was when he was about the age of eighteen years, he was not only master of the Latin tongue, and had read all the poets, and other of the best authors with notable judgment for that age, but he understood, and spake, and writ French, as if he had spent many years in France.

He had another advantage, which was a great ornament to the rest, that was, a good, a plentiful estate, of which he had the early possession. . . .

With these advantages, he had one great disadvantage (which in the first entrance into the world is attended with too much prejudice) in his person and presence, which was in no degree attractive or promising. His stature was low, and smaller than most men; his motion not graceful; and his aspect so far from inviting, that it had somewhat in it of simplicity; and his voice the worst of the three, and so untuned, that instead of reconciling, it offended the ear, so that nobody would have expected music from that tongue; and sure no man was less beholden to nature for its recommendation into the world: but then no man sooner or more disappointed this general and customary prejudice; that little person and small stature was quickly found to contain a great heart, a courage so keen, and a nature so fearless,

that no composition of the strongest limbs, and most harmonious and proportioned presence and strength, ever more
disposed any man to the greatest enterprise; it being his
greatest weakness to be too solicitous for such adventures:
and that untuned tongue and voice easily discovered itself to
be supplied and governed by a mind and understanding so
excellent, that the wit and weight of all he said carried
another kind of lustre and admiration in it, and even another
kind of acceptation from the persons present, than any ornament of delivery could reasonably promise itself, or is usually
attended with; and his disposition and nature was so gentle
and obliging, so much delighted in courtesy, kindness, and
generosity, that all mankind could not but admire and love
him. . . .

He transported himself and his wife into Holland, resolving to buy some military command, and to spend the
remainder of his life in that profession: but being disappointed in the treaty he expected, and finding no opportunity to accommodate himself with such a command,
he returned again into England; resolving to retire to a
country life, and to his books; that since he was not like
to improve himself in arms, he might advance in letters.

In this resolution he was so severe, (as he was always
naturally very intent upon what he was inclined to,) that he
declared, he would not see London in many years, which
was the place he loved of all the world; and that in his
studies, he would first apply himself to the Greek, and
pursue it without intermission, till he should attain to the
full understanding of that tongue: and it is hardly to be
credited, what industry he used, and what success attended
that industry: for though his father's death, by an unhappy
accident, made his repair to London absolutely necessary
in fewer years than he had proposed for his absence, yet

he had first made himself master of the Greek tongue, (in the Latin he was very well versed before,) and had read not only all the Greek historians, but Homer likewise, and such of the poets as were worthy to be perused. . . .

As soon as he had finished all those transactions, which the death of his father had made necessary to be done, he retired again to his country life, and to his severe course of study, which was very delightful to him, as soon as he was engaged in it: but he was wont to say, that he never found reluctancy in any thing he resolved to do, but in his quitting London, and departing from the conversation of those he enjoyed there; which was in some degree preserved and continued by frequent letters, and often visits, which were made by his friends from thence, whilst he continued wedded to the country; and which were so grateful to him, that during their stay with him, he looked upon no book, except their very conversation made an appeal to some book; and truly his whole conversation· was one continued *convivium philosophicum*, or *convivium theologicum*, enlivened and refreshed with all the facetiousness of wit, and good humour, and pleasantness of discourse, which made the gravity of the argument · itself (whatever it was) very delectable. His house where he usually resided, (Tew, or Burford, in Oxfordshire,) being within ten or twelve miles of the university, looked like the university itself, by the company that was always found there. There were Dr. Sheldon, Dr. Morley, Dr. Hammond, Dr. Earles, Mr. Chillingworth, and indeed all men of eminent parts and faculties in Oxford, besides those who resorted thither from London; who all found their lodgings there, as ready as in the colleges; nor did the lord of the house know of their coming or going, nor who were in his house, till he came to dinner, or supper, where all still met; otherwise, there was no troublesome ceremony or constraint, to forbid men to come to the house, or to make them weary of staying there; so that many came thither to study in a better air, finding all the books they could desire in his library, and all the persons together, whose company they could wish, and not find in any other society. Here Mr. Chillingworth wrote, and formed, and modelled, his excellent book against the learned Jesuit Mr. Nott, after frequent debates upon the most important particulars; in many of which, he suffered himself to be overruled by the judgment of his friends, though in others he still adhered to his own fancy, which was sceptical enough, even in the highest points.

In this happy and delightful conversation and restraint, he remained in the country many years; and until he had made so prodigious a progress in learning, that there were very few classic authors in the Greek or Latin tongue that he had not read with great exactness. He had read all the Greek and Latin fathers; all the most allowed and authentic ecclesiastical writers; and all the councils, with wonderful care and observation; for in religion he thought too careful and too curious an inquiry could not be made, amongst those, whose purity was not questioned, and whose authority was constantly and confidently urged, by men who were furthest from being of one mind amongst themselves: and for the mutual support of their several opinions, in which they most contradicted each other; and in all those controversies, he had so dispassioned a consideration, such a candour in his nature, and so profound a charity in his conscience, that in those points, in which he was in his own judgment most clear, he never thought the worse, or in any degree declined the familiarity, of those who were of another mind; which, without question, is an excellent temper for the propagation and advancement of Christianity. With these great advantages of industry, he had a memory retentive of all that he had ever read, and an understanding and judgment to apply it seasonably and appositely, with the most dexterity and address, and the least pedantry and affectation, that ever man, who knew so much, was possessed with, of what quality soever. It is not a trivial evidence of his learning, his wit, and his candour, that may be found in that discourse of his, against the infallibility of the church of Rome, published since his death, and from a copy under his own hand, though not prepared and digested by him for the press, and to which he would have given some castigations.

But all his parts, abilities, and faculties, by art and industry, were not to be valued, or mentioned, in comparison of his most accomplished mind and manners: his gentleness and affability was so transcendent and obliging, that it drew reverence, and some kind of compliance, from the roughest, and most unpolished, and stubborn constitutions; and made them of another temper in debate, in his presence, than they were in other places. He was in his nature so severe a lover of justice, and so precise a lover of truth, that he was superior to all possible temptations for the violation of either; indeed so rigid an exacter of perfection, in all those things which seemed but to border upon either of them, and by the common practice of men were not thought to border upon either, that many who knew him very well, and loved and admired his virtue, (as all who did know him must love and admire it,) did believe that he was of a temper and composition fitter to live in *republica Platonis*, than in *face Romuli:* but this rigidness was only exercised towards himself; towards his friend's infirmities no man was more indulgent. In his conversation, which was the most cheerful and pleasant that can be imagined, though he was young, (for all I have yet spoken of him doth not exceed his age of twenty-five or twenty-six years: what progress he made afterwards will be mentioned in its proper season in this discourse,) and of great gayety in his humour, with a flowing delightfulness of language, he had so chaste a tongue and ear, that there was never known a profane or loose word to fall from him, nor in truth in his company; the integrity and cleanliness of the wit of that time not exercising itself in that license before persons for whom they had any esteem.—*Clarendon's Life.*

4.   A Bull Fight in Madrid in 1649.

BOTH the ambassadors had a box prepared for them to see the *toros ;* which is a spectacle very wonderful, different from what they had seen at Burgos, where the bulls were much tamer, and where they were not charged by men on horseback, and little harm done.

Here the place was very noble, being the market-place, a very large square, built with handsome brick houses, which had all balconies, which were adorned with tapestry and very beautiful ladies. Scaffolds were built round to the first story, the lower rooms being shops, and for ordinary use; and in the division of those scaffolds all the magistrates and officers of the town knew their places. The pavement of the place was all covered with gravel, (which in summer time was upon those occasions watered by carts charged with hogsheads of water.) As soon as the king comes, some officers clear the whole ground from the common people, so that there is no man seen upon the plain but two or three alguazils, magistrates with their small white wands. Then one of the four gates which lead into the streets is opened, at which the

torreadors enter, all persons of quality richly clad, and upon
the best horses in Spain, every one attended by eight or ten
or more lackeys, all clinquant with gold and silver lace, who
carry the spears which their masters are to use against the
bulls; and with this entry many of the common people break
in, for which sometimes they pay very dear. The persons
on horseback have all cloaks folded up upon their left
shoulder, the least disorder of which, much more the letting
it fall, is a very great disgrace; and in that grave order they
march to the place where the king sits, and after they have
made their reverences, they place themselves at a good
distance from one another, and expect the bull. The bulls
are brought in the night before from the mountains by the
people used to that work, who drive them into the town
when nobody is in the streets, into a pen made for them,
which hath a door that opens into that large space; the key
whereof is sent to the king, which the king, when he sees
every thing ready, throws to an alguazil, who carries it to the
officer that keeps the door, and he causes it to be opened,
when a single bull is ready to come out. When the bull
enters, the common people, who sit over the door or near
it, strike him, or throw short darts with sharp points of steel,
to provoke him to rage. He commonly runs with all his
fury against the first man he sees on horseback, who watches
him so carefully, and avoids him so dexterously, that when
the spectators believe him to be even between the horns of
the bull, he avoids by the quick turn of his horse, and with
his lance strikes the bull upon a vein that runs through his
pole, with which in a moment he falls down dead. But this
fatal stroke can never be struck but when the bull comes so
near upon the turn of the horse that his horn even touches
the rider's leg, and so is at such a distance that he can
shorten his lance, and use the full strength of his arm in the

blow.   And they who are the most skilful in the exercise do
frequently kill the beast with such an exact stroke, insomuch
as in a day two or three fall in that manner: but if they miss
the vein, it only gives a wound that the more enrages him.
Sometimes the bull runs with so much fierceness, (for if he
escapes the first man, he runs upon the rest as they are in
his way,) that he gores the horse with his horns that his guts
come out, and he falls before the rider can get from his back.
Sometimes, by the strength of his neck, he raises horse and
man from the ground, and throws both down, and then the
greatest danger is another gore upon the ground.   In any of
these disgraces, or any other by which the rider comes to be
dismounted, he is obliged in honour to take his revenge upon
the bull by his sword, and upon his head, towards which the
standers by assist him by running after the bull and hocking
him, by which he falls upon his hinder legs; but before that
execution can be done, a good bull hath his revenge upon
many poor fellows.   Sometimes he is so unruly that nobody
dares to attack him, and then the king calls for the mastiffs,
whereof two are let out at a time, and if they cannot master
him, but are themselves killed, as frequently they are, the
king then, as a last refuge, calls for the English mastiffs, of
which they seldom turn out above one at a time; and he
rarely misses taking the bull and holding him by the nose
till the men run in; and after they have hocked him, they
quickly kill him.   In one of those days there were no fewer
than sixteen horses, as good as any in Spain, the worst of
which would that very morning have yielded three hundred
pistoles, killed, and four or five men, besides many more of
both hurt: and some men remain perpetually maimed: for
after the horsemen have done as much as they can, they
withdraw themselves, and then some accustomed nimble
fellows, to whom money is thrown when they perform their

feats with skill, stand to receive the bull, whereof the worst are reserved till the last: and it is a wonderful thing to see with what steadiness those fellows will stand a full career of the bull, and by a little quick motion upon one foot avoid him, and lay a hand upon his horn, as if he guided him from him; but then the next standers by, who have not the same activity, commonly pay for it, and there is no day without much mischief. It is a very barbarous exercise and triumph, in which so many men's lives are lost, and always ventured; but so rooted in the affections of that nation, that it is not in the king's power, they say, to suppress it, though, if he disliked it enough, he might forbear to be present at it. There are three festival days in the year, whereof midsummer is one, on which the people hold it to be their right to be treated with these spectacles, not only in great cities, where they are never disappointed, but in very ordinary towns, where there are places provided for it. Besides those ordinary annual days, upon any extraordinary accidents of joy, as at this time for the arrival of the queen, upon the birth of the king's children, or any signal victory, these triumphs are repeated, which no ecclesiastical censures or authority can suppress or discountenance. For pope Pius the Fifth, in the time of Philip the Second, and very probably with his approbation, if not upon his desire, published a bull against the *toros* in Spain, which is still in force, in which he declared, that nobody should be capable of Christian burial who lost his life at those spectacles, and that every clergyman who should be present at them stood excommunicated *ipso facto;* and yet there is always one of the largest galleries assigned to the office of the inquisition and the chief of the clergy, which is always filled; besides that many religious men in their habits get other places; only the Jesuits, out of their submission to the supreme authority of the pope, are never

present there, but on those days do always appoint some
such solemn exercise to be performed, that obliges their
whole body to be together.—*History of the Rebellion.*

5. The Fall of Hampden in Chalgrave Field.

ONE of the prisoners who had been taken in the action
said, ' that he was confident Mr. Hampden was hurt, for he
saw him ride off the field before the action was done, which
he never used to do, and with his head hanging down, and
resting his hands upon the neck of his horse ;' by which he
concluded he was hurt. But the news the next day made the
victory much more important than it was thought to have
been. . . . . . But that which would have been looked upon
as a considerable recompense for a defeat, could not but be
thought a glorious crown of a victory, which was the death
of Mr. Hampden; who, being shot into the shoulder with a
brace of bullets, which brake the bone, within three weeks
after died with extraordinary pain; to as great a consternation of all that party, as if their whole army had been defeated
or cut off.

Many men observed (as upon signal turns of great affairs,
as this was, such observations are frequently made) that
the field in which the late skirmish was, and upon which
Mr. Hampden received his death's wound, Chalgrave field,
was the same place in which he had first executed the
ordinance of the militia, and engaged that county, in which
his reputation was very great, in this rebellion : and it was
confessed by the prisoners that were taken that day, and
acknowledged by all, that upon the alarm that morning, after
their quarters were beaten up, he was exceedingly solicitous
to draw forces together to pursue the enemy; and being
himself a colonel of foot, put himself amongst those horse as

a volunteer, who were first ready; and that when the prince made a stand, all the officers were of opinion to stay till their body came up, and he alone (being second to none but the general himself in the observance and application of all men) persuaded and prevailed with them to advance; so violently did his fate carry him to pay the mulct in the place where he had committed the transgression about a year before.

He was a gentleman of a good family in Buckinghamshire, and born to a fair fortune, and of a most civil and affable deportment. In his entrance into the world, he indulged to himself all the license in sports and exercises, and company, which was used by men of the most jolly conversation. Afterwards, he retired to a more reserved and melancholic society, yet preserving his own natural cheerfulness and vivacity, and above all, a flowing courtesy to all men; though they who conversed nearly with him, found him growing into a dislike of the ecclesiastical government of the church, yet most believed it rather a dislike of some churchmen, and of some introducements of theirs, which he apprehended might disquiet the public peace. He was rather of reputation in his own country than of public discourse or fame in the kingdom before the business of ship-money: but then he grew the argument of all tongues, every man inquiring who and what he was, that durst, at his own charge, support the liberty and property of the kingdom, and rescue his country from being made a prey to the court. His carriage, throughout that agitation, was with that rare temper and modesty, that they who watched him narrowly to find some advantage against his person, to make him less resolute in his cause, were compelled to give him a just testimony. And the judgment that was given against him infinitely more advanced him, than the service for which it was given. When this parliament began, (being returned

knight of the shire for the county where he lived,) the eyes
of all men were fixed on him as their *patriæ pater*, and the
pilot that must steer their vessel through the tempests and
rocks which threatened it.   And I am persuaded his power
and interest, at that time, was greater to do good or hurt
than any man's in the kingdom, or than any man of his rank
hath had in any time : for his reputation of honesty was
universal, and his affections seemed so publicly guided, that
no corrupt or private ends could bias them.

He was of that rare affability and temper in debate, and
of that seeming humility and submission of judgment, as
if he brought no opinions with him, but a desire of information and instruction; yet he had so subtle a way of
interrogating, and under the notion of doubts insinuating his
objections, that he left his opinions with those from whom
he pretended to learn and receive them.   And even with
them who were able to preserve themselves from his infusions, and discerned those opinions to be fixed in him
with which they could not comply, he always left the
character of an ingenious and conscientious person.   He
was indeed a very wise man, and of great parts, and
possessed with the most absolute spirit of popularity, that
is, the most absolute faculties to govern the people, of any
man I ever knew.   For the first year of the parliament,
he seemed rather to moderate and soften the violent
and distempered humours, than to inflame them.   But
wise and dispassioned men plainly discerned that that
moderation proceeded from prudence, and observation that
the season was not ripe, rather than that he approved of
the moderation; and that he begat many opinions and
motions, the education whereof he committed to other
men; so far disguising his own designs, that he seemed
seldom to wish more than was concluded; and in many

gross conclusions, which would hereafter contribute to designs not yet set on foot, when he found them sufficiently backed by majority of voices, he would withdraw himself before the question, that he might seem not to consent to so much visible unreasonableness; which produced as great a doubt in some as it did approbation in others, of his integrity. What combination soever had been originally with the Scots for the invasion of England, and what farther was entered into afterwards in favour of them, and to advance any alteration of the government in parliament, no man doubts was at least with the privity of this gentleman.

After he was amongst those members accused by the king of high treason, he was much altered; his nature and carriage seeming much fiercer than it did before. And without question, when he first drew his sword, he threw away the scabbard; for he passionately opposed the overture made by the king for a treaty from Nottingham, and as eminently, any expedients that might have produced an accommodation in this that was at Oxford; and was principally relied on to prevent any infusions which might be made into the earl of Essex towards peace, or to render them ineffectual if they were made; and was indeed much more relied on by that party than the general himself. In the first entrance into the troubles, he undertook the command of a regiment of foot, and performed the duty of a colonel on all occasions most punctually. He was very temperate in diet, and a supreme governor over all his passions and affections, and had thereby a great power over other men's. He was of an industry and vigilance not to be tired out, or wearied by the most laborious; and of parts not to be imposed upon by the most subtle or sharp; and of a personal courage equal to his best parts; so that he

was an enemy not to be wished wherever he might have
been made a friend, and as much to be apprehended where
he was so as any man could deserve to be. And therefore
his death was no less congratulated on the one party, than
it was condoled on the other. In a word, what was said of
Cinna might well be applied to him; he had a head to contrive, and a tongue to persuade, and a hand to execute, any
mischief. His death therefore seemed to be a great deliverance to the nation.—*History of the Rebellion.*

6. Clarendon's Letter to the Vice-Chancellor of Oxford.

For Mr. Vicechancellor of Oxford.

Good Mr. Vicechancellor,

Having found it necessary to transport myselfe out of
England, and not knowing when it will please God that I
shall returne againe; it becomes me to take care that the
University may not be without the service of a person
better able to be of use to them, then I am like to be;
and I doe therefore hereby surrender the office of Chancellor into the hands of the said University, to the end
that they make choyce of some other person better qualifyed
to assist and protect them then I am, I am sure he can
never be more affectionate to it. I desire you, as the
last suite I am like to make to you, to believe that I
doe not fly my Country for guilt, and how passionately
soever I am pursued, that I have not done any thing to
make the University ashamed of me, or to repent the
good opinion they had once of me, and though I must
have noe farther mention in your publique devotions (which

I have alwayes exceedingly valued) I hope I shall be alwayes remembered in your private prayers as

          Good Mr. Vicechancellor,

                 Your affectionate servant,

                         CLARENDON.

Calice, this $\frac{7}{17}$ Dec. 1667.

                        MS. in Bodleian Library.

XIV.

JOHN MILTON.

1608–1674.

JOHN MILTON, *magnum et venerabile nomen*, was born in Bread Street, London, on the 9th December, 1608. He was descended from an ancient family settled at Milton in Oxfordshire. His father had been disinherited because of his desertion of the Roman Catholic faith, and had settled in London in order to support himself as a scrivener. John Milton, after receiving the first rudiments of learning from a domestic tutor, Thomas Young, was educated at St. Paul's School, and Christ's College, Cambridge. At school he began to distinguish himself by his eager application to his studies, and by his skill in Latin versification. In 1632 he left the University after a residence of seven years, having taken the degree of M.A.

He was deterred from entering the Church, as he had originally intended, by scruples which appear to have referred rather to her order of government and discipline than to her doctrine.

He spent the next five years at Horton, in Buckinghamshire, whither his father had retired from business. These years were devoted to severe study, ranging not only over the widest field of classical and modern literature, but including theology, and more than one Oriental language, in addition to Hebrew. During this time several of his finest poems, *Comus*, *L'Allegro*, *Il Penseroso*, and *Lycidas* were composed.

On his mother's death in 1638 Milton went abroad, visited Grotius in Paris, and passed into Italy, the language and literature of which country had special attraction for him. At Florence,

Sienna, Rome, and Naples he was received with honour by the learned societies of those cities, and gave a favourable impression of the culture and learning of his own country. He was about to visit Sicily and Greece when, as he says, 'the melancholy intelligence of the Civil War recalled me : and I esteemed it dishonourable for me to be lingering abroad, even for the improvement of my mind, when my fellow-citizens were contending for their liberty at home.'

After this tour, which had occupied nearly two years, he settled in London, and very early engaged in the controversies of the time, publishing, in 1641, the *Tractate of Reformation*, which was followed in 1642 by *The Reason of Church Government urged against Prelacy*. His life was strictly retired, almost ascetic, passed in his studies or among his pupils.

In 1643 Milton married Mary Powell, the daughter of a zealous Royalist gentleman. The change of habits and associations displeased the lady, and in a month she left her husband's home, and it was long before she was persuaded to return to it, though when she did so the reconcilement appears to have been complete, and the marriage not unhappy. In 1644 Milton wrote his *Tractate on Education*, followed in the same year by *Areopagitica*, *a Speech of Mr. John Milton for the Liberty of Unlicensed Printing*, the most celebrated perhaps and powerful of his prose writings. Upon the trial and execution of Charles I Milton wrote *The Tenure of Kings and Magistrates*, in vindication of the act and of the new order of things. To strengthen the republican spirit of the nation he had just commenced *The History of England*, when, without any solicitation on his part, he was invited by the Council of State to become their Foreign Secretary. Diplomatic correspondence was then carried on in Latin, and Milton was the first Latinist of his age and country.

In 1652, the blindness which had threatened him for some time became complete, and nearly at the same time his wife died, leaving him with three daughters. Shortly afterwards he was married to the lady whose premature death within the year is the subject of the sonnet, 'Methought I saw my late espoused saint.' After the death of Cromwell, Milton continued to labour in the failing cause of the Commonwealth, until the triumphant return of Charles II. He was thereupon discharged from his office of Secretary, two of his political pamphlets were, on a petition from the Commons, burnt by the common hangman, and he himself was compelled to live for a time in retirement. He now devoted himself to the composition of *Paradise Lost,* which occupied him for nearly five years. *Paradise Regained* and *Samson Agonistes* were published together in 1671. About twelve years before his death Milton married for the third time ; his wife survived him. Milton's last literary work was the republication of some of his earlier treatises, as well as of a volume containing his familiar Latin letters and his College exercises. He died at the age of sixty-six, and was buried in the Church of St. Giles, Cripplegate.

Milton's prose writings are, as appears from what has been said, chiefly polemical and political. His prose, like that of many of our early writers, is of very unequal quality. Mr. Hallam says that his intermixture of familiar with learned phraseology is unpleasing, and the structure of his sentences elaborate ; that he seldom reaches any harmony, and that his wit is poor and without ease. If the justness of Mr. Hallam's strictures must be admitted, we may also accept his praise that these writings glow with an intense love of liberty and truth, and contain frequent passages of the highest imaginative power, in which the majestic soul of Milton breathes such high thoughts as had not been uttered before.

----

1. Education.

THE end then of learning is to repair the ruins of our first parents by regaining to know God aright, and out of that knowledge to love him, to imitate him, to be like him, as we may the nearest by possessing our souls of true virtue, which being united to the heavenly grace of faith makes up the highest perfection. But because our understanding cannot in this body found itself but on sensible things, nor arrive so clearly to the knowledge of God and things invisible, as by orderly conning over the visible and inferior creature, the same method is necessarily to be followed in all discreet teaching. And seeing every nation affords not experience and tradition enough for all kind of learning, therefore we are chiefly taught the languages of those people who have at any time been most industrious after wisdom; so that language is but the instrument conveying to us things useful to be known. And though a linguist should pride himself to have all the tongues that Babel cleft the world into, yet, if he have not studied the solid things in them as well as the words and lexicons, he were nothing so much to be esteemed a learned man, as any yeoman or tradesman competently wise in his mother dialect only. Hence appear the many mistakes which have made learning generally so unpleasing and so unsuccessful: first we do amiss to spend seven or eight years merely in scraping together so much miserable Latin and Greek, as might be learnt otherwise easily and delightfully in one year. And that which casts our proficiency therein so much behind, is our time lost partly in too oft idle vacancies given both to Schools and Universities, partly in a preposterous exaction, forcing the empty wits of children to compose themes, verses and orations, which are the acts of ripest judgment and the final work of a head filled by long reading and observing, with elegant maxims, and copious invention. These are not matters to be wrung from poor striplings, like blood out of the nose, or the plucking of untimely fruit: besides the ill habit whidh they get of wretched barbarizing against the Latin and Greek idiom, with their untutored Anglicisms, odious to be read, yet ·not

to be avoided without a well-continued and judicious conversing among pure authors digested, which they scarce
taste, whereas, if after some preparatory grounds of speech
by their certain forms got into memory, they were led to
the praxis thereof in some chosen short book lessoned
thoroughly to them, they might then forthwith proceed to
learn the substance of good things, and arts in due order,
which would bring the whole language quickly into their
power. This I take to be the most rational and most
profitable way of learning languages, and whereby we may
best hope to give account to God of our youth spent
herein. And for the usual method of teaching arts, I deem
it to be an old error of Universities not yet well recovered
from the scholastic grossness of barbarous ages, that instead of beginning with arts most easy, and those be such
as are most obvious to the sense, they present their young
unmatriculated novices at first coming with the most intel-
lective abstractions of logic and metaphysics: so that they
having but newly left those grammatic flats and shallows
where they stuck unreasonably to learn a few words with
lamentable construction, and now on the sudden transported
under another climate to be tost and turmoiled with their
unballasted wits in fathomless and unquiet deeps of controversy, do for the most part grow into hatred and
contempt of learning, mocked and deluded all this while
with ragged notions and babblements, while they expected
worthy and delightful knowledge; till poverty or youthful
years call them importunately their several ways, and hasten
them with the sway of friends either to an ambitious and
mercenary, or ignorantly zealous divinity; some allured to
the trade of law, grounding their purposes not on the
prudent and heavenly contemplation of justice and equity
which was never taught them, but on the promising and

pleasing thoughts of litigious terms, fat contentions, and flowing fees; others betake them to State affairs, with souls so unprincipled in virtue and true generous breeding, that flattery and Court shifts and tyrannous aphorisms appear to them the highest points of wisdom; instilling their barren hearts with a conscientious slavery, if, as I rather think, it be not fained. Others, lastly, of a more delicious and airy spirit, retire themselves, knowing no better, to the enjoyments of ease and luxury, living out their days in feast and jollity; which indeed is the wisest and the safest course of all these, unless they were with more integrity undertaken. And these are the errors and these are the fruits of mis-spending our prime youth at the Schools and Universities as we do, either in learning mere words, or such things chiefly as were better unlearnt.

I shall detain you no longer in the demonstration of what we should not do, but straight conduct ye to a hill-side, where I will point ye out the right path of a virtuous and noble education; laborious indeed at the first ascent, but else so smooth, so green, so full of goodly prospect and melodious sounds on every side, that the Harp of Orpheus was not more charming. I doubt not but ye shall have more ado to drive our dullest and laziest youth, our stocks and stubbs from the infinite desire of such a happy nurture, than we have now to hale and drag our choicest and hopefullest wits to that asinine feast of sow-thistles and brambles which is commonly set before them, as all the food and entertainment of their tenderest and most docible age. I call therefore a complete and generous education that which fits a man to perform justly, skilfully, and magnanimously all the offices, both private and public, of peace and war. And how all this may be done between twelve and one and twenty, less time than is now bestowed in pure trifling at Grammar and Sophistry, is to be thus ordered.—*Of Education.*

2. Of Unlicensed Printing.

I DENY not, but that it is of greater concernment in the Church and Commonwealth, to have a vigilant eye how books demean themselves, as well as men; and thereafter to confine, imprison, and do sharpest justice on them as malefactors: for books are not absolutely dead things, but do contain a potency of life in them to be as active as that soul was whose progeny they are; nay they do preserve as in a vial the purest efficacy and extraction of that living intellect that bred them. I know they are as lively, and as vigorously productive, as those fabulous dragon's teeth; and being sown up and down, may chance to spring up armed men. And yet, on the other hand, unless wariness be used, as good almost kill a man as kill a good book. Who kills a man kills a reasonable creature, God's image; but he who destroys a good book, kills reason itself, kills the image of God, as it were in the eye. Many a man lives a burden to the earth; but a good book is the precious life-blood of a master spirit, embalmed and treasured up on purpose to a life beyond life. It is true, no age can restore a life, whereof perhaps there is no great loss; and revolutions of ages do not oft recover the loss of a rejected truth, for the want of which whole nations fare the worse. We should be wary therefore what persecution we raise against the living labours of public men, how we spill that seasoned life of man preserved and stored up in books; since we see a kind of homicide may be thus committed, sometimes a martyrdom, and if it extend to the whole impression, a kind of massacre, whereof the execution ends not in the slaying of an elemental life, but strikes at that ethereal and fifth essence, the breath of reason itself, slays an immortality rather than a life.—*Areopagitica.*

3. The Kingdom of Christ.

WHICH way to end I know not, unless I turn mine eyes, and with your help lift up my hand to that eternal and propitious throne, where nothing is readier than grace and refuge to the distresses of mortal suppliants : and it were a shame to leave these serious thoughts less piously than the heathen were wont to conclude their graver discourses.

Thou therefore that sittest in light and glory unapproachable, parent of angels and men ! next thee I implore omnipotent king, redeemer of that lost remnant whose nature thou didst assume, ineffable and everlasting love ! And thou the third subsistence of divine infinitude, illumining spirit, the joy and solace of created things ! one tri-personal Godhead ! look upon this thy poor and almost spent, and expiring church, leave her not thus a prey to these importunate wolves, that wait and think long till they devour thy tender flock, these wild boars that have broke into thy vineyard, and left the print of their polluting hoofs on the souls of thy servants. O let them not bring about their damned designs that stand now at the entrance of the bottomless pit expecting the watch-word to open and let out those dreadful locusts and scorpions, to re-involve us in that pitchy cloud of infernal darkness, where we shall never more see the sun of thy truth again, never hope for the cheerful dawn, never more hear the bird of morning sing. Be moved with pity at the afflicted state of this our shaken monarchy, that now lies labouring under her throes, and struggling against the grudges of more dreaded calamities. . . .

O how much more glorious will those former deliverances appear, when we shall know them not only to have saved us from greatest miseries past, but to have reserved us for greatest happiness to come. Hitherto thou hast but freed us, and that not fully, from the unjust and tyrannous claim of thy foes, now unite us entirely, and appropriate us to thyself, tie us everlastingly in willing homage to the prerogative of thy eternal throne. . . .

Then amidst the hymns and hallelujahs of saints some one may perhaps be heard offering at high strains in new and lofty measures to sing and celebrate thy divine mercies and marvellous judgments in this land throughout all ages; whereby this great and warlike nation, instructed and inured to the fervent and continual practice of truth and righteousness, and casting far from her the rags of her old vices, may press on hard to that high and happy emulation to be found the soberest, wisest, and most Christian people at that day when thou, the eternal and shortly-expected King, shalt open the clouds to judge the several kingdoms of the world, and distributing national honours and rewards to religious and just commonwealths, shalt put an end to all earthly tyrannies, proclaiming thy universal and mild monarchy through heaven and earth. Where they undoubtedly that by their labours, counsels, and prayers have been earnest for the common good of religion and their country, shall receive, above the inferior orders of the blessed, the regal addition of principalities, legions, and thrones into their glorious titles, and in supereminence of beatific vision progressing the dateless and irrevoluble circle of eternity shall clasp inseparable hands with joy, and bliss in over measure for ever.—*Tractate of Reformation touching Church Discipline in England.*

4. Custom.

IF it were seriously asked, and it would be no untimely question, renowned parliament, select assembly, who of all teachers and masters that ever have taught, hath drawn the most disciples after him, both in religion, and in manners, it might be not untruly answered, custom. Though virtue be commended for the most persuasive in her *Theory;* and conscience in the plain demonstration of the spirit, finds most evincing, yet whether it be the secret of divine will, or the original blindness we are born in, so it happens for the most part, that custom still is silently received for the best instructor. Except it be, because her method is so glib and easy, in some manner like to that vision of *Ezekiel,* rolling up her sudden book of implicit knowledge, for him that will, to take and swallow down at pleasure; which proving but of bad nourishment in the concoction, as it was heedless in the devouring, puffs up unhealthily, a certain big face of pretended learning, mistaken among credulous men, for the wholesome habit of soundness and good constitution; but is indeed no other, than that swollen visage of counterfeit knowledge and literature, which not only in private mars our education, but also in public is the common climber into every chair, where either religion is preached, or law reported: filling each estate of life and profession, with abject and servile principles; depressing the high and heaven-born spirit of man, far beneath the condition wherein either God created him, or sin hath sunk him. To pursue the allegory, custom being but a mere face, as echo is a mere voice, rests not in her unaccomplishment, until by secret inclination, she accorporate herself with error, who being a blind and serpentine body without a head, willingly accepts what he wants, and supplies what her incompleteness went seeking. Hence it is, that error supports custom, custom countenances error. And these two between them would persecute and chase away all truth and solid wisdom out of human life, were it not that God, rather than man, once in many ages, calls together the prudent and religious counsels of men, deputed to re-press the encroachments, and to work off the inveterate blots and obscurities wrought upon our minds by the subtle insinuating of error and custom: who with the numerous and vulgar train of their followers, make it their chief design to envy and cry-down the industry of free reasoning, under the terms of humour, and innovation; as if the womb of teeming truth were to be closed up, if she presume to bring forth aught, that sorts not with their unchewed notions and suppositions. Against which notorious injury and abuse of man's free soul to testify and oppose the utmost that study and true labour can attain, heretofore the incitement of men reputed grave hath led me among others; and now the duty and the right of an instructed Christian calls me through the chance of good or evil report, to be the sole advocate of a discountenanced truth: a high enterprise Lords and Commons, a high enterprise and a hard, and such as every seventh son of a seventh son does not venture on.—*Preface to the Doctrine and Discipline of Divorce.*

5. The Prophet's Woe.

How happy were it for this frail, and as it may be truly called, mortal life of man, since all earthly things which have the name of good and convenient in our daily use, are withal so cumbersome and full of trouble, if knowledge yet which is the best and lightsomest possession of the mind, were as the common saying is, no burden, and that what it wanted of being a load to any part of the body, it did not with a heavy advantage overlay upon the spirit. For not to speak of that knowledge that rests in the contemplation of natural causes and dimensions, which must needs be a lower wisdom, as the object is low, certain it is that he who hath obtained in more than the scantiest measure to know anything distinctly of God, and of his true worship, and what is infallibly good and happy in the state of man's life, what in itself evil and miserable, though vulgarly not so esteemed, he that hath obtained to know this, the only high valuable wisdom indeed, remembering also that God even to a strictness requires the improvement of these his entrusted gifts, cannot but sustain a sorer burden of mind, and more pressing than any supportable toil, or weight, which the body can labour under; how and in what manner he shall dispose and employ those sums of knowledge and illumination, which God hath sent him into this world to trade with. And that which aggravates the burden more, is, that having received amongst his allotted parcels certain precious truths of such an orient lustre as no diamond can equal, which nevertheless he has in charge to put off at any cheap rate, yea for nothing to them that will, the great merchants of this world fearing that this course would soon discover, and disgrace the false glitter of their deceitful wares wherewith they abuse the people, like poor Indians with beads and glasses, practise by all means how they may suppress the venting of such rarities and such a cheapness as would undo them, and turn their trash upon their hands. Therefore by gratifying the corrupt desires of men in fleshly doctrines, they stir them up to persecute with hatred and contempt all those that seek to bear themselves uprightly in this their spiritual factory : which they foreseeing, though they cannot but testify of truth and the excellence of that heavenly traffic which they bring, against what opposition, or danger soever, yet needs must it sit heavily upon their spirits, that being in God's prime intention and their own, selected heralds of peace, and dispensers of treasure inestimable without price to them that have no pence, they find in the discharge of their commission that they are made the greatest variance and offence, a very sword and fire both in house and city over the whole earth.—*Reason of Church Government urged against Prelacy.*

6. Truth against Falsehood.

METHINKS I see in my mind a noble and puissant nation rousing herself like a strong man after sleep, and shaking her invincible locks: methinks I see her as an eagle muing her mighty youth, and kindling her undazzled eyes at the full midday beam; purging and unscaling her long abused sight at the fountain itself of heavenly radiance; while the whole noise of timorous and flocking birds, with those also that love the twilight, flutter about, amazed at what she means, and in their envious gabble would prognosticate a year of sects and schisms.

What should ye do then, should ye suppress all this flowery crop of knowledge and new light sprung up and yet springing daily in this city, should ye set an *Oligarchy* of twenty ingrossers over it, to bring a famine upon our minds again, when we shall know nothing but what is measured to us by their bushel? Believe it, Lords and Commons, they who counsel ye to such a suppressing, do as good as bid ye suppress yourselves; and I will soon shew how. If it be desired to know the immediate cause of all this free writing and free speaking, there cannot be assigned a truer than your own mild, and free, and human government; it is the liberty, Lords and Commons, which your own valorous and happy counsels have purchased us, liberty which is the nurse of all great wits; this is that which hath rarified and enlightened our spirits like the influence of heaven; this is that which hath enfranchised, enlarged and lifted up our apprehensions degrees above themselves. Ye cannot make us now less capable, less knowing, less eagerly pursuing of the truth, unless ye first make yourselves, that made us so, less the lovers, less the founders of our true liberty. We can grow ignorant again, brutish, formal, and slavish, as ye found us; but you then must first become that which ye cannot be, oppressive, arbitrary, and tyrannous, as they were from whom ye have freed us. That our hearts are now more capacious, our thoughts more erected to the search and expectation of greatest and exactest things, is the issue of your own virtue propagated in us; ye cannot suppress that unless ye reinforce an abrogated and merciless law, that fathers may despatch at will their own children. And who shall then stick closest to ye, and excite others? not he who takes up arms for cote and conduct, and his four nobles of Danegelt. Although I dispraise not the defence of just immunities, yet love my peace better, if that were all. Give me the liberty to know, to utter, and to argue freely according to conscience, above all liberties. . . . . .

The Temple of *Janus* with his two *controversal* faces might now not unsignificantly be set open. And though all the winds of doctrine were let loose to play upon the earth, so truth be in the field, we do injuriously by licencing and prohibiting to misdoubt her strength. Let her and falsehood grapple; who ever knew truth put to the worse, in a free and open encounter. Her confuting is the best and surest suppressing. He who hears what praying there is for light and clearer knowledge to be sent down among us,

would think of other matters to be constituted beyond the
discipline of *Geneva*, framed and fabriced already to our
hands. Yet when the new light which we beg for shines
in upon us, there be who envy, and oppose, if it come not
first in at their casements. What a collusion is this, whenas
we are exhorted by the wise man to use diligence, *to seek for
wisdom as for hidden treasures* early and late, that another
order shall enjoin us to know nothing but by statute. When
a man hath been labouring the hardest labour in the deep
mines of knowledge, hath furnished out his findings in all
their equipage, drawn forth his reasons as it were a battle
ranged, scattered and defeated all objections in his way, calls
out his adversary into the plain, offers him the advantage of
wind and sun, if he please; only that he may try the matter
by dint of argument, for his opponents then to skulk, to lay
ambushments, to keep a narrow bridge of licencing where
the challenger should pass, though it be valour enough
in soldiership, is but weakness and cowardice in the wars
of truth. For who knows not that truth is strong next to
the Almighty; she needs no policies, nor stratagems, nor
licencings to make her victorious, those are the shifts and
the defences that error uses against her power: give her
but room, and do not bind her when she sleeps, for then
she speaks not true, as the old *Proteus* did, who spake
oracles only when he was caught and bound, but then
rather she turns herself into all shapes, except her own,
and perhaps tunes her voice according to the time, as
Micaiah did before *Ahab*, until she be adjured into her
own likeness. Yet is it not impossible that she may have
more shapes than one. What else is all that rank of things
indifferent, wherein truth may be on this side, or on the
other, without being unlike herself.—*Areopagitica.*

7. The Quest for Truth.

TRUTH indeed came once into the world with her divine master, and was a perfect shape most glorious to look on : but when he ascended, and his apostles after him were laid asleep, then straight arose a wicked race of deceivers, who as that story goes of the ` *Egyptian Typhon* with his conspirators, how they dealt with the good *Osiris*, took the virgin truth, hewed her lovely form into a thousand pieces, and scattered them to the four winds. From that time ever since, the sad friends of truth, such as durst appear, imitating the careful search that *Isis* made for the mangled body of *Osiris*, went up and down gathering up limb by limb still as they could find them. We have not yet found them all, Lords and Commons, nor ever shall do, till her master's second coming ; he shall bring together every joint and member, and shall mould them into an immortal feature of loveliness and perfection. Suffer not these licencing prohibitions to stand at every place of opportunity forbidding and disturbing them that continue seeking, that continue to do our obsequies to the torn body of our martyred saint. We boast our light; but if we look not wisely on the sun itself, it smites us into darkness. Who can discern those planets that are oft *Combust*, and those stars of brightest magnitude that rise and set with the sun, until the opposite motion of their orbs bring them to such a place in the firmament, where they may be seen evening or morning. The light which we have gained, was given us, not to be ever staring on, but by it to discover onward things more remote from our knowledge. . . . . . . There be who perpetually complain of schisms and sects, and make it such a calamity that any man dissents from their maxims. It is their own pride and ignorance which causes the disturbing, who neither will hear with meekness, nor can convince, yet all must be suppressed which is not found in their *Syntagma*. They are the troublers, they are the dividers of unity, who neglect and permit not others to unite those dissevered pieces which are yet wanting to the body of truth. To be still searching what we know not, by what we know, still closing up truth to truth as we find it (for all her body is *homogeneal*, and proportional) this is the golden rule in *Theology* as well as in Arithmetic, and makes up the best harmony in a church; not the forced and outward union of cold, and neutral, and inwardly divided minds.

Lords and Commons of England, consider what nation it is whereof ye are, and whereof ye are the governors: a nation not slow and dull, but of a quick, ingenious, and piercing spirit, acute to invent, subtle and sinewy to discourse, not beneath the reach of any point the highest that human capacity can soar to. Therefore the studies of learning in her deepest sciences have been so ancient, and so eminent among us, that writers of good antiquity and ablest judgment have been persuaded that even the school of *Pythagoras* and the *Persian* wisdom took beginning from the old philosophy of this island. . . . . . Now once again . by all concurrence of signs, and by the general instinct of holy and devout men, as they daily and solemnly express their thoughts, God is decreeing to begin some new and great period in his church, even to the reforming of Reformation itself: what does he then but reveal himself to his servants, and as his manner is, first to his Englishmen; I say as his manner is, first to us, though we mark not the method of his counsels, and are unworthy. Behold now this vast city; a city of refuge, the mansion house of liberty, encompassed and surrounded with his protection; the shop of war hath not there more anvils and hammers waking, to fashion out the plates and instruments of armed justice in defence of beleaguered truth, than there be pens and heads there, sitting by their studious lamps, musing, searching, revolving new notions and ideas wherewith to present, as with their homage and their fealty, the approaching reformation : others as fast reading, trying all things, assenting to the force of reason and convincement. What could a man require more from a nation so pliant and so prone to seek after knowledge. What wants there to such a towardly and pregnant soil, but wise and faithful labourers, to make a knowing people, a nation of prophets, of sages, and of worthies.—*Areopagitica.*

XV.

JEREMY TAYLOR.

1613—1667.

JEREMY TAYLOR was the son of a barber at Cambridge, in which town he was born, August 15, 1613. From the recently founded Grammar School of his native place he passed, at the age of thirteen, to Caius College as a sizar. He took his degree of B.A. in 1631, and was chosen fellow of his college. At twenty-one he was ordained. Soon after this he removed to London, where he was favourably noticed by Laud, who was always remarkable for his encouragement of men of learning and ability. Laud's exertions obtained for Taylor a Fellowship at All Souls' College, Oxford. In 1637 Bishop Juxon appointed him to the living of Uppingham. He followed the fortunes of Charles I during his struggle with Parliament, his living was sequestered, and, like many other royalists, he suffered hardship and poverty during the Commonwealth. In 1655, on account of some expressions in a preface to *The Golden Grove*, a well-known book of devotion, he was imprisoned. At the Restoration, he was made Bishop of Down and Connor. Here he laboured incessantly for the advance of his Church, but with small effect. He died at Lisburne, in 1667.

Jeremy Taylor stands high in the catalogue of English divines. His practical writings preserve their popularity, and, in their own peculiar way, possess a remarkable charm. He is best known to the general reader by his *Manual of Devotion, Holy Living and Dying*, and by his *Sermons*. In his sermons we have, upon the whole, the most favourable specimens of his genius. The learning is abundant, sometimes oppressive. Few writers in any age have used quotation so freely. The rhetorical power of Taylor is certainly, as Mr. Hallam has called it, too Asiatic ; but the distinct personality of the writer is so preserved, that the reader is attracted in spite of himself. There are passages in his sermons which will charm so long as imagination and fancy exert their sway. In *The Liberty of Prophesying*, he pleaded for toleration and freedom of opinion. The *Ductor Dubitantium* exhibits him as a master of casuistic morality. His solution of grave difficulties is often far from satisfactory, and the student of Taylor's writings will turn with pleasure to the hortatory and devotional passages which abound in his purely theological writings.

The great preachers of the Gallican Church are the only divines who have equalled Jeremy Taylor in the composition of funeral orations. His discourse on the death of Lady Carbery, the wife of a nobleman who had shown him great kindness, from which an extract is given below, is unique in English literature. A striking criticism of Bishop Taylor, and a parallel between his characteristics as a writer and those of Milton, will be found later among the extracts from Coleridge.

---

1. Care of our Time.

HE that is choice of his time will also be choice of his company, and choice of his actions; lest the first engage him in vanity and loss, and the latter, by being criminal, be a throwing his time and himself away, and a going back in the accounts of eternity.

God hath given to man a short time here upon earth, and yet upon this short time eternity depends : but so, that for every hour of our life (after we are persons capable of laws, and know good from evil), we must give account to the great judge of men and angels. And this is it which our blessed Saviour told us, that we must account for *every idle*

word: not meaning that every word which is not designed
to edification, or is less prudent, shall be reckoned for a sin;
but that the time which we spend in our idle talking and
unprofitable discoursings, that time which might and ought
to have been employed to spiritual and useful purposes, that
is to be accounted for.

For we must remember that we have a great work to do,
many enemies to conquer, many evils to prevent, much
danger to run through, many difficulties to be mastered,
many necessities to serve, and much good to do, many
children to provide for, or many friends to support, or many
poor to relieve, or many diseases to cure, besides the needs
of nature and of relation, our private and our public cares,
and duties of the world, which necessity and the providence
of God hath adopted into the family of religion.

And that we need not fear this instrument to be a snare
to us, or that the duty must end in scruple, vexation, and
eternal fears, we must remember that the life of every man
may be so ordered (and indeed must), that it may be a
perpetual serving of God: the greatest trouble, and most
busy trade, and worldly incumbrances, when they are necessary, or charitable, or profitable, in order to any of those
ends which we are bound to serve, whether public or private,
being a doing of God's work. For God provides the good
things of the world to serve the needs of nature, by the
labours of the ploughman, the skill and pains of the artizan,
and the dangers and traffic of the merchant: these men are
in their callings the ministers of the Divine Providence, and
the stewards of the creation, and servants of a great family
of God.

God hath given every man work enough to do, that there
shall be no room for idleness; and yet hath so ordered the
world, that there shall be space for devotion. He that hath

the fewest businesses of the world, is called upon to spend
more time in the dressing of his soul; and he that hath the
most affairs, may so order them, that they shall be a service
of God; whilst at certain periods they are blessed with
prayers and actions of religion, and all day long are hallowed
by a holy intention. . . . . Idleness is the greatest
prodigality in the world : it throws away that which is un-
valuable in respect of its present use, and irreparable when
it is past, being to be recovered by no power of art or nature.
—*Holy Living.*

2.   On the Death of Lady Carbery.

THIS descending to the grave is the lot of all men, 'neither
doth God respect the person of any man;' the rich is not
protected for favour, nor the poor for pity, the old man is
not reverenced for his age, nor the infant regarded for his
tenderness; youth and beauty, learning and prudence, wit
and strength, lie down equally in the dishonours of the grave.
All men, and all natures, and all persons resist the addresses
and solennities of death, and strive to preserve a miserable
and unpleasant life; and yet they all sink down and die.
For so have I seen the pillars of a building assisted with
artificial props bending under the pressure of a roof, and
pertinaciously resisting the infallible and prepared ruin,

> Donec longa dies omni compage soluta
> Ipsum cum rebus subruat auxilium,

till the determined day comes, and then the burden sunk
upon the pillars, and disordered the aids and auxiliary rafters
into a common ruin and a ruder grave : so are the desires and
weak arts of man; with little aids and assistances of care
and physic we strive to support our decaying bodies, and to

put off the evil day; but quickly that day will come, and
then neither angels nor men can rescue us from our grave ;
but the roof sinks down upon the walls, and the walls descend
to the foundation; and the beauty of the face, and the dishonours of the belly, the discerning head and the servile feet,
the thinking heart and the working hand, the eyes and the
guts together shall be crushed into the confusion of a heap,
and dwell with creatures of an equivocal production, with
worms and serpents, the sons and daughters of our own
bones, in a house of dirt and darkness.

Let not us think to be excepted or deferred : if beauty, or
wit, or youth, or nobleness, or wealth, or virtue could have
been a defence, and an excuse from the grave, we had not
met here to-day to mourn upon the hearse of an excellent
lady : and God only knows for which of us next the mourners
shall ' go about the streets ' or weep in houses.

We have lived so many years; and every day and every
minute we make an escape from those thousands of dangers
and deaths that encompass us round about, and such escapings
we must reckon to be an extraordinary fortune, and therefore
that it cannot last long.   Vain are the thoughts of man, who
when he is young or healthful thinks he hath a long thread
of life to run over, and that it is violent and strange for
young persons to die, and natural and proper only for the
aged.   It is as natural for a man to die by drowning as by a
fever: and what greater violence or more unnatural thing is
it that the horse threw his rider into the river, than that a
drunken meeting cast him into a fever?   And the strengths
of youth are as soon broken by the strong sicknesses of
youth, and the stronger intemperance, as the weakness of
old age by a cough, or an asthma, or a continual rheum.
Nay, it is more natural for young men and women to die
than for old; because that is more natural which hath more

natural causes, and that is more natural which is most common : but to die with age is an extreme rare thing; and there are more persons carried forth to burial before the five and thirtieth year of their age than after it. And therefore let no vain confidence make you hope for long life: if you have lived but little, and are still in youth, remember that now you are in your biggest throng of dangers both of body and soul; and the proper sins of youth, to which they rush infinitely and without consideration, are also the proper and immediate instruments of death.   But if you be old you have escaped long and wonderfully, and the time of your escaping is out: you must not for ever think to live upon wonders, or that God will work miracles to satisfy your longing follies, and unreasonable desires of living longer to sin and to the world.   Go home and think to die, and what you would choose to be doing when you die, that do daily : for you will all come to that pass to rejoice that you did so, or wish that you had: that will be the condition of every one of us; for ' God regardeth no man's person.'—*Funeral Sermon.*

3. Prayer.

PRAYER is the peace of our spirit, the stillness of our thoughts, the evenness of recollection; the seat of meditation, the rest of our cares, and the calm of our tempest; prayer is the issue of a quiet mind, of untroubled thoughts, it is the daughter of charity, and the sister of meekness; and he that prays to God with an angry, that is, with a troubled and discomposed spirit, is like him that retires into a battle to meditate, and sets up his closet in the out-quarters of an army, and chooses a frontier garrison to be wise in.   Anger is a perfect alienation of the mind from prayer, and therefore is contrary to that attention

which presents our prayers in a right line to God. For
so have I seen a lark· rising from his bed of grass, and
soaring upwards, singing as he rises, and hopes to get to
heaven, and climb above the clouds; but the poor bird
was beaten back with the loud sighings of an eastern wind,
and his motion made irregular and unconstant, descending
more at every breath of the tempest, than it could recover
by the libration and frequent weighing of its wings; till
the little creature was forced to sit down and pant, and
stay till the storm was over; and then it made a prosperous
flight, and did rise and sing, as if it had learned music and
motion from an angel as he passed sometimes through the
air about his ministries here below: so is the prayer of a
good man; when his 'affairs have required business, and
his business was matter of discipline, and his discipline
was to pass upon a sinning person, or had a design of
charity, his duty met with infirmities of a man, and anger
was its instrument, and the instrument became stronger than
the prime agent, and raised a tempest, and overruled the
man; and then his prayer was broken, and his thoughts
were troubled, and his words went up towards a cloud,
and his thoughts pulled them back again, and made them
without intention; and the good man sighs for·his infirmity,
but must be content to lose the prayer, and he must recover
it when his anger is removed, and his spirit is becalmed,
made even as the brow of Jesus, and smooth like the
heart of God; and then it ascends to heaven upon the
wings of the holy Dove, and dwells with God, till it returns,
like the useful bee, loaden with a blessing and the dew of
heaven.—*Sermon on the Return of Prayers.*

4. Marriage.

MARRIAGE is a school and exercise of virtue; and though marriage hath cares, yet the single life hath desires which are more troublesome and more dangerous, and often end in sin, while the cares are but instances of duty and exercises of piety; and therefore if single life hath more privacy of devotion, yet marriage hath more necessities and more variety of it, and is an exercise of more graces. . . . . Here is the proper scene of piety and patience, of the duty of parents and the charity of relatives; here kindness is spread abroad, and love is united and made firm as a centre: marriage is the nursery of heaven; the virgin sends prayers to God, but she carries but one soul to him; but the state of marriage fills up the numbers of the elect, and hath in it the labour of love, and the delicacies of friendship, the blessing of society, and the union of hands and hearts; it hath in it less of beauty, but more of safety, than the single life; it hath more care, but less danger; it is more merry, and more sad; is fuller of sorrows, and fuller of joys; it lies under more burdens, but it is supported by all the strengths of love and charity, and those burdens are delightful. Marriage is the mother of the world, and preserves kingdoms, and fills cities, and churches, and heaven itself. . . . . Marriage, like the useful bee, builds a house and gathers sweetness from every flower, and labours and unites into societies and republics, and sends out colonies, and feeds the world with delicacies, and obeys their king, and keeps order, and exercises many virtues, and promotes the interest of mankind, and is that state of good things to which God hath designed the present constitution of the world. . . . They that enter into the state of marriage cast a die of the greatest contingency, and yet of the greatest interest in the world, next to the last throw for eternity. Life or death, felicity or a lasting sorrow, are in the power of marriage. A woman indeed ventures most, for she hath no sanctuary to retire to from an evil husband; she must dwell upon her sorrow, and hatch the eggs which her own folly or infelicity hath produced; and she is more under it, because her tormentor hath a warrant of prerogative, and the woman may complain to God as subjects do of tyrant princes, but otherwise she hath no appeal in the causes of unkindness. And though the man can run from many hours of his sadness, yet he must return to it again, and when he sits among his neighbours he remembers the objection that lies in his bosom, and he sighs deeply. The boys, and the pedlars, and the fruiterers, shall tell of this man, when he is carried to his grave, that he lived and died a poor wretched person.

Let man and wife be careful to stifle little things, that as fast as they spring they be cut down and trod upon; for if they be suffered to grow by numbers, they make the spirit peevish, and the society troublesome, and the affections loose and easy by an habitual aversation. Some men are more vexed with a fly than with a wound; and when the gnats disturb our sleep, and the reason is disquieted but not perfectly awakened, it is often seen that he is fuller of trouble than if in the daylight of his reason he were to contest with a potent enemy. In the frequent little accidents of a family a man's reason cannot always be awake; and when his discourses are imperfect, and a trifling trouble makes him yet more restless, he is soon betrayed to the violence of passion. It is certain that the man or woman are in a state of weakness and folly then when they can be troubled with a trifling accident, and therefore it is not good to tempt their affections when they

are in that state of danger. In this case the caution is
to subtract fuel from the sudden flame; for stubble though
it be quickly kindled, yet it is as soon extinguished if it
be not blown by a pertinacious breath, or fed with new
materials. Add no new provocations to the accident, and
do not inflame this, and peace will soon return, and the
discontent will pass away soon as the sparks from the
collision of a flint: ever remembering that discontents proceeding from daily little things, do breed a secret undis-
cernible disease which is more dangerous than a fever
proceeding from a discerned notorious surfeit.

Let the husband and wife infinitely avoid a curious
distinction of mine and thine, for this hath caused all
the laws and all the suits and all the wars in the world;
let them who have but one person have also but one
interest. . . . . As the earth, the mother of all creatures here
below, sends up all its vapours and proper emissions at the
command of the sun, and yet requires them again to refresh
her own needs, and they are deposited between them both
in the bosom of a cloud, as a common receptacle, that they
may cool his flames, and yet descend to make her fruitful:
so are the proprieties of a wife to be disposed of by her
lord; and yet all are for her provisions, it being a part of
his need to refresh and supply hers, and it serves the interest
of both while it serves the necessities of either.

These are the duties of them both, which have common
regards and equal necessities and obligations. And indeed
there is scarce any matter of duty but it concerns them both
alike, and is only distinguished by names, and hath its
variety by circumstances and little accidents: and what in
one is called 'love,' in the other is called 'reverence;' and
what in the wife is 'obedience,' the same in the man is
'duty:' he provides, and she dispenses; he gives command-

ments, and she rules by them; he rules her by authority, and she rules him by love; she ought by all means to please him, and he must by no means displease her. For as the heart is set in the midst of the body, and though it strikes to one side by the prerogative of nature, yet those throbs and constant motions are felt on the other side also, and the influence is equal to both: so it is in conjugal duties; some motions are to the one side more than to the other, but the interest is on both, and the duty is equal in the several instances. . . . There is nothing can please a man without love; and, if a man be weary of the wise discourses of the apostles, and of the innocency of an even and a private fortune, or hates peace or a fruitful year, he hath reaped thorns and thistles from the choicest flowers of paradise; 'for nothing can sweeten felicity itself, but love.' . . . No man can tell but he that loves his children, how many delicious accents make a man's heart dance in the pretty conversation of those dear pledges; their childishness, their stammering, their little angers, their innocence, their imperfections, their necessities, are so many little emanations of joy and comfort to him that delights in their persons and society; but he that loves not his wife and children, feeds a lioness at home, and broods a nest of sorrows; and blessing itself cannot make him happy; so that all the commandments of God enjoining a man to love his wife, are nothing but so many necessities and capacities of joy. 'She that is loved is safe, and he that loves is joyful.' Love is a union of all things excellent: it contains in it proportion and satisfaction and rest and confidence.—*Sermon, The Marriage Ring.*

5. Godly Fear.

FEAR is the duty we owe to God, as being the God of power and justice, the great Judge of heaven and earth, the avenger of the cause of widows, the patron of the poor, and the advocate of the oppressed, a mighty God and terrible. . . . . Fear is the great bridle of intemperance, the modesty of the spirit, and the restraint of gaieties and dissolutions; it is the girdle to the soul, and the handmaid to repentance; the arrest of sin, and the cure or antidote to the spirit of reprobation; it preserves our apprehensions of the divine majesty, and hinders our single actions from combining to sinful habits; it is the mother of consideration, and the nurse of sober counsels; and it puts the soul to fermentation and activity, making it to pass from trembling to caution, from caution to carefulness, from carefulness to watchfulness, from thence to prudence; and by the gates and progresses of repentance it leads the soul on to love, and to felicity, and to joys in God, that shall never cease again. Fear is the guard of a man in the days of prosperity, and it stands upon the watch-towers and spies the approaching danger, and gives warning to them that laugh loud, and feast in the chambers of rejoicing, where a man cannot consider by reason of the noises of wine, and jest, and music: and if prudence takes it by the hand and leads it on to duty, it is a state of grace, and a universal instrument to infant religion, and the only security of the less perfect persons; and in all senses is that homage we owe to God, who sends often to demand it, even then when he speaks in thunder, or smites by a plague, or awakens us by threatenings, or discomposes our easiness by sad thoughts, and tender eyes, and fearful hearts, and trembling considerations.

But this so excellent grace is soon abused in the best and

most tender spirits; in those who are softened by nature
and by religion, by infelicities or cares, by sudden accidents
or a sad soul; ... so have I seen a harmless dove, made
dark with an artificial night, and her eyes sealed and locked
up with a little quill, soaring upward and flying with
amazement, fear, and an undiscerning wing; she made
towards heaven, but knew not that she was made a train and
an instrument, to teach her enemy to prevail upon her and
all her defenceless kindred: so is a superstitious man,
zealous and blind, forward and mistaken, he runs towards
heaven as he thinks, but he chooses foolish paths; and out
of fear takes any thing that he is told; or fancies and
guesses concerning God by measures taken from his own
diseases and imperfections.   But fear, when it is inordinate,
is never a good councillor, nor makes a good friend; and
he that fears God as his enemy is the most completely
miserable person in the world. . . . Therefore of all the
evils of the mind fear is certainly the worst and the most
intolerable: levity and rashness have in it some spritefulness,
and greatness of action; anger is valiant: desire is busy
and apt to hope; credulity is oftentimes entertained and
pleased with images and appearances: but fear is dull, and
sluggish, and treacherous, and flattering, and dissembling,
and miserable, and foolish.   Every false opinion concerning
God is pernicious and dangerous; but if it be joined with
trouble of spirit, as fear, scruple, or superstition are, it is like
a wound with an inflammation, or a strain of a sinew
with a contusion or contrition of the part, painful and
unsafe; it puts on two actions when itself is driven; it urges
reason and circumscribes it, and makes it pitiable, and
ridiculous in its consequent follies; which if we consider it
will sufficiently reprove the folly, and declare the danger. . . .
Let the grounds of our actions be noble, beginning upon

reason, proceeding with prudence, measured by the common
lines of men, and confident upon the expectation of a usual
providence. Let us proceed from causes to effects, from
natural means to ordinary events, and believe felicity not to
be a chance but a choice; and evil to be the daughter of sin
and the divine anger, not of fortune and fancy; let us fear
God when we have made him angry, and not be afraid
of him when we heartily and laboriously do our duty; our
fears are to be measured by open revelation and certain
experience, by the threatenings of God and the sayings of
wise men, and their limit is reverence, and godliness is their
end : and then fear shall be a duty, and a rare instrument of
many: in all other cases it is superstition or folly, it is sin
or punishment, the ivy of religion, and the misery of an
honest and a weak heart; and is to be cured only by
reason and good company, a wise guide and a plain rule,
a cheerful spirit and a contented mind, by joy in God
according to the commandments, that is, a 'rejoicing
evermore.'. . . The illusions of a weak piety, or an unskilful
confident soul: they fancy to see mountains of difficulty, but
touch them, and they seem like clouds riding upon the wings
of the wind, and put on shapes as we please to dream.
He that denies to give alms for fear of being poor, or to
entertain a disciple for fear of being suspected of the party,
or to own a duty for fear of being put to venture for a
crown; he that takes part of the intemperance, because he
dares not displease the company, or in any sense fears the
fears of the world, and not the fear of God, this man enters
into his portion of fear betimes, but it will not be finished to
eternal ages. To fear the censures of men when God is ·
your judge, to fear their evil when God is your defence, to
fear Death when he is the entrance to life and felicity, is
unreasonable and pernicious; but if you will turn your

passions into duty, and joy, and security, fear to offend God, to enter voluntarily into temptation; fear the alluring face of lust, and the smooth entertainments of intemperance; fear the anger of God when you have deserved it, and when you have recovered from the snare, then infinitely fear to return into that condition in which whosoever dwells is the heir of fear and eternal sorrow.—*Sermon of Godly Fear.*

6. Toleration.

I END with a story which I find in the Jews' books. 'When Abraham sat at his tent-door, according to his custom, waiting to entertain strangers; he espied an old man stooping and leaning on his staff, weary with age and travel, coming towards him, who was a hundred years of age. He received him kindly, washed his feet, provided supper, caused him to sit down; but observing that the old man eat and prayed not, nor begged for a blessing on his meat, he asked him why he did not worship the God of heaven: the old man told him that he worshipped the fire only, and acknowledged no other god; at which answer Abraham grew so zealously angry that he thrust the old man out of his tent, and exposed him to all the evils of the night and an unguarded condition. When the old man was gone, God called to Abraham, and asked him where the stranger was; he replied, "I thrust him away because he did not worship thee:" God answered him, "I have suffered him these hundred years, although he dishonoured me, and couldst not thou endure him one night when he gave thee no trouble?" Upon this' saith the story 'Abraham fetched him back again and gave him hospitable entertainment and wise instruction.' Go thou and do likewise, and thy charity will be rewarded by the God of Abraham.—*Liberty of Prophesying.*

7. Sickness.

At the first address and presence of sickness, stand still and arrest thy spirit, that it may without amazement or affright consider, that this was that thou lookedst for, and wert always certain should happen; and that now thou art to enter into the actions of a new religion, the agony of a strange constitution; but at no hand suffer thy spirits to be dispersed with fear or wildness of thought, but stay their looseness and dispersion by a serious consideration of the present and future employment. For so doth the Libyan lion, spying the fierce huntsman; first beats himself with the strokes of his tail, and curls up his spirits, making them strong with union and recollection, till, being struck with a Mauritanian spear, he rushes forth into his defence and noblest contention; and either escapes into the secrets of his own dwelling, or else dies the bravest of the forest. Every man when shot with an arrow from God's quiver, must then draw in all the auxiliaries of reason, and know that then is the time to try his strength, and to reduce the words of his religion into action, and consider, that if he behaves himself weakly and timorously, he suffers never the less of sickness; but if he returns to health, he carries along with him the' mark of a coward and a fool; and if he descends into his grave, he enters into the state of the faithless and unbelievers. Let him set his heart firm upon this resolution, 'I must bear it inevitably, and I will, by God's grace, do it nobly.'

Bear in thy sickness all along the same thoughts, pro-positions, and discourses, concerning thy person, thy life and death, thy soul and religion, which thou hadst in the best days of thy health, and when thou didst discourse wisely concerning things spiritual. For it is to be supposed (and if it be not yet done, let this rule remind thee of it, and direct thee) that thou hast cast about in thy health, and considered concerning thy change and the evil day, that thou must be sick and die, that thou must need a comforter, and that it was certain thou shouldst fall into a state in which all the cords of thy anchor should be stretched, and the very rock and foundation of faith should be attempted; and whatsoever fancies may disturb you, or whatsoever weaknesses may invade you, yet consider, when you were better able to judge and govern the accidents of your life, you concluded it necessary to trust in God, and possess your soul with patience. Think of things as they think that stand by you, and as you did when you stood by others; that it is a blessed thing to be patient; that a quietness of spirit hath a certain reward; that still there is infinite truth and reality in the promises of the gospel; that still thou art in the care of God, in the condition of a son, and working out thy salvation with labour and pain, with fear and trembling; that now the sun is under a cloud, but it still sends forth the same influence: and be sure to make no new principles upon the stock of a quick and an impatient sense, or too busy an apprehension: keep your old principles, and upon their stock discourse and practise on towards your conclusion. . . .

If thou fearest thou shalt need, observe and draw together all such things as are apt to charm thy spirit, and ease thy fancy in the sufferance. . . . It may be thou wert moved much to see a person of honour to die untimely; or thou didst love the religion of that death-bed, and it was dressed up in circumstances fitted to thy needs, and hit thee on that part where thou wert most sensible; or some little saying in a sermon or passage of a book was chosen and singled out by a peculiar apprehension, and made consent lodge awhile in thy spirit, even then when thou didst place death in thy meditation, and didst view it in all its dress of fancy. Whatsoever that was which at any time. did please thee in thy most passionate and fantastic part, let not that go, but bring it home at that time especially; because when thou art in thy weakness, such little things will easier move thee than a more severe discourse and a better reason. For a sick man is like a scrupulous: his case is gone beyond the cure of arguments, and it is a trouble, that can only be helped by chance, or a lucky saying. . . . I deny not but this course is most proper to weak persons; but it is a state of weakness for which we are now providing remedies and instruction: a strong man will not need it; but when our sickness hath rendered us weak in all senses, it is not good to refuse a remedy because it supposes us to be sick. But then if to the catalogue of weak persons we add all those who are ruled by fancy, we shall find that many persons in their health, and more in their sickness, are under the dominion of fancy, and apt to be helped by those little things, which themselves have found fitted to their apprehension, and which no other man can minister to their needs, unless by chance, or in a heap of other things. But therefore every man should remember by what instruments he was at any time much moved, and try them upon his spirit in the day of his calamity.—*Holy Dying.*

XVI.

SIR WILLIAM TEMPLE.

1628—1699.

THE family of Temple has contributed many famous names to the political history of England, but Sir William Temple is the only son of his race whose name survives in literature. He was born in London in 1628, and was the eldest child of his father, who was Master of the Rolls in Ireland. His earliest education was conducted by his maternal uncle, Dr. Hammond, the celebrated divine. At seventeen he went into residence at Emmanuel College, Cambridge, where he studied under Cudworth, whose influence may be traced in the Essays of his pupil. His career at the University was that of a young man intended for public life. His principal studies were the modern languages, especially French and Spanish; after two years of residence at Cambridge he left without taking a degree, and went abroad to complete his education by travel, having, as a professed Royalist, no prospect of public employment at home. In 1654 he married Dorothy the daughter of Sir Peter Osborn, a lady of the highest accomplishments, to whom he had been engaged for several years. It is said that she preferred Temple to Henry Cromwell, the younger son of the Protector. After his marriage he lived with his father in Ireland, occupying himself with the study of History and Philosophy, and refusing all solicitation to accept employment under Cromwell. For some time after the Restoration Sir William Temple sat in the Irish Parliament. In 1665 he was sent abroad on a mission of great importance, to negotiate a treaty with the Bishop of Munster for joining the king in a war with Holland. This was the beginning of a series of distinguished diplomatic services. The Triple Alliance, concluded at the Hague between England, Holland, and Sweden in January 1668, a treaty the object of which was to bring about peace between France and Spain and to restrain France from invading the Low Countries, was mainly due to Temple's energy, and established his reputation as a diplomatist. He continued to carry out the policy of the Allied Powers at the Hague, and became, not unnaturally, especially obnoxious to the French Government, at whose instigation he was abruptly recalled in 1669. He retired to Sheen, where he employed himself with gardening and in the composition of several of his best treatises. He was recalled to active service in 1674, and displayed his independence as a statesman by refusing to sign the treaty proposed after the peace of Nimeguen. In 1681 he withdrew finally from public employment. The rest of his life was passed in retirement, from which William III in vain attempted to attract him. He died in 1699.

Sir William Temple has a place of his own among English writers, and will be studied for the purity and elegance of his English when greater thinkers, whose forms of expression are uncouth, are neglected.

Temple is master of a style which is seen to most advantage in memoirs and essays of the lighter kind. This style he may almost be said to have originated. He seldom fails to gratify his reader, and he has occasional passages of great splendour and dignity.

Sir James Mackintosh says of Temple, ' in an age of extremes he was attached to liberty, and yet averse from endangering the public quiet.' It is not altogether fanciful to say that the political and domestic character of Temple is reflected in his Letters, Essays, and Memoirs. In an evil hour for his reputation as a critic, he lavished praise on the so-called Letters of Philaris, and provoked a controversy for ever memorable in literary annals. He was the patron of Swift, who has hardly done justice to his memory.

---

1. Giants in Wit and Genius exceptional productions of Nature.

I have long thought, that the different abilities of men, which we call wisdom or prudence, for the conduct of public affairs or private life, grow directly out of that little grain of intellect or good sense which they bring with them into the world; and that the defect of it in men comes from some want in their conception or birth.

> Dixitque semel nascentibus auctor,
> Quicquid scire licet.

And though this may be improved or impaired in some degree, by accidents of education, of study, and of conversation and business, yet it cannot go beyond the reach of its native force, no more than life can beyond the period to which it was destined by the strength or weakness of the seminal virtue.

If these speculations should be true, then I know not what advantages we can pretend to modern knowledge by any we receive from the ancients; nay it is possible, men may lose rather than gain by them; may lessen the force and growth of their own genius by constraining and forming it upon that of others; may have less knowledge of their own, for contenting themselves with that of those before them. So a man that only translates, shall never be a poet, nor a painter that only copies, nor a swimmer that swims always with bladders. So people that trust wholly to other's charity, and without industry of their own, will be always poor. Besides who can tell, whether learning may not even weaken invention in a man that has great advantages from nature and birth; whether the weight and number of so many other men's thoughts and notions may not suppress his own, or hinder the motion and agitation of them, from which all invention arises; as heaping on wood, or too many sticks, extinguishes a little spark that would otherwise have grown up to a noble flame. The strength of mind, as well as of body, grows more from the warmth of exercise than of clothes; nay, too much of this foreign heat rather makes men faint, and their constitutions tender or weaker than they would be without them. Let it come about how it will, if we are dwarfs, we are still so though we stand upon a giant's shoulders; and even so placed, yet we see less than he, if we are naturally shorter sighted, or if we do not look as much about us, or if we are dazzled with the height, which often happens from weakness either of heart or brain.

In the growth and stature of souls, as well as bodies, the common productions are of indifferent sizes, that occasion no gazing, nor no wonder : but though there are or have been sometimes dwarfs and sometimes giants in the world, yet it does not follow, that there must be·such in every age, nor in every country; this we can no more conclude, than that there never have been any, because there are none now, at least in the compass of our present knowledge or enquiry. As I believe there may have been giants at some time and some place or other in the world, or such a stature, as may not have been equalled perhaps again in several thousands of years, or in any other parts, so there may be giants in wit and knowledge, of so over-grown a size, as not to be equalled again in many successions of ages, or any compass of place or country. Such, I am sure, Lucretius esteems and describes Epicurus to have been, and to have risen, like a prodigy of invention and knowledge, such as had not been before, nor was like to be again; and I know not why others of the ancients may not be allowed to have been as great in their kinds, and to have built as high, though upon different schemes or foundations. Because there is a stag's head at Amboyse of a most prodigious size, and a large table at Memorancy cut out of the thickness of a vine stock, is it necessary that there must be, every age, such a stag in every great forest, or such a vine in every large vineyard'; or that the productions of nature, in any kind, must be still alike, or something near it, because nature is still the same? May there not many circumstances concur to one production that do not to any other, in one or many ages? In the growth of a tree, there is the native strength of the seed, both from the kind, and from the perfections of its ripening, and from the health and vigour of the plant that bore it : there is the, degree of strength and excellence in that vein of earth where it first took root; there is a propriety of soil, suited to the kind of tree that grows in it; there is a great favour or disfavour to its growth from accidents of water and of shelter, from the kindness or unkindness of seasons, till it be past the need or the danger of them. All these, and perhaps many others, joined with the propitiousness of climate to that sort of tree, and the length of age it shall stand and grow, may produce an oak, a fig, or a plane-tree, that shall deserve to be renowned in story, and shall not perhaps be paralleled in other countries or times.

May not the same have happened in the production, growth, and size of wit and genius in the world, or in some parts or ages of it, and from many more circumstances that contributed towards it, than what may concur to the stupendous growth of a tree or animal?—*Essay, Upon the Ancient and Modern Learning.*

2. Of Gardening.

I may perhaps be allowed to know something of this trade, since I have so long allowed myself to be good for nothing else, which few men will do, or enjoy their gardens, without often looking abroad to see how other matters play, what motions in the state, and what invitations they may hope for into other's scenes.

For my own part, as the country life, and this part of it more particularly, were the inclination of my youth itself, so they are the pleasure of my age; and I can truly say, that, among many great employments that have fallen to my share, I have never asked or sought for any one of them, but often endeavoured to escape from them into the ease and freedom of a private scene, where a man may go his own way and his own pace, in the common paths or circles of life.

The measure of choosing well is, whether a man likes what he has chosen; which, I thank God, has befallen me; and though, among the follies of my life, building and planting have not been the least, and have cost me more than I have the confidence to own, yet they have been fully recompensed by the sweetness and satisfaction of this retreat, where, since my resolution taken of never entering again into any public employments, I have passed five years without ever going once to town, though I am almost in sight of it, and have a house there always ready to receive me. Nor has this been any sort of affectation, as some have thought it, but a mere want of desire or humour to make so small a remove.

That which makes the cares of gardening more necessary, or at least more excusable, is, that all men eat fruit that can get it; so as the choice is only, whether one will eat good or ill; and between these the difference is not greater in point of taste and delicacy, than it is of health: for the first I will only say, that whoever has used to eat good will do very great penance when he comes to ill: and for the other, I think nothing is more evident, than as ill or unripe fruit is extremely unwholesome, and causes so many untimely deaths, or so much sickness about autumn, in all great cities where it is greedily sold as well as eaten; so no part of diet, in any season, is so healthful, so natural, and so agreeable to the stomach, as good and well-ripened fruits; for this I make the measure of their being good: and let the kinds be what they will, if they will not ripen perfectly in our climate, they are better never planted, or never eaten. Now whoever will be sure to eat good fruit, must do it out of a garden of his own; for besides the choice so necessary in the sorts, the soil, and so many other circumstances that go to compose a good garden, or produce good fruits, there is something very nice in gathering them, and choosing the best even from the same tree. The best sorts of all among us, which I esteem the white figs and the soft peaches, will not carry without suffering. The best fruit that is bought, has no more of the master's care than how to raise the greatest gains; his business is to have as much fruit as he can upon a few trees, whereas the way to have it excellent is to have but little upon many trees. So that for all things out of a garden, either of salads or fruits, a poor man will eat better, that has one of his own, than a rich man that has none. And this is all I think of necessary and useful to be known upon this subject.—*Essay, Of Gardening.*

3. Retirement from Public Life.

Upon the survey of all these circumstances, conjunctures, and dispositions, both at home and abroad, I concluded in cold blood, that I could be of no further use or service to the king my master, and my country, whose true interests I always thought were the same, and would be both in danger when they came to be divided, and for that reason had ever endeavoured the uniting them; and had compassed it, if the passions of some few men had not lain fatally in the way, so as to raise difficulties that I saw plainly were never to be surmounted. Therefore, upon the whole, I took that firm resolution, in the end of the year 1680, and the interval between the Westminster and Oxford parliaments, never to

charge myself more with any public employments; but retiring wholly to a private life, in that posture take my fortune
with my country, whatever it should prove: which as no
man can judge, in the variety of accidents that attend human
affairs, and the chances of every day, to which the greatest
lives, as well as actions, are subject; so I shall not trouble
myself so much as to conjecture: *fata viam invenient.*

Besides all these public circumstances, I considered myself in my own humour, temper, and dispositions, which
a man may disguise to others, though very hardly, but cannot to himself. I had learned by living long in courts and
public affairs, that I was fit to live no longer in either. I
found the arts of a court were contrary to the frankness and
openness of my nature; and the constraints of public business too great for the liberty of my humour and my life.
The common and proper ends of both are the advancement
of men's fortunes ; and that I never minded, having as much
as I needed, and, which is more, as I ' desired. The talent
of gaining riches I ever despised, as observing it to belong
to the most despisable men in other kinds : and I had the
occasions of it so often in my way, if I would have made
use of them, that I grew to disdain them, as a man does
meat that he has always before him. Therefore, I never
could go to service for nothing but wages, nor endure to be
fettered in business when I thought it was to no purpose. I
knew very well the arts of a court are, to talk the present
language, to serve' the present turn, and to follow the present humour of the prince, whatever it is: of all these I
found myself so incapable, that I could not talk a language
I did not mean, nor serve a turn I did not like, nor follow
any man's humour wholly against my own. Besides, I have
had, in twenty years' experience, enough of the uncertainty
of princes, the caprices of fortune, the corruption of ministers,

the violence of factions, the unsteadiness of counsels, and
the infidelity of friends; nor do I think the rest of my life
enough to make any new experiments. . . .

And so I take leave of all those airy visions which have
so long busied my head about mending the world; and at
the same time, of all those shining toys or follies that employ
the thoughts of busy men: and shall turn mine wholly to
mend myself; and, as far as consists with a private condition, still pursuing that old and excellent counsel of Pythagoras, that we are, with all the cares and endeavours of our
lives, to avoid diseases in the body, perturbations in the mind,
luxury in diet, factions in the house, and seditions in the
state.—*Memoirs.*

4. Holland.

WHATEVER it was, whether nature or accident, and upon
what occasion soever it arrived, the soil of the whole Province
of Holland is generally flat, like the sea in a calm, and looks
as if, after a long contention between land and water, which
it should belong to, it had at length been divided between
them: for to consider the great rivers, and the strange
number of canals that are found in this province, and do
not only lead to every great town, but almost to every
village, and every farm-house in the country; and the
infinity of sails that are seen everywhere coursing up and
down upon them; one would imagine the water to have
shared with the land, and the people that live in boats to
hold some proportion with those that live in houses. And
this is one great advantage towards trade, which is natural to
the situation, and not to be attained in any country where
there is not the same level and softness of soil, which makes
the cutting of canals so easy work, as to be attempted almost
by every private man: and one horse shall draw in a boat

more than fifty can do in a cart; whereas carriage makes a great part of the price in all heavy commodities : and, by this easy way of travelling, an industrious man loses no time from his business, for he writes, eats, or sleeps, while he goes; whereas the time of labouring or industrious men is the greatest native commodity of any country. . . . . .

Another advantage of their situation for trade is made by those two great rivers of the Rhine and the Macs, reaching up, and navigable so mighty a length, into so rich and populous countries of the higher and lower Germany; which as it brings down all the commodities from those parts to the magazines of Holland, that vent them by their shipping into all parts of the world, where the market calls for them; so, with something more labour and time, it returns all the merchandizes of other parts into those countries that are seated upon those streams. For their commodious seat, as to the trade of the Straits, or Baltic, or any parts of the ocean, I see no advantage they have of most parts of England; and they must certainly yield to many we possess, if we had other equal circumstances to value them.

The lowness and flatness of their lands makes in a great measure the richness of their soil, that is easily overflowed every winter, so as the whole country, at that season, seems to lie under water, which, in spring, is driven out again by mills. But that which mends the earth, spoils the air, which would be all fog and mist, if it were not cleared by the sharpness of their frosts, which never fail with every east wind for about four months of the year, and are much fiercer than in the same latitude with us, because that wind comes to them over a mighty length of dry continent; but is moistened by the vapours, or softened by the warmth of the sea's motion, before it reaches us.

And this is the greatest disadvantage of trade they receive

from their situation, though necessary to their health; because many times their havens are all shut up for two or three months with ice, when ours are open and free.

The fierce sharpness of these winds makes the changes of their weather and seasons more violent and surprising, than in any place I know; so as a warm faint air turns in a night to a sharp frost, with the wind coming into the north-east: and the contrary with another change of wind. The spring is much shorter, and less agreeable, than with us; the winter much colder, and some parts of the summer much hotter; and I have known, more than once, the violence of one give way to that of the other, like the cold fit of an ague to the hot, without any good temper between.

The flatness of their land exposes it to the danger of the sea, and forces them to infinite charge in the continual fences and repairs of their banks to oppose it; which employ yearly more men, than all the corn of the Province of Holland could maintain (as one of their chief ministers has told me). They have lately found the common sea-weed to be the best material for these dykes, which, fastened with a thin mixture of earth, yields a little to the force of the sea, and returns when the waves give back: whether they are thereby the safer against water, as, they say, houses that shake are against wind; or whether, as pious naturalists observe, all things carry about them that which serves for a remedy against the mischief they do in the world.

The extreme moisture of the air I take to be the occasion of the great neatness of their houses, and cleanliness in their towns. For without the help of those customs their country would not be habitable by such crowds of people, but the air would corrupt upon every hot season, and expose the inhabitants to general and infectious diseases; which they hardly escape three summers together, especially about

Leyden, where the waters are not so easily renewed; and for this reason, I suppose, it is, that Leyden is found to be the neatest and cleanliest kept of all their towns.

The same moisture of air makes all metals apt to rust and wood to mould; which forces them, by continual pains of rubbing and scouring, to seek a prevention, or cure: this makes the brightness and cleanness that seems affected in their houses, and is called natural to them, by people who think no further. So the deepness of their soil, and wetness of seasons, which would render it unpassable, forces them, not only to exactness of paving in their streets, but to the expense of so long causeways between many of their towns, and in their highways: as, indeed, most national customs are the effect of some unseen or unobserved natural causes or necessities.—*Observations upon the United Provinces.*

5. Length of Life in Britain.

For the honour of our climate it has been observed by ancient authors, that the Britons were longer-lived than any other nation to them known. And in modern times there have been more and greater examples of this kind than in any other countries of Europe. The story of old Parr is too late to be forgotten by many now alive, who was brought out of Derbyshire to the court in King Charles I's time, and lived to a hundred and fifty-three years old; and might have, as was thought, gone further, if the change of country air and diet for that of the town had not carried him off, perhaps untimely at that very age. The late Robert Earl of Leicester, who was a person of great learning and observation, as well as of truth, told me several stories very extraordinary upon this subject; one, of a Countess of Desmond, married out of England in Edward IV's time,

and who lived far in King James's reign, and was counted
to have died some years above a hundred and forty; at
which age she came from Bristol to London to beg some
relief at Court, having long been very poor by the ruin
of that Irish family into which she was married.

Another he told me was of a beggar at a bookseller's
shop, where he was some weeks after the death of Prince
Henry; and observing those that passed by, he was saying
to his company, that never such a mourning had been seen
in England: this beggar said, no, never since the death of
Prince Arthur. My Lord Leicester, surprised, asked what
she meant, and whether she remembered it: she said, very
well: and upon his more curious inquiry told him that her
name was Rainsford, of a good family in Oxfordshire: that,
when she was about twenty years old, upon the falseness
of a lover, she fell distracted; how long she had been so,
nor what passed in that time, she knew not; that, when
she was thought well enough to go abroad, she was fain
to beg for her living: that she was some time at this trade
before she recovered any memory of what she had been, or
where bred: that, when this memory returned, she went
down into her country, but hardly found the memory of any
of her friends she had left there; and so returned to a parish
in Southwark, where she had some small allowance among
other poor, and had been for many years; and once a week
walked into the city, and took what alms were given her.
My Lord Leicester told me, he sent to inquire at the parish,
and found their account agree with the woman's: upon
which he ordered her to call at his house once a week,
which she did for some time; after which he heard no
more of her. This story raised some discourse upon a
remark of some in the company, that mad people are apt
to live long. They alleged examples of their own know-

ledge : but the result was, that, if it were true, it must proceed from the natural vigour of their tempers, which disposed them to passions so violent as ended in frenzies: and from the great abstinence and hardships of diet they are forced upon by the methods of their cure, and severity of those who had them in care; no other drink but water being allowed them, and very little meat.

The last story I shall mention from that noble person, upon this subject, was of a morrice-dance in Herefordshire ; whereof, he said, he had a pamphlet still in his library, written by a very ingenious gentleman of that county: and which gave an account how such a year of King James's reign, there went about the country a set of morrice-dancers, composed of ten men who danced, a maid Marian, and a tabor and pipe: and how these twelve, one with another, made up twelve hundred years. 'Tis not so much, that so many, in one small county, should live to that age, as that they should be in vigour and in humour to travel and to dance.

I have, in my life, met with two of above a hundred and twelve ; whereof the woman had passed her life in service ; and the man, in common labour, till he grew old, and fell upon the parish. But I met with one who had gone a much greater length, which made me more curious in my inquiries. 'Twas an old man who begged usually at a lonely inn, upon the road in Staffordshire ; who told me, he was a hundred and twenty-four years old: that he had been a soldier in the Cales voyage, under the Earl of Essex, of which he gave me a sensible account. That, after his return, he fell to labour in his own parish, which was about a mile from the place where I met him. That he continued to work till a hundred and twelve, when he broke one of his ribs, by a fall from a cart, and, being

thereby disabled, he fell to beg. This agreeing with what
the master of the house told me, was reported and believed
by all his neighbours. I asked him what his usual food
was; he said, milk, bread, and cheese, and flesh when it
was given him. I asked him what he used to drink; he
said, O sir, we have the best water in our parish that is
in all the neighbourhood: whether he never drank any thing
else? he said, yes, if any body gave it him, but not otherwise: and the host told me, he had got many a pound in
his house, but never spent one penny. I asked if he had
any neighbours as old as he; and he told me, but one,
who had been his fellow soldier at Cales, and was three
years older; but he had been most of his time in a good
service, and had something to live on now he was old.—
Of Health and Long Life.

XVII.

ISAAC BARROW.

1630—1677.

ISAAC BARROW, the son of a linen-draper in London, but descended of an ancient Suffolk family, was born in 1630. His education, which was commenced at Charterhouse, where he was remarkable only for fighting and idleness, was continued with better success at Felstead. His progress there was so great that his master appointed him at the age of thirteen as a little tutor to Viscount Fairfax, of Emly in Ireland. Whilst in Ireland, in 1643, he was admitted a Pensioner of Peterhouse, in Cambridge, of which College his uncle, afterwards Bishop of St. Asaph, was then Fellow. His uncle's ejection from the College for writing against the Covenant led to his withdrawing from it, and he entered, when he came to Cambridge in 1645, as a Pensioner of Trinity. The losses incurred by his father through adherence to the royal cause brought him into pecuniary difficulty, through which he was helped by the liberality of Dr. Hammond. In 1647 he was elected a Scholar of the House. By his good conduct he preserved the good-will and esteem of his superiors in spite of the obnoxiousness of the party to which he belonged, and though he had never taken the Covenant, in 1649 he was elected Fellow.

Perceiving that the times were unfavourable to persons of royalist opinions, he resolved to devote himself to medicine, and began the studies preliminary to that profession; but he soon returned to divinity, to which, with mathematics and astronomy, he devoted himself for the rest of his life. He travelled for some years in France, Italy, and Turkey, selling his books to defray the cost of his journeys. Soon after his return to England, in 1659, he took orders.

In 1660 he was appointed Professor of Greek at Cambridge, and in 1662 elected Gresham Professor of Geometry, which office he held until 1669, when he resigned the chair, resolving henceforward to confine himself to the study of divinity. He was succeeded in it by Isaac Newton, whose talents when an undergraduate at Cambridge he had been the first to recognise and encourage. He was nominated Master of Trinity by the King in 1672, and died in his forty-seventh year in 1677.

Isaac Barrow was equally celebrated as a mathematician and divine. As a divine, he is principally known as the author of the *Treatise of the Pope's Supremacy*, published by the care of Bishop Tillotson after its writer's death, a standard work, which occupies one of the foremost places in our controversial theology. As a moral and practical writer, he is discriminating, as well as earnest, vigorous, and copious; he exhibits great resources of language, and brings out the whole contents of a subject with clearness, freedom, and vivacity. His style, though it tends to looseness and diffuseness, is still always animated and rich. His readers are often cautioned against his redundancy, but it is the redundancy of an original and fertile genius. The characteristic qualities of his mind are best exhibited in his *Sermons*, in which he handles moral as well as doctrinal subjects, and enters with heartiness into questions of life and practice.

---

1. Prayer.

WE cannot ever be framing or venting long prayers with our lips, but almost ever our mind can throw pious glances, our heart may dart good wishes upwards; so that hardly any moment (any considerable space of time) shall pass without some lightsome flashes of devotion. As bodily respiration, without intermission or impediment, doth concur with all our actions ; so may that breathing of soul, which · preserveth our spiritual life, and ventilateth that holy flame within us, well conspire with all other occupations.

For devotion is of a nature so spiritual, so subtle, and penetrant, that no matter can exclude or obstruct it. Our minds are so exceedingly nimble and active, that no business can hold pace with them, or exhaust their attention and activity. We can never be so fully possessed by any employment, but that divers vacuities of time do intercur, wherein our thoughts and affections will be diverted to other matters. ⸱ As a covetous man, whatever beside he is doing, will be carking about his bags and treasures ; an ambitious man will be devising on his plots and projects ; a voluptuous man will have his mind in his dishes ; a lascivious man will be doting on his amours ; a studious man will be musing on his notions,—every man according to his particular inclination, will lard his business and besprinkle all his actions with cares and wishes tending to the enjoyment of what he most esteemeth and affecteth ; so may a good Christian, through all his undertakings, wind in devout reflections and pious motions of soul toward the chief object of his mind and affection. Most businesses have wide gaps, all have some chinks, at which devotion may slip in. Be we never so urgently set or closely intent upon any work, (be we feeding, be we travelling, be we trading, be we studying,) nothing yet can forbid, but that we may together wedge in a thought concerning God's goodness.—*Sermon, The Duty of Prayer.*

2. A Peaceable Temper.

It much conduceth to the preservation of peace, and upholding amicable correspondence in our dealings and transactions with men, liable to doubt and debate, not to insist upon nice and rigorous points of right, not to take all advantage offered us, not to deal hard measure, not to use extremities, to the damage or hindrance of others, especially when no comparable benefit will thence accrue to ourselves. For such proceedings, as they discover in us little kindness to, or tenderness of, our neighbours' good, so they exceedingly exasperate them, and persuade them we are their enemies, and render them ours, and so utterly destroy peace between us. Whereas abating something from the height and strictness of our pretences, and a favourable recession in such cases, will greatly engage men to have an honourable opinion, and a peaceable affection towards us.

If we would attain to this peaceable estate of life, we must use toward all men such demonstrations of respect and courtesy, which according to their degree and station custom doth entitle them to, or which upon the common score of humanity they may be reasonably deemed to expect from us; respective gestures, civil salutations, free access, affable demeanour, cheerful looks, and ,courteous discourse. These, as they betoken good-will in them that use them, so they beget, cherish, and increase it in those whom they refer to : and the necessary fruit of mutual good-will is peace.

But the contrary carriages, contemptuous or disregardful behaviour, difficulty of admission to converse, a tetrical or sullen aspect, rough and fastidious language, as they discover a mind averse from friendly commerce, so they beget a more potent disdain in others: men generally (especially those of generous and hearty temper) valuing their due respect beyond all other interests, and more contentedly brooking injury than neglect.

He that would effectually observe the apostolic rule, must

be disposed to overlook such lesser faults committed against him, as make no great breach upon his interest or credit, yea, to forget or forgive the greatest and most grievous injuries : to excuse the mistakes, and connive at the neglects, and bear patiently the hasty passions of his neighbour, and to embrace readily any seasonable overture, and accept any tolerable conditions of reconcilement. For even in common life that observation of our Saviour most exactly holds, *It is impossible that offences should not come ;* the air may sooner become wholly fixed, and the sea continue in a perfect rest, without waves or undulations, than human conversation be altogether free from occasions of distaste, which he that cannot either prudently dissemble, or patiently digest, must renounce all hopes of living peaceably here. He that like tinder is inflammable by the least spark, and is enraged by every angry word, and resents deeply every petty affront, and cannot endure the memory of a past unkindness should upon any terms be defaced, resolves surely to live in eternal tumult and combustion, to multiply daily upon himself fresh quarrels, and to perpetuate all enmity already begun. Whereas by total passing by those little causes of disgust the present contention is altogether avoided, or instantly appeased, our neighbour's passion suddenly evaporates and consumes itself; no remarkable footsteps of dissension remain; our neighbour, reflecting upon what is past, sees himself obliged by our discreet forbearance.

If we desire to live peaceably, we must restrain our pragmatical curiosity within the bounds of our proper business and concernment, not (being *curiosi in aliena republica*) invading other men's provinces, and without leave or commission intermeddling with their affairs; not rushing into their closets, prying into their concealed designs, or dictating counsel to them without due invitation thereto.

If we would live peaceably with all men, it behoves us not
to engage ourselves so deeply in any singular friendship, or
in devotion to any one party of men, as to be entirely partial
to their interests, and prejudiced in their behalf, without
distinct consideration of the truth and equity of their pretences in the particular matters of difference; not to approve,
favour, or applaud that which is bad in some; to dislike,
discountenance, or disparage that which is good in others:
not, out of excessive kindness to some, to give just cause of
distaste to others: not, for the sake of a fortuitous agreement in disposition, opinion, interest, or relation, to violate
the duties of justice or humanity. For he that upon such
terms is a friend to any one man, or party of men, as to be
resolved, with an implicit faith or blind obedience, to maintain whatever he or they shall do to be good, doth in a
manner undertake enmity against all men beside, and as it
may happen, doth oblige himself to contradict plain truth, to
deviate from the rules of virtue, and to offend Almighty God
himself. This unlimited partiality we owe only to truth and
goodness, and to God (the fountain of them), in no case to
swerve from their dictates and prescriptions. He that
followed Tiberius Gracchus in his seditious practices, upon
thè bare account of friendship, and alleged in his excuse,
that, if his friend had required it of him, he should as readily
have put fire to the Capitol, was much more abominable for
his disloyalty to his country, and horrible impiety against
God, than commendable for his constant fidelity to his
friend.—*Sermon, Of a Peaceable Temper and Carriage.*

3. Not easy to be good.

VIRTUE is not a mushroom, that springeth up of itself
in one night when we are asleep, or regard it not; but a

delicate plant, that groweth slowly and tenderly, needing much pains to cultivate it, much care to guard it, much time to mature it, in our untoward soil, in this world's unkindly weather: happiness is a thing too precious to be purchased at an easy rate; heaven is too high to be come at without much climbing; the crown of bliss is a prize too noble to be won without a long and a tough conflict. Neither is vice a spirit that will be conjured down by a charm, or with a presto driven away; it is not an adversary that can be knocked down at a blow, or despatched with a stab. Whoever shall pretend that at any time, easily, with a celerity, by a kind- of legerdemain, or by any mysterious knack, a man may be settled in virtue, or converted from vice, common experience abundantly will confute him; which sheweth, that a habit otherwise (setting miracles aside) cannot be produced or destroyed, than by a constant exercise of acts suitable or opposite thereto; and that such acts cannot be exercised without voiding all impediments, and framing all principles of action, (such as temper of body, judgment of mind, influence of custom,) to a compliance ; that who by temper is peevish or choleric, cannot, without mastering that temper, become patient or meek ; that who from vain opinions is proud, cannot, without considering away those opinions, prove humble; that who by custom is grown intemperate, cannot, without weaning himself from that custom, come to be sober; that who, from the concurrence of a sorry nature, fond conceits, mean breeding, and scurvy usage, is covetous, cannot, without draining all those sources of his fault, be turned into liberal. The change of our mind is one of the greatest alterations in nature, which cannot be compassed in any way or within any time we please; but it must proceed on leisurely and regularly, in such order, by such steps, as the nature of things doth permit; it must be wrought by a resolute and laborious perseverance; by a watchful application of mind, in voiding prejudices, in waiting for advantages, in attending to all we do; by forcible wresting our nature from its bent, and swimming against the current of impetuous desires; by a patient disentangling ourselves from practices most agreeable and familiar to us; by a wary fencing with temptations, by long struggling with manifold oppositions and difficulties; whence the holy scripture termeth our practice a warfare, wherein we are to fight many a bloody battle with most redoubtable foes; a combat, which must be managed with our best skill and utmost might: a race, which we must pass through with incessant activity and swiftness. '

If therefore we mean to be good or to be happy, it behoveth us to lose no time; to be presently up at our great task; to snatch all occasions, to embrace all means incident of reforming our hearts and lives. As those, who have a long journey to go, do take care to set out early, and in their way make good speed, lest the night overtake them before they reach their home; so it being a great way from hence to heaven, seeing we must pass over so many obstacles, through so many paths of duty, before we arrive thither, it is expedient to set forward as soon as can be, and to proceed with all expedition; the longer we stay, the more time we shall need, and the less we shall have.

We may consider, that no future time which we can fix upon will be more convenient than the present is for our reformation. Let us pitch on what time we please, we shall be as unwilling and unfit to begin as we are now; we shall find in ourselves the same indispositions, the same averseness, or the same listlessness toward it, as now : there will occur the like hardships to deter us, and the like pleasures to allure us from our duty; objects will then be as present, and will strike as smartly upon our senses; the case will appear just the same, and the same pretences for delay will obtrude themselves; so that we shall be as apt then as now to prorogue the business. We shall say then, to-morrow I will mend; and when that morrow cometh, it will be still to-morrow, and so the morrow will prove endless. If, like the simple rustic, (who stayed by the river-side waiting till it had done running, so that he might pass dry-foot over the channel,) we do conceit that the sources of sin (bad inclinations within, and strong temptations abroad) will of themselves be spent, or fail, we shall find ourselves deluded. If ever we come to take up, we must have a beginning with some difficulty and trouble; we must courageously break through the present with all its enchantments; we must undauntedly plunge into the cold stream; we must rouse ourselves from our bed of sloth; we must shake off that brutish improvidence, which detaineth us; and why should we not assay it now? There is the same reason now that ever we can have; yea, far more reason now; for if that we now begin, hereafter at any determinate time some of the work will be done, what remaineth will be shorter and easier to us.—*Sermon, The Danger and Mischief of delaying Repentance.*

4. Wit.

But first it may be demanded what the thing we speak of is, or what this facetiousness doth import? To which question I might reply as Democritus did to him that asked the definition of a man, *It is that which we all see and know;* any one better apprehends what it is by acquaintance, than I can inform him by description. It is indeed a thing so versatile and multiform, appearing in so many shapes, so many postures, so many garbs, so variously apprehended

by several eyes and judgments, that it seemeth no less hard
to settle a clear and certain notion thereof, than to make a
portrait of Proteus, or to define the figure of the fleeting air.
Sometimes it lieth in pat allusion to a known story, or in
seasonable application of a trivial saying, or in forging an
ᴀpposite tale : sometimes it playeth in words and phrases,
taking advantage from the ambiguity of their sense, or the
affinity of their sound : sometimes it is wrapped in a dress of
humorous expression : sometimes it lurketh under an odd
similitude : sometimes it is lodged in a sly question, in a
smart answer, in a quirkish reason, in a shrewd intimation,
in cunningly diverting or cleverly retorting an objection :
sometimes it is couched in a bold scheme of speech, in a
tart irony, in a lusty hyperbole, in a startling metaphor, in a
plausible reconciling of contradictions, or an acute nonsense :
sometimes a scenical representation of persons or things, a
counterfeit speech, a mimical look or gesture passeth for it :
sometimes an affected simplicity, sometimes a presumptuous
bluntness giveth it being : sometimes it riseth from a lucky
hitting upon what is strange, sometimes from a crafty wresting obvious matter to the purpose : often it consisteth in one
knows not what, and springeth up one can hardly tell how.
Its ways are unaccountable and inexplicable, being answerable to the numberless rovings of fancy and windings of
language.   It is, in short, a manner of speaking out of the
simple and plain way, (such as reason teacheth and proveth
things by,) which by a pretty surprising uncouthness in conceit or expression doth affect and amuse the fancy, stirring
in it some wonder, and breeding some delight thereto.   It
raiseth admiration, as signifying a nimble sagacity of apprehension, a special felicity of invention, a vivacity of spirit,
and reach of wit more than vulgar : it seeming to argue a
rare quickness of parts, that one can fetch in remote con-

ceits applicable; a notable skill, that he can dexterously accommodate them to the purpose before him; together with a lively briskness of humour, not apt to damp those sportful flashes of imagination. It also procureth delight, by gratifying curiosity with its rareness or semblance of difficulty; (as monsters, not for their beauty, but their rarity; as juggling tricks, not for their use, but their abstruseness, are beheld with pleasure;) by diverting the mind from its road of serious thoughts; by instilling gaiety and airiness of spirit; by provoking to such dispositions of spirit in way of emulation or complaisance; and by seasoning matters, otherwise distasteful or insipid, with an unusual, and thence grateful tang.—*Sermon against Foolish Talking and Jesting.*

XVIII.

JOHN TILLOTSON.

1630—1694.

JOHN TILLOTSON was the son of a clothier at Sowerby in Yorkshire. He was born in October, 1630, and educated at Clare Hall, Cambridge. At the Restoration he became Chaplain to Charles II, Dean of Canterbury in 1672, and Archbishop of that see in 1691, holding the Deanery of St. Paul's for a brief period prior to his appointment to this highest dignity of the Church. After the Revolution of 1688 he was admitted to a high degree of confidence in the counsels of William III.

Tillotson's father was a zealous Calvinist, and his son's first impressions and early education among the Puritans had connected him with the Presbyterians; when he gradually receded from their principles, and at last, on the deprivation of Sancroft for refusing to take the oaths to the new government, succeeded him as Archbishop of Canterbury, he became the object of the attacks of the nonjurors. But the discretion of his conduct and his exemplary life gained him general esteem and confidence. His indifference to money was such that, on his death in 1694, his debts could not have been paid by his widow, had not the King forgiven his first-fruits. The copyright of his *Sermons*, which produced £2500, was the only provision which remained for his widow, a niece of Oliver Cromwell, to whom he had been married for upwards of thirty years.

Tillotson ranks among the foremost of the latitudinarian divines, and his reputation as a preacher was very high among his contemporaries. He left three folio volumes of sermons, but his general style, though highly commended both by Dryden and

Addison, seems to us in the present day frigid, and familiar, in comparison with the luxuriant style of the preachers of the preceding generation, or even with South and Barrow. He was, if not the first, the best example of the perspicuous and popular preaching which came in after the Restoration, in contradistinction to the style of learned allusion which stamps the Caroline divines.

---

1. The Uncertainty of Earthly Happiness.

But, setting aside these, and the like melancholy considerations, when we are in the health and vigour of our age, when our blood is warm, and our spirits quick, and the humours of our body not yet turned and soured by great disappointments, and grievous losses of our estates, or nearest friends and relations, by a long course of afflictions, by many cross events and calamitous accidents; yet we are continually liable to all these, and the perpetual fear and danger of them is no small trouble and uneasiness to our minds, and does, in a great measure, rob us of the comfort, and eat out the pleasure and sweetness of all our enjoyments; and, by degrees, the evils we fear overtake us; and as one affliction and trouble goes off, another succeeds in the place of it, like Job's messengers, whose bad tidings and reports of calamitous accidents came so thick upon him, that they overtook one another.

If we have a plentiful fortune, we are apt to abuse it to intemperance and luxury, and this naturally breeds bodily pains and diseases, which take away all the comfort and enjoyment of a great estate. If we have health, it may be we are afflicted with losses or deprived of friends, or crossed in our interests and designs, and one thing or other happens

to impede or interrupt the contentment and happiness of
our lives. Sometimes an unexpected storm, or some other
sudden calamity, sweepeth away, in an instant, all that
which with so much industry and care we have been
gathering many years. Or if an estate stand firm, our
children are taken away, to whose comfort and advantage
all the pains and endeavours of our lives were devoted.
Or if none of these happen (as it is very rare to escape
most, or some of them), yet for a demonstration to us that
God intended this world to be uneasy, to convince us that
a perfect state of happiness is not to be had here below,
we often see in experience that those who seem to be in
a condition as happy as this world can put them into, by
the greatest accommodations towards it, are yet as far or
farther from happiness as those who are destitute of most
of those things wherein the greatest felicity of this world
is thought to consist. Many times it so happens, that they
who have all the furniture and requisites, all the materials
and ingredients of a worldly felicity at their command, and
in their power, yet have not the skill and ability out of
all these to frame a happy condition of life to themselves.
They have health, and friends, and reputation, and estate
in abundance, and all outward accommodations that heart
can wish; and yet, in the midst of all these circumstances
of outward felicity, they are uneasy in their minds, and,
as the wise man expresseth it, in their sufficiency they are
in straits, and are, as it were, surfeited even with happiness
itself, and do so fantastically and unaccountably nauseate
the good condition they are in, that though they want
nothing to make them happy, yet they cannot think themselves so; though they have nothing in the world to molest
and disgust them, yet they can make a shift to create as
much trouble to themselves out of nothing, as they who

have the real and substantial causes of 'discontent.—*Sermon,
Good Men Strangers and Sojourners upon Earth.*

2. The Dignity of Man.

CONSIDER him in himself, as compounded of soul and
body. Consider man in his outward and worse part, and
you shall find that to be admirable, even to astonishment;
in respect of which the Psalmist cries out (Psal. cxxxix. 14),
'I am fearfully and wonderfully made: marvellous are thy
works; and that my soul knoweth right well.' The frame
of our bodies is so curiously wrought, and every part of
it so full of miracle, that Galen (who was otherwise backward enough to the belief of a God), when he had
anatomized man's body, and carefully surveyed the frame
of it, viewed the fitness and usefulness of every part of it,
and the many several intentions of every little vein, and
bone, and muscle, and the beauty of the whole; he fell
into a pang of devotion, and wrote a hymn to his Creator.
And those excellent books of his, *De Usu Partium,* 'of
the usefulness and convenient contrivance of every part of
the body,' are a most exact demonstration of the Divine
wisdom, which appears in the make of our body; of which
books, Gassendus saith, the whole work is writ with a kind
of enthusiasm. The wisdom of God, in the frame of our
bodies, very much appears by a curious consideration of
the several parts of it; but that requiring a very accurate
skill in anatomy, I choose rather wholly to forbear it,
than by my unskilfulness to be injurious to the Divine
wisdom.

But this *domicilium corporis,* 'the house of our body,'
though it be indeed a curious piece, yet it is nothing to
the noble inhabitant that dwells in it. The cabinet, though

it be exquisitely wrought, and very rich; yet it comes infinitely short in value of the jewel, that is hid and laid up in it. How does the glorious faculty of reason and understanding exalt us above the rest of the creatures! Nature hath not made that particular provision for man, which it hath made for other creatures, because it hath provided for him in general, in giving him a mind and reason. Man is not born clothed, nor armed with any considerable weapon for defence; but he hath reason and understanding to provide these things for himself; and this alone excels all the advantages of other creatures: he can keep himself warmer and safer; he can foresee dangers, and provide against them; he can provide weapons that are better than horns, and teeth, and paws, and, by the advantage of his reason, is too hard for all other creatures, and can defend himself against their violence.

If we consider the mind of man yet nearer, how many arguments of divinity are there in it! That there should be at once in our understandings distinct comprehensions of such variety of objects; that it should pass in its thoughts from heaven to earth in a moment, and retain the memory of things past, and take a prospect of the future, and look forward as far as eternity! Because we are familiar to ourselves, we cannot be strange and wonderful to our-selves; but the great miracle of the world is the mind of man, and the contrivance of it an eminent instance of God's wisdom.

Consider man with relation to the universe, and you shall find the wisdom of God doth appear, in that all things are made so useful for man, who was designed to be the chief inhabitant of this visible world, the guest whom God designed principally to entertain in this house which he built. Not that we are to think, that God hath so made all things for man, that he hath not made them at all for himself, and possibly for many other uses than we can imagine ; for we much overvalue ourselves, if we think them to be only for us; and we diminish the wisdom of God, in restraining it to one end: but the chief and principal end of many things is the use and service of man; and in reference to this end, you shall find that God hath made abundant and wise provision.

More particularly we will consider man, in his natural capacity as a part of the world. How many things are there in the world for the service and pleasure, for the use and delight of man, which, if man were not in the world, would be of little use? Man is by nature a contemplative creature, and God has furnished him with many objects to exercise his understanding upon, which would be so far useless and lost, if man were not. Who should observe the motions of the stars, and the courses of those heavenly bodies, and all the wonders of nature? Who should pry into the secret virtues of plants, and other natural things, if there were not in the world a creature endowed with reason and understanding? Would the beasts of the field study astronomy, or turn chymists, and try experiments in nature?

What variety of beautiful plants and flowers is there! which can be imagined to be of little other use but for the pleasure of man. And if man had not been, they would have lost their grace, and been trod down by the beasts of the field, without pity or observation; they would not have made them into garlands and nosegays. How many sorts of fruits are there which grow upon high trees out of the reach of beasts! and, indeed, they take no pleasure in them. What would all the vast bodies of trees have served for, if man had not been to build with them, and make dwellings of them? Of what use would all the mines of metal have been, and of coal, and the quarries of stone? would the mole have admired the fine gold? would the beasts of the forest have built themselves palaces, or would they have made fires in their dens?—*Sermon, The Wisdom of God in the Creation of the World.*

3. The Souls of Beasts.

But there is one difficulty in this: for it may be said, if sensitive perception be an argument of the soul's immateriality, and consequently immortality, then the souls of beasts will be immortal, as well as the souls of men. For answer to this, I shall say these things.

That the most general and common philosophy of the world, hath always acknowledged something in beasts besides their bodies, and that the faculty of sense and perception which is in them, is founded in a principle of a higher nature than matter. And as this was always the common philosophy of the world, so we find it to be a supposition of scripture, which frequently attributes souls to beasts as well as to men, though of a much inferior nature. And therefore those particular philosophers, who have denied any immaterial principle, or a soul to beasts, have also denied them to have sense, any more than a clock, or watch, or any other engine; and have imagined them to be nothing else but a finer and more complicated kind of engines, which by reason of the curiosity and tenderness of their frame, are more easily susceptible of all kind of motions and impressions from without, which impressions are the cause of all those actions that resemble those sensations which we men find in our selves: which is to say, that birds, and beasts, and fishes, are nothing

else but a more curious sort of puppets, which by certain
secret and hidden weights and springs do move up and
down, and counterfeit the actions of life and sense. This
I confess seems to me to be an odd kind of philosophy;
and it hath this vehement prejudice against it, that if this
were true, every man would have great cause to question
the reality of his own perceptions, for to all appearance
the sensations of beasts are as real as ours, and in many
things their senses much more exquisite than ours; and
if nothing can be a sufficient argument to a man, that
he is really endowed with sense, besides his own consciousness of it, then every man hath reason to doubt whether
all men in the world besides himself be not mere engines;
for no man hath any other evidence, that another man is
really endowed with sense, than he hath that brute creatures
are so; for they appear to us to see, and hear, and feel,
and smell, and taste things as truly and as exactly as any
man in the world does.—*Sermon, Of the Immortality of the
Soul.*

4. The Providence of God.

WE are, indeed, liable to many things in this world, which
have a great deal of evil and affliction in them, to poverty,
and pain, and reproach, and restraint, and the loss of our
friends and near relations; and these are great afflictions,
and very cross and distasteful to us; and therefore, when we
are in danger of any of these, and apprehend them to be
making towards us, we are apt to be anxious, and full of
trouble; and when they befall us, we are prone to censure
the providence of God, and to judge rashly concerning it,
as if all things were not ordered by it for the best: but we
should consider, that we are very ignorant and short-sighted
creatures, and see but a little way before us, are not able to

penetrate into the designs of God, and to look to the end of his providence.   We cannot (as *Solomon* expresseth it) *see the work of God from the beginning to the end;* whereas, if we saw the whole design of providence together, we should strangely admire the beauty and proportion of it, and should see it to be very wise and good.   And that which, upon the whole matter, and in the last issue and result of things, is most for our good, is certainly best, how grievous soever it may seem for the present.   Sickness caused by physic is, many times, more troublesome for the present, than the disease we take it for; but every wise man composeth himself to bear it as well as he can, because it is in order, to his health: the evils and afflictions of this life are the physic, and means of cure, which the providence of God is often necessitated to make use of; and if we did trust ourselves in the hands of this great physician, we should quietly submit to all the severities of his providence, in confidence that they would *all work together for our good.*

When children are under the government of parents, or the discipline of their teachers, they are apt to murmur at them, and think it very hard to be denied so many things which they desire, and to be constrained by severities to a great many things which are grievous and tedious to them: but the parent and the master know very well, that it is their ignorance and inconsiderateness which makes them to think so, and that when they come to years, and to understand themselves better, then they will acknowledge, that all that which gave them so much discontent, was really for their good, and that it was their childishness and folly, which made them to think otherwise, and that they had, in all probability, been undone, had they been indulged in their humour, and permitted in everything to have their own will; they had not wit and consideration enough to trust the discretion of their parents and governors, and to believe that even those things which were so displeasing to them, would at last tend to their good.

There is a far greater distance between the wisdom of God and men, and we are infinitely more ignorant and childish in respect of God, than our children are in respect of us; and being persuaded of this, we ought to reckon, that while we are in this world, under God's care and discipline, it is necessary for our good, that we be restrained in many things, which we eagerly desire: and suffer many things that are grievous to us; and that when we come to heaven, and are grown up to be men, and *have put away childish thoughts*, and are come to understand things as they truly are, and not *in a riddle*, and darkness, as we now do; then *the judgment of God will break forth as the light, and the righteousness* of all his dealings *as the noon-day;* then all the riddles of providence will be clearly expounded to us, and we shall see a plain reason for all those dispensations which were so much stumbled at, and acknowledge the great wisdom and goodness of them.—*Sermon, The Wisdom of God in his Providence.*

5. Public and Private Life.

ONE would be apt to wonder, that Nehemiah (Chap. v. Ver. 16, 17, 18.) should reckon a huge bill of fare and a vast number of promiscuous guests amongst his virtues and good deeds, for which he desires God to remember him. But upon better consideration, besides the bounty, and sometimes charity, of a great table, (provided there be nothing of vanity or ostentation in it) there may be exercised two very considerable virtues; one is, *temperance*, and the other *self-denial*, in a man's being contented for the sake of the public, to deny himself so much, as to sit down every day to a feast, and to eat continually in a crowd, and almost never to be alone, especially when, as it often happens, a great part of the company, that a man must have, is the company, that a man would not have. I doubt it will prove but a melancholy business, when a man comes to die, to have made a great noise and bustle in the world, and to have been known far and near; but all this while to have been hid and conceal'd from himself. It is a very odd and fantastical sort of life for a man to be continually from home, and most of all a stranger at his own house.

It is surely an uneasy thing to sit always in a frame, and to be perpetually upon a man's guard; not to be able to speak a careless word, or to use a negligent posture, without observation and censure.

Men are apt to think, that they, who are in highest places, and have the most power, have most liberty to say and do what they please. But it is quite otherwise, for they have the least liberty, because they are most observed. It is not mine own observation; a much wiser man (I mean Tully) says, *In maximâ quâque fortunâ minimum licere.* They, that are in the highest and greatest condition, have of all others the least liberty.

In a moderate station it is sufficient for a man to be indifferently wise. Such a man has the privilege to commit little follies and mistakes without having any great notice taken of them. But he, that lives in the light, *i. e.* in the view of all men, his actions are exposed to every body's observation and censure.

We ought to be glad, when those, that are fit for government, and called to it, are willing to take the burden of it upon them; yea, and to be very thankful to them too, that they will be at the pains, and can have the patience, to govern, and to live publicly. Therefore it is happy for the world, that there are some, who are born and bred up to, it; and that custom hath made it easy, or at least tolerable to them. Else who, that is wise, would undertake it, since it is certainly much easier of the two to obey a just and wise government (I had almost said any government) than to govern justly and wisely. Not that I find fault with those, who apply themselves to public business and affairs. They do well, and we are beholden to them. Some by their education, and being bred up to great things, and to be able to bear and manage great business with more ease than others, are peculiarly fitted to serve God and the public in this way: and they, that do, are worthy of double honour.

The advantage, which men have by a more devout, and retired, and contemplative life, is, that they are not distracted about many things; their minds and affections are set upon one thing; and the whole stream and force of their affections run one way. All their thoughts and endeavours are united in one great end and design, which makes their life all of a piece, and to be consistent with itself throughout.

Nothing but necessity, or the hope of doing more good than a man is capable of doing in a private station (which a modest man will not easily presume concerning himself) can recompense the trouble and uneasiness of a more public and busy life.

Besides that many men, if they understand themselves right, are at the best in a lower and more private condition, and make a much more awkward figure in a higher and more public station; when perhaps, if they had not been advanced, every one would have thought them fit and worthy to have been so.

And thus I have considered and compared impartially `

both these conditions, and upon the whole matter, without any thing either of disparagement or discouragement to the wise and great. · And in my poor judgment the more retired and private condition is the better and safer, the more easy and innocent, and consequently the more desirable of the two.

Those, who are fitted and contented to serve mankind in the management and government of public affairs, are called benefactors, and if they govern well, deserve to be called so, and to be so accounted, for denying themselves in their own ease, to do good to many.—*Commonplace Book.*

XIX.

JOHN DRYDEN.

1631—1700.

JOHN DRYDEN was born in 1631 at Aldwincle in Northampton-shire. He received the rudiments of education at Tichmarsh in his native county. He was afterwards admitted King's Schòlar at Westminster, and under the celebrated Dr. Busby made rapid progress in classical learning. From Westminster he was elected, 1650, Scholar ·of Trinity College, Cambridge. He took his degree in 1654, and three years later finally left his University for London, where he at once entered on the career of a literary man, which he pursued to the very end of his life. He occupied in his relations with men of genius, of rank, and political influence as high a station in the very foremost circles as literary reputation could gain for its owner.

Dryden attached himself to the Court party in the reigns of Charles II and James II, in the latter of which he left the Church of England for the Church of Rome. At the Revolution he was dismissed from the place of Poet Laureate, which he had held since the death of Sir William Davenant in 1668, and lived in comparative obscurity, though he was still patronized by several of the nobility. By the loss of this office he became again almost wholly dependent on literary labour for bread. Dryden was married to Lady Elizabeth Howard, daughter of the Earl of Berkshire, and had several children, none however of whom long survived him. He died in 1700, and was buried in Westminster Abbey.

Dryden was the most popular and (putting aside Milton, who belongs to an earlier period) most eminent poet of the latter half of the seventeenth century. His works consist of plays, satires, translations, and occasional poems. Of these, the plays are much the most voluminous, and in their time were doubtless considered the most important; but later generations have bestowed very little attention on them. They, however, gave occasion to several of those compositions which have made him distinguished as a prose writer, critical prefaces, explaining the nature of the works they introduce, and vindications, rebutting the attacks of literary rivals or political opponents. These prose pieces have had very warm admirers, including Gray and Charles James Fox; and are characterised by Johnson in words that may be worth quoting: 'Criticism, either didactic or defensive, occupies almost all his prose, except those pages which he has devoted to his patrons: but none of his prefaces were ever thought tedious. They have not the formality of a settled style, in which the first half of the sentence betrays the other. The clauses are never balanced, nor the periods modelled; every word seems to drop by chance, though it falls into its proper place. Nothing is cold or languid; the whole is airy, animated, and vigorous; what is little is gay; what is great is splendid. He may be thought to mention himself too frequently; but while he forces himself upon our esteem, we cannot refuse him to stand high in his own. Everything is excused by the play of images and the sprightliness of expression. Though all is easy, nothing is feeble; though all seems careless, there is nothing harsh; and though, since his earlier works, more than a century has passed, they have nothing yet uncouth or obsolete.' Perhaps the only abatements that need be made from this elaborate eulogy are contained in the admissions that in his prose writings, as in his poems, he is sometimes coarse and vulgar, that 'the play of images' of which Johnson speaks, arises not so much from a fervid imagination as from a well-stored mind familiar with its own resources, and that now, at the distance of a second century, the absence of uncouth or obsolete expressions cannot be affirmed quite so unhesitatingly as when Johnson wrote.

1. Great Men as Poets and Patrons.

DIONYSIUS and Nero had the same longing, but with all their power they could never bring their business well about. 'Tis true, they proclaimed themselves poets by sound of trumpet; and poets they were, upon pain of death to any man who durst call them otherwise. The audience had a fine time on't, you may imagine; they sat in a bodily fear, and looked as demurely as they could: for it was a hanging matter to laugh unseasonably; and the tyrants were suspicious, as they had reason, that their subjects had them in the wind; so, every man, in his own defence, set as good a face upon the business as he could. It was known beforehand that the monarchs were to be crowned laureats; but when the show was over, and an honest man was suffered to depart quietly, he took out his laughter which he had stifled; with a firm resolution never more to see an emperor's play, though he had been ten years a making it. In the meantime the true poets were they who made the best markets, for they had wit enough to yield the prize with a good grace, and not contend with him who had thirty legions. They were sure to be rewarded, if they confessed themselves bad writers, and that was somewhat better than to be martyrs for their reputation. Lucan's example was enough to teach them manners; and after he was put to death, for overcoming Nero, the emperor carried it without dispute for the best poet in his dominions. No man was ambitious of that grinning honour; for if he heard the malicious trumpeter proclaiming his name before his betters, he knew there was but one way with him. Mecaenas took another course, and we know he was more than a great man, for he was witty too: but finding himself far gone in poetry, which Seneca assures us was not his talent, he

thought it his best way to be well with Virgil and with
Horace; that at least he might be a poet at the second
hand: and we see how happily it has succeeded with him;
for his own bad poetry is forgotten, and their panegyrics
of him still remain.   But they who should be our patrons,
are for no such expensive ways to fame; they have much of
the poetry of Mecaenas, but little of his liberality.   They
are for persecuting Horace and Virgil, in the persons of
their successors; for such is every man, who has any part
of their soul and fire, though in a less degree.   Some of
their little zanies yet go farther; for they are persecutors
even of Horace himself, as far as they are able, by their
ignorant and vile imitations of him; by making an unjust
use of his authority, and turning his artillery against his
friends.   But how would he disdain to be copied by such
hands!   I dare answer for him, he would be more uneasy
in their company, than he was with Crispinus, their fore-
father, in the Holy Way; and would no more have allowed
them a place amongst the critics, than he would Demetrius
the mimic, and Tigellius the buffoon;

> ————Demetri, teque, Tigelli,
> Discipularum inter jubeo plorare cathedras.

With what scorn would he look down upon such miserable
translators, who make doggrel of his Latin, mistake his
meaning, misapply his censures, and often contradict their
own?   He is fixed as a landmark to set out the bounds
of poetry:

> ————Saxum antiquum, ingens,——
> Limes agro positus, litem ut discerneret arvis.

But other arms than theirs, and other sinews are required,
to raise the weight of such an author; and when they would
toss him against their enemies,

Genua labant, gelirus cancrevit frigore sanguis.
Tum lapis ipse, viri vacuum per inane volutus,
Nec spatium evasit totum, nec pertulit ictum.
Preface to 'All for Love.'

2. Horace and Juvenal.

THIS last consideration seems to incline the balance on
the side of Horace, and to give him the preference to
Juvenal, not only in profit, but in pleasure. But, after
all, I must confess, that the delight which Horace gives
me is but languishing. Be pleased still to understand,
that I speak of my own taste only: he may ravish other
men; but I am too stupid and insensible to be tickled.
Where he barely grins himself, and, as Scaliger says, only
shows his white teeth, he cannot provoke me to any laughter.
His urbanity, that is, his good manners, are to be commended, but his wit is faint; and his salt, if I may dare to
say so, almost insipid. Juvenal is of a more vigorous and
masculine wit; he gives me as much pleasure as I can bear;
he fully satisfies my expectation; he treats his subject home;
his spleen is raised, and he raises mine: I have the
pleasure of concernment in all he says; he drives his
reader along with him; and when he is at the end of his
way, I willingly stop with him. If he went another stage,
it would be too far: it would make a journey of a progress,
and turn delight into fatigue. When he gives over, it is a
sign the subject is exhausted, and the wit of man can carry
it no farther. If a fault can be justly found in him, it is,
that he is sometimes too luxuriant, too redundant; says
more than he needs, like my friend the *Plain Dealer*, but
never more than pleases. Add to this, that his thoughts
are as just as those of Horace, and much more elevated.
His expressions are sonorous and more noble; his verse

more numerous, and his words are suitable to his thoughts, sublime and lofty. All these contribute to the pleasure of the reader; and the greater the soul of him who reads, his transports are the greater. Horace is always on the amble, Juvenal on the gallop; but his way is perpetually on carpet-ground. He goes with more impetuosity than Horace, but as securely; and the swiftness adds a more lively agitation to the spirits.—*Essay on Satire.*

3. Private Greatness and Ambition.

To be nobly born, and of an ancient family, is in the extremes of fortune, either good or bad; for virtue and descent are no inheritance. A long series of ancestors shews the native with great advantage at the first; but, if he any way degenerate from his line, the least spot is visible on ermine. But, to preserve this whiteness in its original purity, you, my lord, have, like that ermine, forsaken the common tract of business, which is not always clean: you have chosen for yourself a private greatness, and will not be polluted with ambition. It has been observed in former times, that none have been so greedy of employments, and of managing the public, as they who have least deserved their stations. But such only merit to be called patriots, under whom we see their country flourish. I have laughed sometimes, (for who would always be a Heraclitus?) when I have reflected on those men, who from time to time have shot themselves into the world. I have seen many successions of them; some bolting out upon the stage with vast applause, and others hissed off, and quitting it with disgrace. But, while they were in action, I have constantly observed, that they seemed desirous to retreat from business: greatness, they said, was nauseous, and a crowd was troublesome:

a quiet privacy was their ambition. Some few of them, I believe, said this in earnest, and were making a provision against future want, that they might enjoy their age with ease. They saw the happiness of a private life, and promised to themselves a blessing, which every day it was in their power to possess. But they deferred it, and lingered still at court, because they thought they had not yet enough to make them happy: they would have more, and laid in, to make their solitude. luxurious :—a wretched philosophy, which Epicurus never taught them in his garden. They loved the prospect of this quiet in reversion, but were not willing to have it in possession: they would first be old, and make as sure of health and life, as if both of them were at their dispose. But put them to the necessity of a present choice, and they preferred continuance in power; like the wretch who called Death to his assistance, but refused him when he came.—*Dedication of the Georgics to the Earl of Chesterfield.*

4. The Italian Language.

IT is almost needless to speak anything of that noble language, in which this musical drama was first invented and performed. All, who are conversant in the Italian, cannot but observe, that it is the softest, the sweetest, the most harmonious, not only of any modern tongue, but even beyond any of the learned. It seems indeed to have been invented for the sake of poetry and music ; the vowels are so abounding in all words, especially in terminations of them, that, excepting some few monosyllables, the whole language ends in them. Then the pronunciation is so manly, and so sonorous, that their very speaking has more of music in it than Dutch poetry and song. It has withal derived so much copiousness and eloquence from the Greek and Latin, in the composition of words, and the formation of them, that if, after all, we must call it barbarous, it is the most beautiful and most learned of any barbarism in modern tongues; and we may, at least, as justly praise it, as Pyrrhus did the Roman discipline and martial order, that it was of barbarians, (for so the Greeks called all other nations,) but had nothing in it of barbarity. This language has in a manner been refined and purified from the Gothic ever since the time of Dante, which is above four hundred years ago; and the French, who now cast a longing eye to their country, are not less ambitious to possess their elegance in poetry and music; in both which they labour at impossibilities. It is true, indeed, they have reformed their tongue, and brought both their prose and poetry to a standard; the sweetness, as well as the purity, is much improved, by throwing off the unnecessary consonants, which made their spelling tedious, and their pronunciation harsh: but, after all, as nothing can be improved beyond its own *species*, or farther than its original nature will allow; as an ill voice, though ever so thoroughly instructed in the rules of music, can never be brought to sing harmoniously, nor many an honest critic ever arrive to be a good poet; so neither can the natural harshness of the French, or their perpetual ill accent, be ever refined into perfect harmony like the Italian. The English has yet more natural disadvantages than the French; our original Teutonic, consisting most in monosyllables, and those incumbered with consonants, cannot possibly be freed from those inconveniences. The rest of our words, which are derived from the Latin chiefly, and the French, with some small sprinklings of Greek, Italian, and Spanish, are some relief in poetry, and help us to soften our uncouth numbers; which, together with our English genius, incomparably beyond the trifling of the French, in all the nobler parts of verse, will justly give us the pre-eminence. But, on the other hand, the effeminacy of our pronunciation, (a defect common to us and to the Danes,) and our scarcity of female rhymes, have left the advantage of musical composition for songs, though not for recitative, to our neighbours.—*Preface to Albion and Albanius.*

5. The Office of the Poet.

But these little critics do not well consider what is the work of a poet, and what the graces of a poem: the story is the least part of either: I mean the foundation of it, before it is modelled by the art of him who writes it; who forms it with more care, by exposing only the beautiful parts of it to view, than a skilful lapidary sets a jewel. On this foundation of the story, the characters are raised: and, since no story can afford characters enough for the variety of the English stage, it follows, that it is to be altered and enlarged with new persons, accidents, and designs, which will almost make it new. When this is done, the forming it into acts and scenes, disposing of actions and passions into their proper places, and beautifying both with descriptions, similitudes, and propriety of language, is the principal employment of the poet; as being the largest field of fancy, which is the principal quality required in him: for so much the word ποιητὴs implies. Judgment, indeed, is necessary in him; but it is fancy that gives the life-touches, and the secret graces to it; especially in serious plays, which depend not much on observation. For, to write humour in comedy, (which is the theft of poets from mankind) little of fancy is required; the poet observes only what is ridiculous and pleasant folly, and by judging exactly what is so, he pleases in the representation of it.

T 2

But, in general, the employment of a poet is like that of a curious gunsmith, or watchmaker: the iron or silver is not his own; but they are the least part of that which gives the value: the price lies wholly in the workmanship. And he who works dully on a story, without moving laughter in a comedy, or raising concernment in a serious play, is no more to be accounted a good poet, than a gunsmith of the Minories is to be compared with the best workman of the town.— *Preface to the Mock Astrologer.*

6. Blank Verse and Rhyme.

I know not whether I have been so careful of the plot and language as I ought; but, for the latter, I have endeavoured to write English, as near as I could distinguish it from the tongue of pedants, and that of affected travellers. Only I am sorry, that (speaking so noble a language as we do) we have not a more certain measure of it, as they have in France, where they have an academy erected for that purpose, and endowed with large privileges by the present king. I wish we might at length leave to borrow words from other nations, which is now a wantonness in us, not a necessity; but so long as some affect to speak them, there will not want others, who will have the boldness to write them.

But I fear, lest, defending the received words, I shall be accused for following the new way, I mean, of writing scenes in verse. Though, to speak properly, it is not so much a new way amongst us, as an old way new revived; for, many years before Shakspeare's plays, was the tragedy of Queen Gorboduc, in English verse, written by that famous Lord Buckhurst, afterwards earl of Dorset. . . . . . But, supposing our countrymen had not received this writing till of late; shall we oppose ourselves to the most polished and civilised nations of Europe? Shall we, with the same singularity, oppose the world in this, as most of us do in pronouncing Latin? Or do we desire that the brand, which Barclay has (I hope unjustly) laid upon the English, should still continue? *Angli suos ac sua omnia impense mirantur; cæteras nationes despectui habent.* All the Spanish and Italian tragedies, I have yet seen, are writ in rhyme. For the French, I do not name them, because it is the fate of our countrymen to admit little of theirs among us, but the basest of their men, the extravagancies of their fashions, and the frippery of their merchandise. Shakspeare (who, with some errors not to be avoided in that age, had undoubtedly a larger soul of poesy than ever any of our nation) was the first who, to shun the pains of continual rhyming, invented that kind of writing which we call blank verse, but the French, more properly, *prose mesuré;* into which the English tongue so naturally slides, that, in writing prose, it is hardly to be avoided. And therefore, I admire some men should perpetually stumble in a way so easy, and, inverting the order of their words, constantly close their lines with verbs, which, though commended sometimes in writing Latin, yet we were whipt at Westminster if we used it twice together. I knew some, who, if they were to write in blank verse, *Sir, I ask your pardon,* would think it sounded more heroically to write, *Sir, I your pardon ask.* I should judge him to have little command of English, whom the necessity of a rhyme should force often upon this rock; though sometimes it cannot easily be avoided; and indeed this is the only inconvenience with which rhyme can be charged. This is that which makes them say, rhyme is not natural, it being only so, when the poet either makes a vicious choice of words, or places them, for rhyme sake, so unnaturally as no man would in ordinary speaking; but when it is so judiciously ordered, that the first word in the verse

seems to beget the second, and that the next, till that becomes
the last word in the line, which, in the negligence of prose,
would be so; it must then be granted, rhyme has all the
advantages of prose, besides its own. . . . . .

The advantages which rhyme has over blank verse are so
many, that it were lost time to name them. Sir Philip Sidney,
in his Defence of Poesy, gives us one, which, in my opinion,
is not the least considerable; I mean the help it brings to
memory, which rhyme so knits up, by the affinity of sounds, '
that, by remembering the last word in one line, we often
call to mind both the verses. Then, in the quickness of
repartees (which in discoursive scenes fall very often), it has
so particular a grace, and is so aptly suited to them, that the
sudden smartness of the answer, and the sweetness of the
rhyme, set off the beauty of each other. But that benefit
which I consider most in it, because I have not seldom found
it, is, that it bounds and circumscribes the fancy. For imagination in a poet is a faculty so wild and lawless, that, like
an high-ranging spaniel, it must have clogs tied to it, lest it
outrun the judgment. The great easiness of blank verse
renders the poet too luxuriant; he is tempted to say many
things, which might better be omitted, or at least shut up in
fewer words; but when the difficulty of artful rhyming is
interposed, where the poet commonly confines his sense to
his couplet, and must contrive that sense into such words,
that the rhyme shall naturally follow them, not they the
rhyme; the fancy then gives leisure to the judgment to come
in, which, seeing so heavy a tax imposed, is ready to cut off
all unnecessary expences. This last consideration has already
answered an objection which some have made, that rhyme
is only an embroidery of sense, to make that, which is ordinary in itself, pass for excellent with less examination. But
certainly, that, which most regulates the fancy, and gives the

judgment its busiest employment, is like to bring forth the richest and clearest thoughts. The poet examines that most, which he produceth with the greatest leisure, and which, he knows, must pass the severest test of the audience, because they are aptest to have it ever in their memory; as the stomach makes the best concoction when it strictly embraces the nourishment, and takes account of every little particle as it passes through. But, as the best medicines may lose their virtue, by being ill applied, so is it with verse, if a fit subject be not chosen for it.—*Dedication to the Rival Ladies.*

XX.

JOHN LOCKE.

1632—1704.

JOHN LOCKE was born at Wrington in Somersetshire in 1632. He was educated at Westminster, from which he was removed to a Studentship at Christ Church, Oxford, where he was greatly distinguished no less by industry than by superior ability. The writings of Descartes appear early to have excited his interest in the study of philosophy. After having taken the degree of M.A. in 1658 he applied himself to the study of Medicine, but his health prevented his pursuing that profession. In 1666 he formed the acquaintance of Lord Ashley, afterwards Earl of Shaftesbury, to whose fortunes he was attached for many years, sharing his prosperity and his disgrace, and for a time acting first as tutor to his son, and then to his grandson the future author of the *Characteristics*. Locke commenced his famous *Essay Concerning Human Understanding* in 1670, but it was not till 1687 that he was able to complete it. It attracted great and immediate attention, not only in philosophical circles, but in the wider world of thoughtful readers. It was followed in the next few years by the *Letters on Toleration* and the *Treatises on Government* and *Thoughts on Education*, as well as by several minor essays in vindication of opinions advanced in his larger works. He suffered severely from asthma during the later part of his life, and lived at Oates in the retirement of Sir Francis Masham's house for the last fourteen years. He died in 1704 in the seventy-third year of his age.

Locke is one of the most prominent of our philosophical and political authors; there is probably no writer on philosophy who has produced such a broad and solid effect on the mind of the English people. Few have turned their attention to metaphysical enquiries without reading his *Essay Concerning Human Under-*

standing, which has lent to such enquiries whatever popularity they possess. D'Alembert says that Locke created the science of Metaphysics in somewhat the same way as Newton created that of Physics; and his enquiry into the origin, development and combination of our thoughts justly entitle him to be called the founder of Psychology in England. There is scarcely any English writer whose works bear such an impress of originality, power, patient sagacity, and good sense. The style of Locke has fine qualities, but is too incorrect to be taken as a model of English language. It is homely, racy and masculine, though wanting in philosophical precision and sometimes too idiomatic and colloquial, or too indefinite and figurative for the abstruse subjects with which he has to deal.

---

1. The Opening of the Essay of Human Understanding.

SINCE it is the understanding, that sets man above the rest of sensible beings, and gives him all the advantage and dominion which he has over them; it is certainly a subject, even for its nobleness, worth our labour to inquire into. The understanding, like the eye, whilst it makes us see and perceive all other things, takes no notice of itself; and it requires art and pains to set it at a distance, and make it its own object. But, whatever be the difficulties that lie in the way of this inquiry; whatever it be, that keeps us so much in the dark to ourselves; sure I am, that all the light we can let in upon our own minds, all the acquaintance we can make with our own understandings, will not only be very pleasant, but bring us great advantage in directing our thoughts in search of other things.

This, therefore, being my purpose; to inquire into the original, certainty, and extent of human knowledge, together with the grounds and degrees of belief, opinion and assent— I shall not at present meddle with the physical consideration of the mind, or trouble myself to examine, wherein its essence consists, or by what motions of our spirits, or alterations of our bodies, we come to have any sensation by our organs, or any ideas in our understandings; and whether those ideas do, in their formation, any, or all of them, depend on matter or no. These are speculations, which, however curious and entertaining, I shall decline, as lying out of my way in the design I am now upon. It shall suffice to my present purpose, to consider the discerning faculties of a man, as they are employed about the objects which they have to do with : and I shall imagine I have not wholly misemployed myself in the thoughts I shall have on this occasion, if, in this historical, plain method, I can give any account of the ways whereby our understandings come to attain those notions of things we have, and can set down any measures of the certainty of our knowledge, or the grounds of those persuasions, which are to be found amongst men, so various, different, and wholly contradictory; and yet asserted, somewhere or other, with such assurance and confidence, that he that shall take a view of the opinions of mankind, observe their opposition, and at the same time consider the fondness and devotion wherewith they are embraced, the resolution and eagerness wherewith they are maintained—may perhaps have reason to suspect, that either there is no such thing as truth at all, or that mankind hath no sufficient means to attain a certain knowledge of it.

If, by this inquiry into the nature of the understanding, I can discover the powers thereof, how far they reach, to what things they are in any degree proportionate, and where they fail us; I suppose it may be of use to prevail with the busy mind of man, to be more cautious in meddling with things exceeding its comprehension; to stop when it is at the utmost extent of its tether; and to sit down in a quiet ignorance of those things which, upon examination, are found to be beyond the reach of our capacities. ᐧ We should not then perhaps be so forward, out of an affectation of an universal knowledge, to raise questions, and perplex ourselves and others with disputes about things to which our understandings are not suited, and of which we cannot frame in our minds any clear or distinct perceptions, or whereof (as it has perhaps too often happened) we have not any notions at all. If we can find out how far the understanding can extend its view, how far it has faculties to attain certainty, and in what cases it can only judge and guess, we may learn to content ourselves with what is attainable by us in this state.

For, though the comprehension of our understandings comes exceeding short of the vast extent of things; yet we shall have cause enough to magnify the bountiful Author of our being, for that proportion and degree of knowledge he has bestowed on us, so far above all the rest of the inhabitants of our mansion. Men have reason to be well satisfied with what God hath thought fit for them, since he hath given them (as St. Peter says) πάντα πρὸς ζωὴν καὶ εὐσέβειαν, whatsoever is necessary for the conveniences of life and information of virtue; and has put within the reach of their discovery the comfortable provision for this life, and the way that leads to a better. How short soever their knowledge may come of an universal or perfect comprehension of whatsoever is, it yet secures their great concernments, that they have light enough to lead them to the knowledge of their Maker, and the sight of their own duties. Men may find matter sufficient to busy their heads, and employ their hands with variety, delight, and satisfaction, if they will not boldly quarrel with their own constitution, and throw away the blessings their hands are filled with, because they are not big enough to grasp everything. We shall not have much reason to complain of the narrowness of our minds, if we will but employ them about what may be of use to us; for of that they are very capable : and it will be an unpardonable, as well as childish peevishness, if we undervalue the advantages of our knowledge, and neglect to improve it to the ends for which it was given us, because there are some things that are set out of the reach of it. It will be no excuse to an idle and untoward servant, who would not attend his business by candle-light, to plead that he had not broad sunshine. The candle that is set up in us, shines bright enough for all our purposes. The discoveries we can make with this, ought to satisfy us : and we shall then use our understandings right, when we entertain all objects in that way and proportion that they are suited to our faculties, and upon those grounds they are capable of being proposed to us ; and not peremptorily or intemperately require demonstration, and demand certainty, where probability only is to be had, and which is sufficient to govern all our concernments. If we will disbelieve everything, because we cannot certainly know all things, we shall do much what as wisely as he, who would not use his legs, but sit still and perish, because he had no wings to fly.

When we know our own strength, we shall the better know what to undertake with hopes of success; and when we have well surveyed the powers of our own minds, and made some estimate what we may expect from them, we shall not be inclined either to sit still, and not set our thoughts on work at all, in despair of knowing anything; or, on the other side, question everything, and disclaim all knowledge, because some things are not to be understood. It is of great use to the sailor, to know the length of his line, though he cannot with it fathom all the depths of the ocean. It is well he knows that it is long enough to reach the bottom, at such places as are necessary to direct his voyage, and caution him against running upon shoals that may ruin him. Our business here is not to know all things, but those which concern our conduct. If we can find out those measures, whereby a rational creature, put in that state in which man is in this world, may, and ought to govern his opinions, and actions depending thereon, we need not to be troubled that some other things escape our knowledge.—*Essay Concerning Human Understanding.*

2. Opposition to Government sometimes desirable.

THE end of government is the good of mankind: and which is best for mankind, that the people should be always exposed to the boundless will of tyranny; or that the rulers should be sometimes liable to be opposed, when they grow exorbitant in the use of their power, and employ it for the destruction, and not the preservation of the properties of their people?

Nor let any one say, that mischief can arise from hence, as often as it shall please a busy head, or turbulent spirit, to desire the alteration of the government. It is true, such men may stir, whenever they please; but it will be only to their own just ruin and perdition : for till the mischief be grown general, and the ill designs of the rulers become visible, or their attempts sensible to the greater part, the people, who are more disposed to suffer than right themselves by resistance, are not apt to stir. The examples of particular injustice or oppression, of here and there an unfortunate man, moves them not. But if they universally have a persuasion, grounded upon manifest evidence, that designs are carrying on against their liberties, and the general course and tendency of things cannot but give them strong suspicions of the evil intention of their governors, who is to be blamed for it? Who can help it, if they, who might avoid it, bring themselves into this suspicion? Are the people to be blamed, if they have the sense of rational creatures, and can think of things no otherwise than as they find and feel them? And is it not rather their fault, who put things into such a posture, that they would not have them thought to be as they are? I grant, that the pride, ambition, and turbulency of private men, have sometimes caused great disorders in commonwealths, and factions have been fatal to states and kingdoms. But whether the mischief hath oftener begun in the people's wantonness, and a desire to cast off the lawful authority of their rulers, or in the rulers' insolence, and endeavours to get and exercise an arbitrary power over their people; whether oppression, or disobedience, gave the first rise to the disorder; I leave it to impartial history to determine. This I am sure, whoever, either ruler or subject, by force goes about to invade the rights of either prince or people, and lays the foundation for overturning the constitution and frame of any just government; is highly guilty of the greatest crime, I think, a man is capable of; being to answer for all those mischiefs of blood, rapine, and desolation, which the breaking to pieces of governments brings on a country. And he who does it, is justly to be esteemed the common enemy and pest of mankind, and is to be treated accordingly.—*Essay concerning the true Original, Extent and End of Civil Government.*

3.　Of Recreation.

RECREATION is as necessary as labour or food: but because there can be no recreation without delight, which depends not always on reason, but oftener on fancy, it must be permitted children not only to divert themselves, but to do it after their own fashion, provided it be innocently, and without prejudice to their health; and therefore in this case they should not be denied, if they proposed any particular kind of recreation; though I think, in a well-ordered education, they will seldom be brought to the necessity of asking any such liberty. Care should be taken, that what is of advantage to them, they should always do with delight; and, before they are wearied with one, they should be timely diverted to some other useful employment. But if they are not yet brought to that degree of perfection, that one way of improvement can be made a recreation to them, they must be let loose to the childish play they fancy; which they should be weaned from, by being made surfeited of it: but from things of use, that they are employed in, they should always be sent away with an appetite; at least be dismissed before they are tired, and grow quite sick of it; that so they may return to it again, as to a pleasure that diverts them. For you must never think them set right, till they can find delight in the practice of laudable things; and the useful exercises of the body and mind, taking their turns, make their lives and improvement pleasant in a continued train of recreations, wherein the wearied part is constantly relieved and refreshed. Whether this can be done in every temper, or whether tutors and parents will be at the pains, and have the discretion and patience to bring them to this, I know not; but that it may be done in most children, if a right course be taken to raise in them the desire of credit, esteem, and reputation, I do not at all doubt. And when they have so much true life put into them, they may freely be talked with, about what most delights them, and be directed, or let loose to it, so that they may perceive that they are beloved and cherished, and that those under whose tuition they are,

are not enemies to their satisfaction. Such a management will make them in love with the hand that directs them, and the virtue they are directed to. . . . Our short lives will not serve us for the attainment of all things; nor can our minds be always intent on something to be learned. The weakness of our constitutions, both of mind and body, requires that we should be often unbent: and he that will make a good use of any part of his life, must allow a large portion of it to recreation. At least this must not be denied to young people, unless, whilst you with too much haste make them old, you have the displeasure to set them in their graves, or a second childhood, sooner than you could wish. And therefore I think, that the time and pains allotted to serious improvements, should be employed about things of most use and consequence, and that too in the methods the most easy and short, that could be at any rate obtained; and perhaps, as I have above said, it would be none of the least secrets of education, to make the exercises in the body and the mind, the recreation one to another. I doubt not but that something might be done in it, by a prudent man, that would well consider the temper and inclination of his pupil. For he that is wearied either with study or dancing, does not desire presently to go to sleep; but to do something else which may divert and delight him. But this must be always remembered, that nothing can come into the account of recreation, that is not done with delight. . . .

I have one thing more to add, which as soon as I mention, I shall run the danger of being suspected to have forgot what I am about, and what I have above written concerning education, all tending towards a gentleman's calling, with which a trade seems wholly to be inconsistent. And yet, I cannot forbear to say, I would have him learn a trade, a manual trade; nay, two or three, but one more particularly.

The busy inclination of children being always to be directed to something that may be useful to them, the advantages proposed from what they are set about may be considered of two kinds; 1. Where the skill itself, that is got by exercise, is worth the having. Thus skill not only in languages,, and learned sciences, but in painting, turning, gardening, tempering and working in iron, and all other useful arts, is worth the having. 2. Where the exercise itself, without any consideration, is necessary or useful for health. Knowledge in some things is so necessary to be got by children, whilst they are young, that some part of their time is to be allotted to their improvement in them, though those employments contribute nothing at all to their health: such as reading, and writing, and all other sedentary studies, for the cultivating of the mind, which unavoidably take up a great part of gentlemen's time, quite from their cradles. Other manual arts, which are both got and exercised by labour, do many of them, by that exercise, not only increase our dexterity and skill, but contribute to our health too; especially such as employ us in the open air. In these, then, health and improvement may be joined together; and of these should some fit ones be chosen, to be made the recreations of one, whose chief business is with books and study. In this choice, the age and inclination of the person is to be considered, and constraint always to be avoided in bringing him to it. For command and force may often create, but can never cure aversion; and whatever any one is brought to by compulsion, he will leave as soon as he can, and be little profited, and less recreated by, whilst he is at it. . . .

Nor let it be thought, that I mistake, when I call these or the like exercises of manual arts, diversions or recreations: for recreation is not being idle, (as every one may

observe) but easing the wearied part by change of business:
and he that thinks diversion may not lie in hard and painful
labour, forgets the early rising, hard riding, heat, cold and
hunger of huntsmen, which is yet known to be the constant
recreation of men of the greatest condition.   Delving,
planting, inoculating, or any the like profitable employments,
would be no less a diversion, than any of the idle sports in
fashion, if men could but be brought to delight in them,
which custom and skill in a trade will quickly bring any one
to do.   And I doubt not but there are to be found those,
who, being frequently called to cards, or any other play,
by those they could not refuse, have been more tired with
these recreations, than with any the most serious employment of life; though the play has been such as they have
naturally had no aversion to, and with which they could
willingly sometimes divert themselves. . . .

Recreation belongs not to people who are strangers to
business, and are not wasted and wearied with the employment of their calling.   The skill should be, so to order their
time of recreation, that it may relax and refresh the part
that has been exercised, and is tired; and yet do something,
which, besides the present delight and ease, may produce
what will afterwards be profitable.   It has been nothing but
vanity and pride of greatness and riches, that has brought
unprofitable and dangerous pastimes (as they are called) into
fashion, and persuaded people into a belief, that the learning
or putting their hands to any thing that was useful, could
not be a diversion fit for a gentleman.   This has been that
which has given cards, dice, and drinking, so much credit in
the world; and a great many throw away their spare hours
in them, through the prevalency of custom, and want of
some better employment to fill up the vacancy of leisure,
more than from any real delight is to be found in them.

They cannot bear the dead weight of unemployed time lying upon their hands, nor the uneasiness it is to do nothing at all; and having never learned any laudable manual art, wherewith to divert themselves, they have recourse to those foolish or ill ways in use, to help off their time, which a rational man, till corrupted by custom, could find very little pleasure in.

I say not this, that I would never have a young gentleman accommodate himself to the innocent diversions in fashion, amongst those of his age and condition. I am so far from having him austere and morose to that degree, that I would persuade him to more than ordinary complaisance for all the gaieties and diversions of those he converses with, and be averse or testy in nothing they should desire of him, that might become a gentleman, and an honest man : though, as to cards and dice, I think the safest and best way is never to learn any play upon them, and so to be incapacitated for those dangerous temptations, and incroaching waters of useful time. But allowance being made for idle and jovial conversation, and all fashionable becoming recreations, I say, a young man will have time enough, from his serious and main business, to learn almost any trade. It is for want of application, and not of leisure, that men are not skilful in more arts than one; and an hour in a day, constantly employed in such a way of diversion, will carry a man in a short time a great deal farther than he can imagine : which, if it were of no other use but to drive the common, vicious, useless, and dangerous pastimes out of fashion, and to shew there was no need of them, would deserve to be encouraged. If men from their youth were weaned from that sauntering humour, wherein some, out of custom, let a good part of their lives run uselessly away, without either business or recreation; they would find time enough to acquire dexterity and skill in hundreds of things, which, though remote from their proper callings, would not at all interfere with them. And therefore, I think, for this, as well as other reasons before-mentioned, a lazy, listless humour, that idly dreams away the days, is of all others the least to be indulged, or permitted in young people. It is the proper state of one sick, and out of order in his health, and is tolerable in nobody else, of what age or condition soever. . . .

Amongst the great variety there is of ingenious manual arts, it will be impossible that no one should be found to please and delight him, unless he be either idle or debauched, which is not to be supposed in a right way of education. And since he cannot be always employed in study, reading, and conversation, there will be many an hour, besides what his exercises will take up, which, if not spent this way, will be spent worse. For, I conclude, a young man will seldom desire to sit perfectly still and idle; or if he does, it is a fault that ought to be mended.—*Some Thoughts concerning Education.*

4. Memory.

ATTENTION and repetition help much to the fixing any ideas in the memory: but those which naturally at first make the deepest and most lasting impression, are those which are accompanied with pleasure or pain. The great business of the senses being to make us take notice of what hurts or advantages the body, it is wisely ordered by nature (as has been shewn) that pain should accompany the reception of several ideas; which supplying the place of consideration and reasoning in children, and acting quicker than consideration in grown men, makes both the old and young avoid painful objects, with that haste which is necessary for their preservation; and, in both, settles in the memory a caution for the future.

Concerning the several degrees of lasting, wherewith ideas are imprinted on the memory, we may observe, that some of them have been produced in the understanding, by an object affecting the senses once only, and no more than once; others that have more than once offered themselves to the senses, have yet been taken little notice of: the mind either heedless, as in children, or otherwise employed, as in men, intent only on one thing, not setting the stamp deep into itself. And in some, where they are set on with care and repeated impressions, either through the temper of the body, or some other fault, the memory is very weak. In all these cases, ideas in the mind quickly fade, and often vanish quite out of the understanding, leaving no more footsteps or remaining characters of themselves, than shadows do flying over fields of corn; and the mind is as void of them, as if they had never been there. . . . .

The memory of some, it is true, is very tenacious, even to a miracle: but yet there seems to be a constant decay of all our ideas, even of those which are struck deepest, and in minds the most retentive; so that if they be not sometimes renewed by repeated exercise of the senses, or reflection on those kind of objects which at first occasioned them, the print wears out, and at last there remains nothing to be seen. Thus the ideas, as well as children, of our youth, often die before us: and our minds represent to us those tombs, to which we are approaching; where though the brass and marble remain, yet the inscriptions are effaced by time, and the imagery moulders away. The pictures drawn in our minds are laid in fading colours, and, if not sometimes refreshed, vanish and disappear. How much the constitution of our bodies and the make of our animal spirits are concerned in this, and whether the temper of the brain makes this difference, that in some it retains the characters drawn on it like marble, in others like free-stone, and in others little better than sand, I shall not here enquire: though it may seem probable, that the constitution of the body does sometimes influence the memory; since we oftentimes find a disease quite strip the mind of all its ideas, and the flames of a fever in a few days calcine all those images to dust and confusion, which seemed to be as lasting as if graved in marble. . . .

Memory, in an intellectual creature, is necessary in the next degree to perception. It is of so great moment, that where it is wanting, all the rest of our faculties are in a great measure useless: and we in our thoughts, reasonings, and knowledge, could not proceed beyond present objects, were it not for the assistance of our memories, wherein there may be two defects.

First, That it loses the idea quite, and so far it pro-duces perfect ignorance. For since we can know nothing farther than we have the idea of it, when that is gone, we are in perfect ignorance.

Secondly, That it moves slowly, and retrieves not the ideas that it has, and are laid up in store, quick enough to serve the mind upon occasions. This, if it be to a great degree, is stupidity; and he, who through this default in his memory, has not the ideas that are really preserved there, ready at hand when need and occasion calls for them, were almost as good be without them quite, since they serve him to little purpose. The dull man, who loses the opportunity whilst he is seeking in his mind for those ideas that should serve his turn, is not much more happy in his knowledge than one that is perfectly ignorant. It is the business therefore of the memory to furnish to the mind those dormant ideas which it has present occasion for; in the having them ready at hand on all occasions, consists that which we call invention, fancy, and quickness of parts.

These are defects, we may observe, in the memory of one man compared with another. There is another defect which we may conceive to be in the memory of man in general, compared with some superior created intellectual beings, which in this faculty may so far excel man, that they may have constantly in view the whole scene of all their former actions, wherein no one of the thoughts they have ever had may slip out of their sight. The omniscience of God, who knows all things past, present, and to come, and to whom the thoughts of men's hearts always lie open, may satisfy us of the possibility of this. For who can doubt but God may communicate to those glorious spirits, his immediate attendants, any of his perfections, in what proportions he pleases, as far as created finite beings can be capable? It is reported of that prodigy of parts, Monsieur Pascal, that, till the decay of his health had impaired his memory, he forgot nothing of what he had done, read, or thought, in any part of his rational age. This is a privilege so little known to most men, that it seems almost incredible to those, who, after the ordinary way, measure all others by themselves; but yet, when considered, may help us to enlarge our thoughts towards greater perfection of it in superior ranks of spirits. For this of Mr. Pascal was still with the narrowness that human minds are confined to here, of having great variety of ideas only by succession, not all at once: whereas the several degrees of angels may probably have larger views, and some of them be endowed with capacities able to retain together, and constantly set before them, as in one picture all 'their past knowledge at once. This, we may conceive, would be no small advantage to the knowledge of a thinking man, if all his past thoughts and reasonings could be always present to him. And therefore we may suppose it one of those ways, wherein the knowledge of separate spirits may exceedingly surpass ours.

This faculty of laying up and retaining the ideas that are brought into the mind, several other animals seem to have to a great degree, as well as man. For to pass by other instances, birds learning of tunes, and the endeavours one may observe in them to hit the notes right, put it past doubt with me, that they have perception, and retain ideas in their memories, and use them for patterns. For it seems to me impossible, that they should endeavour to conform their voices to notes (as it is plain they do) of which they had no ideas. For though I should grant sound may mechanically cause a certain motion of the animal spirits, in the brains of those birds, whilst the tune is actually playing; and that motion may be continued on to the muscles of the wings, and so the bird mechanically be driven away by certain noises, because this may tend to the bird's preservation: yet that can never be supposed a reason, why it should cause mechanically, either whilst the tune was playing, much less after it has ceased, such a motion of the organs in the bird's voice, as should conform it to the notes of a foreign sound; which imitation can be of no use to the bird's preservation. But which is more, it cannot with any appearance of reason be supposed (much less proved) that birds, without sense and memory, can approach their notes nearer and nearer by degrees to a tune played yesterday; which if they have no idea of in their memory, is nowhere, nor can be a pattern for them to imitate, or which any repeated essays can bring them nearer to. Since there is no reason why the sound of a pipe should leave traces in their brains, which not at first, but by their after-endeavours, should produce the like sounds; and why the sounds they make themselves, should not make traces which they should follow, as well as those of the pipe, is impossible to conceive.—*Essay Concerning Human Understanding.*

XXI.

ROBERT SOUTH.

1633—1716.

ROBERT SOUTH, the son of a London merchant, was born in 1633. He was educated at Westminster, under Dr. Busby, and elected Student at Christ Church, Oxford, together with John Locke. He took Holy Orders in 1658, and, as Public Orator of the University, attracted the notice of the Chancellor, Clarendon, whose Domestic Chaplain he became. During his residence in the University, which lasted through the Interregnum, South attached himself in turn to every theological party which rose to the ascendant ; the Restoration, however, helped to cure him of these inconsistencies, and he settled down as a steady adherent of High Church and high prerogative doctrines. But his former versatility drew upon him the dislike, and his rapid promotion the envy, of that section of the Oxford Cavaliers who had abided by their principles, when those principles entailed much obloquy and many inconveniences upon their professors. These feelings find adequate expression in the sketch of South's life, from the pen of that most zealous of Royalists, Anthony-a-Wocd, which is much more an invective than a biography.

South was a Prebend of Westminster, and in 1670 he was made a Canon of Christ Church, and was afterwards presented with the living of Islip by the Dean and Chapter of Westminster.

Subsequently, he declined the Bishopric of Rochester and the Deanery of Westminster, saying that such a chair would be too uneasy for an old infirm man to sit in. He died in 1716, and was buried near his old master, Dr. Busby, in Westminster Abbey.

South is chiefly known by his *Sermons;* Mr. Hallam says of them—'They were much celebrated at the time, and retain a portion of their renown. This is by no means surprising. South had great qualifications for that popularity which attends the pulpit, and his manner was at that time original. Not diffuse, nor learned, nor formal in argument, like Barrow; with a more natural structure of sentences, a more pointed, though by no means a more fair and satisfactory turn of reasoning; with a style clear and English, free from all pedantry, but abounding with those colloquial novelties of idiom, which, though now become vulgar and offensive, the age of Charles II affected; sparing no personal or temporary sarcasm, but if he seems for a moment to tread on the verge of buffoonery, recovering himself by some stroke of vigorous sense and language: such was the worthy Dr. South, whom the courtiers delighted to hear. His sermons want all that is called unction, and sometimes even earnestness; but there is a masculine spirit about them, which, combined with their peculiar characteristics, would naturally fill the churches where he might be heard.' To this it may be added that in his finer passages, such as the following extracts, South shows himself one of the greatest and subtlest masters of the English tongue.

---

1. The Understanding.

AND first for its noblest faculty, the understanding: it was then sublime, clear, and aspiring, and, as it were, the soul's upper region, lofty and serene, free from the vapours and disturbances of the inferior affections. It was the leading, controlling faculty; all the passions wore the colours of reason; it did not so much persuade, as command; it was not consul, but dictator. Discourse was then almost as quick as intuition; it was nimble in proposing, firm in concluding; it could sooner determine than now it can dispute. Like the sun, it had both light and agility; it knew no rest, but in motion; no quiet, but in activity. It did not so properly apprehend, as irradiate the object; not so much find, as make things intelligible. It did arbitrate upon the several reports of sense, and all the varieties of imagination; not like a drowsy judge, only hearing, but also directing their verdict. In sum, it was vegete, quick, and lively; open as the day, untainted as the morning, full of the innocence and sprightliness of youth; it gave the soul a bright and a full view into all things; and was not only a window, but itself the prospect. Briefly, there is as much difference between the clear representations of the understanding then, and the obscure discoveries that it makes now, as there is between the prospect of a casement and of a key-hole. . . . .

Study was not then a duty, night-watchings were needless; the light of reason wanted not the assistance of a candle. This is the doom of fallen man, to labour in the fire, to seek truth *in profundo*, to exhaust his time and impair his health, and perhaps to spin out his days, and himself, into one pitiful, controverted conclusion. There was then no poring, no struggling with memory, no straining for invention: his faculties were quick and expedite; they answered without knocking, they were ready upon the first summons, there was freedom and firmness in all their operations. I confess, it is difficult for us, who date our ignorance from our first being, and were still bred up with the same infirmities about us with which we were born, to raise our thoughts and imagination to those intellectual perfections that attended our nature in the time of innocence; as it is for a peasant bred up in the obscurities of a cottage, to fancy in his mind the unseen splendours of a court. But by rating positives by their privatives, and other arts of reason, by which discourse supplies the want of the reports of sense, we may collect the excellency of the understanding then, by the glorious re-

mainders of it now, and guess at the stateliness of the building, by the magnificence of its ruins. All those arts, rarities,
and inventions, which vulgar minds gaze at, the ingenious
pursue, and all admire, are but the reliques of an intellect
defaced with sin and time. We admire it now, only as
antiquaries do a piece of old coin, for the stamp it once
bore, and not for those vanishing lineaments and disappear-
ing draughts that remain upon it at present. And certainly
that must needs have been very glorious, the decays of which
are so admirable. He that is comely, when old and decrepid, surely was very beautiful when he was young. An
Aristotle was but the rubbish of an Adam, and Athens but
the rudiments of Paradise.—*Sermon, The Creation of Man in
the Image of God.*

2. The Will.

DOUBTLESS the will of man in the state of innocence had
an entire freedom, a perfect equipendency and indifference
to either part of the contradiction, to stand, or not to stand;
to accept, or not accept the temptation. I will grant the
will of man now to be as much a slave as any one will have
it, and be only free to sin; that is, instead of a liberty, to
have only a licentiousness; yet certainly this is not nature,
but chance. We were not born crooked; we learnt these
windings and turnings of the serpent: and therefore it
cannot but be a blasphemous piece of ingratitude to ascribe
them to God, and to make the plague of our nature the condition of our creation.

The will was then ductile, and pliant to all the motions of
right reason; it met the dictates of a clarified understanding
half way. And the active informations of the intellect,
filling the passive reception of the will, like form closing
with matter, grew actuate into a third, and distinct perfection

of practice: the understanding and will never disagreed; for the proposals of the one never thwarted the inclinations of the other. Yet neither did the will servilely attend upon the understanding, but as a favourite does upon his prince, where the service is privilege and preferment; or as Solomon's servants waited upon him, it admired its wisdom, and heard its prudent dictates and counsels, both the direction and the reward of its obedience. It is indeed the nature of this faculty to follow a superior guide, to be drawn by the intellect; but then it was drawn as a triumphant chariot, which at the same time both follows and triumphs; while it obeyed this, it commanded the other faculties. It was subordinate, not enslaved to the understanding: not as a servant to a master, but as a queen to her king, who both acknowledges a subjection, and yet retains a majesty.—*Sermon, The Creation of Man in the Image of God.*

3. The Body.

HAVING thus surveyed the image of God in the soul of man, we are not to omit now those characters of majesty that God imprinted upon the body. He drew some traces of his image upon this also; as much as a spiritual substance could be pictured upon a corporeal. As for the sect of the Anthropomorphites, who from hence ascribe to God the figure of a man, eyes, hands, feet, and the like, they are too ridiculous to deserve a confutation. They would seem to draw this impiety from the letter of the scripture sometimes speaking of God in this manner. Absurdly; as if the mercy of scripture expressions ought to warrant the blasphemy of our opinions. And not rather show us, that God condescends to us, only to draw us to himself; and clothes himself in our likeness, only to win us to his own. The practice of the papists is much of the same nature, in their absurd and impious picturing of God Almighty: but the wonder in them is the less, since the image of a deity may be a proper object for that, which is but the image of a religion. But to the purpose: Adam was then no less glorious in his externals: he had a beautiful body, as well as an immortal soul. The whole compound was like a well-built temple, stately without, and sacred within. The elements were at perfect union and agreement in his body; and their contrary qualities served not for the dissolution of the compound, but the variety of the composure. Galen, who had no more divinity than what his physic taught him, barely upon the consideration of this so exact frame of the body, challenges any one upon an hundred years study, to find how any the least fibre, or most minute particle, might be more commodiously placed, either for the advantage of use or comeliness; his stature erect, and tending upwards to his centre; his countenance majestic and comely, with the lustre of a native beauty, that scorned the poor assistance of art, or the attempts of imitation; his body of so much quickness and agility, that it did not only contain, but also represent the soul: for we might well suppose, that where God did deposit so rich a jewel, he would suitably adorn the case. It was a fit workhouse for sprightly vivid faculties to exercise and exert themselves in. A fit tabernacle for an immortal soul, not only to dwell in, but to contemplate upon: where it might see the world without travel; it being a lesser scheme of the creation, nature contracted, a little cosmography, or map of the universe. Neither was the body then subject to distempers, to die by piecemeal, and languish under coughs, catarrhs, or consumptions. Adam knew no disease, so long as temperance from the forbidden fruit secured him. Nature was his physician; and innocence

and abstinence would have kept him healthful to immortality.—*Sermon, The Creation of Man in the Image of God.*

4. Inclination and Idleness.

To will a thing therefore, is certainly much another thing
from what the generality of men, especially in their spiritual
concerns, take it to be.　I say, in their spiritual concerns;
for in their temporal, it is manifest that they think and judge
much otherwise; and in the things of this woild, no man is
allowed or believed to will any thing heartily, which he 'does
not endeavour after proportionably.　A wish is properly a
man of desire, sitting, or lying still; but an act of the will, is
a man of business vigorously going about his work: and
certainly there is a great deal of difference between a man's
stretching out his arms to work, and his stretching them out
only to yawn. . . .

Labour is confessedly a great part of the curse; and therefore, no wonder, if men fly from it: which they do with so
great an aversion, that few men know their own strength for
want of trying it; and, upon that account, think themselves
really unable to do many things, which experience would
convince them, they have more ability to effect, than they
have will to attempt.

It is idleness that creates impossibilities; and, where men
care not to do a thing, they shelter themselves under a persuasion, that it cannot be done.　The shortest and the surest
way to prove a work possible, is strenuously to set about it;
and no wonder, if that proves it possible, that, for the most
part, makes it so.

Dig, says the unjust steward, *I cannot.*　But why?　Did
either his legs or his arms fail him?　No; but day-labour
was but an hard and a dry kind of livelihood to a man

that could get an estate with two or three strokes of his
pen; and find so great a treasure as he did, without dig-
ging for it.

But such excuses will not pass muster with God, who will
allow no man's humour or idleness to be the measure of possible or impossible. And to manifest the wretched hypocrisy
of such pretences, those very things, which upon the bare
obligation of duty are declined by men as impossible, presently become not only possible, but readily practicable too,
in a case of extreme necessity. As no doubt that foremen-
tioned instance of fraud and laziness, the unjust steward,
who pleaded that he could neither dig nor beg, would quickly
have been brought both to dig and to beg too, rather than
starve. And if so, what reason could such an one produce
before God, why he could not submit to the same hardships,
rather than cheat and lie? The former being but destruc-
tive of the body, this latter of the soul: and certainly the
highest and dearest concerns of a temporal life are infinitely
less valuable than those of an eternal; and consequently
ought, without any demur at all, to be sacrificed to them,
whensoever they come in competition with them. He who
can digest any labour, rather than die, must refuse no labour,
rather than sin.—*Sermon, Good Inclinations no Excuse for
Bad Actions.*

5. Considerations against Despondency.

THE other extreme, which these considerations should
arm the heart of man against, is, utter despondency of mind
in a time of pressing adversity.

As he who presumes, steps into the throne of God; so he
that despairs, limits an infinite power to a finite apprehension,
and measures Providence by his own little, contracted model.

But the contrivances of Heaven are as much above our politics, as beyond our arithmetic.

Of those many millions of casualties, which we are not aware of, there is hardly one, but God can make an instrument of our deliverance. And most men, who are at length delivered from any great distress indeed, find that they are so, by ways that they never thought of; ways above or beside their imagination.

And therefore let no man, who owns the belief of a providence, grow desperate or forlorn under any calamity or strait whatsoever; but compose the anguish of his thoughts, and rest his amazed spirits upon this one consideration, that he knows not *which way the lot may fall*, or what may happen to him; he comprehends not those strange unaccountable methods, by which Providence may dispose of him.

In a word. To sum up all the foregoing discourse: since the interest of governments and nations, of princes and private persons, and that, both as to life and health, reputation and honour, friendships and enmities, employments and preferments, (notwithstanding all the contrivance and power that human nature can exert about them,) remain so wholly contingent, as to. us; surely all the reason of mankind cannot suggest any solid ground of satisfaction, but in making that God our friend, who is the sole and absolute disposer of all these things: and in carrying a conscience so clear towards him, as may encourage us with confidence to cast ourselves upon him: and in all casualties still to promise ourselves the best events from his providence, to whom nothing is casual: who constantly wills the truest happiness to those that trust in him, and works all things according to the counsel of that blessed will.—*Sermon, All Contingencies under the direction of God's Providence.*

6. Friendships Human and Divine.

PEOPLE at first, while they are young and raw, and soft-natured, are apt to think it an easy thing to gain love, and reckon their own friendship a sure price of another man's. But when experience shall have once opened their eyes, and shewed them the hardness of most hearts, the hollowness of others, and the baseness and ingratitude of almost all, they will then find that a friend is the gift of God; and that he only, who made hearts, can unite them. For it is he who creates those sympathies and suitablenesses of nature, that are the foundation of all true friendship, and then by his providence brings persons so affected together.

It is an expression frequent in scripture, but infinitely more significant than at first it is usually observed to be; namely, that God gave such or such a person grace or favour in another's eyes. It is an invisible hand from heaven that ties this knot, and mingles hearts and souls, by strange, secret, and unaccountable conjunctions.

That heart shall surrender itself and its friendship to one man, at first view, which another has in vain been laying siege to for many years, by all the repeated acts of kindness imaginable.

Nay, so far is friendship from being of any human production, that, unless nature be predisposed to it by its own propensity or inclination, no arts of obligation shall be able to abate the secret hatreds and hostilities of some persons towards others. No friendly offices, no addresses, no benefits whatsoever, shall ever alter or allay that diabolical rancour that frets and ferments in some hellish breasts, but that upon all occasions it will foam out at its foul mouth in slander and invective, and sometimes bite too in a shrewd turn or a secret blow. This is true and undeniable upon frequent experience; and happy those who can learn it at the cost of other men's.

But now, on the contrary, he who will give up his name to Christ in faith unfeigned, and a sincere obedience to all his righteous laws, shall be sure to find love for love, and friendship for friendship. The success is certain and infallible; and none ever yet miscarried in the attempt. For Christ freely offers his friendship to all, and sets no other rate upon so vast a purchase, but only that we would suffer him to be our friend. Thou perhaps spendest thy precious time in waiting upon such a great one, and thy estate in presenting him, and probably, after all, hast no other reward, but sometimes to be smiled upon, and always to be smiled at; and when thy greatest and most pressing occasions shall call for succour and relief, then to be deserted and cast off, and not known.

Now, I say, turn the stream of thy endeavours another way, and bestow but half that hearty, sedulous attendance upon thy Saviour in the duties of prayer and mortification, and be at half that expense in charitable works, by relieving Christ in his poor members; and, in a word, study as much to please him who died for thee, as thou dost to court and humour thy great patron, who cares not for thee, and thou shalt make him thy friend for ever; a friend who shall own thee in thy lowest condition, speak comfort to thee in all thy sorrows, counsel thee in all thy doubts, answer all thy wants, and, in a word, *never leave thee, nor forsake thee.* But when all the hopes that thou hast raised upon the promises or supposed kindnesses of the fastidious and fallacious great ones of the world, shall fail, and upbraid thee to thy face, he shall then take thee into his bosom, embrace, cherish, and support thee, and, as the Psalmist expresses it, *he shall guide thee with his counsel here, and afterwards receive thee into glory.—Sermon, Of the love of Christ to his Disciples.*

XXII.

FRANCIS ATTERBURY.

1662-3—1731-2.

FRANCIS ATTERBURY holds a conspicuous place in the political, ecclesiastical, and literary history of England. He was born at Middleton in Buckinghamshire, in 1662-3. He was admitted a King's Scholar at Westminster under Dr. Busby in 1676, and thence elected in 1680 a Student of Christ Church, Oxford, under Dr. Fell.

His application to study was intense, and he is known to have excelled in literature and even in mathematics. He remained at Oxford filling various offices at Christ Church and in the University, but an academic life was unsuited to his active and aspiring nature, and in 1691 he left the University and was ordained. He soon became distinguished as a preacher, and the controversies to which some of his sermons gave rise contributed to spread his reputation: in 1699 and for ten years after his efforts were directed to the vindication and restoration of the rights of Convocation and to the establishment of the independent action of the Lower House, in which for a time he succeeded. He was appointed Dean of Christ Church in 1711, and Bishop of Rochester with the Deanery of Westminster *in commendam* in 1713. At the Rebellion of 1715, on the accession of George the First, the tide of Atterbury's fortune began to turn. His refusal to sign the Declaration against Rebellion, and his persistent opposition to the Court and violent protests against its measures, made him the object of both fear and hatred to the Whigs. In 1722 he was committed to the Tower on a charge of high treason—a bill for his deposition and banishment passed the

Commons, and, after he had eloquently but unsuccessfully defended himself in the Lords, in a great speech, of which a portion is given below, the bill was passed, and Atterbury was put on board a man of war and landed in France. At Paris he threw himself into the cause of the Pretender, but met with such disgusts and ill treatment that he withdrew to Montpellier. He returned to Paris in 1730, and died there in his seventieth year, in 1731–2. His body was brought to England, and buried in Westminster Abbey.

Atterbury was an accomplished scholar, an ingenious and acute controversialist, and an eloquent preacher. His ability and energy were confessed even by his opponents, Burnet and Hoadly. His style has great rhetorical vigour, and no objection can be taken to it on the score of purity or refinement. If he wants depth and originality, his language is always clear and intelligible, and in his letters especially distinguished by elegance.

1. King Charles the First.

THE mind of man, filled with vain ideas of worldly pomp and greatness, is apt to admire those princes most, who are most fortunate, and have filled the world with the fame of their successful achievements.

But to those who weigh things in the balance of right reason and true religion, it will, I am persuaded, appear that the character of this excellent king, even while he was in his lowest and most afflicted state, had something in it, more truly great and noble, than all the triumphs of conquerors: something that raised him as far above the most prosperous princes, as they themselves are raised above the rest of mankind.

Many kings there have been, as happy as all worldly felicity could make them; and some of these have distinguished themselves as much by their virtues, as their happiness. But the possessors of those virtues, being seated on a throne, displayed them from thence with all manner of advantage; their good actions appeared in the best light, by reason of the high orb, in which they moved, while performing them: whereas, the royal virtues, which we this day celebrate, shone brightest in affliction, and when all external marks of royal state and dignity were wanting to recommend them. Others, perhaps, may have been as just, as beneficent, as merciful, in the exercise of their royal power, as this good king was: but none surely did ever maintain such a majestic evenness and serenity of mind, when despoiled of that power; when stript of everything but a good cause, and a good conscience; when destitute of all hopes of succour from his friends, or of mercy from his enemies : then, even then, did he possess his soul in peace, and patiently expect the event, without the least outward sign of dejection or discomposure. He remembered himself to be a king, when all the world besides seemed to have forgotten it; when his inferiors treated him with insolence, and his equals with indifference; when he was brought before that infamous tribunal, where his own subjects sat as his judges; and even when he came to die by their sentence. In all these sad circumstances, on all these trying occasions, he spake, he did nothing, which misbecame the high character he bore, and will always bear, of a great king, and one of the best of Christians. And this mixture of unaffected greatness and goodness, in the extremity of misery, was, I say, his peculiar and distinguishing excellence: other royal qualities, that adorn prosperity, he shared in common with others of his rank : but in the decent and kingly exercise of these passive graces, he had, among the list of princes, no superior, no equal, no rival.

Indeed, the last scene of his sufferings was very dismal;

and such, from which mere human nature, unsupported by extraordinary degrees of grace, musts need have shrunk back a little affrighted, and seemed desirous of declining. But those succours were not wanting to him; for he went even through this last trial, unshaken; and submitted his royal head to the stroke of the executioner, with as much tranquillity and meekness, as he had borne lesser barbarities.- The passage through this Red Sea was bloody, but short; a divine hand strengthened him in it, and conducted him through it; and he soon reached the shore of bliss and immortality.—*Sermon on the Martyrdom of King Charles the First.*

2. Before the House of Lords, May 11, 1723.

LET me speak, my Lords, (always, I hope, with that modesty which becomes an accused person, but ·yet) with the freedom of an Englishman. Had nothing been opened to you concerning this man's character and secret trans-actions, could you possibly have believed the romantic tales he has told? Could this pretender to secrets have had, or shall he still have, any weight with you? who threw away his life, rather than venture to stand to the truth of what he had said? Shall this man do more mischief by his death, than he could have done, if living? For then he would have been confronted, puzzled, confounded. Shame and consciousness might have made him unsay what he had said : but a dead man can retract nothing. What he has written, he has written : the accusation must stand just as it is; and we are deprived of the advantages of those confessions, which truth and remorse had once extorted, and would again have extorted from him. However, I could have been glad to have had all that even this witness said; and would have hoped, that, by a comparison of the several parts of the story he at several times told, some light might have been gained that now is wanting.

But he is gone to his place, and has answered for what he said at another Tribunal. I desire not to blemish his character, any farther than is absolutely necessary to my own just defence. . . .

Our Law has taken care that there should be a more clear and full proof of Treason than of any other crime whatsoever. And reasonable it is, that a crime attended with the highest penalties should be made out by the clearest and fullest evidence. And yet here is a charge of high treason brought against me, not only without full evidence, but without any evidence at all, that is, any such evidence as the law of the land knows and allows. And what is not evidence at law (pardon me what I am going to say) can never be made such, in order to punish what is past, but by a violation of the law: for the law which prescribes the nature of the proof required, is as much the law of the land, as that which declares the crime ; and both must join to convict a man of guilt. And it seems equally unjust to declare any sort of proof legal, which was not so before a prosecution commenced for any act done, as it would be to declare the act itself *ex-post-facto* to be criminal.

Now there never was a charge of so high a nature so strongly pressed and so weakly supported—supported, not by any living or dead witness, speaking from his own knowledge, but by mere hearsays and reports from others ; contradicted by the very persons from whom they are said to be derived—supported not by any one criminal deed proved to have been done, not by any one criminal line proved to have been either written or received, not even by any one criminal word proved to have been spoken by me ; but by intercepted letters in a correspondence, to which it appears not that I was, and to which it is certain that I was not privy; some of these letters shewn to have been contrived with a design of fastening them upon me, as a foundation of the scheme which was to follow; others written with the same view, employing the same fictitious names, and throwing out dark and suspicious hints, concerning the persons meant by those names, and endeavouring by little facts and circumstances, sometimes true, sometimes doubtful, and often false, to point out that person to such as should intercept those letters, who continues all this time a stranger to the whole transaction, and never makes the discovery till he feels it, and finds it advanced into a solemn accusation; till 'the pestilence that walked in darkness becomes the arrow that flyeth by noonday.' . . .

My Lords, this is my case; I have shewed it so to be; though I had the hard task upon me of proving a negative, and had no other lights to guide me but those the Report affords. And shall I stand convicted before your Lordships upon such an evidence as this? by the hearsay of an hearsay (for this often is the case), and that denied by the very person into whose testimony all must be resolved; by strained reasonings and inferences, from obscure passages, and fictitious names in letters, the contents of which were entirely a secret to me, till I saw them in print. . . .

Shall I, my Lords, be deprived of all that is valuable to an Englishman (for in the circumstances to which I am to be reduced, life itself is scarce valuable) by such an evidence as this! such an evidence as would not be admitted in any other cause, in any other court; nor allowed, I verily believe, to condemn a Jew in the Inquisitions of Spain or Portugal; shall it be received against me, a Bishop of this Church, and a member of this House, in a charge of high treason brought in the High Court of Parliament? God forbid! . . .

Doubtless the Legislature is without bounds. It may do what it pleases; and whatever it does is binding. Nay, in some respects it has greater power (with reverence be it spoken) than the Sovereign Legislator of the Universe; for he can do nothing unjustly! But though no limits can be set to Parliaments, yet they have generally thought fit to prescribe limits to themselves; and so to guide even their proceedings by bill in criminal cases, as to depart as little as possible from the known laws and usages of the realm. The Parliament may, if it pleases, by a particular act, order a criminal to be tortured who will not confess; for who shall gainsay them? But they never did it: nor, I presume, ever will; because torture, though practised in other countries, is unknown in ours, and repugnant to the temper and genius of our mild and free Government: and yet, my Lords, it looks, methinks, somewhat like torture, to inflict grievous pains and penalties on a person only suspected of guilt, but not legally proved guilty, in order to extort some confession or discovery from him. This, in other countries, is called putting to the question; and it matters not much by what engines or method such an experiment is made.

The Parliament may (if it pleases) by an express law adjudge a man to absolute perpetual imprisonment, as well as to perpetual exile; without reserving to the Crown any power of determining such imprisonment. They have enacted the one; I find not they ever enacted the other. And the reason seems to have been, because our Law, which above all others provides for the liberty of the subject's person, knows nothing of such absolute perpetual imprisonment.

The Parliament may in like manner condemn a man upon a charge of accumulative and constructive treason. They did so once, in the case of the Earl of Strafford; but they repented of it afterwards, and ordered 'all the records and proceedings of Parliament relating thereto to be wholly cancelled, defaced,' and obliterated, to the intent the same might not be visible in after-ages, or brought into example to the prejudice of any person whatsoever.' My Lords, it was the fate of that great person thus to fall by accumulative and constructive treason. A much less now stands before you, who is attacked by accumulative and constructive proofs of his guilt; that is, by such proofs as in themselves, and when taken single and apart, are allowed to prove nothing; but when taken together, and well interpreted and explained, are said to give mutual light and strength to each other, and by the help of certain inferences and deduction to have the force, though not the formality, of legal evidence. Will such proofs be ever admitted by your Lordships, in order to deprive a fellow-subject of his fortunes, his fame, his friends, and his country, and send him in his old age, without language, without limbs, without health, and without a provision for the necessaries of life, to live, or rather starve, amongst foreigners? I say again, God forbid!

My ruin is not of that moment to any man, or any number of men, as to make it worth their while to violate (or even *seem* to violate) the constitution in any degree to procure it. In preserving and guarding *that* against all attempts, the safety and the happiness of every Englishman lies. But when once, by such extraordinary steps as these, we depart from the fixed rules and forms of justice, and try untrodden paths, no man knows whither they will lead him, or where he shall be able to stop, when pressed by the crowd that follow him.

Though I am worthy of no regard; though whatever is done to me may be looked upon as just; yet your Lordships will have some regard to your own lasting interests, and those of the State; and not introduce into criminal cases a sort of evidence with which our constitution is not acquainted, and which, under the appearance of supporting it at first, may be afterwards made use of (I speak · my honest fears) gradually to undermine and destroy it.

For God's sake, my Lords, lay aside these extraordinary proceedings! set not these new and dangerous precedents! And I for my part will voluntarily and cheerfully go into perpetual exile, and please myself with the thought that I have in some measure preserved the constitution by quitting my country; and I will live, wherever I am, praying for its prosperity, and die with the words of Father Paul in my mouth, which he used of the Republic of Venice, 'Esto perpetua!' The way to perpetuate it is, not to depart from it. Let *me* depart; but let *that* continue fixed on the immoveable foundations of Law and Justice, and stand for ever.

Had indeed the charge been as fully proved as it is strongly asserted, it had been in vain to think of encountering well-attested facts by protestation to the contrary, though never so solemnly made. But, as that charge is enforced by flights and probabilities, and cannot be disproved in many circumstances without proving a negative, your Lordships will, in such a case, allow the solemn asseverations of a man in behalf of his own innocence to have their due weight. And I ask no more of God than to grant them as much influence with you as they have truth in themselves.

If, after all, it shall be still thought by your Lordships that there is any seeming strength in any of the proofs produced against me ; if by private persuasions of my guilt, founded on unseen, unknown motives, which ought not certainly to influence public judgements; if by any reasons and necessities of state (of the expedience, wisdom, and justice of which I am no competent judge) your Lordships shall be induced to proceed on this bill, and to pass it in any shape; I shall dispose myself quietly and patiently to submit to what is determined. ' God's will be done! Naked came I out of my mother's womb, and naked shall I return thither; the Lord gave, and the Lord hath taken away; and (whether in giving or taking) blessed be the name of the Lord!'

3. Letters to Pope.

Dec. 1716.

I RETURN your Preface, which I have read twice with pleasure. The modesty and good sense there is in it must please every one who reads it; and since there is nothing that can offend, I see not why you should balance a moment about printing it—always provided, that there is nothing said there which you may have occasion to unsay hereafter: of which you yourself are the best and the only judge. This is my sincere opinion, which I give because you ask it: and which I would not give, though asked, but to a man I value as much as I do you; being sensible how improper it is, on many accounts, for me to interpose in things of this nature; which I never understood well, and now understand somewhat less than ever I did. But I can deny you nothing; especially since you have had the goodness often and patiently to hear what I have said against rhyme, and in behalf of blank verse; with little discretion perhaps, but I am sure without the least prejudice: being myself equally incapable of writing well in either of those ways, and leaning therefore to neither side of the question but as the appearance of reason inclines me. Forgive me this error, if it be one; an error of above thirty years' standing, and which therefore I shall be very loth to part with.

In other matters which relate to polite writing, I shall seldom differ from you; or, if I do, shall, I hope, have the prudence to conceal my opinion.

.   .   .   .

The Tower, April 10, 1723.

I THANK you for all the instances of your friendship both before and since my misfortunes. A little time will complete them, and separate you and me for ever. But in what part of the world soever I am, I will live mindful of your sincere kindness to me; and will please myself with the thought, that I still live in your esteem and affection, as much as ever I did; and that no accidents of life, no distance of time or place, will alter you in that respect. It never can me; who have loved and valued you ever since I knew you, and shall not fail to do it when I am not allowed to tell you so; as the case will soon be. Give my faithful services to Dr. Arbuthnot, and thanks for what he sent me, which was much to the purpose, if any thing can be said to be to the purpose in a case that is already determined. Let him know my defence will be such, that neither my friends need blush for me, nor will my enemies have great occasion of triumph, though sure of the victory. I shall want his advice before I go abroad, in many things. But I question whether I shall be permitted to see him, or any body but such as are absolutely necessary towards the despatch of my private affairs. If so, God bless you both! and may no part of the ill fortune that attends me pursue either of you! I know not but I may call upon you at my hearing, to say somewhat about my way of spending my time at the Deanery, which did not seem calculated towards managing plots and conspiracies. But of that I shall consider.——You and I have spent many hours together upon much pleasanter subjects; and, that I may preserve the old custom, I shall not part with you now

till I have closed this letter with three lines of Milton, which
you will, I know, readily and not without some degree of
concern apply to your ever affectionate, &c.   Fr. Roffen.

> ' Some natural tears he dropt, but wip'd them soon :
> The world was all before him, where to chuse
> His place of rest, and Providence his Guide.'

.   .   .   .

Paris, Nov. 23, 1731.

WHAT are they doing in England to the honour of letters?
and particularly what are you doing?

> ' Ipse quid audes?
> Quae circumvolitas agilis thyma ? '

Do you pursue the Moral Plan [the Essay on Man] you
marked out, and seemed sixteen months ago so intent upon?
Am I to see it perfected ere I die? and are you to enjoy the
reputation of it while you live? or do you rather choose to
leave the marks of your friendship, like the legacies of a will,
to be read and enjoyed only by those who survive you?   Were
I as near you as I have been, I should hope to peep into the
manuscript before it was finished.   But, alas! there is, and will
ever probably be, a great deal of land and sea between us.
How many books have come out of late in your parts, which
you think I should be glad to peruse?   Name them: the
Catalogue, I believe, will not cost you much trouble.   They
must be good ones indeed to challenge any part of my time,
now I have so little of it left.   I, who squandered whole
days heretofore, now husband hours, when the glass begins
to run low, and care not to mis-spend them on trifles.   At
the end of the lottery of life, our last minutes, like tickets
left in the wheel, rise in their valuation.   They are not of so
much worth, perhaps, in themselves, as those which preceded; but we are apt to prize them more, and with reason.
I do so, my dear friend, and yet think the most precious

minutes of my life well employed in reading what you write. . . .

My country, at this distance, seems to me a strange sight: I know not how it appears to you, who are in the midst of the scene, and yourself a part of it: I wish you would tell me. . . .

After all, I do and must love my country, with all its faults and blemishes; even that part of the constitution which wounded me unjustly, and itself through my side, shall ever be dear to me. My last wish will be like that of Father Paul, 'Esto perpetua!' and when I die at a distance from it, it will be in the same manner as Virgil describes the expiring Peloponnesian,

> 'Sternitur———
> ———et dulces moriens reminiscitur Argos.'

Do I still live in the memory of my friends, as they do in mine?—*Epistolary Correspondence.*

XXIII.

DANIEL DEFOE.

CIRCA 1663—1731.

DANIEL DEFOE was born in London about 1663. His father, James Foe, was a citizen and butcher of the parish of St. Giles, Cripplegate.

Little is known of his early life except that his family were Protestant Dissenters, and that he was educated at a dissenting academy at Newington. He became an author before he was twenty-one, and is said to have devoted to literature and politics time which was necessary for the conduct of his business, which was that of a hosier. In 1692 he became a bankrupt, and was obliged to abscond ' from his creditors. A composition was entered into, and by unwearied diligence he succeeded in making the payments with punctuality.

In 1683 he took arms as a follower of the Duke of Monmouth, and in 1688 he zealously favoured the Revolution. He was more than once the object of prosecution for his political writings, and in 1703 he was sentenced to the pillory, and to be fined and imprisoned, but he did not lose heart, and his time in Newgate was fruitful of literary projects.

The formerly current opinion that Defoe's political career came to a close immediately, or very soon after, the accession of the House of Hanover, is now known to be erroneous. From 1715 to 1726 he contributed largely to various Jacobite journals, with the connivance and in the pay of the ministries who held power during that period. In this employment it was expected of him to restrain the violence of the malcontent party for whom he ostensibly worked, and to keep the Government duly informed of the movements and projects of the partisans of the Stuarts. This course of conduct has left a deep stain on the memory of

Defoe; nevertheless it is difficult to believe that he was not a man of a naturally simple, straightforward, earnest character. Such a character is reflected in his language, which though careless and hasty, is always that of a clear thinker, and of one who writes only because he has something to say. He is an excellent example of a plain style. The bulk of his voluminous works is political. It was not until he was fifty-eight that he commenced a new career of authorship as a writer of fiction, and among other works of that class produced the *History of the Plague*, from which two of the following extracts are taken. *Robinson Crusoe* first appeared in 1719, and was succeeded by several other tales, which, if showing equal power, neither obtained nor perhaps deserved the same wide-spread popularity. His narrative style has the same merits, after its kind, as his political style. Defoe died in the parish in which he was born in 1731.

---

1. The Plague of London.

INDEED, the poor people were to be pitied in one particular thing, in which they had little or no relief, and which I desire to mention with a serious awe and reflection, which, perhaps, every one that reads this may not relish; namely, that whereas Death now began not, *as we may say*, to hover over every one's head only, but to look into their houses, and chambers, and stare in their faces; though there might be some stupidity, and dulness of the mind, and there was so, a great deal; yet, there was a great deal of just alarm, sounded in the very inmost soul, *if I may so say*, of others. Many consciences were awakened; many hard hearts melted into tears; and many a penitent confession was made of crimes long concealed. It would have wounded the soul of any Christian to have heard the dying groans of many a despairing creature; and none durst come near to comfort them. Many a robbery, many a murder, was then confessed aloud, and nobody surviving

Y 2

to record the accounts of it. People might be heard, even
in the streets as we passed along, calling upon God for
mercy, and saying, 'I have been a thief,—I have been an
adulterer,—I have been a murderer,'—and the like ; and
none durst stop to make the least inquiry into such things,
or to administer comfort to the poor creatures, that in the
anguish both of soul and body thus cried out. Some of
the ministers did visit the sick at first, and for a little
while, but it was not to be done; it would have been
present death to have gone into some houses. The very
buryers of the dead, who were the most hardened creatures
in town, were sometimes beaten back, and so terrified,
that they durst not go into the houses where whole families
were swept away together, and where the circumstances
were more particularly horrible, as some were; but this was,
indeed, at the first heat of the distemper.

Time inured them to it all; and they ventured everywhere
afterwards, without hesitation, as I shall have occasion to
mention at large hereafter.

I am supposing now the Plague to be begun, as I have
said, and that the magistrates began to take the condition
of the people into their serious consideration. What they
did as to the regulation of inhabitants, and of infected
families, I shall speak to by itself; but as to the affair of
health, it is proper to mention it here, that having seen
the foolish humour of the people in running after quacks,
and mountebanks, wizards, and fortune-tellers, (which they
did as above, even to madness,) the Lord Mayor, a very
sober and religious gentleman, appointed physicians and
surgeons for relief of the poor ; I mean, the diseased poor ;
and, in particular, ordered the College of Physicians to
publish directions for cheap remedies for the poor, in all
circumstances of the distemper. This, indeed, was one of

the most charitable and judicious things that could be done at that time; for this drove the people from haunting the doors of every disperser of bills, and from taking down blindly, and without consideration, poison for physic, and death instead of life.

This direction of the physicians was done by a consultation of the whole College; and, as it was particularly calculated for the use of the poor, and for cheap medicines, it was made public, so that everybody might see it; and copies were given gratis to all that desired it. But as it is public, and to be seen on all occasions, I need not give the reader of this the trouble of it.

I shall not be supposed to lessen the authority or capacity of the physicians when I say that the violence of the distemper, when it came to its extremity, was like the Fire the next year. The Fire which consumed what the Plague could not touch, defied all the application of remedies; the fire-engines were broken, the buckets thrown away, and the power of man was baffled and brought to an end: so the Plague defied all medicines; the very physicians were seized with it, with their preservatives in their mouths; and men went about prescribing to others, and telling them what to do, till the tokens were upon them, and they dropped down dead; destroyed by that very enemy they directed others to oppose. This was the case of several physicians, even some of them the most eminent, and of several of the most skilful surgeons. Abundance of quacks too died, who had the folly to trust to their own medicines, which they must needs be conscious to themselves, were good for nothing; and who rather ought, like other sorts of thieves, to have run away, sensible of their guilt, from the justice that they could not but expect should punish them, as they knew they had deserved.

Not that it is any derogation from the labour, or application of the physicians, to say they fell in the common calamity: nor is it so intended by me; it rather is to their praise, that they ventured their lives so far as even to lose them in the service of mankind. They endeavoured to do good, and to save the lives of others; but we were not to expect that the physicians could stop God's judgments, or prevent a distemper evidently armed from Heaven, from executing the errand it was sent about.

Doubtless, the physicians assisted many by their skill, and by their prudence and applications, to the saving of their lives, and restoring their health; but it is not lessening their character, or their skill, to say, they could not cure those that had the tokens upon them, or those who were mortally infected before the physicians were sent for, as was frequently the case.—*History of the Plague.*

2. The Abatement and End of the Pestilence.

I would be glad if I could close the account of this melancholy year with some particular examples historically; I mean of the thankfulness to God our Preserver, for our being delivered from this dreadful calamity. Certainly, the circumstances of the deliverance, as well as the terrible enemy we were delivered from, called upon the whole nation for it; the circumstances of the deliverance were, indeed, very remarkable, as I have in part mentioned already; and particularly, the dreadful condition which we were all in, when we were, to the surprise of the whole town, made joyful with the hope of a stop of the infection.

Nothing but the immediate finger of God, nothing but omnipotent power could have done it; the contagion despised all medicine, death raged in every corner; and had it gone on as it did then, a few weeks more would have cleared the town of all and everything that had a soul. Men began to despair, every heart failed them for fear; people were made desperate through the anguish of their souls, and the terror of death sat in the countenances of the people.

In that very moment when we might very well say, Vain was the help of man; I say, in that very moment it pleased God, with a most agreeable surprise, to cause the fury of it to abate, even of itself; and the malignity declining, as I have said, though infinite numbers were sick, yet fewer died; and the very first week's bill decreased 1843, a vast number indeed.

It is impossible to express the change that appeared in the very countenances of the people, that Thursday morning when the weekly bill came out: it might have been perceived in their countenances, that a secret surprise and smile of joy sat on everybody's face; they shook one another by the hands in the streets, who would hardly go on the same side of the way with one another before; where the streets were not too broad, they would open their windows, and call from one house to another, and asked how they did, and if they had heard the good news that the plague was abated; some would return, when they said good news, and ask, What good news? And when they answered that the plague was abated, and the bills decreased almost two thousand, they would cry out, God be praised; and would weep aloud for joy, telling them they had heard nothing of it; and such was the joy of the people, that it was as it were to them life from the grave. I could almost set down as many extravagant things done in the excess of their joy, as of their grief, but that would be to lessen the value of it.

It is now, as I said before, the people had cast off all

apprehension, and that too fast; indeed we were no more afraid now to pass by a man with a white cap upon his head, or with a cloth wrapt round his neck, or with his leg limping, occasioned by the sores in his groin, all which were frightful to the last degree but the week before; but now the street was full of them, and these poor recovering creatures, give them their due, appeared very sensible of their unexpected deliverance; and I should wrong them very much, if I should not acknowledge, that I believe many of them were really thankful; but I must own, that for the generality of the people, it might too justly be said of them as was said of the children of Israel, after their being delivered from the host of Pharaoh, when they passed the Red Sea, and looked back, and saw the Egyptians overwhelmed in the water; viz., that they sang but they soon forgot His works.—*History of the Plague.*

3. The Trader.

TRADE must not be entered into as a thing of light concern; it is called business very properly, for it is a business for life, and ought to be followed as one of the great businesses of life.   He that trades in jest, will certainly break in earnest; and this is one reason why so many tradesmen come to so hasty a conclusion of their affairs.   It must be followed with a full attention of the mind, and full attendance of the person; nothing but what are to be called the necessary duties of life are to intervene; and even those are to be limited so as not to be prejudicial to business.

The duties of life, which are either spiritual or secular, must not interfere with, nor jostle one another out of its place.   It is the duty of every Christian to worship God, to pay his homage morning and evening to his Maker, and at all other proper seasons to behave as becomes a sincere

worshipper of God; nor must any avocation, however necessary, interfere with this duty, either in public or in private. Nor,
on the other hand, must a man be so intent upon religious
duties as to neglect the proper times and seasons of business.
There is a medium to be observed in everything, and works
of supererogation are not required at any man's hands;
though it must be confessed, there is far less need of cautions
to be given on this side of the question than on the other;
for alas! so little danger are we in generally of being hurt
by too much religion, that it is more than twenty times for
once that tradesmen neglect their shops and business to
follow the track of their vices and extravagances, by taverns,
gaming-houses, balls, masquerades, plays, harlequinery, and
operas, insomuch that this may be truly called an age of gallantry and gaiety. The playhouses and balls are now filled
with citizens and young tradesmen, more than with gentlemen and families of distinction; the shopkeepers wear different garbs than what they were wont to do, are decked out
with long wigs and swords, and all the fugal badges of trade
are quite disdained and thrown aside.

But what is the consequence? You did not see in those
days such frequent acts of grace for the relief of insolvent
debtors, and yet the jails filled with insolvents before the next
year, though ten or twelve thousand have been released at a
time by those acts. Nor did you see so many commissions of
bankrupt in the *Gazette* as now. The wise man said long
ago, *He that loves pleasure shall be a poor man.* But nothing
ruins a tradesman so effectually as the neglect of his business; he, therefore, who is not determined to pursue his
trade diligently, had much better never begin it.

Nor can a man, without diligence, ever thoroughly understand his business; and how should he thrive when he
does not perfectly know what he is doing, or how to do it?

Application to his trade teaches him how to carry it on as much as his going apprentice taught him how to set it up. The diligent tradesman is always the knowing and complete tradesman.

Now in order to have a man apply heartily, and pursue earnestly the business he is engaged in, there is yet another thing necessary, namely, that he should delight in it. To follow a trade, and not to love and delight in it, is making it a slavery or bondage, not a business; the shop becomes a bridewell, and the warehouse a house of correction to the tradesman, if he does not delight in his trade.

To delight in business is making business pleasant and agreeable, and such a tradesman cannot but be diligent in it. This, according to Solomon, makes him certainly rich, raises him above the world, and makes him able to instruct and encourage those who come after him. . . .

Such a man as this, as he rose by steps of wisdom and prudence, so he will stand upon the same bottom, and go on to act by the same rules, and not run into the vices of trade, when he has thriven by the virtues of it.

As he got an estate by honesty, so he will enjoy it with modesty. He is convinced that to boast of his own wisdom in the amassing his money, and insult the senses and understanding of every man that has miscarried, is not only a token of immodesty, but the infallible mark of irreligion, as it is sacrificing to his own net and to his own drag, to his own head and to his own hands.

A wise, sober, modest tradesman, when he is thriven and grown rich, is really a valuable man, and he is valued on all occasions; as he went on with everybody's good wishes when he was getting it, so he has everybody's blessing and good word when he has got it.

If he retains the character when he has retired from business, which he deserved and gained when he was in business, he is a public good in the place where he lives; as he was useful to himself before, he is useful to everybody else after. Such a man has more opportunity of doing good than almost any other person I can name. He is useful a thousand ways, and many of them are such, by his experience and knowledge of business, as men of ten times his learning and education, in other things, cannot know.

He is, in the first place, a kind of a natural magistrate in the town where he lives; and all the little causes, which in matters of trade are innumerable, and which often, for want of such a judge, go on to suits at law, and so ruin the people concerned in them by the expense, the delay, the wounds in substance, and the wounds in reputation which they often bring with them; I say, all these causes are brought before him, and he not only hears and determines them, but in many of them his determination shall be as effectual among the contending tradesmen, and his vote as decisive, as that of any lord chancellor whatever.

He is the general peacemaker of the country, the common arbitrator of all trading differences, family breaches, and private injuries; and, in general, he is the domestic judge, in trade especially; and by this he gains a general respect, an universal kind of reverence in all the families about him, and he has the blessings and prayers of poor and rich.

Again, he is the trade-counsellor of the country where he lives. It must be confessed, in matters of commerce, lawyers make but very poor work, when they come to be consulted about the little disputes which continually happen among tradesmen, and are so far from setting things to rights, that they generally, by their ignorance in the usage and customs of trade, make breaches wider rather than close them, and leave things worse than they find them.

But the old, approved, experienced tradesman, who has the reputation of an honest man, and has left off business, and gone out of trade, with a good reputation for judgment, integrity, and modesty, is the oracle for trade. Every one goes to him for advice, refers to his opinion, and consults with him in difficult and intricate cases. In short, he may be said to be the trade-chancellor of the place; differences are adjusted, enemies reconciled, equitable questions resolved by him. He is not the arbiter, but the umpire; he is the last resort. Even when arbitrators cannot make it up, he is chosen to arbitrate between the arbitrators, and not only adjusts differences before they come to a height, and so prevents the people going to law, saving them from the expense of their money, and the wasting extravagances of violent, and perhaps malicious prosecutions, but makes men friends, when they are, as it were, just beginning to be enemies; and before the breaches are come to a head, he stops the irruption, acts the part of a moderator, calms the passions of the furious, checks the spirits of the contentious, and, finding out the healing medium which satisfies both sides, brings them to yield to one another, and so does justice to both.

Thus he is, in a word, a kind of a common peacemaker, and is the father of the trading world in the orb or circle wherein he moves. His presence has a kind of peacemaking aspect in it, and he is more necessary than a magistrate, whether he is in office or not.—*Complete English Tradesman.*

4. China Ware.

THE road all on this side of the country is very populous, and is full of potters and earth-makers, that is to say, people that temper the earth, for the China-ware; and as I was coming along, our Portugal pilot, who had always something

or other to say to make us merry, came sneering to me, and
told me, he would show me the greatest rarity in all the
country, and that I should have this to say of China, after all
the ill-humoured things I had said of it, that I had seen one
thing which was not to be seen in all the world beside. I
was very importunate to know what it was. At last he told
me it was a gentleman's house built all with China-ware.
' Well,' says I, 'are not the materials of their buildings the
product of their own country; and so is all China-ware; is
it not?' ' No, no,' says he, ' I mean it is a house all made
of China-ware, such as you call it in England; or, as it is
called in our country, porcelain.' ' Well,' says I, 'such a
thing may be. How big is it? Can we carry it in a box
upon a camel? If we can, we will buy it.' ' Upon a camel!'
says the old pilot, holding up both his hands, ' why there is
a family of thirty people in it.'

I was then curious indeed to see it, and when I came to
it, it was nothing but this. It was a timber house, or a house
built, as we call it in England, with, lath and plaster, but all
this plastering was really China-ware, that is to say, it was
plastered with the earth that makes China-ware.

The outside, which the sun shone hot upon, was glazed,
and looked very well, perfectly white, and painted with blue
figures, as the large China-ware in England is painted, and
hard, as if it had been burned. As to the inside, all the
walls, instead of wainscot, were lined up with hardened and
painted tiles, like the little square tiles we call galley-tiles in
England, all made of the finest China, and the figures exceeding fine indeed, with extraordinary variety of colours
mixed with gold, many tiles making but one figure, but joined
so artificially, the mortar being made of the same earth, that
it was very hard to see where the tiles met. The floors of
the rooms were of the same composition, and as hard as the

earthen floors we have in use in several parts of England, especially Lincolnshire, Nottinghamshire, Leicestershire, &c., as hard as a stone, and smooth, but not burned and painted, except some smaller rooms, like closets, which were all as it were paved with the same tile. The ceiling, and in a word, all the plastering work in the whole house were of the same earth; and after all, the roof was covered with tiles of the same, but of a deep shining black.

This was a China warehouse indeed, truly and literally to be called so ; and had I not been upon the journey, I could have stayed some days to see and examine the particulars of it. They told me there were fountains and fish-ponds in the garden, all paved at the bottom and sides with the same, and fine statues set up in rows on the walks, entirely formed of the porcelain earth, and burned whole.

As this is one of the singularities of China, so they may be allowed to excel in it; but I am very sure they excel in their accounts of it; for they told me such incredible things of their performance in crockery-ware, for such it is, that I care not to relate, as knowing it could not be true. They told me in particular, of one workman that made a ship with all its tackle, and masts and sails, in earthen-ware, big enough to carry fifty men. If they had told me he launched it, and made a voyage to Japan in it, I might have said something to it indeed ; but as it was, I knew the whole of the story ; which was in short, asking pardon for the word, that the fellow lied.—*Robinson Crusoe, Second Part.*

XXIV.

JONATHAN SWIFT.

1667—1745.

JONATHAN SWIFT, born in 1667, was the son of an English gentleman settled in Ireland; he began life as secretary to Sir William Temple (1689-1699). After that statesman's death, he obtained some small preferment in Ireland; but in 1710 came back to England, and for some years supported Harley and Bolingbroke, the heads of the Tory party, by a series of political pamphlets. With the accession of George I, the Tory Ministry was irretrievably ruined, and Swift was compelled to return to Ireland, to the Deanery of St. Patrick, the only reward he had received for his services. The rest of his life was spent in what he regarded as banishment, and was further embittered by his unhappy relations with two ladies, Esther Johnson and Hester Vanhomrigh, the Stella and Vanessa of his journals and his verse. To the former, whom he had first known in the house of Sir William Temple, in which she was brought up, he was united for many years in marriage, but the tie was never acknowledged during his lifetime, and was thus the cause of much suffering if also of much happiness to both. With the latter he formed a friendship of the most ardent kind, which the lady desired should lead to marriage, and she died broken-hearted on discovering the fact that he was already legally bound to another. Later in life, disease of the brain came on, and he died mad in 1745.

There is no greater master of satire than Swift. He thought clearly, wrote a singularly pure English, and could make every sentence an epigram, without impairing the continuous flow

of his argument. Two of his best-known works have an alle-
gorical character. The *Tale of a Tub* is directed against religious
sects, and was written with such licence of illustration, that
Queen Anne would never permit the author to obtain the preferment he coveted in England. In *Gulliver's Travels*, the satire
is rather against abuses of Government and the pleasant vices of
society. In the latter part of this, as in several of his minor
pieces, he is at times very coarse. This fault grew upon him in
later life, perhaps partly in connection with a diseased brain, and
has caused his writings to be regarded with suspicion. Yet,
judged by the standard of his better works, Swift is a moralist of
high stamp. He attacked the sceptics of his day with scathing
irony. He was the first man who had the heart to feel for the
oppressed Irish peasantry, and the courage to denounce the injustice of English mis-rule. His *Drapier's Letters* form an epoch
in constitutional history; and the peaceful struggle for Irish independence dates from them. The *Journal to Stella* has passages
of infinite tenderness. There have been more faultless and
purer-minded men than Swift; but few have seen more clearly
where wrong lay, or have attacked it more fearlessly.

---

1. The Lawyers.

THERE was another point which a little perplexed him at
present. I had informed him that some of our crew left
their country on account of being ruined by law; that I had
already explained the meaning of the word; but he was at
a loss how it should come to pass, that the law, which was
intended for every man's preservation, should be any man's
ruin. Therefore he desired to be farther satisfied what I
meant by law, and the dispensers thereof, according to the
present practice in my own country; because he thought
nature and reason were sufficient guides for a reasonable
animal, as we pretended to be, in shewing us what he ought
to do, and what to avoid.

I assured his honour, that law was a science in which I had not much conversed, farther than by employing advocates, in vain, upon some injustices that had been done me : however, I would give him all the satisfaction I was able.

I said, there was a society of men among us, bred up from their youth in the art of proving, by words multiplied for the purpose, that white is black, and black is white, according as they are paid. To this society all the rest of the people are slaves. For example, if my neighbour hath a mind to my cow, he hires a lawyer to prove that he ought to have my cow from me. I must then hire another to defend my right, it being against all rules of law that any man should be allowed to speak for himself. Now, in this case, I, who am the right owner, lie under two great disadvantages : first, my lawyer, being practised almost from his cradle in defending falsehood, is quite out of his element when he would be an advocate for justice, which is an unnatural office he always attempts with great awkwardness, if not with ill will. The second disadvantage is, that my lawyer must proceed with great caution, or else he will be reprimanded by the judges, and abhorred by his brethren, as one that would lessen the practice of the law. And therefore I have but two methods to preserve my cow. The first is, to gain over my adversary's lawyer with a double fee, who will then betray his client, by insinuating that he hath justice on his side. The second way is, for my lawyer to make my cause appear as unjust as he can by allowing the cow to belong to my adversary: and this, if it be skilfully done, will certainly bespeak the favour of the bench. Now, your honour is to know, that these judges are persons appointed to decide all controversies of property, as well as for the trial of criminals, and picked out from the most dexterous lawyers, who are grown old or lazy; and having been biassed all their lives against truth and equity, lie under such a fatal necessity of favouring fraud, perjury, and oppression, that I have known some of them refuse a large bribe from the side where justice lay, rather than injure the faculty, by doing anything unbecoming their nature or their office.

It is a maxim among these lawyers, that whatever has been done before may legally be done again; and therefore they take special care to record all the decisions formerly made against common justice and the general reason of mankind. These, under the name of precedents, they produce as authorities to justify the most iniquitous opinions; and the judges never fail of directing accordingly.

In pleading, they studiously avoid entering into the merits of the cause, but are loud, violent, and tedious in dwelling upon all circumstances which are not to the purpose. For instance, in the case already mentioned, they never desire to know what claim or title my adversary has to my cow; but whether the said cow were red or black; her horns long or short; whether the field I graze her in be round or square; whether she was milked at home or abroad; what diseases she is subject to, and the like; after which they consult precedents, adjourn the cause from time to time, and in ten, twenty, or thirty years come to an issue.

It is likewise to be observed, that this society has a peculiar cant and jargon of their own, that no other mortal can understand, and wherein all their laws are written, which they take special care to multiply; whereby they have wholly confounded the very essence of truth and falsehood, of right and wrong; so that it will take thirty years to decide whether the field left me by my ancestors for six generations belongs to me, or to a stranger three hundred miles off.

In the trial of persons accused for crimes against the state, the method is much more short and commendable : the judge first sends to sound the disposition of those in power, after which he can easily hang or save a criminal, strictly preserving all due forms of law.

Here my master interposing, said, it was a pity that creatures endued with such prodigious abilities of mind, as these lawyers, by the description I gave of them, must certainly be, were not rather encouraged to be instructors of others in wisdom and knowledge. In answer to which I assured his honour, that in all points out of their own trade they were usually the most ignorant and stupid generation among us, the most despicable in common conversation, avowed enemies to all knowledge and learning, and equally disposed to pervert the general reason of mankind in every other subject of discourse as in that of their own profession.— *Voyage to the Houyhnhnms.*

2. The Academy of Laputa.

WE crossed a walk to the other part of the academy, where, as I have already said, the projectors in speculative learning resided.

The first professor I saw, was in a very large room, with forty pupils about him. After salutation, observing me to look earnestly upon a frame, which took up the greatest part of both the length and breadth of the room, he said, 'Perhaps I might wonder to see him employed in a project for improving speculative knowledge, by practical mechanical operations. But the world would soon be sensible of its usefulness; and he flattered himself, that a more noble exalted thought never sprang in any other man's head. Every one knew how laborious the usual method is of attaining to arts and sciences; whereas, by his contrivance, the most ignorant person, at a reasonable charge, and with a little bodily labour, might write books in philosophy, poetry, politics, laws, mathematics, and theology, without the least assistance from genius or study.' He then led me to the frame, about the sides whereof all his pupils stood in ranks. It was twenty feet square, placed in the middle of the room. The superficies was composed of several bits of wood, about the bigness of a die, but some larger than others. They were all linked together by slender wires. These bits of wood were covered, on every square, with paper pasted on them; and on these papers were written all the words of their language, in their several moods, tenses, and declensions, but without any order. The professor then desired me to observe; for he was going to set his engine at work. The pupils, at his command, took each of them hold of an iron handle, whereof there were forty fixed round the edges of the frame, and giving them a sudden turn, the whole disposition of the words was entirely changed. He then commanded six-and-thirty of the lads to read the several lines softly, as they appeared upon the frame; and, where they found three or four words together that might make part of a sentence, they dictated to the four remaining boys, who were scribes. This work was repeated three or four times, and, at every turn, the engine was so contrived, that the words shifted into new places, as the square bits of wood moved upside down.

Six hours a-day the young students were employed in this labour; and the professor shewed me several volumes in large folio, already collected, of broken sentences, which he intended to piece together, and, out of those rich materials, to give the world a complete body of all arts and sciences; which, however, might be still improved, and much expedited, if the public would raise a fund for making and employing five hundred such frames in Lagado, and oblige the managers to contribute in common their several collections.

He assured me, that this invention had employed all his thoughts from his youth; that he had emptied the whole vocabulary into his frame, and made the strictest computation of the general proportion there is in books between the number of particles, nouns, and verbs, and other parts of speech.

I made my humblest acknowledgment to this illustrious person, for his great communicativeness; and promised, if ever I had the good fortune to return to my native country, that I would do him justice, as the sole inventor of this wonderful machine; the form and contrivance of which I desired leave to delineate on paper, as in the figure here annexed. I told him, although it were the custom of our learned in Europe to steal inventions from each other, who had thereby at least this advantage, that it became a controversy which was the right owner; yet I would take such caution, that he should have the honour entire, without a rival.

We next went to the school of languages, where three professors sat in consultation upon improving that of their own country.

The first project was to shorten discourse, by cutting polysyllables into one, and leaving out verbs and participles, because, in reality, all things imaginable are but nouns.

The other project was a scheme for entirely abolishing all words whatsoever, and this was urged as a great advantage in point of health, as well as brevity. For it is plain, that every word we speak is, in some degree, a diminution of our lungs by corrosion, and, consequently, contributes to the shortening of our lives. An expedient was therefore offered, that, since words are only names for things, it would be more convenient for all men. to carry about them such things as were necessary to express a particular business they are to discourse on. And this invention would certainly have taken place, to the great ease, as well as health of the subject, if the women, in conjunction with the vulgar and illiterate, had not threatened to raise a rebellion, unless they might be allowed the liberty to speak with their tongues, after the manner of their forefathers ; such constant irre-concilable enemies to science are the common people. However, many of the most learned and wise adhere to the new scheme of expressing themselves by things, which has only this inconvenience attending it, that, if a man's business be very great, and of various kinds, he must be obliged, in proportion, to carry a greater bundle of things upon his back, unless he can afford one or two strong servants to attend him. I have often beheld two of these sages almost sinking under the weight of their packs, like pedlars among us; who, when they meet in the street, would lay down their loads, open their sacks, and hold conversation for an hour together, then put up their implements, help each other to resume their burdens, and take their leave.

But for short conversations, a man may carry implements in his pockets, and under his arms, enough to supply him ; and in his house, he cannot be at a loss. Therefore the room where company meet who practise this art, is full of all things, ready at hand requisite to furnish matter for this kind of artificial converse.

Another great advantage proposed by this invention was, that it would serve as a universal language, to be understood in all civilized nations, whose goods and utensils are generally of the same kind, or nearly resembling, so that their uses might easily be comprehended. And thus ambassadors would be qualified to treat with foreign princes, or ministers of state, to whose tongues they were utter strangers.

In the school of political projectors, I was but ill entertained; the professors appearing, in my judgment, wholly out of their senses, which is a scene that never fails to make me melancholy. These unhappy people were proposing schemes for persuading monarchs to choose favourites upon the score of their wisdom, capacity, and virtue; of teaching ministers to consult the public good: of rewarding merit, great abilities, and eminent services; of instructing princes to know their true interest, by placing it on the same foundation with that of their people; of choosing for employments persons qualified to exercise them; with many other wild impossible chimeras, that never entered before into the heart of man to conceive; and confirmed in me the old observation, 'That there is nothing so extravagant and irrational, which some philosophers have not maintained for truth.'

I heard a very warm debate between two professors, about the most commodious and effectual ways and means of raising money, without grieving the subject. The first affirmed, 'The justest method would be, to lay a certain tax upon vices and folly; and the sum fixed upon every man to be rated, after the fairest manner, by a jury of his neighbours.' The second was of an opinion directly contrary; 'To tax those qualities of body and mind, for which men chiefly value themselves; the rate to be more or less, according to the degrees of excelling; the decision whereof should be left entirely to their own breast.' The highest tax was upon men who are the greatest favourites of the other sex, and the assessments, according to the number and nature of the favours they have received; for which they are allowed to be their own vouchers. Wit, valour, and politeness were likewise proposed to be largely taxed, and collected in the same manner, by every person's giving his own word for the quantum of what he possessed. But as to honour, justice, wisdom, and learning, they should not be taxed at all, because they are qualifications of so singular a kind, that no man will either allow them in his neighbour, or value them in himself.

The women were proposed to be taxed according to their beauty and skill in dressing, wherein they had the same privilege with the men, to be determined by their own judgment. But constancy, chastity, good sense, and good nature, were not rated, because they would not bear the charge of collecting.

To keep senators in the interest of the crown, it was proposed that the members should raffle for employments; every man first taking an oath, and giving security, that he would vote for the court, whether he won or not; after which, the losers had, in their turn, the liberty of raffling upon the next vacancy. Thus, hope and expectation would be kept alive; none would complain of broken promises, but impute their disappointments wholly to fortune, whose shoulders are broader and stronger than those of a ministry.—*Voyage to Laputa.*

3. · English Notions of Ireland.

THERE is a vein of industry and parsimony, that runs through the whole people of England, which, added to the easiness of their rents, makes them rich and sturdy. As to Ireland, they know little more of it than they do of Mexico; further than that it is a country subject to the king of England, full of bogs, inhabited by wild Irish papists, who are kept in awe by mercenary troops sent from thence : and their opinion is, that it were better for England if this whole island were sunk into the sea : for they have a tradition, that every forty years there must be a rebellion in Ireland. I have seen the grossest suppositions pass upon them : that the wild Irish were taken in toils ; but that in some time they would grow so tame as to eat out of your hands : I have been asked by hundreds, and particularly by my neighbours your tenants at Pepperhara, whether I had come from Ireland by sea : and, upon the arrival of an Irish man to a country town, I have known crowds coming about him, and wondering to see him look so much better than themselves.

A gentleman now in Dublin affirms, that, passing some months ago through Northampton, and finding the whole town in a flurry, with bells, bonfires, and illumination ; upon asking the cause, he was told, it was for joy that the Irish had submitted to receive Wood's half-pence. This, I think, plainly shews what sentiments that large town hath of us, and how little they made it their own case ; although they lie directly in our way to London, and therefore cannot but be frequently convinced that we have human shapes.— *Sixth Drapier's Letter.*

4. The Advantages of Public Education.

THERE is one young lord in this town, who by an un-exampled piece of good fortune was miraculously snatched out of the gulph of ignorance, confined to a public school for a due term of years, well whipped when he deserved it, clad no better than his comrades, and always their playfellow on the same foot, had no precedence in the school, but what was given him by his merit, and lost it whenever he was

negligent. It is well known, how many mutinies were bred
at this unprecedented treatment, what complaints among his
relations, and other great ones of both sexes; that his stockings with silver clocks were ravished from him; that he wore
his own hair; that his dress was undistinguished; that he
was not fit to appear at a ball or assembly, nor suffered to
go to either: and it was with the utmost difficulty, he became qualified for his present removal, where he may probably be farther persecuted, and possibly with success, if
the firmness of a very worthy governor and his own good
dispositions, will not preserve him. I confess, I cannot but
wish, he may go on in the way he began; because I have
a curiosity to know by so singular an experiment, whether
truth, honour, justice, temperance, courage, and good sense,
acquired by a school and college education, may not produce a very tolerable lad, although he should happen to fail
in one or two of those accomplishments, which, in the
general vogue, are held so important to the finishing of
a gentleman.

It is true, I have known an academical education to have
been exploded in public assemblies; and have heard more
than one or two persons of high rank declare, they could
learn nothing more at Oxford and Cambridge, than to drink
ale and smoke tobacco; wherein I firmly believed them, and
could have added some hundred examples from my own
observation in one of those universities ; but they all were of
young heirs sent thither only for form; either from schools,
where they were not suffered by their careful parents to
stay above three months in the year; or from under the
management of French family tutors, who yet often attended
them to their college, to prevent all possibility of their improvement; but I never yet knew any one person of quality,
who followed his studies at the university, and carried away

his just proportion of learning, that was not ready upon all occasions to celebrate and defend that course of education, and to prove a patron of learned men.

There is one circumstance in a learned education, which ought to have much weight, even with those who have no learning at all. The books read at school and college are full of incitements to virtue, and discouragements from vice, drawn from the wisest reasons, the strongest motives, and the most influencing examples. Thus young minds are filled early with an inclination to good, and an abhorrence of evil, both which increase in them, according to the advances they make in literature; and although they may be, and too often are, drawn by the temptations of youth, and the opportunities of a large fortune, into some irregularities, when they come forward into the great world, yet it is ever with reluctance and compunction of mind; because their bias to virtue still continues. They may stray sometimes, out of infirmity or compliance; but they will soon return to the right road, and keep it always in view. ·I speak only of those excesses, which are too much the attendants of youth and warmer blood; for as to the points of honour, truth, justice, and other noble gifts of the mind, wherein the temperature of the body has no concern, they are seldom or ever known to be wild.

I have engaged myself very unwarily in too copious a subject for so short a paper. The present scope I would aim at, is, to prove that some proportion of human knowledge appears requisite to those, who by their birth or fortune are called to the making of laws, and, in a subordinate way, to the execution of them; and that such knowledge is not to be obtained, without a ,miracle, under the frequent, corrupt, and sottish methods of educating those, who are born to wealth or titles. For I would have it re-

membered, that I do by no means confine these remarks
to young persons of noble birth ; the same errors running
through all families, where there is wealth enough to afford,
that their sons (at least the eldest) may be good for nothing.
Why should my son be a scholar, when it is not intended
that he should live by his learning? By this rule, if what
is commonly said be true, that ' money answers all things,'
why should my son be honest, temperate, just, or charitable,
since he has no intention to depend upon any of these
qualities for a maintenance?

When all is done, perhaps, upon the whole, the matter is
not so bad as I would make it; and God, who works good
out of evil, acting only by the ordinary course and rule of
nature, permits this continual circulation of human things, for
his own unsearchable ends. The father grows rich by avarice,
injustice, oppression; he is a tyrant in the neighbourhood
over slaves and beggars, whom he calls his tenants. Why
should he desire to have qualities infused into his son, which
himself never possessed, or knew, or found the want of, in
the acquisition of his wealth? The son, bred in sloth and
idleness, becomes a spendthrift, a cully, a profligate, and goes
out of the world a beggar, as his father came in ; thus the
former is punished for his own sins, as well as for those of
the latter. The dunghill, having raised a huge mushroom
of short duration, is now spread to enrich other men's lands.
It is indeed of worse consequence, where noble families are
gone to decay; because their titles and privileges outlive
their estates: and politicians tell us, that nothing is more
dangerous to the public, than a numerous nobility without
merit or fortune. But even here God has likewise prescribed some remedy in the order of nature ; so many great
families coming to an end, by the sloth, luxury and abandoned
lusts, which enervated their breed through every succession,

producing gradually a more effeminate race wholly unfit for propagation.—*An Essay on Modern Education.*

5. Advice to a Young Lady.

IF you are in company with men of learning, though they happen to discourse of arts and sciences out of your compass, yet you will gather more advantage by listening to them, than from all the nonsense and frippery of your own sex; but if they be men of breeding, as well as learning, they will seldom engage in any conversation where you ought not to be a hearer, and in time have your part. If they talk of the manners and customs of the several kingdoms of Europe, of travels into remoter nations, of the state of your own country, or of the great men and actions of Greece and Rome; if they give their judgment upon English and French writers either in verse or prose, of the nature and limits of virtue and vice; it is a shame for an English lady not to relish such discourses, not to improve by them, and endeavour by reading and information to have her share in those entertainments, rather than turn aside, as it is the usual custom, and consult with the woman who sits next her about a new cargo of fans.

It is a little hard, that not one gentleman's daughter in a thousand should be brought to read or understand her own natural tongue, or to be judge of the easiest books that are written in it; as any one may find, who can have the patience to hear them, when they are disposed to mangle a play or novel, where the least word out of the common road is sure to disconcert them; and it is no wonder, when they are not so much as taught to spell in their childhood, nor can ever attain to it in their whole lives. I advise you therefore to read aloud, more or less, every day to your husband, if he will permit you, or to any other friend (but not a female one) who is able to set you right.; and as for spelling, you may compass it in time by making collections from the books you read.

I know very well, that those who are commonly called learned women, have lost all manner of credit by their impertinent talkativeness and conceit of themselves; but there is an easy remedy for this, if you once consider, that after all the pains you may be at, you never can arrive in point of learning to the perfection of a schoolboy. The reading I would advise you to, is only for improvement of your own good sense, which will never fail of being mended by discretion. It is a wrong method, and ill choice of books, that makes those learned ladies just so much the worse for what they have read; and therefore it shall be my care to direct you better, a task for which I take myself to be not ill-qualified; because I have spent more time, and have had more opportunities, than many others, to observe and discover from what source the various follies of women are derived.

Pray observe, how insignificant things are the common race of ladies, when they have passed their youth and beauty; how contemptible they appear to the men, and yet more contemptible to the younger part of their own sex; and have no relief, but in passing their afternoons in visits, where they are never acceptable; and their evenings at cards among each other; while the former part of the day is spent in spleen and envy, or in vain endeavours to repair by art and dress the ruins of time. Whereas I have known ladies at sixty, to whom all the polite part of the court and town paid their addresses, without any farther view than that of enjoying the pleasure of their conversation.

I am ignorant of any one quality that is amiable in a man, which is not equally so in a woman: I do not except even modesty and gentleness of nature. Nor do I know one vice or folly, which is not equally detestable in both. There is indeed one infirmity which is generally allowed you, I mean that of cowardice; yet there should seem to be something very capricious, that when women profess their admiration for a colonel or a captain, on account of his valour, they should fancy it a very graceful and becoming quality in themselves, to be afraid of their own shadows; to scream in a barge when the weather is calmest, or in a coach at a ring: to run from a cow at a hundred yards' distance; to fall into fits at the sight of a spider, an earwig, or a frog. At least, if cowardice be a sign of cruelty, (as it is generally granted,) I can hardly think it an accomplishment so desirable, as to be thought worth improving by affectation.

And as the same virtues equally become both sexes, so there is no quality whereby women endeavour to distinguish themselves from men, for which they are not just so much the worse, except that only of reservedness; which, however, as you generally manage it, is nothing else but affectation or hypocrisy. For, as you cannot too much discountenance those of our sex who presume to take unbecoming liberties before you; so you ought to be wholly unconstrained in the company of deserving men, when you have had sufficient experience of their discretion. . . .

I will add one thing, although it be a little out of place, which is to desire, that you will learn to value and esteem your husband for those good qualities, which he really possesses, and not to fancy others in him which he certainly has not. For, although this latter is generally understood to be a mark of love, yet it is indeed nothing but affectation or ill judgment. It is true, he wants so very few accomplishments, that you are in no great danger of erring on this side; but my caution is occasioned by a lady of your acquaintance, married to a very valuable person, whom yet she is so unfortunate as to be always commending for those perfections to which he can least pretend.—*Letter to a Very Young Lady on her Marriage.*

6. Ill bred Hospitality.

THOSE inferior duties of life, which the French call *les petites morales,* or the smaller morals, are with us distinguished by the name of good manners or breeding.   This I look upon, in the general notion of it, to be a sort of artificial good sense, adapted to the meanest capacities, and introduced to make mankind easy in their commerce with each other.   Low and little understandings, without some rules of this kind, would be perpetually wandering into a thousand indecencies and irregularities in behaviour; and in their ordinary conversation fall into the same boisterous familiarities that one observes amongst them when a debauch hath quite taken away the use of their reason. In other instances it is odd to consider, that, for want of common discretion, the very end of good breeding is wholly perverted; and civility, intended to make us easy, is employed in laying chains and fetters upon us, in debarring us of our wishes, and in crossing our most reasonable desires and inclinations.   This abuse reigns chiefly in the country, as I found to my vexation, when I was last there, in a visit I made to a neighbour about two miles from my cousin.   As soon as I entered the parlour, they put me into the great chair that stood close by a huge fire, and kept me there by force until I was almost stifled.   Then a boy came in great hurry to pull off my boots, which I in vain opposed, urging that I must return soon after dinner. In the meantime the good lady whispered her eldest daughter, and slipped a key into her hand; the girl returned instantly with a beer-glass half full of *aqua mirabilis* and syrup of gillyflowers. I took as much as I had a mind for, but madam vowed I should drink it off; for she was sure it would do me good after coming out of the cold air; and I was forced to obey, which absolutely took away my stomach. When dinner came in, I had a mind to sit at a distance from the fire; but they told me it was as much as my life was worth, and set me with my back just against it. Although my appetite was quite gone, I was resolved to force down as much as I could, and desired the leg of a pullet. 'Indeed, Mr. Bickerstaff (says the lady), you must eat a wing, to oblige me;' and so put a couple upon my plate. I was persecuted at this rate during the whole meal; as often as I called for small beer, the master tipped the wink, and the servant brought me a brimmer of October. Some time after dinner I ordered my cousin's man, who came with me, to get ready the horses; but it was resolved I should not stir that night; and when I seemed pretty much bent upon going, they ordered the stable door to be locked, and the children hid my cloak and boots. The next question was, What would I have for supper? I said I never eat anything at night: but was at last, in my own defence, obliged to name the first thing that came into my head. After three hours spent chiefly in apologies for my entertainment, insinuating to me, 'That this was the worst time of the year for provisions; that they were at a great distance from any market; that they were afraid I should be starved; and that they knew they kept me to my loss;' the lady went, and left me to her husband; for they took special care I should never be alone. As soon as her back was turned, the little misses ran backwards and forwards every moment, and constantly as they came in, or went out, made a courtesy directly at me, which, in good manners, I was forced to return with a bow and Your humble servant, pretty miss. Exactly at eight the mother came up, and discovered, by the redness of her face, that supper was not far off. It was twice as large as the dinner, and my persecution doubled in proportion. I desired at my usual hour to go to my repose, and was conducted to my chamber by the gentleman, his lady, and the whole train of children. They importuned me to drink something before I went to bed; and, upon my refusing, at last left a bottle of *stingo* as they called it, for fear I should wake and be thirsty in the night. I was forced in the morning to rise and dress myself in the dark, because they would not suffer my kinsman's servant to disturb me at the hour I desired to be called. I was now resolved to break through all measures to get away; and, after sitting down to a monstrous breakfast of cold beef, mutton, neats tongues, venison pasty, and stale beer, took leave of the family. But the gentleman would needs see me part of the way, and carry me a short cut through his own ground, which he told me would save half a mile's riding. This last piece of civility had like to have cost me dear, being once or twice in danger of my neck by leaping over his ditches, and at last forced to alight in the dirt, when my horse, having slipped his bridle, ran away, and took us up more than an hour to recover him again. It is evident that none of the absurdities I met with in this visit proceeded from an ill intention, but from a wrong judgment of complaisance and a misapplication of the rules of it.—*Tatler.*

XXV.

ANTHONY ASHLEY COOPER, EARL OF SHAFTESBURY.

1671–1713.

ANTHONY ASHLEY COOPER, the author of the *Characteristics*, was the grandson of the great statesman, Dryden's Achitophel, who was the first Earl of Shaftesbury. He had the best means of becoming versed in classical literature and in philosophy. He was taught Greek and Latin orally by a Mrs. Birch, who is said to have been able to speak them fluently, and to have taught her pupil to do so by the time he was eleven years old. In his grandfather's household he had constant opportunity of intercourse with Locke, and had already at the age of eighteen begun a regular correspondence with him on philosophical questions.

He lived a studious and retired life, spending much of his time abroad, either in Italy, where he studied the fine arts elaborately, or in Holland, where he conversed with Bayle, and other free spirits, who found a refuge there. He took little part in English politics. He sate in the Commons during one Parliament (1694–1698), but broke down as a speaker. Afterwards, as a Peer, he was active in the election of William's last Parliament (1701), and is said to have had a hand in the composition of the celebrated speech in which the King called on this Parliament for support in the new war with France. He was a friend of Somers, to whom he addressed the letter on *Enthusiasm*, and a faithful Whig.

He died at Naples in 1713. His treatises were all written

A a 2

(at least in their complete form) during the last five years of his life. The letter on *Enthusiasm* (1708) was occasioned by the excitement about the 'French Prophets,' and was followed by the *Essay on the Freedom of Wit and Humour*. Both deal with the legitimacy of the application of ridicule to religious pretensions. The *Advice to an Author*, which exhibits true self-knowledge as the basis of literary art, was published in 1710. Then came his two distinctly philosophical treatises, the *Inquiry concerning Virtue*, and the *Moralists, a Rhapsody*. The above, with Miscellaneous Reflections, and an essay on Art, purporting to be a 'notion' of a possible 'Tablature of the Judgment of Hercules,' form the *Characteristics*, which were first published complete after his death.

He had a real love for classical literature, and believed himself, as he was believed by his contemporaries, to write a specially classical style. To later readers he has seemed to have lost vernacular vigour without acquiring classical ease. Questions of religion and philosophy he approached too much in the attitude of a well-bred connoisseur to get to the bottom of them. He vigorously maintained, however, as against Hobbes, the 'disinterestedness' of virtue, and introduced the doctrine of a 'moral sense,' i. e. of a specific feeling of pleasure in good actions, as the source of moral judgments. He was a great student of Epictetus and Antoninus, and had a genuine stoical belief in one divine mind, expressed in nature and communicated to man.

---

1. The Masque of Society.

IF a native of Ethiopia were on a sudden transported into Europe, and placed either at Paris or Venice at a time of carnival, when the general face of mankind was disguised, and almost every creature wore a mask; it is probable he would for some time be at a stand, before he discovered the cheat: not imagining that a whole people could be so fantastical, as upon agreement, at an appointed time, to transform themselves by a variety of habits, and make it a solemn practice to impose on one another, by this universal confusion of characters and persons. Though he might at first perhaps have looked on this with a serious eye, it would be hardly possible for him to hold his countenance, when he had perceived what was carrying on. The Europeans, on their side, might laugh perhaps at this simplicity. But our Ethiopian would certainly laugh with better reason. It is easy to see which of the two would be ridiculous. For he who laughs, and is himself ridiculous, bears a double share of ridicule. However, should it so happen, that in the transport of ridicule, our Ethiopian, having his head still running upon masks, and knowing nothing of the fair complexion and common dress of the Europeans, should upon the sight of a natural face and habit, laugh just as heartily as before; would not he in his turn become ridiculous, by carrying the jest too far; when by a silly presumption he took nature for mere art, and mistook perhaps a man of sobriety and sense for one of those ridiculous mummers?

There was a time when men were accountable only for their actions and behaviour. Their opinions were left to themselves. They had liberty to differ in these, as in their faces. Every one took the air and look which was natural to him. But in process of time, it was thought decent to mend men's countenances, and render their intellectual complexions uniform and of a sort. Thus the magistrate became a dresser, and in his turn was dressed too, as he deserved; when he had given up his power to a new order of tiremen. But though in this extraordinary conjuncture it was agreed that there was only one certain and true dress, one single peculiar air, to which it was necessary all people should conform ; yet the misery was, that neither the magistrate nor the tire-men themselves, could resolve, which of the various modes was the exact true one. Imagine now, what the effect of this must needs be; when men became persecuted thus on every side about their air and feature, and were put to their shifts how to adjust and compose their mien, according to the right mode; when a thousand models, a thousand patterns of dress were current, and altered every now and then, upon occasion, according to fashion and the humour of the times. Judge whether men's countenances were not like to grow constrained, and the natural visage of mankind, by this habit, distorted, convulsed, and rendered hardly knowable.

But as unnatural or artificial as the general face of things may have been rendered by this unhappy care of dress, and over-tenderness for the safety of complexions; we must not therefore imagine that all faces are alike besmeared or plaistered. All is not fucus, or mere varnish. Nor is the face of Truth less fair and beautiful, for all the counterfeit vizards which have been put upon her. We must remember the carnival, and what the occasion has been of this wild concourse and medley; who were the institutors of it; and to what purpose men were thus set a-work and amused. We may laugh sufficiently at the original cheat; and, if pity will suffer us, may make ourselves diversion enough with the folly and madness of those who are thus caught, and practised on, by these impostures. But we must remember withal our Ethiopian, and beware, lest by taking plain nature for a vizard, we become more ridiculous than the people whom we ridicule.—' *Sensus Communis,' an Essay on the Freedom of Wit and Humour.*

2. God in the Universe.

THUS I continue then, said Theocles, addressing myself, as you would have me, to that guardian Deity and inspirer, whom we are to imagine present here; but not here only. For ' O mighty Genius ! sole-animating and inspiring Power ! author and subject of these thoughts ! thy influence is universal, and in all things thou art inmost. From thee depend their secret springs of action. Thou movest them with an irresistible, unwearied force, by sacred and inviolable laws, framed for the good of each particular being, as best may suit with the perfection, life, and vigour of the whole. The vital principle is widely shared, and infinitely varied; dispersed throughout; no where extinct. All lives, and by succession still revives. The temporary beings quit their borrowed forms, and yield their elementary substance to new comers. Called, in their several turns, to life, they view the light, and viewing pass ; that others too may be spectators of the goodly scene, and greater numbers still enjoy the privilege of Nature. Munificent and great, she imparts herself to most ; and makes the subjects of her bounty infinite. Nought stays her hastening hand. No time nor substance is lost or unimproved. New forms arise ; and when the old dissolve, the matter whence they were composed, is not left useless, but wrought with equal management and art, even in corruption, Nature's seeming waste, and vile abhorrence. The abject state appears merely as the way or passage to some better. But could we nearly view it, and with indifference, remote from the antipathy of sense, we then perhaps should highest raise our admiration ; convinced that even the way itself was equal to the end. Nor can we judge less favourably of that consummate art exhibited through all the works of nature ; since our weak eyes, helped by mechanic art, discover in these works a hidden scene of wonders; worlds within worlds, of infinite minuteness, though as to art still equal to the greatest, and pregnant with more wonders than the most discerning sense, joined with the greatest art, or the acutest reason, can penetrate or unfold.

But it is in vain for us to search the bulky mass of matter; seeking to know its nature; how great the whole itself, or even how small its parts.

If, knowing only some of the rules of motion, we seek to trace it further, it is in vain we follow it into the bodies it has reached. Our tardy apprehensions fail us, and can reach nothing beyond the body itself, through which it is diffused. Wonderful being, (if we may call it so,) which bodies never receive, except from others which lose it; nor ever lose, unless by imparting it to others. Even without change of place it has its force; and bodies big with motion labour to move, yet stir not; whilst they express an energy beyond our comprehension.

In vain too we pursue that phantom Time, too small, and yet too mighty for our grasp; when shrinking to a narrow point, it escapes our hold, or mocks our scanty thought by swelling to eternity an object unproportioned to our capacity, as is thy being, O thou ancient Cause! older than Time, yet young with fresh Eternity.

In vain we try to fathom the abyss of space, the seat of thy extensive being; of which no place is empty, no void which is not full.

In vain we labour to understand that principle of sense and thought, which seeming in us to depend so much on motion, yet differs so much from it, and from matter itself, as not to suffer us to conceive how thought can more result from this, than this arise from thought. But thought we own preeminent, and confess the reallest of beings; the only existence of which we are made sure, by being conscious. All else may be only dream and shadow. All which even sense suggests may be deceitful. The sense itself remains still; reason subsists; and thought maintains its eldership of being. Thus are we in a manner conscious of that original and externally existent thought, whence we derive our own. And thus the assurance we have of the existence of beings above our sense, and of Thee (the great exemplar of thy works), comes from Thee, the all-true, and perfect, who hast thus communicated thyself more immediately to us, so as in some manner to inhabit within our souls; Thou who art original soul, diffusive, vital in all, inspiriting the whole!

All nature's wonders serve to excite and perfect this idea of their Author. It is here He suffers us to see, and even converse with Him, in a manner suitable to our frailty. How glorious is it to contemplate Him, in this noblest of His works apparent to us, the system of the bigger world!'
—*From The Moralists, a Philosophical Rhapsody.*

3. Common-Sense Morality.

A MAN of thorough good-breeding, whatever else he be, is incapable of doing a rude or brutal action. He never deliberates in this case, or considers of the matter by prudential rules of self-interest and advantage. He acts from his nature, in a manner necessarily, and without reflection: and if he did not, it were impossible for him to answer his character, or be found that truly well-bred man, on every occasion. It is the same with the honest man. He cannot deliberate in the case of a plain villany. A plum is no temptation to him. He likes and loves himself too well, to change hearts with one of those corrupt miscreants, who amongst them gave that name to a round sum of money gained by rapine and plunder of the commonwealth. He who would enjoy a freedom of mind, and be truly possessor of himself, must be above the thought of stooping to what is villanous or base. He, on the other side, who has a heart to stoop, must necessarily quit the thought of manliness, resolution, friendship, merit, and a character with himself and others. But to affect these enjoyments and advantages, together with the privileges of a licentious principle; to pretend to enjoy society, and a free mind, in company with a knavish heart, is as ridiculous as the way of children, who eat their cake, and afterwards cry for it. When men begin to deliberate about dishonesty, and finding it go less against their stomach, ask slyly, 'Why they should stick at a good piece of knavery, for a good sum?' they should be told, as children, that they cannot eat their cake, and have it.

When men, indeed, are become accomplished knaves, they are past crying for their cake. They know themselves, and are known by mankind. It is not these who are so much envied or admired. The moderate kind are the more taking with us. Yet, had we sense, we should consider, it is in reality the thorough profligate knave, the very complete unnatural villain alone, who can any way bid for happiness with the honest man. True interest is wholly on one side, or the other. All between is inconsistency, irresolution, remorse, vexation, and an ague-fit; from hot to cold; from one passion to another quite contrary; a perpetual discord of life; and an alternate disquiet and self-dislike. The only rest or repose must be through one, determined, considerate resolution: which when once taken, must be courageously kept, and the passions and affections brought under obedience to it; the temper steeled and hardened to the mind; the disposition to the judgment. Both must agree; else all must be disturbance and confusion. So that to think with one's self, in good earnest, 'Why may not one do this little villany, or commit this one treachery, and but for once?' is the most ridiculous imagination in the world, and contrary to common sense. For a common honest man whilst left to himself, and undisturbed by philosophy, and subtile reasonings about his interest, gives no other answer to the thought of villany, than that he cannot possibly find in his heart to set about it, or conquer the natural aversion he has to it. And this is natural and just.

The truth is, as notions stand now in the world, with respect to morals, honesty is like to gain little by philosophy, or deep speculations of any kind. In the main, it is best to stick to common sense, and go no further. Men's first thoughts, in this matter, are generally better than their second; their natural notions better than those refined by study, or consultation with casuists. According to common speech, as well as common sense, Honesty is the best policy: but, according to refined sense, the only well-advised persons, as to this world, are errant knaves; and they alone are thought to serve themselves, who serve their passions, and indulge their loosest appetites and desires.—Such, it seems, are the wise, and such the wisdom of this world!

An ordinary man talking of a vile action, in a way of common sense, says naturally and heartily, 'He would not be guilty of such a thing for the whole world.' But speculative men find great modifications in the case; many ways of evasion; many remedies; many alleviations. A good gift rightly applied; a right method of suing out a pardon;

good almshouses, and charitable foundations erected for right worshippers ; and a good zeal shown for the right belief, may sufficiently atone for one wrong practice; especially when it is such as raises a man to a considerable power (as they say) of doing good, and serving the true cause.

Many a good estate, many a high station has been gained upon such a bottom as this. Some crowns too may have been purchased on these terms : and some great emperors (if I mistake not) there have been of old, who were much assisted by these or the like principles; and in return were not ungrateful to the cause and party which had assisted them. The forgers of such morals have been amply endowed : and the world has paid roundly for its philosophy; since the original plain principles of humanity, and the simple honest precepts of peace and mutual love, have, by a sort of spiritual chymists, been so sublimated, as to become the highest corrosives; and passing through their limbecs, have yielded the strongest spirit of mutual hatred and malignant persecution.—'*Sensus Communis,*' *or an Essay on the Freedom of Wit and Humour.*

4. Egotism in Writing.

It is observable, that the writers of Memoirs and Essays are chiefly subject to this frothy distemper. Nor can it be doubted that this is the true reason why these gentlemen entertain the world so lavishly with what relates to themselves. For having had no opportunity of privately conversing with themselves, or exercising their own genius, so as to make acquaintance with it, or prove its strength ; they immediately fall to work in a wrong place, and exhibit on the stage of the world that practice which they should have kept to themselves; if they designed that either they, or the world, should be the better for their moralities. Who indeed can endure to hear an empiric talk of his own constitution, how he governs and manages it, what diet agrees best with it, and what his practice is with himself? The proverb, no doubt, is very just, 'Physician cure thyself.' Yet methinks one should have but an ill time, to be present at these bodily operations. Nor is the reader in truth any better entertained, when he is obliged to assist at the experimental discussions of his practising author, who all the while is in reality doing no better, than taking his physic in public.

For this reason, I hold it very indecent for any one to publish his meditations, occasional reflections, solitary thoughts, or other such exercises as come under the notion of this self-discoursing practice. And the modestest title I can conceive for such works, would be that of a certain author who called them his crudities. . . . For so public-spirited they are, that they can never afford themselves the least time to think in private, for their own particular benefit and use. For this reason, though they are often retired, they are never by themselves. The world is ever of the party. They have their author-character in view, and are always considering how this or that thought would serve to complete some set of contemplations, or furnish out the common-place book, from whence these treasured riches are to flow in plenty on the necessitous world.

But if our candidates for authorship happen to be of the sanctified kind, it is not to be imagined how much farther still their charity is apt to extend. So exceeding great is their indulgence and tenderness for mankind, that they are unwilling the least sample of their devout exercise should be lost. Though there are already so many formularies and rituals appointed for this species of soliloquy; they can allow nothing to lie concealed, which passes in this religious commerce and way of dialogue between them and their soul.

These may be termed a sort of pseudo-ascetics, who can have no real converse either with themselves, or with heaven; whilst they look thus asquint upon the world, and carry titles and editions along with them in their meditations. And although the books of this sort, by a common idiom, are called good books; the authors, for certain, are a sorry race: for religious crudities are undoubtedly the worst of any. A saint-author of all men least values politeness. He scorns to confine that spirit in which he writes, to rules of criticism and profane learning. Nor is he inclined in any respect to play the critic on himself, or regulate his style or language by the standard of good company, and people of the better sort. He is above the consideration of that which in a narrow sense we call manners. Nor is he apt to examine any other faults than those which he calls sins; though a sinner against good breeding, and the laws of decency, will no more be esteemed a good author, than will a sinner against grammar, good argument, or good sense. And if moderation and temper are not of the party with a writer, let his cause be ever so good, I doubt whether he will be able to recommend it with great advantage to the world. . . . . .

A remarkable instance of the.want of this sovereign remedy may be drawn from our common great talkers, who engross the greatest part of the conversations of the world, and are the forwardest to speak in public assemblies. . Many of these have a sprightly genius, attended with a mighty heat and ebullition of fancy. But it is a certain observation in our science, that they who are great talkers in company, have never been any talkers by themselves, nor used to these.private discussions of our home-regimen. For which reason their froth abounds. Nor can they discharge any thing without some mixture of it. But when they carry their attempts beyond ordinary discourse, and would rise to the capacity of authors, the case grows worse with them. Their page can carry none of the advantages of their person. They can no way bring into paper those airs they give themselves in discourse. The turns of voice and action, with which they help out many a lame thought and incoherent sentence, must here be laid aside; and the speech taken to pieces, compared together, and examined from head to foot. So that unless the party has been used to play the critic thoroughly upon himself, he will hardly be found proof against the criticisms of others. His thoughts can never appear very correct, unless they have been used to sound correction by themselves, and been well formed and disciplined before they are brought into the field. It is the hardest thing in the world to be a good thinker, without being a strong self-examiner, and thorough-paced dialogist, in this solitary way.—*Soliloquy, or Advice to an Author.*

XXVI.

SIR RICHARD STEELE.

1671—1729.

RICHARD STEELE was born in 1671, of English parents, in Dublin, where his father was secretary to the Duke of Ormond. He lost his father when he was very young, and was sent by the Duke of Ormond to the Charterhouse, where he was the school-fellow of Addison. He was admitted a Postmaster of Merton College, Oxford, in 1691, but left the University without taking a degree, and entered the army, enlisting as a private in the horse-guards. For this he was disinherited by a rich relation, but his convivial and popular qualities attracted the good-will of his officers, and he obtained a commission and rose to the rank of captain ere he quitted the service in 1703. At the beginning of the reign of Queen Anne he obtained the appointment of Gazetteer. In 1713 Steele entered Parliament as member for Stockbridge, but two years later was expelled from the House for alleged seditious libels, contained in the *Englishman* and the *Crisis*, for which he was certainly only in part responsible. On the accession of George the First he obtained some minor offices, received a gratuity, and was knighted. In 1715 he again entered Parliament as member for Boroughbridge in Yorkshire.

Some years before his death he was struck with paralysis, and retired to his country-seat in Wales, where he died in 1729.

Steele commenced his career as an author with a Poem on the Funeral of Queen Mary. It was quickly followed by a treatise in prose, The Christian Hero—written in the first instance for his own use while in the army, and then published in order that

he might̨thus bind himself publicly to the principles he had advo-
cated. Steele's first comedy, 'Grief à la Mode,' had much success
and long held a place on the stage. It was followed by several
other pieces with varying fortune. As a dramatic writer Steele
was anxious, as many of his papers show, together with Addison
and others, to hasten the time when the morals of the age should
be reformed by a well-regulated theatre. But though Steele had
considerable success both as a play-writer and as a pamphleteer,
he owes his chief reputation to his efforts as an essayist. The
Tatler, which he commenced in 1709, was the beginning of a
new era in periodical writing. The paper appeared three times
a week, with some items of news especially on foreign affairs,
respecting which his position as Gazetteer enabled him to
obtain the earliest information ; but the distinctive point of the
Tatler was the papers which it contained on the moral, social, and
economical topics of the day, interspersed with literary and
theatrical notices; the model thus formed has been copied
down to the present day in many contemporary weekly journals.
The *Tatler* was followed in 1711 by the *Spectator*, in 1713 by the
Guardian, and by a succession of other journals of similar nature,
among which were the *Rambler* and the *Idler*. To his association
with the great name of Addison, even more than to his own
merits, Steele owes the reputation he has acquired in English
Literature. He possesses considerable dramatic and descriptive
power ; his style is ordinarily light and graceful, well-fitted to the
somewhat ephemeral subjects about which he commonly writes.
But in his more serious moods, he is not without a certain unaffected tenderness, which has the powerful charm of sincerity.

---

1. Impudence and False Modesty.

IF we would examine into the secret springs of action
in the *impudent* and the *absurd*, we shall find, though they
bear a great resemblance in their behaviour, that they move
upon very different principles. The *impudent* are pressing,
though they know they are disagreeable; the *absurd* are

importunate, because they think they are acceptable. *Impudence* is a vice, and *Absurdity* a folly. Sir Francis Bacon talks very agreeably on the subject of *Impudence.* He takes notice, that the orator being asked, what was the first, second, and third requisite to make a fine speaker? still answered, *Action.* This, said he, is the very outward form of speaking; and yet it is what with the generality has more force than the most consummate abilities. *Impudence* is to the rest of mankind, of the same use which *action* is to orators.

The truth is, the gross of men are governed more by appearances than realities; and the impudent man in his air and behaviour undertakes for himself that he has ability and merit, while the modest or diffident gives himself up as one who is possessed of neither. For this reason, men of front carry things before them with little opposition; and make so skilful a use of their talent, that they can grow out of humour like men of consequence, and be sour, and make their dissatisfaction do them the same service as desert. This way of thinking has often furnished me with an apology for great men who confer favours on the impudent. In carrying on the government of mankind, they are not to consider what men they themselves approve in their closets and private conversations; but what men will extend themselves farthest, and more generally pass upon the world for such as their patrons want in such and such stations, and consequently take so much work off the hands of those who employ them.

Far be it that I should attempt to lessen the acceptance which men of this character meet with in the world; but I humbly propose only, that they who have merit of a different kind would accomplish themselves in some degree with this quality, of which I am now treating. Nay, I allow these gentlemen to press as forward as they please in the advancement of their interests and fortunes, but not to intrude upon others in conversation also. Let them do what they can with the rich and the great, as far as they are suffered; but let them not interrupt the easy and agreeable. They may be useful as servants in ambition, but never as associates in pleasure. However, as I would still drive at something instructive in every lucubration, I must recommend it to all men who feel in themselves an impulse towards attempting laudable actions, to acquire such a degree of assurance, as never to lose the possession of themselves in public or private, so far as to be incapable of acting with a due decorum on any occasion they are called to. It is a mean want of fortitude in a good man, not to be able to do a virtuous action with as much confidence as an impudent fellow does an ill one. There is no way of mending such false modesty, but by laying it down for a rule, that there is nothing shameful but what is criminal.

The Jesuits, an order whose institution is perfectly calculated for making a progress in the world, take care to accomplish their disciples for it, by breaking them of all impertinent bashfulness, and accustoming them to a ready performance of all indifferent things. I remember in my travels, when I was once at a public exercise in one of their schools, a young man made a most admirable speech, with all the beauty of action, cadence of voice, and force of argument imaginable, in defence of the love of glory. We were all enamoured with the grace of the youth, as he came down from the desk where he spoke, to present a copy of his speech to the head of the society. The principal received it in a very obliging manner, and bid him go to the market-place and fetch a joint of meat, for he should dine with him.   He bowed, and in a trice the orator returned, full of the sense of glory in this obedience, and with the best shoulder of mutton in the market.

This treatment capacitates them for every scene of life. I therefore recommend it to the consideration of all who have the instruction of youth, which of the two is the more inexcusable, he who does everything by the mere force of his impudence, or he who performs nothing through the oppression of his modesty?   In a word, it is weakness not to be able to attempt what a man thinks he ought, and there is no modesty but in self-denial.—*Tatler, No.* 168.

2.   The Remembrance of lost Friends.

THERE are those among mankind, who can enjoy no relish of their being, except the world is made acquainted with all that relates to them, and think everything lost that passes unobserved; but others find a solid delight in stealing by the crowd, and modelling their life after such a manner, as is as much above the approbation as the practice of the vulgar.   Life being too short to give instances great enough of true friendship or good-will, some sages have thought it pious to preserve a certain reverence for the *manes* of their deceased friends; and have withdrawn themselves from the rest of the world at certain seasons, to commemorate in their own thoughts such of their acquaintance who have gone before them out of this life.   And indeed, when we are advanced in years, there is not a more pleasing entertainment, than to recollect in a gloomy moment the many we have parted with, that have been dear and agreeable to us, and to cast a melancholy thought or two after those with whom, perhaps, we have indulged ourselves in whole nights of mirth and jollity.   With such inclinations in my heart I went to my closet yesterday evening, and resolved to be sorrowful; upon which occasion I could not but look with disdain upon myself, that though all the reasons which I had to lament the loss of many of my friends are now as forcible as at the moment of their departure, yet did not my heart swell with the same sorrow which I felt at that time: but I could, without tears, reflect upon many pleasing adventures I have had with some, who have long been blended with common earth. Though it is by the benefit of nature, that length of time blots out the violence of afflictions; yet with tempers too much given to pleasure, it is almost necessary to revive the old places of grief in our memory; and ponder step by step on past life, to lead the mind into that sobriety of thought which poises the heart, and makes it beat with due time, without being quickened with desire, or retarded with despair, from its proper and equal motion. When we wind up a clock that is out of order, to make it go well for the future, we do not immediately set the hand to the present instant, but we make it strike the round of all its hours, before it can recover the regularity of its time. Such, thought I, shall be my method this evening; and since it is that day of the year, which I dedicate to the memory of such in another life as I much delighted in when living, an hour or two shall be sacred to sorrow and their memory, while I run over all the melancholy circumstances of this kind which have occurred to me in my whole life.

The first sense of sorrow I ever knew was upon the death of my father, at which time I was not quite five years of age; but was rather amazed at what all the house meant, than possessed with a real understanding why nobody was willing to play with me. I remember I went into the room where his body lay, and my mother sat weeping alone by it. I had my battledore in my hand, and fell a-beating the coffin, and calling Papa; for, I know not how, I had some slight idea that he was locked up there. My mother catched me in her arms, and, transported beyond all patience of the silent grief she was before in, she almost smothered me in her embraces; and told me in a flood of tears, 'Papa could not hear me, and would play with me no more, for they were going to put him under ground, whence he could never come to us again.' She was a very beautiful woman, of a noble spirit, and there was a dignity in her grief, amidst all the wildness of her transport, which, methought, struck me with an instinct of sorrow, that before I was sensible of what it was to grieve, seized my very soul, and has made pity the weakness of my heart ever since. The mind in infancy is, methinks, like the body in embryo; and receives impressions so forcible, that they are as hard to be removed by reason, as any mark, with which a child is born, is to be taken away by any future application. Hence it is, that good nature in me is no merit; but having been so frequently overwhelmed with her tears before I knew the cause of any affliction, or could draw defences from my own judgment, I imbibed commiseration, remorse, and an unmanly gentleness of mind, which has since ensnared me into ten thousand calamities; from whence I can reap no advantage, except it be, that, in such a humour as I am now in, I can the better indulge myself in the softness of humanity, and enjoy that sweet anxiety which arises from the memory of past afflictions.

We, that are very old, are better able to remember things which befel us in our distant youth, than the passages of later days. For this reason it is, that the companions of my strong and vigorous years present themselves more immediately to me in this office of sorrow. Untimely or unhappy deaths are what we are most apt to lament: so little are we able to make it indifferent when a thing happens, though we know it must happen. Thus we groan under life, and bewail those who are relieved from it. Every object that returns to our imagination raises different passions, according to the circumstance of their departure. Who can have lived in an army, and in a serious hour reflect upon the many gay and agreeable men that might long have flourished in the arts of peace, and not join with the imprecations of the fatherless and widow on the tyrant to whose ambition they fell sacrifices? But gallant men, who are cut off by the sword, move rather our veneration than our pity: and we gather relief enough from their own contempt of death, to make it no evil, which was approached with so much cheerfulness, and attended with so much honour. But when we turn our thoughts from the great parts of life on such occasions, and instead of lamenting those who stood ready to give death to those from whom they had the fortune to receive it; I say, when we let our thoughts wander from such noble objects, and consider the havoc which is made among the tender and the innocent, pity enters with an unmixed softness, and possesses all our souls at once.—*Tatler, No.* 181.

3. The True Fine Gentleman.

It is a most vexatious thing to an old man, who endeavours to square his notions by reason, and to talk from reflection and experience, to fall in with a circle of young ladies at their afternoon tea-table. This happened very lately to be my fate. The conversation, for the first half-hour, was so very rambling, that it is hard to say what was talked of, or who spoke least to the purpose. The various motions of the fan, the tossings of the head, intermixed with all the pretty kinds of laughter, made up the greatest part of the discourse. At last, this modish way of shining, and being witty, settled into something like conversation, and the talk ran upon fine gentlemen. From the several characters that were given, and the exceptions that were made, as this or that gentleman happened to be named, I found that a lady is not difficult to be pleased, and that the town swarms with fine gentlemen. A nimble pair of heels, a smooth complexion, a full-bottom wig, a laced shirt, an embroidered suit; a pair of fringed gloves, a hat and feather; any one or more of these and the like accomplishments ennobles a man, and raises him above the vulgar, in a female imagination. On the contrary, a modest serious behaviour, a plain dress, a thick pair of shoes, a leathern belt, a waistcoat not lined with silk, and such like imperfections, degrade a man, and are so many blots in his escutcheon. I could not forbear smiling at one of the prettiest and liveliest of this gay assembly, who excepted to the gentility of Sir William Hearty, because he wore a frize coat, and breakfasted upon toast and ale. I pretended to admire the fineness of her taste; and to strike in with her in ridiculing those awkward healthy gentlemen, that seem to make nourishment the chief end of eating. I gave her an account of an honest Yorkshire gentleman, who, when I was a traveller, used to invite his acquaintance at Paris to break their fast with him upon cold roast beef and mum. There was, I remember, a little French marquis, who was often pleased to rally him unmercifully upon beef and pudding, of which our country-man would despatch a pound or two with great alacrity, while his antagonist was piddling at a mushroom, or the haunch of a frog. I could perceive the lady was pleased with what I said, and we parted very good friends by virtue of a maxim I always observe: never to contradict or reason with a sprightly female. I went home, however, full of a great many serious reflections upon what had passed: and though, in complaisance, I disguised my sentiments, to keep up the good humour of my fair companions, and to avoid being looked upon as a testy old fellow, yet out of the good-will I bear to the sex, and to prevent for the future their being imposed upon by counterfeits, I shall give them the distinguishing marks of 'a true fine gentleman.'

When a good artist would express any remarkable character in sculpture, he endeavours to work up his figure into all the perfection his imagination can form; and to imitate not so much what is, as what may or ought to be. I shall follow their example, in the idea I am going to trace out of a fine gentleman, by assembling together such qualifications as seem requisite to make the character complete. In order to this I shall premise in general, that by a fine gentleman I mean a man completely qualified as well for the service and good, as for the ornament and delight, of society. When I consider the frame of mind peculiar to a gentleman, I suppose it graced with all the dignity and elevation of spirit that human nature is capable of. To this I would have joined a clear understanding, a reason free from prejudice, a steady judgment, and an extensive knowledge. When I think of the heart of a gentleman, I imagine it firm and intrepid, void of all inordinate passions, and full of tenderness, compassion, and benevolence. When I view the fine gentleman with regard to his manners, methinks I see him modest without bashfulness, frank and affable without impertinence, obliging and complaisant without servility, cheerful and in good humour without noise. These amiable qualities are not easily obtained; neither are there many men that have a genius to excel this way. A finished gentleman is perhaps the most uncommon of all the great characters in life. Besides the natural endowments with which this distinguished man is to be born, he must run through a long series of education. Before he makes his appearance and shines in the world, he must be principled in religion instructed in all the moral virtues, and led through the whole course of the polite arts and sciences. He should be no stranger to courts and to camps: he must travel to open his mind, to enlarge his views, to learn the policies and interests of foreign states, as well as to fashion and polish himself, and to get clear of national prejudices; of which every country has its share. To all these more essential improvements, he must not forget to add the fashionable ornaments of life, such as are the languages and the bodily exercises most in vogue; neither would I have him think even dress itself beneath his notice.

It is no very uncommon thing in the world to meet with men of probity; there are likewise a great many men of honour to be found. Men of courage, men of sense, and men of letters are frequent: but a true fine gentleman is what one seldom sees. He is properly a compound of the various good qualities that embellish mankind. As the great poet animates all the different parts of learning by the force of his genius, and irradiates all the compass of his knowledge by the lustre and brightness of his imagination; so all the great and solid perfections of life appear in the finished gentleman, with a beautiful gloss and varnish; every thing he says or does is accompanied with a manner, or rather a charm, that draws the admiration and good-will of every beholder.—*Guardian, No.* 34.

4. Desultory Reading.

THERE is nothing in which men deceive themselves more ridiculously, than in the point of reading, and which, as it is commonly practised under the notion of improvement, has less advantage. The generality of readers, who are pleased with wandering over a number of books, almost at the same instant, or if confined to one, who pursue the author with much hurry and impatience to his last page, must without doubt be allowed to be notable digesters. This unsettled way of reading naturally seduces us into as undetermined a. manner of thinking, which unprofitably fatigues the imagination, when a continued chain of thought would probably produce inestimable conclusions. All authors are eligible either for their matter or style; if for the first, the elucidation and disposition of it into proper lights ought to employ a judicious reader: if for the last, he ought to observe how some common words are started into a new signification, how such epithets are beautifully reconciled to things that seemed incompatible, and must often remember the whole structure of a period, because by the least transposition, that assemblage of words which is called a style becomes utterly annihilated. The swift despatch of common readers not only eludes their memory, but betrays their apprehension, when the turn of thought and expression would insensibly grow natural to them, would they but give themselves time to receive the impression. Suppose we fix one of these readers in his easy chair, and observe him passing through a book with a grave ruminating face, how ridiculously must he look, if we desire him to give an account of an author he has just read over! and how unheeded must the general character of it be, when given by one of these serene unobservers! The common defence of these people is, that they have no design in reading but for pleasure, which I think should rather arise from the reflection and remembrance of what one has read, than from the transient satisfaction of what one does, and we should be pleased proportionably as we are profited. It is prodigious arrogance in any one to imagine, that by one hasty course through a book he can fully enter into the soul and secrets of a writer, whose life, perhaps, has been busied in the birth of such production. Books that do not immediately concern some profession or science, are generally run over as mere empty entertainments, rather than as matter of improvement; though, in my opinion, a refined speculation upon morality, or history, requires as much time and capacity to collect and digest, as the most abstruse treatise of any profession; and I think, besides, there can be no book well written, but what must necessarily improve the understanding of the reader, even in the very profession to which he applies himself. For to reason with strength, and express himself with propriety, must equally concern the divine, the physician, and the lawyer. My own course of looking into books has occasioned these reflections, and the following account may suggest more.

Having been bred up under a relation that had a pretty large study of books, it became my province once a week to dust them. In the performance of this duty, as I was obliged to take down every particular book, I thought there was no way to deceive the toil of my journey through the different abodes and habitations of these authors but by reading something in every one of them; and in this manner to make my passage easy from the comely folio in the upper shelf or region, even through the crowd of duodecimos in the lower. By frequent exercise I became so great a pro-

ficient in this transitory application to books, that I could
hold open half a dozen small authors in my hand, grasping .
them with as secure a dexterity as a drawer doth his glasses,
and feasting my curious eye with all of them at the same
instant. Through these methods the natural irresolution of
my youth was much strengthened, and having no leisure,
if I had had inclination, to make pertinent observations in
writing, I was thus confirmed a very early wanderer. When
I was sent to Oxford, my chiefest expense ran upon books,
and my only consideration in such expense upon numbers,
so that you may be sure that I had what they call a choice
collection, sometimes buying by the pound, sometimes by
the dozen, at other times by the hundred. For the more
pleasant use of a multitude of books, I had, by frequent
conferences with an ingenious joiner, contrived a machine
of an orbicular structure, that had its particular receptions
for a dozen authors, and which, with the least touch of the
finger would whirl round, and present the reader at once
with a delicious view of its full furniture. Thrice a day
did I change, not only the books, but the languages; and
had used my eye to such a quick succession of objects,
that in the most precipitate twirl I could catch a sentence
out of each author, as it passed fleeting by me. Thus my
hours, days, and years, flew unprofitably away, but yet were
agreeably lengthened by being distinguished with this en-
dearing variety; and I cannot but think myself very fortunate
in my contrivance of this engine, with its several new editions
and amendments, which have contributed so much to the
delight of all studious vagabonds. When I had been resident the usual time at Oxford that gains one admission
into the public library, I was the happiest creature on earth,
promising to myself most delightful travels through this new
world of literature. Sometimes you might see me mounted

upon a ladder, in search of some Arabian manuscripts, which
had slept in a certain corner undisturbed for many years.
Once I had the misfortune to fall from this eminence, and
catching at the chains of the books, was seen hanging in
a very merry posture, with two or three large folios rattling
about my neck, till the humanity of Mr. Crab the librarian
disentangled us.

As I always held it necessary to read in public places, by
way of ostentation, but could not possibly travel with a
library in my pockets, I took the following method to
gratify this errantry of mine. I contrived a little pocket-
book, each leaf of which was a different author, so that
my wandering was indulged and concealed within the same
enclosure.

This extravagant humour, which should seem to pronounce
me irrecoverable, had the contrary effect; and my hand and
eye being thus confined to a single book, in a little time reconciled me to the perusal of a single author. However,
I chose such a one as had as little connexion as possible,
turning to the Proverbs of Solomon, where the best instructions are thrown together in the most beautiful range
imaginable, and where I found all that variety which I had
before sought in so many different authors, and which was
so necessary to beguile my attention. By these proper
degrees, I have made so glorious a reformation in my
studies, that I can keep company with Tully in his most
extended periods, and work through the continued narrations
of the most prolix historian. I now read nothing without
making exact collections, and shall shortly give the world
an instance of this in the publication of the following
discourses. The first is a learned controversy about the
existence of griffins, in which I hope to convince the
world, that notwithstanding such a mixed creature has been

allowed by Ælian, Solinus, Mela, and Herodotus, that they have been perfectly mistaken in that matter, and shall support myself by the authority of Albertus, Pliny, Aldrovandus, and Matthias Michovius, which two last have clearly argued that animal out of the creation.

The second is a treatise of sternutation or sneezing, with the original custom of saluting or blessing upon that motion: as also with a problem from Aristotle, showing why sneezing from noon to night was innocent enough, from night to noon, extremely unfortunate.

The third and most curious is my discourse upon the nature of the lake Asphaltites, or the lake of Sodom, being a very careful inquiry whether brickbats and iron will swim in that lake, and feathers sink; as Pliny and Mandeville have averred.

The discussing these difficulties without perplexity or prejudice, the labour in collecting and collating matters of this nature, will, I hope, in a great measure atone for the idle hours I have trifled away in matters of less importance.—*Guardian, No.* 60.

XXVII.

JOSEPH ADDISON.

1672—1719.

JOSEPH ADDISON was born at Milstone, his father's rectory, in Wiltshire, in 1672. He learned the rudiments of education at schools in the neighbourhood of his home, and was then sent to the Charter-house. At fifteen he was entered at Queen's College, Oxford, but he had not been there many months, when a copy of Latin Verses, which attracted the notice of Dr. Lancaster, gained him admittance at Magdalen College. As Demy and afterwards as Fellow he resided for ten years at Magdalen, and his College is still proud of his name. During his residence at the University, he appears to have concentrated his attention on the study of the Latin poets, and to have had some thought of devoting himself to poetry; his position as fellow of a College, rich in preferment, would naturally have led him to the Church as a profession, but the influence of the Lord Keeper Somers and of Montague, Chancellor of the Exchequer, together with a pension obtained for him through Lord Somers, determined his choice otherwise. In 1699, he left Oxford and remained on the Continent for more than four years, studying the language in Paris, and enjoying the society of philosophers and poets, and in Italy making himself familiar with the monuments of ancient and modern art, and strengthening himself by the observation of superstition and misrule in the love which he had early conceived for truth and freedom. Whilst on the Continent he collected the materials for his *Dialogues upon the Usefulness of Ancient Medals*, and also wrote the greater part of his tragedy of *Cato*.

On his return to England, at the end of 1703, Addison's prospects of employment were for a while clouded by the fall of his friend Lord Somers and rise of Godolphin to power at the accession of Anne. But this exclusion from office did not last long, and in 1705 he was made Under Secretary and employed on a foreign mission. He became afterwards Chief Secretary for Ireland—an office which he filled twice—Secretary to the Lord Justices, and finally, in 1717, Secretary of State. This completes the tale of Addison's public career. It was like his private life—unblemished and stainless in its integrity. He married, in 1716, the Countess of Warwick, and died in 1719, having just completed his forty-seventh year.

As an author, Addison has left poems, among which was the *Campaign*, written to celebrate Marlborough's victory at Blenheim; plays, of which the most successful was *Cato*; his *Italian Travels*; and lastly, the immortal papers which have given enduring fame to the *Tatler*, *Spectator*, *Guardian*, and one or two other short-lived periodicals.

Addison's style has always been looked upon as the model of classical English. 'His prose,' in the words of Dr. Johnson, 'is the model of the middle style; on grave subjects not formal, on light occasions not grovelling, pure without scrupulosity, and exact without apparent elaboration; always equable and always easy, it was apparently his principal endeavour to avoid all harshness and severity of diction.' In delicacy of wit, fertility of imagination, and grace of expression, his best essays, Lord Macaulay truly says, approach near to absolute perfection. Mr. Thackeray holds Addison to have been ' one of the most enviable of mankind. A life prosperous and beautiful—a calm death—an immense fame and affection afterwards for his happy and spotless name.'

The extent and variety of his powers is such that it is impossible to give an adequate idea of them in the following brief extracts.

1. The Papal States at the close of the Seventeenth Century.

In my way from Rome to Naples I found nothing so
remarkable as the beauty of the country, and the extreme
poverty of its inhabitants. It is indeed an amazing thing to
see the present desolation of Italy, when one considers what
incredible multitudes of people it abounded with during the
reigns of the Roman Emperors : and notwithstanding the
removal of the Imperial seat, the irruptions of the barbarous
nations, the civil wars of this country, with the hardships of
its several governments, one can scarce imagine how so
plentiful a soil should become so miserably unpeopled in
comparison of what it once was. We may reckon, by a
very moderate computation, more inhabitants in the Campania of old Rome than are now in all Italy. And if we
could number up those prodigious swarms that had settled
themselves in every part of this delightful country, I question
not but that they would amount to more than can be found,
at present, in any six parts of Europe of the same extent.
This desolation appears nowhere greater than in the Pope's
territories, and yet there are several reasons would make a
man expect to see these dominions the best regulated and
most flourishing of any other in Europe. Their Prince is
generally a man of learning and virtue, mature in years and
experience, who has seldom any vanity or pleasure to gratify
at his people's expense, and is neither encumbered with wife,
children or mistresses ; not to mention the supposed sanctity
of his character, which obliges him in a more particular
manner to consult the good and happiness of mankind.
The direction of church and state are lodged entirely in his
own hands, so that his government is naturally free from
those principles of faction and division which are mixed in

the very composition of most others. His subjects are always ready to fall in with his designs, and are more at his disposal than any others of the most absolute government, as they have a greater veneration for his person, and not only court his favour but his blessing. His country is extremely fruitful, and has good havens both for the Adriatic and Mediterranean, which is an advantage peculiar to himself and the Neapolitans above the rest of the Italians. There is still a benefit the Pope enjoys above all other sovereigns, in drawing great sums out of Spain, Germany, and other countries that belong to foreign Princes, which one would fancy might be no small ease to his own subjects. We may here add, that there is no place in Europe so much frequented by strangers, whether they are such as come out of curiosity, or such who are obliged to attend the court of Rome on several occasions, as are many of the cardinals and prelates, that bring considerable sums into the Pope's dominions. But notwithstanding all these promising circumstances, and the long peace that has reigned so many years in Italy, there is not a more miserable people in Europe than the Pope's subjects. His state is thin of inhabitants, and a great part of his soil uncultivated. His subjects are wretchedly poor and idle, and have neither sufficient manufactures, nor traffic to employ them. These ill effects may arise, in a great measure, out of the arbitrariness of the government, but I think they are chiefly to be ascribed to the very genius of the Roman Catholic religion, which here shews itself in its perfection. It is not strange to find a country half unpeopled, where so great a proportion of the inhabitants of both sexes is tied under such vows of chastity, and where at the same time an inquisition forbids all recruits out of any other religion. Nor is it less easy to account for the great poverty and want that are to be met with in a country which invites into it such swarms of vagabonds, under the title of Pilgrims, and shuts up in cloisters such an incredible multitude of young and lusty beggars, who, instead of increasing the common stock by their labour and industry, lie as a dead weight on their fellow-subjects, and consume the charity that ought to support the sickly, old and decrepid. The many hospitals, that are everywhere erected, serve rather to encourage idleness in the people, than to set them at work; not to mention the great riches which lie useless in churches and religious houses, with the multitude of festivals that must never be violated by trade or business. To speak truly, they are here so wholly taken up with men's souls, that they neglect the good of their bodies; and when, to these natural evils in the government and religion, there arises among them an avaricious Pope, who is for making a family, it is no wonder if the people sink under such a complication of distempers. Yet it is to this humour of nepotism that Rome owes its present splendour and magnificence; for it would have been impossible to have furnished out so many glorious palaces with such a profusion of pictures, statues, and the like ornaments, had not the riches of the people at several times fallen into the hands of many different families, and of particular persons; as we may observe, though the bulk of the Roman people was more rich and happy in the times of the commonwealth, the city of Rome received all its beauties and embellishments under the Emperors. It is probable the Campania of Rome, as well as other parts of the Pope's territories, would be cultivated much better than it is, were there not such an exorbitant tax on corn, which makes them plough up only such spots of ground as turn to the most advantage: whereas were the money to be raised on lands, with an exception to some of the more barren parts, that might be tax free for a certain term of years, every one would turn his ground to the best account, and in a little time perhaps bring more money into the Pope's treasury.— *Remarks on several Parts of Italy.*

2. Reading a Dance.

I was this morning awaked by a sudden shake of the house; and as soon as I had got a little out of my consternation, I felt another, which was followed by two or three repetitions of the same convulsion. I got up as fast as possible, girt on my rapier, and snatched up my hat, when my landlady came up to me, and told me, that the gentlewoman of the next house begged me to step thither, for that a lodger she had taken in was run mad, and she desired my advice; as indeed everybody in the whole lane does upon important occasions. I am not like some artists, saucy, because I can be beneficial, but went immediately. Our neighbour told us, she had the day before let her second floor to a very genteel youngish man, who told her he kept extraordinary good hours, and was generally at home most part of the morning and evening at study; but that this morning he had for an hour together made this extravagant noise which we then heard. I went up stairs with my hand upon the hilt of my rapier, and approached this new lodger's door. I looked in at the key-hole, and there I saw a well-made man look with great attention on a book, and on a sudden, jump into the air so high, that his head almost touched the ceiling. He came down safe on his right foot, and again flew up alighting on his left; then looked again at his book, and holding out his right leg, put it into such a quivering motion, that I thought he would have shaked it off. He used the left after the same manner; when on a sudden,

to my great surprise, he stooped himself incredibly low, and
turned gently on his toes. After this circular motion, he
continued bent in that humble posture for some time, looking
on his book. After this, he recovered himself with a sudden
spring and flew round the room in all the violence and
disorder imaginable, till he made a full pause for want of
breath. In this interim my woman asked what I thought: I
whispered, that I thought this learned person an enthusiast,
who possibly had his first education in the Peripatetic way,
which was a sect of philosophers who always studied when
walking. But observing him much out of breath, I thought
it the best time to master him if he were disordered, and
knocked at his door. I was surprised to find him open it,
and say with great civility, and good mien, that he hoped he
had not disturbed us. I believed him in a lucid interval, and
desired he would please to let me see his book. He did so,
smiling. I could not make anything of it, and therefore
asked in what language it was writ. He said, it was
one he studied with great application; but it was his profession to teach it, and could not communicate his knowledge without a consideration. I answered, that I hoped he
would hereafter keep his thoughts to himself; for his meditation this morning had cost me three coffee-dishes, and a clean
pipe. He seemed concerned at that, and told me he was a
dancing-master, and had been reading a dance or two before
he went out, which had been written by one who taught at
an Academy in France. He observed me at a stand, and
went on to inform me, that now articulate motions, as well as
sounds, were expressed by proper characters; and that there
is nothing so common as to communicate a dance by a letter.
I beseeched him hereafter to meditate in a ground room, for
that otherwise it would be impossible for an artist of any
other kind to live near him; and that I was sure, several of

his thoughts this morning would have shaken my spectacles off my nose, had I been myself at study.

I then took my leave of this virtuoso, and returned to my chamber, meditating on the various occupations of rational creatures.— *Tatler, No.* 88.

3. Frozen Words.

THE present paper I intend to fill with an extract of Sir John's Journal, in which that learned and worthy knight gives an account of the freezing and thawing of several short speeches which he made in the territories of Nova Zembla. I need not inform my reader, that the author of *Hudibras* alludes to this strange quality in that cold climate, when, speaking of abstracted notions clothed in a visible shape, he adds that apt simile,

Like words congeal'd in northern air.

Not to keep my reader any longer in suspense, the relation put into modern language is as follows :—

We were separated by a storm in the latitude of 73, insomuch that only the ship which I was in, with a Dutch and a French vessel, got safe into a creek of Nova Zembla. We landed in order to refit our vessels, and store ourselves with provisions. The crew of each vessel made themselves a cabin of turf and wood, at some distance from each other, to fence themselves against the inclemencies of the weather, which was severe beyond imagination. We soon observed, that in talking to one another we lost several of our words, and could not hear one another at above two yards distance, and that too when we sat very near the fire. After much perplexity, I found that our words froze in the air before they could reach the ears of the person to whom they were spoken. I was soon confirmed in this conjecture, when, upon the increase of the cold, the whole company grew dumb, or rather deaf; for every man was sensible, as we afterwards found, that he spoke as well as ever; but the sounds no sooner took air, than they were condensed and lost. It was now a miserable spectacle to see us nodding and gaping at one another, every man talking, and no man heard. One might observe a seaman, that could hail a ship at a league distance, beckoning with his hands, straining with his lungs, and tearing his throat, but all in vain.

————Nec vox, nec verba sequuntur.

We continued here three weeks in this dismal plight. At length, upon a turn of wind, the air about us began to thaw. Our cabin was immediately filled with a dry clattering sound, which I afterwards found to be the crackling of consonants that broke above our heads, and were often mixed with a gentle hissing which I imputed to the letter S, that occurs so frequently in the English tongue. I soon after felt a breeze of whispers rushing by my ear; for those being of a soft and gentle substance, immediately liquified in the warm wind that blew across our cabin. These were soon followed by syllables and short words, and at length by entire sentences, that melted sooner or later, as they were more or less congealed; so that we now heard everything that had been spoken during the whole three weeks that we had been silent, if I may use that expression. It was now very early in the morning, and yet, to my surprise, I heard somebody say, 'Sir John, it is midnight, and time for the ship's crew to go to bed.' This I knew to be the pilot's voice, and upon recollecting myself, I concluded that he had spoken these words to me some days before, though I could not hear them before the present thaw. My reader will easily imagine how the whole crew was amazed, to hear every man talking, and see no man opening his mouth. In the midst of this great surprise we were all in, we heard a volley of oaths and curses, lasting for a long while, and uttered in a very hoarse voice, which I knew belonged to the boatswain, who was a very choleric fellow, and had taken his opportunity of cursing and swearing at me when he thought I could not hear him; for I had several times given him the strappado on that account, as I did not fail to repeat it for these his pious soliloquies when I got him on ship-board.

I must not omit the names of several beauties in Wapping, which were heard every now and then, in the midst of a long sigh that accompanied them; as ' Dear Kate !' ' Pretty Mrs. Peggy !' ' When shall I see my Sue again?' This betrayed several amours which had been concealed till that time, and furnished us with a great deal of mirth in our return to England.

When this confusion of voices was pretty well over, though I was afraid to offer at speaking, as fearing I should not be heard, I proposed a visit to the Dutch cabin, which lay about a mile farther up into the country. My crew were extremely rejoiced to find they had again recovered their hearing, though every man uttered his voice with the same apprehensions that I had done :

———Et timide verba intermissa retentat.

At about half a mile's distance from our cabin, we heard the groanings of a bear, which at first startled us; but upon enquiry we were informed by some of our company, that he was dead, and now lay in salt, having been killed upon that very spot about a fortnight before, in the time of the frost. Not far from the same place we were likewise entertained with some posthumous snarls and barkings of a fox.

We at length arrived at the little Dutch settlement, and

upon entering the room, found it filled with sighs that smelt of brandy, and several other unsavoury sounds that were altogether inarticulate. My valet, who was an Irishman, fell into so great a rage at what he heard, that he drew his sword; but not knowing where to lay the blame, he put it up again. We were stunned with these confused noises, but did not hear a single word till about half an hour after; which I ascribed to the harsh and obdurate sounds of that language, which wanted more time than ours to melt and become audible.

After having here met with a very hearty welcome, we went to the French cabin, who, to make amends for their three weeks' silence, were talking and disputing with greater rapidity and confusion than ever I heard in an assembly even of that nation. Their language, as I found upon the first giving of the weather, fell asunder and dissolved. I was here convinced of an error into which I had before fallen; for I fancied, that for the freezing of the sound, it was necessary for it to be wrapped up, and, as it were, preserved in breath; but I found my mistake, when I heard the sound of a kit playing a minuet over our heads. I asked the occasion of it; upon which one of the company told me, that it would play there above a week longer if the thaw continued; for, says he, finding ourselves bereft of speech, we prevailed upon one of the company, who had this musical instrument about him, to play to us from morning to night; all which time we employed in dancing, in order to dissipate our chagrin, *et tuer le temps.*—*Tatler, No.* 254.

4. Vision of the Palace of Fame.

THERE are two kinds of immortality; that which the soul really enjoys after this life, and that imaginary existence by

which men live in their fame and reputation. The best
and greatest actions have proceeded from the prospect of
the one or the other of these; but my design is to treat
only of those who have chiefly proposed to themselves the
latter, as the principal reward of their labours. It was for
this reason that I excluded from my Tables of Fame all the
great founders and votaries of religion; and it is for this
reason also, that I am more than ordinarily anxious to do
justice to the persons of whom I am now going to speak;
for, since fame was the only end of all their enterprizes and
studies, a man cannot be too scrupulous in allotting them
their due proportion of it. It was this consideration which
made me call the whole body of the learned to my assistance;
to many of whom I must own my obligations for the cata-
logues of illustrious persons which they have sent me in upon
this occasion. I yesterday employed the whole afternoon
in comparing them with each other; which made so strong
an impression upon my imagination, that they broke my sleep
for the first part of the following night, and at length threw
me into a very agreeable vision, which I shall beg leave to
describe in all its particulars.

I dreamed that I was conveyed into a wide and boundless
plain, that was covered with prodigious multitudes of people,
which no man could number. In the midst of it there stood
a mountain, with its head above the clouds. The sides were
extremely steep, and of such a particular structure, that no
creature which was not made in a human figure could
possibly ascend it. On a sudden there was heard from the
top of it a sound like that of a trumpet; but so exceeding
sweet and harmonious, that it filled the hearts of those
who heard it with raptures, and gave such high and delightful sensations, as seemed to animate and raise human
nature above itself. This made me very much amazed to

find so very few in that innumerable multitude, who had
ears fine enough to hear, or relish this music with pleasure:
but my wonder abated, when, upon looking round me, I saw
most of them attentive to three Syrens, clothed like God-
desses, and distinguished by the names of Sloth, Ignorance,
and Pleasure. They were seated on three rocks, amidst
a beautiful variety of groves, meadows, and rivulets, that
lay on the borders of the mountain. While the base and
grovelling multitude of different nations, ranks, and ages,
were listening to these delusive deities, those of a more
erect aspect, and exalted spirit, separated themselves from
the rest, and marched in great bodies towards the mountain
from whence they heard the sound, which still grew sweeter, -
the more they listened to it.

On a sudden methought this select band sprang forward,
with a resolution to climb the ascent, and follow the call
of that heavenly music. Every one took something with
him that he thought might be of assistance to him in his
march. Several had their swords drawn, some carried rolls
of paper in their hands, some had compasses, others quad-
rants, others telescopes, and others pencils. Some had
laurels on their heads, and others buskins on their legs;
in short, there was scarce any instrument of a mechanic
art, or liberal science, which was not made use of on this
occasion. My good demon, who stood at my right hand
during this course of the whole vision, observing in me
a burning desire to join that glorious company, told me,
'he highly approved that generous ardour with which I
seemed transported; but at the same time advised me to
cover my face with a mask all the while I was to labour
on the ascent.' I took his counsel, without inquiring into his
reasons. The whole body now broke into different parties,
and began to climb the precipice by ten thousand different

paths. Several got into little alleys, which did not reach far up the hill, before they ended, and led no further; and I observed, that most of the artizans, which considerably diminished our number, fell into these paths.

We left another considerable body of adventurers behind us who thought they had discovered by-ways up the hill, which proved so very intricate and perplexed, that after having advanced in them a little, they were quite lost among the several turns and windings; and though they were as active as any in their motions, they made but little progress in the ascent. These, as my guide informed me, were men of subtle tempers, and puzzled politics, who would supply the place of real wisdom with cunning and artifice. Among those who were far advanced in their way, there were some that by one false step fell backward, and lost more ground in a moment than they had gained for many hours, or could be ever able to recover. We were now advanced very high, and observed that all the different paths which ran about the sides of the mountain began to meet in two great roads: which insensibly gathered the whole multitude of travellers into two great bodies. At a little distance from the entrance of each road there stood a hideous phantom, that opposed our further passage. One of these apparitions had his right hand filled with darts, which he brandished in the face of all who came up that way. Crowds ran back at the appearance of it, and cried out 'Death.' The spectre that guarded the other road was Envy. She was not armed with weapons of destruction, like the former; but by dreadful hissings, noises of reproach, and a horrid distracted laughter, she appeared more frightful than Death itself, insomuch, that abundance of our company were discouraged from passing any further, and some appeared ashamed of having come so far. As for

myself, I must confess, my heart shrunk within me at the
sight of these ghastly appearances; but, on a sudden, the
voice of the trumpet came more full upon us, so that we
felt a new resolution reviving in us; and, in proportion as
this resolution grew, the terrors before us seemed to vanish.
Most of the company who had swords in their hands,
marched on with great spirit, and an air of defiance, up
the road that was commanded by Death; while others,
who had thought and contemplation in their looks, went
forward, in a more composed manner, up the road possessed by Envy. The way above these apparitions grew
smooth and uniform, and was so delightful, that the
travellers went on with pleasure, and in a little time arrived
at the top of the mountain. They here began to breathe
a delicious kind of ether, and saw all the fields about them
covered with a kind of purple light, that made them reflect
with satisfaction on their past toils; and diffused a secret
joy through the whole assembly, which showed itself in
every look and feature. In the midst of these happy fields
there stood a palace of a very glorious structure. It had
four great folding-doors, that faced the four several quarters
of the world. On the top of it was enthroned the Goddess
of the mountain, who smiled upon her votaries, and sounded
the silver trumpet which had called them up, and cheered
them in their passage to her palace. They had now formed
themselves into several divisions: a band of historians taking
their stations at each door, according to the persons whom
they were to introduce.

On a sudden, the trumpet, which had hitherto sounded
only a march, or a point of war, now swelled all its notes
into triumph and exultation. The whole fabric shook, and
the doors flew open. The first who stepped forward, was
a beautiful and blooming hero, and, as I heard by the

murmurs round me, Alexander the Great. He was conducted by a crowd of historians. The person who immediately walked before him was remarkable for an embroidered
garment, who, not being well acquainted with the place, was
conducting him to an apartment appointed for the reception
of fabulous heroes. The name of this false guide was
Quintus Curtius. But Arrian and Plutarch, who knew
better the avenues of this palace, conducted him into the
great hall, and placed him at the upper end of the first
table. My good demon, that I might see the whole ceremony, conveyed me to a corner of this room, where I might
perceive all that passed, without being seen myself. The
next who entered was a charming virgin, leading in a
venerable old man that was blind. Under her left arm
she bore a harp, and on her head a garland. Alexander,
who was very well acquainted with Homer, stood up at
his entrance, and placed him on his right hand. The
virgin, who it seems was one of the Nine Sisters that
attended on the Goddess of Fame, smiled with an ineffable
grace at their meeting, and retired.

Julius Cæsar was now coming forward; and though most
of the historians offered their service to introduce him, he
left them at the door, and would have no conductor but
himself.

The next who advanced was a man of a homely but
cheerful aspect, and attended by persons of greater figure
than any that appeared on this occasion. Plato was on
his right hand, and Xenophon on his left. He bowed to
Homer, and sat down by him. It was expected that Plato
would himself have taken a place next to his master Socrates:
but on a sudden there was heard a great clamour of dispu-
tants at the door, who appeared with Aristotle at the head
of them. That philosopher, with some rudeness, but great

strength of reason, convinced the whole table, that a title to the fifth place was his due, and took it accordingly.

He had scarce sat down, when the same beautiful virgin that had introduced Homer, brought in another, who hung back at the entrance, and would have excused himself, had not his modesty been overcome by the invitation of all who sat at the table. His guide and behaviour made me easily conclude it was Virgil. Cicero next appeared, and took his place. He had inquired at the door for Lucceius to introduce him; but not finding him there, he contented himself with the attendance of many other writers, who all, except Sallust, appeared highly pleased with the office.

We waited some time in expectation of the next worthy, who came in with a great retinue of historians, whose names I could not learn, most of them being natives of Carthage. The person thus conducted, who was Hannibal, seemed much disturbed, and could not forbear complaining to the board, of the affronts he had met with among the Roman historians, 'who attempted,' says he, 'to carry me into the subterraneous apartment; and perhaps, would have done it, had it not been for the impartiality of this gentleman,' pointing to Polybius, 'who was the only person, except, my own countrymen, that was willing to conduct me hither.'

The Carthaginian took his seat, and Pompey entered, with great dignity in his own person, and preceded by several historians. Lucan the poet was at the head of them, who observing Homer and Virgil at the table, was going to sit down himself, had not the latter whispered him, that whatever pretence he might otherwise have had, he forfeited his claim to it, by coming in as one of the historians. Lucan was so exasperated with the repulse, that he muttered something to himself; and was heard to say, 'that since he could not have a seat among them himself he would bring in one who alone had more merit than their whole assembly:' upon which he went to the door and brought in Cato of Utica. That great man approached the company with such an air, that showed he contemned the honour which he laid a claim to. Observing the seat opposite to Cæsar was vacant, he took possession of it, and spoke two or three smart sentences upon the nature of precedency, which, according to him, consisted not in place, but in intrinsic merit: to which he added, 'that the most virtuous man, wherever he was seated, was always at the upper end of the table.' Socrates, who had a great spirit of raillery with his wisdom, could not forbear smiling at a virtue which took so little pains to make itself agreeable. Cicero took the occasion to make a long discourse in praise of Cato, which he uttered with much vehemence. Cæsar answered him with a great deal of seeming temper; but, as I stood at a great distance from them, I was not able to hear one word of what they said. But I could not forbear taking notice, that, in all the discourse which passed at the table, a word or nod from Homer decided the controversy.

After a short pause, Augustus appeared, looking round him, with a serene and affable countenance, upon all the writers of his age, who strove among themselves which of them should show him the greatest marks of gratitude and respect. Virgil rose from the table to meet him; and though he was an acceptable guest to all, he appeared more such to the learned than the military worthies.

The next man astonished the whole table with his appearance. He was slow, solemn, and silent in his behaviour, and wore a raiment curiously wrought with hieroglyphics. As he came into the middle of the room, he threw back the skirt of it, and discovered a golden thigh.

Socrates, at the sight of it, declared against keeping company
with any who were not made of flesh and blood; and, therefore desired Diogenes the Laertian to lead him to the apartment allotted for fabulous heroes, and worthies of dubious
existence. At his going out, he told them, 'that they did'
not know whom they dismissed; that he was now Pythagoras
the first of philosophers, and that formerly he had been a
very brave man at the siege of Troy.'—'That may be very
true,' said Socrates; 'but you forget that you have likewise
been a very great harlot in your time.' This exclusion made
way for Archimedes, who came forward with a scheme of
mathematical figures in his hand; among which I observed
a cone and a cylinder.

Seeing this table full, I desired my guide, for variety, to
lead me to the fabulous apartment, the roof of which was
painted with Gorgons, Chimeras, and Centaurs, with many
other emblematical figures, which I wanted both time and
skill to unriddle. The first table was almost full; at the
upper end sat Hercules, leaning an arm upon his club; on
his right hand were Achilles and Ulysses, and between them
Æneas; on his left were Hector, Theseus, and Jason: the
lower end had Orpheus, Æsop, Phalaris, and Musæus. The
ushers seemed at a loss for a twelfth man, when, methought,
to my great joy and surprise, I heard some at the lower end
of the table mention Isaac Bickerstaff; but those of the
upper end received it with disdain, and said, 'if they must
have a British worthy, they would have Robin Hood.'—
Tatler, No. 81.

5. National Thanksgiving.

YESTERDAY was set apart as a day of public thanksgiving
for the late extraordinary successes, which have secured to

us everything that can be esteemed, and delivered us from everything that can be apprehended by a Protestant and free people. I cannot but observe, upon this occasion, the natural tendency in such a national devotion, to inspire men with sentiments of religious gratitude, and to swell their hearts with inward transports of joy and exultation.

When instances of Divine favour are great in themselves, when they are fresh upon the memory, when they are peculiar to a certain country, and commemorated by them in large and solemn assemblies; a man must be of a very cold or degenerate temper, whose heart doth not burn within him in the midst of that praise and adoration, which arises at the same hour in all the different parts of the nation, and from the many thousands of the people.

It is impossible to read of extraordinary and national acts of worship without being warmed with the description, and feeling some degree of that divine enthusiasm, which spreads itself among a joyful and religious multitude. A part of that exuberant devotion, with which the whole assembly raised and animated one another, catches a reader at the greatest distance of time, and makes him a kind of sharer in it. . . . .

Henry the Fifth (who at the beginning of his reign made a public prayer in the presence of his Lords and Commons, that he might be cut off by an immediate death, if Providence foresaw he would not prove a just and good governor, and promote the welfare of his people) manifestly derived his courage from his piety, and was scrupulously careful not to ascribe the success of it to himself. When he came within sight of that prodigious army, which offered him battle at Agincourt, he ordered all his cavalry to dismount, and with the rest of his forces to implore upon their knees a blessing on their undertaking. In a noble speech, which he made to his followers immediately before the first onset, he took notice of a very remarkable circumstance, namely, that this very day of battle was the day appointed in his own kingdom to offer up public devotions for the prosperity of his arms, and therefore bid them not doubt of victory, since at the same time that they were fighting in the field, all the people of England were lifting up their hands to heaven for their success. Upon the close of that memorable day, in which the king had performed wonders with his own hand, he ordered the hundred and fifteenth psalm to be repeated in the midst of his victorious army, and at the words, 'Not unto us, not unto us, but unto Thy name be the praise,' he himself, with his whole host, fell to the earth upon their faces, ascribing to Omnipotence the whole glory of so great an action.—*Freeholder, No.* 49.

XXVIII.

HENRY ST. JOHN, LORD BOLINGBROKE.

1678—1751.

HENRY ST. JOHN, LORD BOLINGBROKE, is best known as a Tory politician, of great fame for oratory, and as the friend of Pope, who dedicated to him the 'Essay on Man,' and to whom he in turn addressed his Philosophical Essays. He represented an ancient family, of which Oliver St. John, the great Republican lawyer, was a cadet, and was born and died in the family house at Battersea. His primary interest was not in literature, but in politics. He entered Parliament in 1700, and attached himself to the Tories from the first. From 1710 to the death of Anne he was Secretary of State, and in alliance with Harley, Earl of Oxford, whom he hated, governed England. He was the real author of the desertion by England of her allies in the war of succession which led to the Peace of Utrecht. On the establishment of George I, having notoriously intrigued with the Pretender, he withdrew to Paris. In his absence, he was, at Walpole's instance, attainted for high treason, and his name erased from the Peerage. Finding himself contemptuously discarded by the Pretender, he spent many years in retirement in France, during which he wrote his 'Reflections on Exile,' and the 'Letter to Sir W. Windham.' He came back to England in 1725, upon a pardon from the King, but never got his attainder reversed, and in consequence could not sit in the House of Lords. In England, he employed himself in writing vehement papers against Walpole, and also in the composition of his 'Remarks on the History of England,' till 1735, when he again withdrew to France. There he wrote his letters on 'the Spirit of Patriotism,' 'the Idea of a Patriot King' (designed to influence Frederick,

Prince of Wales), and 'the Study and Use of History.' On the death of his father in 1744, he returned to England, and lived at Battersea till his death. His philosophical works, consisting of Essays and Minutes of Essays, were not published till after his death.

His style is a model for popular writing on topics of the day. It never rises to great heights, but is always clear, vigorous and sustained. On philosophical subjects, however, a flowing style could not conceal the poverty of his thoughts. His equipment consisted of a theory of knowledge taken simply from Locke, and a doctrine of the comparative insignificance of man's place in nature suggested by the Newtonian Physics. With this he waged war against ' Metaphysical jargon ' (which included all Theology), and in particular against theories which 'made God man's image, man the final cause.' In effect, he denied the moral government of the world, and may therefore be more justly charged with ' infidelity ' than some others against whom the charge is brought. His great adversaries were Cudworth, Archbishop King, Clarke, and Wollaston. An argument of the last of these for a future life, drawn from the unequal allotment of happiness and misery in this, is referred to in one of the following extracts.

1. Harley, Earl of Oxford.

INSTEAD of gathering strength, either as a ministry or as a party, we grew weaker every day. The peace had been judged with reason to be the only solid foundation whereupon we could erect a tory system: and yet when it was made we found ourselves at a full stand. Nay the very work, which ought to have been the basis of our strength, was in part demolished before our eyes, and we were stoned with the ruins of it. Whilst this was doing, Oxford looked on, as if he had not been a party to all which had passed; broke now and then a jest, which savoured of the inns of

court and the bad company in which he had been bred:
and on those occasions, where his station obliged him to
speak of business, was absolutely unintelligible.

Whether this man ever had any determined view besides
that of raising his family is, I believe, a problematical question
in the world. My opinion is, that he never had any other.
The conduct of a minister, who proposes to himself a great
and noble object, and who pursues it steadily, may seem for
a while a riddle to the world; especially in a government
like ours, where numbers of men different in their characters
and different in their interests are at all times to be managed :
where public affairs are exposed to more accidents and
greater hazards than in other countries; and where, by consequence, he who is at the head of business will find himself
often distracted by measures which have no relation to his
purpose, and obliged to bend himself to things which are in
some degree contrary to his main design. The ocean which
environs us is an emblem of our government: and the pilot
and the minister are in similar circumstances. It seldom
happens, that either of them can steer a direct course, and
they both arrive at their port by means which frequently seem
to carry them from it. But as the work advances, the conduct of him who leads it on with real abilities clears up, the
appearing inconsistencies are reconciled, and when it is once
consummated, the whole shows itself so uniform, so plain,
and so natural, that every dabbler in politics will be apt to
think he could have done the same. But on the other hand,
a man who proposes no such object, who substitutes artifice
in the place of ability, who, instead of leading parties and
governing accidents, is eternally agitated backwards and forwards by both, who begins every day something new, and
carries nothing on to perfection, may impose a while on the
world : but a little sooner or a little later the mystery will be

revealed, and nothing will be found to be couched under it but a thread of pitiful expedients, the ultimate end of which never extended farther than living from day to day. Which of these pictures resembles Oxford most, you will determine. I am sorry to be obliged to name him so often; but how is it possible to do otherwise, while I am speaking of times wherein the whole turn of affairs depended on his motions and character?

I have heard, and I believe truly, that when he returned to Windsor in the autumn of 1713, after the marriage of his son, he pressed extremely to have him created duke of Newcastle or earl of Clare: and the queen presuming to hesitate on so extraordinary a proposal, he resented this hesitation in a manner which little became a man who had been so lately raised by the profusion of her favours upon him. Certain it is, that he began then to shew a still greater remissness in all parts of his ministry, and to affect to say, that from such a time, the very time I am speaking of, he took no share in the direction of affairs, or words to that effect.

He pretended to have discovered intrigues which were set on foot against him, and particularly he complained of the advantage which was taken of his absence, during the journey he made at his son's marriage, to undermine him with the queen. He is naturally inclined to believe the worst, which I take to be a certain mark of a mean spirit and a wicked soul: at least I am sure that the contrary quality, when it is not due to weakness of understanding, is the fruit of a generous temper, and an honest heart. Prone to judge ill of all mankind, he will rarely be seduced by his credulity; but I never knew a man so capable of being the bubble of his distrust and jealousy. He was so in this case, although the queen, who could not be ignorant of the truth, said enough to undeceive him. But to be undeceived, and to own himself so, was not his play. He hoped by cunning to varnish over his want of faith and of ability. He was desirous to make the world impute the extraordinary part, or to speak more properly, the no part which he acted with the staff of treasurer in his hand, to the queen's withdrawing her favour from him, and to his friends abandoning him : pretences utterly groundless, when he first made them, and which he brought to be real at last. Even the winter before the queen's death, when his credit began to wane apace, he might have regained it ; he might have reconciled himself perfectly with all his ancient friends, and have acquired the confidence of the whole party. I say he might have done all this; because I am persuaded that none of those I have named were so convinced of his perfidy, so jaded with his yoke, or so much piqued personally against him as I was : and yet if he would have exerted himself in concert with us, to improve the few advantages which were left us, and to ward off the visible danger which threatened our persons and our party, I would have stifled my private animosity, and would have acted under him with as much zeal as ever. But he was incapable of taking such a turn. The sum of all his policy had been to amuse the Whigs, the Tories, and the Jacobites, as long as he could, and to keep his power as long as he amused them. When it became impossible to amuse mankind any longer, he appeared plainly at the end of his line.—*Letter to Sir W. Windham.*

2. A faint and selfish Opposition.

My Lord, I have insisted the more on this duty which men owe to their country, because I came out of England, and continue still, strongly affected with what I saw when

I was there. Our government has approached nearer, than ever before, to the true principles of it, since the revolution of one thousand six hundred and eighty eight: and the accession of the present family to the throne has given the fairest opportunities, as well as the justest reasons, for completing the scheme of liberty, and improving it to perfection. But it seems to me, that in our separate world, as the means of asserting and supporting liberty are increased, all concern for it is diminished. I beheld, when I was among you, more abject servility, in the manners and behaviour of particular men, than I ever saw in France, or than has been seen there, I believe, since the days of that Gascon, who, being turned out of the minister's door, leaped in again at his window. As to bodies of men, I dare challenge your Lordship, and I am sorry for it, to produce any instances of resistance to the unjust demands, or wanton will of a court, that British parliaments have given, comparable to such as I am able to cite to the honour of the parliament of Paris, and the whole body of the law in that country, within the same compass of time. This abject servility may appear justly the more wonderful in Britain, because the government of Britain has, in some sort, the appearance of an oligarchy: and monarchy is rather hid behind it than shewn, rather weakened than strengthened, rather imposed upon than obeyed. The wonder, therefore, is to observe, how imagination and custom, a giddy fool and a formal pedant, have rendered these cabals, or oligarchies, more respected than majesty itself. That this should happen in countries where princes, who have absolute power, may be tyrants themselves, or substitute subordinate tyrants, is not wonderful. It has happened often: but that it should happen in Britain, may be justly an object of wonder. In these countries, the people had lost the armour of their constitution: they were naked and defenceless. Ours is more complete than ever. But though we have preserved the armour, we have lost the spirit, of our constitution: and therefore we bear, from little engrossers of delegated power, what our fathers would not have suffered from true proprietors of the royal authority. Parliaments are not only, what they always were, essential parts of our constitution, but essential parts of our administration too. They do not claim the executive power: no; but the executive power cannot be exercised without their annual concurrence. How few months, instead of years, have princes and ministers now to pass, without inspection and controul? How easy, therefore, is it become to check every growing evil in the bud; to change every bad administration, to keep such farmers of government in awe; to maintain, and revenge, if need be, the constitution? It is become so easy, by the present form of our government, that corruption alone could not destroy us. We must want spirit, as well as virtue, to perish. Even able knaves would preserve liberty in such circumstances as ours, and highwaymen would scorn to receive the wages, and do the drudgery of pick-pockets.· But all is little, and low, and mean among·us! Far from having the virtues, we have not even the vices, of great men. He who had pride instead of vanity, and ambition but equal to his desire of wealth, could never bear, I do not say, to be the under-strapper to any farmer of royal authority, but to see patiently one of them, at best his fellow, perhaps his inferior in every respect, lord it over him, and the rest of mankind, dissipating the wealth, and trampling on the liberties of his country, with impunity. This could not happen, if there was the least spirit among us. But there is none. What passes among us for ambition, is an odd mixture of avarice and vanity: the moderation we have seen practised is pusillanimity, and the philosophy that some men affect, is sloth. Hence it comes that corruption, has spread, and prevails.

I expect little from the principal actors that tread the stage at present. They are divided, not so much as it has seemed, and as they would have it believed, about measures: the true division is about their different ends. Whilst the minister was not hard pushed, nor the prospect of succeeding to him near, they appeared to have but one end, the reformation of the government. The destruction of the minister was pursued only as a preliminary, but of essential and indispensable necessity to that end. But when his destruction seemed to approach, the object of his succession interposed to the sight of many, and the reformation of the government was no longer their point of view. They divided the skin, at least in their thoughts, before they had taken the beast : and the common fear of hunting him down for others, made them all faint in the chace. It was this, and this alone, that has saved him, or has put off his evil day. Corruption, so much, and so justly complained of, could not have done •it alone.

When I say that I expect little from the principal actors that tread the stage at present, I am far from applying to all of them what I take to be true of the far greatest part. There are men among them who certainly intend the good of their country, and whom I love and honour for that reason. But these men have been clogged, or misled, or over-borne by others ; and, seduced by natural temper to inactivity, have taken any excuse, or yielded to any pretence that favoured it. That they should rouse, therefore, in themselves, or in any one else, the spirit they have suffered, nay, helped to die away, I do not expect. I turn my eyes from the generation that is going off, to the generation that is coming on the stage. I expect good from them.—*Letter on the Spirit of Patriotism.*

3. A King, his Court, and his Ministers.

HE must begin to govern as soon as he begins to reign. For the very first steps he makes in government will give the first impression, and as it were the presage of his reign; and may be of great importance in many other respects besides that of opinion and reputation. His first care will be, no doubt, to purge his court, and to call into the administration such men as he can assure himself will serve on the same principles on which he intends to govern.

As to the first point; if the precedent reign has been bad, we know how he will find the court composed. The men in power will be some of those adventurers, busy and bold, who thrust and crowd themselves early into the intrigue of party and the management of affairs of state, often without true ability, always without true ambition, or even the appearances of virtue: who mean nothing more than what is called making a fortune, the acquisition of wealth to satisfy avarice, and of titles and ribbands to satisfy vanity. Such as these are sure to be employed by a weak, or a wicked king: they impose on the first, and are chosen by the last. Nor is it marvellous that they are so, since every other want is supplied in them by the want of good principles and a good conscience; and since these defects become ministerial perfections, in a reign when measures are pursued and designs carried on that every honest man will disapprove. All the prostitutes who set themselves to sale, all the locusts who devour the land, with crowds of spies, parasites, and sycophants, will surround the throne under the patronage of such ministers; and whole swarms of little, nuisome, name-less insects will hum and buzz in every corner of the court. Such ministers will be cast off, and such abettors of a ministry will be chased away together, and at once, by a Patriot King.

Some of them perhaps will be abandoned by him; not to party-fury, but to national justice; not to sate private resentments, and to serve particular interests, but to make satisfaction for wrongs done to their country, and to stand as examples of terror to future administrations. Clemency makes, no doubt, an amiable part of the character I attempt to draw; but clemency, to be a virtue, must have its bounds, like other virtues: and surely these bounds are extended enough by a maxim I have read somewhere, that frailties and even vices may be passed over, but not enormous crimes; 'multa donanda ingeniis puto, sed donanda vitia, non portenta.'

Among the bad company, with which such a court will abound, may be reckoned a sort of men too low to be much regarded, and too high to be quite neglected; the lumber of every administration, the furniture of every court. These gilt carved things are seldom answerable for more than the men on a chess-board, who are moved about at will, and on whom the conduct of the game is not to be charged. Some of these every prince must have about him. The pageantry of a court requires that he should: and this pageantry, like many other despicable things, ought not to be laid aside. But as much sameness as there may appear in the characters of this sort of men, there is one distinction that will be made, whenever a good prince succeeds to the throne after an iniquitous administration: the distinction I mean is, between those who have affected to dip themselves deeply in precedent iniquities, and those who have had the virtue to keep aloof from them, or the good luck not to be called to any share in them. And thus much for the first point, that of purging his court.

As to the second, that of calling to his administration such men as he can assure himself will serve on the same principles on which he intends to govern, there is no need to enlarge much upon it. A good prince will no more choose ill men, than a wise prince will choose fools. Deception in one case is indeed more easy than in the other; because a knave may be an artful hypocrite, whereas a silly fellow can never impose himself for a man of sense. And least of all, in a country like ours, can either of these deceptions happen, if any degree of the discernment of spirits be employed to choose. The reason is, because every man here, who stands forward enough in rank and reputation to be called to the councils of his king, must have given proofs beforehand of his patriotism, as well as of his capacity, if he has either, sufficient to determine his general character.

There is, however, one distinction to be made as to the capacity of ministers, on which I will insist a little: because I think it very important at all times, particularly so at this time; and because it escapes observation most commonly. The distinction I mean is that between a cunning man and a wise man: and this distinction is built on a manifest difference in nature, how imperceptible soever it may become to weak eyes, or to eyes that look at their object through the false medium of custom and habit. My Lord Bacon says, that cunning is left-handed or crooked wisdom. I would rather say, that it is a part, but the lowest part, of wisdom; employed alone by some, because they have not the other parts to employ; and by some, because it is as much as they want, within those bounds of action which they prescribe to themselves, and sufficient to the ends that they propose. The difference seems to consist in degree, and application, rather than in kind. Wisdom is neither left-handed, nor crooked: but the heads of some men contain little, and the hearts of others employ it wrong. To use my Lord Bacon's own comparison, the cunning man knows how to pack the cards, the wise man how to play the game better: but it would be of no use to the first to pack the cards, if his knowledge stopped here, and he had no skill in the game; nor to the second to play the game better, if he did not know how to pack the cards, that he might unpack them by new shuffling. Inferior wisdom or cunning may get the better of folly: but superior wisdom will get the better of cunning. Wisdom and cunning have often the same objects; but a wise man will have more and greater in his view. The least will not fill his soul, nor ever become the principal there; but will be pursued in subserviency, in subordination at least, to the other. Wisdom and cunning may employ sometimes the same means too: but the wise man stoops to these means, and the other cannot rise above them. Simulation and dissimulation, for instance, are the chief arts of cunning: the first will be esteemed always by a wise man unworthy of him, and will be therefore avoided by him, in every possible case; for, to resume my Lord Bacon's comparison, simulation is put on that we may look into the cards of another, whereas dissimulation intends nothing more than to hide our own. Simulation is a stiletto, not only an offensive, but an unlawful weapon; and the use of it may be rarely, very rarely, excused, but never justified. Dissimulation is a shield, as secrecy is armour: and it is no more possible to preserve secrecy in the administration of public affairs without some degree of dissimulation, than it is to succeed in it without secrecy. Those two arts of cunning are like the alloy mingled with pure ore. A little is necessary, and will not debase the coin below its proper standard; but if more than that little be employed, the coin loses its currency, and the coiner his credit.

We may observe much the same difference between wisdom and cunning, both as to the objects they propose and to the means they employ, as we observe between the visual powers of different men. One sees distinctly the objects that are near to him, their immediate relations, and their direct tendencies : and a sight like this serves well enough the purpose of those who concern themselves no further. The cunning minister is one of those : he neither sees, nor is concerned to see, any further than his personal interests, and the support of his administration, require. If such a man overcomes any actual difficulty, avoids any immediate distress, or, without doing either of these effectually, gains a little time, by all the low artifice which cunning is ready to suggest and baseness of mind to employ, he triumphs, and is flattered by his mercenary train, on the great event; which amounts often to no more than this, that he got into distress by one series of faults, and out of it by another. The wise minister sees, and is concerned to see further, because government has a further concern: he sees the objects that are distant as well as those that are near, and all their remote relations, and even their indirect tendencies. He thinks of fame as well as of applause, and prefers that, which to be enjoyed must be given, to that which may be bought. He considers his administration as a single day in the great year of government; but as a day that is affected by those which went before, and that must affect those which are to follow. He combines, therefore, and compares all these objects, relations, and tendencies; and the judgment he makes, on an entire not a partial survey of them, is the rule of his conduct. That scheme of the reason of state, which lies

open before a wise minister, contains all the great principles
of government, and all the great interests of his country: so
that, as he prepares some events, he prepares against others,
whether they be likely to happen during his administration,
or in some future time.—*The Idea of a Patriot King.*

4. Immortality without terrors for the Reason.

THE ancient and modern Epicureans provoke my indignation, when they boast, as a mighty acquisition, their pretended certainty that the body and the soul die together. If
they had this certainty then, would the discovery be so very
comfortable? When I consult my reason, I am ready to ask
these men, as Tully asked their predecessors, where that old
doating woman is who trembles at the '*acherontia templa,*' the
'*alta orci,*' and all the infernal hobgoblins, furies with their
snakes and whips, devils with their cloven feet and lighted
torches? Was there need of so much philosophy to keep
these mighty genii from living under the same terrors? I
would ask further, is the middle between atheism and superstition so hard to find? Or may not these men serve as
examples to prove what Plutarch affirms, 'that superstition
leads to atheism?' For me, who am no philosopher, nor
presume to walk out of the high road of plain common
sense, but content myself to be governed by the dictates of
nature, and am, therefore, in no danger of becoming atheistical, superstitious, or sceptical, I should have no difficulty
which to choose, if the option was proposed to me, to exist
after death, or to die whole, as it has been called. Be there
two worlds, or be there twenty, the same God is the God of
all, and wherever we are, we are equally in His power. Far
from fearing my Creator, that all-perfect Being whom I
adore, I should fear to be no longer His creature.—*Fragments or Minutes of Essays.*

5. The superiority and right use of Human Reason.

NECESSARY agents employ all their powers conformably to the laws of nature, in promoting the same end, that is, in carrying on the physical system. So rational agents should employ all their faculties in preserving the order of the moral system, which reason discovers to be their common duty, and reason and experience to be their common interest. There are great deviations in both, with a double difference relatively to the state of mankind. The former are wholly independent, the latter in great measure dependent on man, notwithstanding the strength of his passions, and the weakness of his reason. The former are not only rare, and the latter frequent; but the consequences of the latter become much more fatal to the happiness of mankind in general, than those of the former. From hence it results very evidently that the wisdom of God, which you may call his goodness, has given man by what is in his power very ample means to make himself amends for that which is out of his power. Atheists and divines find fault with the whole. They cannot, or they will not conceive, that the seeming imperfection of the parts is necessary to the real perfection of the whole. The entire scheme of the works of God must be altered to please them. Nothing, even inconvenient to these delicate persons, must be suffered in it. They must be physically invulnerable, and morally impeccable, or the divine providence must interpose continually to shield every particular man from evils of one sort, and to check him, like the daemon of Socrates, when he is about to commit those of another. . . .

If men come helpless into the world like other animals; if they require even longer than other animals to be nursed and educated by the tender instinct of their parents, and if they are able much later to provide for themselves; it is because they have more to learn and more to do; it is because they are prepared for a more improved state and for greater happiness. Sense and instinct direct all animals to their several ends. Some of them profit more by experience, acquire more knowledge, and think and reason better than others both in different species and in the same. Man is at the head of these, he profits still more by experience, he acquires still more knowledge, he thinks and reasons better than all other animals; for he who is born too stupid to do so, is not a human creature: he sinks into an inferior species, though he be made after the image of man. Man is able by his intellectual superiority to foresee, and to provide more effectually against the evils that threaten him, as well as to procure to himself the necessaries, the comforts, and the pleasures of life. All his natural wants are easily supplied, and God has proportioned them to the abilities of those who remain in the lowest form of rational creatures. The Tartar under his tent, and the Savage in his hut enjoys them. Such is the general state of mankind. Of what then do we complain? His happiness exceeds that of his fellow creatures, at least as much as the dignity of his nature exceeds the dignity of theirs: and is not this enough?

We ought to think that it is enough: and yet God has done more for us. He has made us happy, and he has put it into our power to make ourselves happier by a due use of our reason, which leads us to the practice of moral virtue and of all the duties of society. We are designed to be social, not solitary creatures. Mutual wants unite us: and natural benevolence and political order, on which our happiness depends, are founded in them. This is the law of our nature; and though every man is not able for different reasons to discern it, or discerning it to apply it, yet so many are able to do this that they serve as guides to the rest. The rest submit, for the advantages they find in this submission. They learn by experience that servitude to law is real liberty, and that the regulation of pleasure is real happiness. Pleasures are the objects of self-love, happiness that of reason. Reason is so far from depriving us of the first, that happiness consists in a series of them : and as this can be neither attained nor enjoyed securely out of society, a due use of our reason makes social and self-love coincide, or even become in effect the same. The condition wherein we are born and bred, the very condition so much complained of prepares us for this coincidence, the foundation of all human happiness; and our whole nature, appetite, passion, and reason concur to promote it. As our parents loved themselves in us, so we love ourselves in our children, and in those to whom we are most nearly related by blood. Thus far instinct improves self-love. Reason improves it further. We love ourselves in our neighbours, and in our friends too, with Tully's leave ; for if friendship is formed by a kind of sympathy, it is cultivated by good offices. Reason proceeds. We love ourselves in loving the political body whose members we are, and we love ourselves when we extend our benevolence to all mankind. . . .

Human reason is given for several necessary uses, and principally to lead us to all the happiness we are made capable of attaining, by a proper application of it, which rational experience is sufficient to teach us. . . .

Neither the strength of our reason, nor the too frequent use of it, but the contrary, are to be apprehended : and if the sick man's wine must be mingled with water to do him good, reason, the *medicina animi*, must be employed pure and unmixed. . . .

It is not reason, but perverse will, that makes us fall short

of attainable happiness. The rule is so certain, and the
means so sufficient, that they who deviate from them are
self-condemned at the time they do so; for he, who breaks
the laws of nature, or of his country, will concur to preserve
them inviolate from others. As a member of society, he
acknowledges the general rule. As an individual, he endeavours to be a particular exception to it. . . .

It is true, indeed, that governments shift and change not
only their administrations, but their forms. Good princes
and magistrates carry on the work of God, and by making
men better make them happier. When these are corrupt,
the infection spreads. They corrupt the people, the people
them, social love is extinguished, and passion divides those
whom reason united. When the abuse is confined within
certain bounds, the condition of many men may be happy,
and that of all may be still tolerable : and when the abuse
exceeds such degrees, and when confusion or oppression
becomes intolerable, we are to consider that they who
suffer deserve to suffer. Good government cannot grow
excessively bad, nor liberty be turned into slavery, unless the
body of a people co-operate to their own ruin. The laws,
by which societies are governed regard particulars, and indi-
viduals are rewarded, or punished, by men. But the laws
by which the moral as well as the physical world is governed,
regard generals : and communities are rewarded or punished
by God according to the nature of things in the ordinary
course of his providence, and even without any extraordinary
interposition. Look round the world ancient and modern,
you will observe the general state of mankind to increase in
happiness, or decline to misery, as virtue or vice prevails in
their several societies. Thus the author of nature has been
pleased to constitute the human system, and he must be mad
who thinks that any of the atheistical, theological, or philo-

sophical makers, and menders of worlds, could have constituted it better. The saying of Alphonsus, king of Castile,
who found so many faults in the construction of the material
world that he pronounced himself able to have given the
supreme architect a better plan, has been heard with horror
by every theist. ...

My meditations would have been very different, more just,
and more reverential towards the Supreme Being. I should
have been very sure that neither lifeless matter nor the vege-
tative tribe have any reflex thoughts, nor any thoughts at all.
I should have been convinced that the faculty of thinking is
given to sensitive animals, as we call them, in a lower degree
than to man. But I should not have been convinced that
they have the power of exercising it in respect of present
objects only. The contrary would appear to me, on some
occasions, as manifest in them, or in some of them, as it
appears on others, and on more, in the man who is born
dumb. I should feel the superiority of my species, but I
should acknowledge the community of our kind. I should
rouse in my mind a grateful sense of these advantages above,
all others, that I am a creature capable of knowing, of
adoring, and worshipping my Creator, capable of discovering
his will in the law of my nature, and capable of promoting
my happiness by obeying it. I should acknowledge thank-
fully that I am able, by the superiority of my intellectual
faculties, much better than my fellow-creatures, to avoid
some evils and to soften others, which are common to us
and to them. I should confess that as I proved myself more
rational than they by employing my reason to this purpose,
so I should prove myself less rational by repining at my
state here, and by complaining that there are any unavoidable
evils. I should confess that neither perfect virtue, nor perfect happiness are to be found among the sons of men : and

that we ought to judge of the continuance of one, as we may judge of our perseverance in the other, according to a maxim in the ethics of Confucius; not by this, that we never fall from either, since in that sense there would be no one good nor no one happy man in the world; but by this, that when we do fall we rise again, and pursue the journey of life, in the same road. Let us pursue it contentedly, and learn that, as the softest pillow, on which we can lay our heads has been said by Montagne to be ignorance, we may say more properly that it is resignation. He alone is happy, and he is truly so, who can say, Welcome life, whatever it brings! welcome death, whatever it is! ' Aut transfert, aut finit.'—*Fragments or Minutes of Essays.*

XXIX.

JOHN ARBUTHNOT.

1675—1734-5.

JOHN ARBUTHNOT, an eminent physician and one of the most celebrated wits in the reign of Queen Anne, was the son of an episcopal clergyman of Scotland, and was born in 1675. He studied at the University of Aberdeen, where he took the degree of M.D. The Revolution deprived his father of his preferment, and young Arbuthnot left Scotland to settle as physician at Doncaster, a place noted in that day for its salubrity. Finding, as he humorously said, that he 'could neither live nor die there,' he removed to London, where he first became known by *The Examination of Dr. Woodward's Account of the Deluge.* This work brought him into notice, and introduced him to practice. His elegant and agreeable manners, his wit and pleasantry, and the learning which he combined with these qualities, soon made him the associate of the chief literary men of the day, and the friend of Pope, Swift, Gay, Atterbury, Congreve, Addison, Parnell, and others. He was also the friend both of Harley and of Bolingbroke, and in politics was always faithful to the Tory party. He became physician to Prince George of Denmark, and also to Queen Anne, whom he attended in her last illness.

His most important work is entitled *Tables of Ancient Coins, Weights, and Measures;* it has still some authority. He wrote several successful treatises on Hygiene, but his pieces of Wit and Humour—among which is his *History of John Bull,* a political allegory of great merit—have, together with his Letters, established his place in literature. Many of Arbuthnot's pieces were written in partnership with Swift and **Pope,** and are often

ascribed to them; but Mr. Wharton calls him the author of the
History of John Bull, and of the best parts of *Martinus Scriblerus,*
and adds that 'they abound in strokes of the most exquisite
humour.' His friends were warmly attached to him, and not
more for his intellectual endowments and brilliant wit, than for
his manly and honourable nature. Pope says 'that he was fitter
to live or die than any man he knew; that his good morals were
equal to any man's; but his wit and humour superior to all mankind.' During a great part of his life his health was bad; he
died in 1734.

1. The Usefulness of Mathematical Learning.

MATHEMATICAL knowledge adds a manly vigour to the
mind, frees it from prejudice, credulity, and superstition.
This it does two ways: first, by accustoming us to examine, and not to take things upon trust; secondly, by
giving us a clear and extensive knowledge of the system of
the world; which, as it creates in us the most profound
reverence of the almighty and wise Creator, so it frees us
from the mean and narrow thoughts which ignorance and
superstition are apt to beget. How great an enemy mathematics are to superstition appears from this, that in those
countries where Romish priests exercise their barbarous
tyranny over the minds of men, astronomers, who are fully
persuaded of the motion of the earth, dare not speak out:
but though the Inquisition may extort a recantation, the
Pope and a general Council, too, will not find themselves
able to persuade to the contrary opinion. Perhaps this may
have given occasion to a calumnious suggestion, as if mathematics were an enemy to religion, which is a scandal thrown
both on the one and the other; for truth can never be an

enemy to true religion, which appears always to the best advantage when it is most examined.

————Si propius stes,
Te capiet magis. ————

On the **contrary**, the mathematics are friends to religion ; inasmuch as they charm the passions, restrain the impetuosity of imagination, and purge the mind from error and prejudice. Vice is error, confusion, and false reasoning; and all truth is more or less opposite to it. Besides, mathematical studies may serve for a pleasant entertainment for those hours which young men are apt to throw away upon their vices, the delightfulness of them being such as to make solitude not only easy but desirable. . . .

The next thing that is necessary for the improvement of mathematical learning is, that mathematics be more generally studied at our Universities than hitherto they have been. From those seminaries the State justly expects and demands those who are acquainted both with the speculation and practice. In those are all the encouragements to them imaginable, leisure and assistance. There are still at hand books and instruments, as also other scholars that have made equal progress, and may be comrades in study, and the direction of the professors. There are also in perfection all the incitements to this study, and especially an acquaint-. ance with the works of the ancients, where this learning is so much recommended. There other faculties are studied, to which it is subservient. There, also, are the nobility and gentry bred, who, in due time, must be called to their share in the government of the Fleets, Army, Treasury, and other public employments, where mathematical learning is absolutely necessary, and without which they, though of never so great natural parts, must be at the mercy and discretion of their servants and deputies, who will first cheat them, and then laugh at them. And not only public employments, but their private concerns demand mathematical knowledge. If their fortunes lie in woods, coal, salt, manufactures, &c., the necessity of this knowledge is open and known: and even in land estates, no undertaking for improvement can be securely relied upon without it. It not only makes a man of quality and estate his whole life more illustrious, and more useful for all affairs, but in particular, it is the best companion for a country life. Were this once become a fashionable study (and the *mode* exercises its empire over learning as well as other things), it is hard to tell how far it might influence the morals of our nobility and gentry, in rendering them serious, diligent, curious, taking them off from the more fruitless and airy exercises of the fancy which they are apt to run into.

The only objection I can think of that is brought against these studies is, that mathematics require a particular turn of head, and a happy genius that few people are masters of, without which all the pains bestowed upon the study of them are in vain. They imagine that a man must be a mathematician. I answer, that this exception is common to mathematics and other arts. That there are persons that have a particular capacity and fitness to one more than another, everybody owns: and from experience I dare say, it is not in any higher degree true concerning mathematics than the others. A man of good sense and application is the person that is by nature fitted for them, especially if he begins betimes: and if his circumstances have been such that this did not happen, by prudent direction the defect may be supplied as much as in any art whatsoever. The only advantage this objection has is, that it is on the side of softness and idleness, those two powerful allies. There is nothing further remains, Sir, but that I give you my thoughts in general concerning the order and method of studying mathematics, which I shall do very shortly, as knowing that you are already acquainted with the best methods, and others with you may have them easily from the best and ablest hands.

First, then, I lay down for a principle, that nobody at an University is to be taught the practice of any rule without the true and solid reason and demonstration of the same. Rules without demonstration must and ought to be taught to seamen, artizans, &c., as I have already said; and schools for such people are fit in sea-ports and trading towns; but it is far below the dignity of an University, which is designed for solid and true learning, to do this. It is from the Universities that they must come who are able to remedy the defects of the arts, and therefore nothing must be taken on trust there. Seamen and surveyors, &c., remember their rules, because they are perpetually practising them; but scholars, who are not thus employed, if they know not the demonstration of them, presently forget them.

Secondly, no part of mathematics ought to be taught by compendiums. This follows from the former. Compendiums are fit to give a general and superficial knowledge, not a thorough one. It is time, and not the bulk of books, we ought to be sparing of; and I appeal to any person of experience, whether solid knowledge is not acquired in shorter time by books treating fully of their subjects, than by Compendiums and Abridgments.—*An Essay on the Usefulness of Mathematical Learning.*

2. Letters of the Free-thinkers to Martinus Scriblerus.

WE must not omit taking notice here, that these 'Inquiries into the Seat of the Soul' gave occasion to his first correspondence with the society of Free-thinkers, who were then in their infancy in England, and so much taken with the promising endowments of Martin, that they ordered their Secretary to write him the following letter:—

To the learned Inquisitor into Nature, Martinus Scriblerus:
the society of Free-thinkers greeting.

Grecian Coffee-house, May 7.

It is with unspeakable joy we have heard of your inquisitive genius, and we think it great pity that it should not be better employed, than in looking after that theological nonentity commonly called the soul: since, after all your inquiries, it will appear you have lost your labour in seeking the residence of such a chimera, that never had being but in the brains of some dreaming philosophers. Is it not demonstration to a person of your sense, that, since you cannot find it, there is no such thing? In order to set so hopeful a genius right in this matter, we have sent you an answer to the ill-grounded sophisms of those crack-brained fellows, and likewise an easy mechanical explication of perception or thinking.

One of their chief arguments is, that self-consciousness cannot inhere in any system of matter, because all matter is made up of several distinct beings, which never can make up one individual thinking being.

This is easily answered by a familiar instance. In every *jack* there is a meat-roasting quality, which neither resides in the fly, nor in the weight, nor in any particular wheel of the jack, but is the result of the whole composition: so in an animal, the self-consciousness is not a real quality inherent in one being (any more than meat-roasting in a jack), but the result of several modes or qualities in the same subject. As the fly, the wheels, the chain, the weight, the cords, etc., make one jack, so the several parts of the body make one animal. As perception, or consciousness, is said to be inherent in this animal, so is meat-roasting said to be inherent in the jack. As sensation, reasoning, volition, memory, etc., are the several modes of thinking; so roasting of beef, roasting of mutton, roasting of pullets, geese, turkey, etc., are the several modes of meat-roasting. And as the general quality of meat-roasting, with its several modifications as to beef, mutton, pullets, etc., does not inhere in any one part of the jack; so neither does consciousness, with its several modes of sensation, intellection, volition, etc., inhere in any one, but is the result from the mechanical composition of the whole animal.

The parts (say they) of an animal body are perpetually changed, and the fluids which seem to be the subject of consciousness, are in a perpetual circulation: so that the same individual particles do not remain in the brain; from whence it will follow, that the idea of individual consciousness must be constantly translated from one particle of matter to another, whereby the particle A, for example, must not only be conscious, but conscious that it is the same being with the particle B that went before.

We answer, this is only a fallacy of the imagination, and is to be understood in no other sense than that maxim of the English law, that the *King never dies.* This power of thinking, self-moving, and governing the whole machine, is communicated from every particle to its immediate successor; who, as soon as he is gone, immediately takes upon him the government, which still preserves the unity of the whole system.

They make a great noise about this individuality: how a man is conscious to himself that he is the same individual he was twenty years ago; notwithstanding the flux state of the

particles of matter that compose his body. We think this is
capable of a very plain answer, and may be easily illustrated
by a familiar example.

Sir John Cutler · had a pair of black worsted stockings,
which his maid darned so often with silk, that they became
at last a pair of silk stockings. Now suppose those stockings of Sir John's endued with some degree of consciousness
at every particular darning, they would have been sensible
that they were the same individual pair of stockings, both
before and after the darning; and this sensation would have
continued in them through all the succession of darnings;
and yet after the last of all, there was not perhaps one thread
left of the first pair of stockings, but they were grown to
be silk stockings as was said before.

And whereas it is affirmed, that every animal is conscious
of some individual, self-moving, self-determining principle;
it is answered, that, as in a House of Commons all things
are determined by a majority, so it is in every animal system.
As that which determines the House is said to be the reason
of the whole assembly; it is no otherwise with thinking
beings, who are determined by the greater force of several
particles, which, like so many unthinking members, compose
one thinking system.

And whereas it is likewise objected, that punishments
cannot be just that are not inflicted upon the same individual, which cannot subsist without the notion of a spiritual
substance: we reply, that this is no greater difficulty to conceive, than that a corporation, which is likewise a flux body,
may be punished for the faults, and liable to the debts, of
their predecessors.

We proceed now to explain, by the structure of the brain,
the several modes of thinking. It is well known to ana-
tomists, that the brain is a congeries of glands, that separate

the finer parts of the blood, called animal spirits; that a gland is nothing but a canal of a great length, variously intorted and wound up together. From the arietation and motion of the spirits in those canals proceed all the different sorts of thoughts. Simple ideas are produced by the motion of the spirits in one simple canal; when two of these canals disembogue themselves into one, they make what we call a proposition; and when two of these propositional canals empty themselves into a third, they form a syllogism, or a ratiocination. Memory is formed in a distinct apartment of the brain, made up of vessels similar, and like situated to the ideal, propositional, and syllogistical vessels in the primary parts of the brain. After the same manner it is easy to explain the other modes of thinking; as also why some people think so wrong and perversely, which proceeds from the bad configuration of those glands. Some, for example, are born without the propositional or syllogistical canals; in others, that reason ill, they are of unequal capacities; in dull fellows, of too great a length, whereby the motion of the spirits is retarded; in trifling geniuses, weak and small; in the over-refining spirits, too much intorted and winding; and so of the rest.

We wait with the utmost impatience for the honour of having you a member of our society, and beg leave to assure you that we are, etc.

What return Martin made to this obliging letter we must defer to another occasion.—*Memoirs of Martinus Scriblerus.*

XXX.

GEORGE BERKELEY, BISHOP OF CLOYNE.

1684—1752.

GEORGE BERKELEY, the celebrated metaphysician, was born in Ireland, in 1684, of a family of English extraction.

He received his early education in Kilkenny School, and at the age of fifteen entered Trinity College, Dublin, of which he became Fellow in 1707. He was ordained in 1709. In the following years he appeared as the author of a *Treatise on Arithmetic*, and of another on the *Theory of Vision*, in which he investigated the interdependence of the senses with great skill and sagacity. In 1710 he gave to the world the celebrated Treatise on the *Principles of Human Knowledge*. This work sets forth the theory of matter which was henceforth associated with Berkeley's name as the Berkeleian Theory. This Theory represents matter as not being an external substance, but only existing in the ideas of the human mind. The Dialogues between Hylas and Philonous followed, in which the same theory is applied to detect and expose the irreligious and immoral conceits of the day.

Berkeley's support of the Stuarts and advocacy of the doctrines of non-resistance and passive obedience was not likely to serve his interests with the House of Hanover, and on the accession of George the First, he took a tutorship and travelled for some years in France and Italy. He witnessed the eruption of Vesuvius in 1717, and his report, which was communicated to the Royal Society by Dr. Arbuthnot, is the earliest authentic one from the pen of an Englishman, and almost the first of any detail since the days of Pliny. It is given on this account, as well as because of its intrinsic interest, among the extracts which follow. On Berkeley's return to

England in 1721, his efforts to counteract the ruin caused by the failure of the South Sea Scheme brought him again into notice and favour. In 1724 he became Dean of Derry. In 1728 his generous and devoted spirit led him to offer to resign his Deanery and to enter upon a scheme for the foundation of a Missionary College at Bermuda, with the object of converting the North-American Indians. He resided for three years in Rhode Island for the execution and superintendence of this plan, which, however, fell to the ground through the failure of pecuniary aid promised by the government. The masterly series of Dialogues, *Alciphron, or the Minute Philosopher,* were the fruit of his leisure while in the new world. Soon after his return to Europe, the see of Cloyne became vacant, and to it Berkeley was consecrated in 1733. On his return to Ireland he devoted himself to charitable and patriotic objects, and especially to the improvement of the condition of the Irish labourer. He continued to reside at Cloyne until within a few months of his death, when he retired to Oxford, where he died early in 1753.

In addition to the works already mentioned, Berkeley contributed numerous brief essays on moral, social, and economical questions to the discussions of the day. His style is singularly adapted to the character of his philosophy, expressing as it does, the subtlest and finest philosophical ideas with the most felicitous freedom and ease, and even elegance and grace, which he combines, however, with great precision, and with a clear order and arrangement. As an exponent of philosophical thought, he is thus distinguished from former great writers in the same department; and he may be said to have created a new metaphysical style. He combined, however, with this philosophical temper an extraordinary practical enthusiasm, energy, and benevolence.

---

1. That Man can see God.

IT seems to be a general pretence of the unthinking herd, that they cannot see God. Could we but see him, say they, as we see a man, we should believe that he is, and believing, obey his commands.   But alas, we need only open our eyes to see the Sovereign Lord of all things with a more full and clear view, than we do any of our fellow-creatures.   A human spirit or person is not perceived by sense, as not being an idea; when, therefore, we see the colour, size, figure, and motions of a man, we perceive only certain sensations or ·ideas excited in our own minds; and these being exhibited to our view in sundry distinct collections, serve to mark out unto us the existence of finite and created spirits like ourselves.   Hence it is plain, we do not see a man, if by *man* is meant that which lives, moves, perceives, and thinks as we do: but only such a certain collection of ideas, as directs us to think there is a distinct principle of thought and motion like to ourselves, accompanying and represented by it.   And after the same manner we see God; all the difference is, that whereas some one finite and narrow assemblage of ideas denotes a particular human mind, whithersoever we direct our view, we do at all times and in all places perceive manifest tokens of the Divinity: every thing we see, hear, feel, or anywise perceive by sense, being a sign or effect of the power of God; as is our perception of those very motions, which are produced by men.

It is therefore plain, that nothing can be more evident to anyone that is capable of the least reflection, than the existence of God, or a spirit who is intimately present to our minds, producing in them all that variety of ideas and sensations which continually affect us, on whom we have an absolute, an entire dependance; in short, 'in whom we live and move, and have our being.'

That the discovery of this great truth which lies so near and obvious to the mind, should be attained to by the reason of so very few, is a sad instance of the stupidity and inattention of men, who, though they are surrounded with such clear manifestations of the Deity, are yet so little affected by them, that they seem, as it were, blinded with excess of light.

But you will say, Hath Nature no share in the production of natural things, and must they be all ascribed to the immediate and sole operation of God? I answer, if by *Nature* is meant only the visible *series* of effects or sensations imprinted on our minds, according to certain fixed and general laws, then it is plain that Nature, taken in this sense, cannot produce anything at all. But, if by *Nature* is meant some being distinct from God, as well as from the laws of nature, and things perceived by sense, I must confess that word is to me an empty sound without any intelligible meaning annexed to it. Nature, in this acceptation, is a vain chimera, introduced by those heathens who had not just notions of the omnipresence and infinite perfection of God.—*Treatise concerning the Principles of Human Knowledge.*

2. Appeal to the Roman Catholic Clergy of Ireland.

BE not startled, reverend Sirs, to find yourselves addressed to by one of a different communion. We are indeed (to our shame be it spoken) more inclined to hate for those articles wherein we differ, than to love one another for those wherein we agree.

But if we cannot extinguish, let us at least suspend our animosities, and, forgetting our religious feuds, consider ourselves in the amiable light of countrymen and neighbours. Let us for once turn our eyes on those things in which we have one common interest. Why should disputes about faith interrupt the duties of civil life? or the different roads we take to heaven prevent our taking the same steps on earth? Do we not inhabit the same spot of ground, breathe the same air, and live under the same government? Why then should we not conspire in one and the same design, to promote the common good of our country?

We are all agreed about the usefulness of meat, drink, and clothes, and without doubt, we all sincerely wish our poor neighbours were better supplied with them. Providence and nature have done their part; no country is better qualified to furnish the necessaries of life, and yet no people are worse provided. In vain is the earth fertile, and the climate benign, if human labour be wanting. Nature supplies the materials, which art and industry improve to the use of man, and it is the want of this industry that occasions all our other wants. The public hath endeavoured to excite and encourage this most useful virtue. Much hath been done; but whether it be from the heaviness of the climate, or from the Spanish or Scythian blood that runs in their veins, or whatever else may be the cause, there still remains in the natives of this island a remarkable antipathy to labour.

You, gentlemen, can alone conquer their innate, hereditary sloth. Do you, then, as you love your country, exert yourselves. Certainly, planting and tilling the earth is an exercise not less pleasing than useful; it takes the peasant from his smoky cabin into the fresh air and the open field, rendering his lot far more desirable than that of the sluggard, who lies in the straw, or sits whole days by the fire. Convince your people, that not only pleasure invites, but necessity also drives them to labour. If you have any compassion for these poor creatures, put them in mind how many of them perished in a late memorable distress, through want of that provident care against a hard season, observable not only in all other men, but even in irrational animals. Set before their eyes, in lively colours, their own indigent and sordid lives, compared with those of other people, whose industry hath procured them hearty food, warm clothes, and decent dwellings. Make them sensible what a reproach it is, that a nation which makes so great pretensions to antiquity, and is said to have flourished many years ago in arts and learning, should in these days turn out a lazy, destitute, and degenerate race. Raise your voices, reverend Sirs, exert your influence, shew your authority over the multitude, by engaging them to the practice of an honest industry, a duty necessary to all, and required in all, whether Protestants or Roman Catholics, whether Christians, Jews, or Pagans.

It will be alleged in excuse of their idleness, that the country people want encouragement to labour, as not having a property in the lands. There is small encouragement, say you, for them to build or plant upon another's land, wherein they have only a temporary interest. How many industrious persons are there in all civilized countries without any property in lands, or any prospect of estates, or employments! Industry never fails to reward her votaries. There is no one but can earn a little, and little added to little makes a heap. In this fertile and plentiful island, none can perish for want but the idle and improvident. None who have industry, frugality, and foresight, but may get into tolerable if not wealthy circumstances. Are not all trades and manufactures open to those of your communion? Have you not the same free use, and may you not make the same advantage, of fairs and markets as other men? Do you pay higher duties, or are you liable to greater impositions, than your fellow-subjects? And are not the public premiums and encouragements given indifferently to artists of all communions? Have not, in fact, those of your communion a very great share of the commerce of this kingdom in their hands? And is not more to be got by this than by purchasing estates, or possessing civil employments, whose incomes are often attended with large expenses?

A tight house, warm apparel, and wholesome food, are sufficient motives to labour. If all had them, we should be a flourishing nation. And if those who take pains may have them, those who will not take pains are not to be pitied; they are to be looked on and treated as drones, the pest and disgrace of society. . . .

Many suspect your religion to be the cause of that notorious idleness which prevails so generally among the natives of this island, as if the Roman Catholic faith were inconsistent with an honest diligence in a man's calling. But whoever considers the great spirit of industry that reigns in Flanders and France, and even beyond the Alps, must acknowledge this to be a groundless suspicion. In Piedmont and Genoa, in the Milanese and the Venetian state, and indeed throughout all Lombardy, how well is the soil cultivated, and what manufactures of silk, velvet, paper, and other commodities, flourish? The King of Sardinia will suffer no idle hands in his territories, no beggar to live by the sweat of another's brow; it has even been made penal at Turin to relieve a strolling beggar. To which I might add that the person whose authority will be of the greatest weight with you, even the pope himself, is at this day endeavouring to put new life into the trade and manufactures of his country.

Though I am in no secret of the Court of Rome, yet I will venture to affirm, that neither pope, nor cardinals, will be pleased to hear that those of their Communion are distinguished, above all others, by sloth, dirt, and beggary; or be displeased at your endeavouring to rescue them from the reproach of such an infamous distinction.

The case is as clear as the sun; what we urge is enforced

by every motive that can work on a reasonable mind. The good of your country, your own private interest, the duty of your function, the cries and distresses of the poor, do with one voice call for your assistance. And, if it is on all hands allowed to be right and just, if agreeable both to reason and religion, if coincident with the views both of your temporal and spiritual superiors, it is to be hoped this Address may find a favourable reception, and that a zeal for disputed points will not hinder your concurring to propagate so plain and useful a doctrine, wherein we are all agreed.

When a leak is to be stopped, or a fire extinguished, do not all hands co-operate without distinction of sect or party? Or if I am fallen into a ditch, shall I not suffer a man to help me out, until I have first examined his creed? Or when I am sick, shall I refuse the physic, because my physician doth or doth not believe the pope's supremacy?

Fas est et ab hoste doceri. But, in truth, I am no enemy to your persons, whatever I may think of your tenets. On the contrary, I am your sincere well-wisher. I consider you as my countrymen, as fellow-subjects, as professing belief in the same Christ. And I do most sincerely wish, there was no other contest between us but—who shall most completely practise the precepts of him by whose name we are called, and whose disciples we all profess to be.—*A Word to the Wise: or, an Exhortation to the Roman Catholic Clergy of Ireland.*

3. Thoughts in Westminster School.

Upon the late election of king's scholars, my curiosity drew me to Westminster School. The sight of a place where I had not been for many years revived in my thoughts the tender images of my childhood, which by a great length of time had contracted a softness that rendered them inexpressibly agreeable. As it is usual with me to draw a secret unenvied pleasure from a thousand incidents overlooked by other men, I threw myself into a short transport, forgetting my age, and fancying myself a school-boy.

This imagination was strongly favoured by the presence of so many young boys, in whose looks were legible the sprightly passions of that age, which raised in me a sort of sympathy. Warm blood thrilled through every vein; the faded memory of those enjoyments that once gave me pleasure put on more lively colours, and a thousand gay amusements filled my mind.

It was not without regret that I was forsaken by this waking dream. The cheapness of puerile delights, the guiltless joy they leave upon the mind, the blooming hopes that lift up the soul in the ascent of life, the pleasure that attends the gradual opening of the imagination and the dawn of reason, made me think most men found that stage the most agreeable part of their journey.

When men come to riper years, the innocent diversions which exalted the spirits, and produced health of body, indolence of mind, and refreshing slumbers, are too often exchanged for criminal delights which fill the soul with anguish and the body with disease. The grateful employment of admiring and raising themselves to an imitation of the polite style, beautiful images, and noble sentiments of ancient authors, is abandoned for law-Latin, the lucubrations of our paltry newsmongers, and that swarm of vile pamphlets which corrupt our taste, and infest the public. The ideas of virtue which the characters of heroes had imprinted on their minds insensibly wear out, and they come to be influenced by the nearer examples of a degenerate age.

In the morning of life, when the soul first makes her

entrance into the world, all things look fresh and gay; their novelty surprises, and every little glitter or gaudy colour transports the stranger. But by degrees the sense grows callous, and we lose that exquisite relish of trifles, by the time our minds should be supposed ripe for rational entertainments. I cannot make this reflection without being touched with a commiseration of that species called Beaus, the happiness of those men necessarily terminating with their childhood; who, from a want of knowing other pursuits, continue a fondness for the delights of that age after the relish of them is decayed.

Providence hath with a bountiful hand prepared variety of pleasures for the various stages of life. It behoves us not to be wanting to ourselves, in forwarding the intention of nature, by the culture of our minds, and a due preparation of each faculty for the enjoyment of those objects it is capable of being affected with.

As our parts open and display by gentle degrees, we rise from the gratifications of sense to relish those of the mind. In the scale of pleasure, the lowest are sensual delights, which are succeeded by the more enlarged views and gay portraitures of a lively imagination; and these give way to the sublimer pleasures of reason, which discover the causes and designs, the frame, connection, and symmetry of things, and fill the mind with the contemplation of intellectual beauty, order, and truth.

Hence I regard our public schools and universities, not only as nurseries of men for the service of the church and state, but also as places designed to teach mankind the most refined luxury, to raise the mind to its due perfection, and give it a taste for those entertainments which afford the highest transport, without the grossness or remorse that attend vulgar enjoyments.

In those blessed retreats men enjoy the sweets of solitude, and yet converse with the greatest *Genii* that have appeared in every age, wander through the delightful mazes of every art and science, and as they gradually enlarge their sphere of knowledge, at once rejoice in their present possessions, and are animated by the boundless prospect of future discoveries. *There* a generous emulation, a noble thirst of fame, a love of truth and honourable regards, reign in minds as yet untainted from the world. *There* the stock of learning transmitted down from the ancients is preserved, and receives a daily increase; and it is *thence* propagated by men who, having finished their studies, go into the world, and spread that general knowledge and good taste throughout the land, which is so distant from the barbarism of its ancient inhabitants, or the first genius of its invaders. And as it is evident that our literature is owing to the schools and universities, so it cannot be denied that these are owing to our religion.

It was chiefly, if not altogether, upon religious considerations that princes, as well as private persons, have erected Colleges, and assigned liberal endowments to students and professors. Upon the same account they meet with encouragement and protection from all christian states, as being esteemed a necessary means to have the sacred oracles and primitive traditions of Christianity preserved and understood. And it is well known that, after a long night of ignorance and superstition, the reformation of the church and that of learning began together, and made proportionable advances, the latter having been the effect of the former, which of course engaged men in the study of the learned languages and of antiquity.—*Guardian, No.* 62.

4. The Eruption of Vesuvius in 1717.

With much difficulty I reached the top of Mount Vesuvius, in which I saw a vast aperture full of smoke, which hindered the seeing its depth and figure. I heard within that horrid gulf certain odd sounds, which seemed to proceed from the belly of the mountain; a sort of murmuring, sighing, throbbing, churning, dashing (as it were) of waves, and between whiles a noise, like that of thunder or cannon, which was constantly attended with a clattering like that of tiles falling from the tops of houses on the streets. Sometimes, as the wind changed, the smoke grew thinner, discovering a very ruddy flame, and the jaws of the pan or *crater* streaked with red and several shades of yellow. After an hour's stay, the smoke, being moved by the wind, gave us short and partial prospects of the great hollow, in the flat bottom of which I could discern two furnaces almost contiguous: that on the left, seeming about three yards in diameter, glowed with red flame, and threw up red-hot stones with a hideous noise, which, as they fell back, caused the fore-mentioned clattering. May 8, in the morning, I ascended to the top of Vesuvius a second time, and found a different face of things. The smoke ascending upright gave a full prospect of the crater, which, as I could judge, is about a mile in circumference, and an hundred yards deep. A conical mount had been formed since my last visit, in the middle of the bottom: this mount, I could see, was made of the stones thrown up and fallen back again into the crater. In this new hill remained the two mounts or furnaces already mentioned: that on our left was in the vertex of the hill which it had formed round it, and raged more violently than before, throwing up, every three or four minutes, with a dreadful bellowing, a vast number of red-hot stones, sometimes in appearance above a thousand, and at least three thousand feet higher than my head as I stood upon the brink: but, there being little or no wind, they fell back perpendicularly into the crater, increasing the conical hill. The other mouth to the right was lower in the side of the same new-formed hill. I could discern it to be filled with red-hot liquid matter, like that in the furnace of a glass-house, which raged and wrought as the waves of the sea, causing a short abrupt noise like what may be imagined to proceed from a sea of quicksilver dashing among uneven rocks. This stuff would sometimes spew over and run down the convex side of the conical hill; and appearing at first red-hot, it changed colour, and hardened as it cooled, shewing the first rudiments of an eruption, or, if I may say so, an eruption in miniature. Had the wind driven in our faces, we had been in no small danger of stifling by the sulphureous smoke, or being knocked on the head by lumps of molten minerals, which we saw had sometimes fallen on the brink of the crater, upon those shots from the gulf at the bottom. But, as the wind was favourable, I had an opportunity to survey this odd scene for above an hour and a half together; during which it was very observable that all the volleys of smoke, flame, and burning stones, came only out of the hole to our left, while the liquid stuff in the other mouth wrought and overflowed, as hath been already described. ... The 10th, when we thought all would have been over, the mountain grew very outrageous again, roaring and groaning most dreadfully. You cannot form a juster idea of this noise in the most violent fits of it, than by imagining a mixed sound made up of the raging of a tempest, the murmur of a troubled sea, and the roaring of thunder and artillery, confused all together. It was very terrible as we heard it in the further end of Naples, at the distance of above twelve miles: this moved my curiosity to approach the mountain. Three or four of us got into a boat, and were set ashore at *Torre del Greco*, a town situate at the foot of Vesuvius to the south-west, whence we rode four or five miles before we came to the burning river, which was about midnight. The roaring of the volcano grew exceeding loud and horrible as we approached. I observed a mixture of colours in the cloud over the crater, green, yellow, red, and blue; there was likewise a ruddy dismal light in the air over that tract of land where the burning river flowed; ashes continually showered on us all the way from the sea-coast: all which circumstances, set off and augmented by the horror and silence of the night, made a scene the most uncommon and astonishing I ever saw, which grew still more extraordinary as we came nearer the stream. Imagine a vast torrent of liquid fire rolling from the top down the side of the mountain, and with irresistible fury bearing down and consuming vines, olives, fig-trees, houses; in a word, every thing that stood in its way. This mighty flood divided into different channels, according to the inequalities of the mountain: the largest stream seemed half a mile broad at least, and five miles long. . . . I walked so far before my companions up the mountain, along the side of the river of fire, that I was obliged to retire in great haste, the sulphureous stream having surprised me, and almost taken away my breath. During our return, which was about three o'clock in the morning, we constantly heard the murmur and groaning of the mountain, which between whiles would burst out into louder peals, throwing up huge spouts of fire and burning stones, which falling down again, resembled the stars in our rockets. Sometimes I observed two, at others three, distinct columns of flames; and sometimes one vast one that seemed to fill the whole crater. These burning columns and the fiery stones seemed to be shot 1000 feet perpendicular above the summit of the volcano.—*Letter to Dr. Arbuthnot.*

END OF THE FIRST VOLUME.

www.ingramcontent.com/pod-product-compliance
Lightning Source LLC
Chambersburg PA
CBHW022019110726
47901CB00006B/1586